IN LOVE BY CHRISTMAS

ALSO BY SANDY NATHAN

Stepping Off the Edge: A Roadmap for the Soul

Numenon: A Tale of Mysticism & Money
(Bloodsong 1)

Mogollon: A Tale of Mysticism & Mayhem
(Bloodsong 2)

Leroy Watches Jr. & the Badass Bull
(A Bloodsong Novella)

Tecolote: The Little Horse That Could

The Angel & the Brown-Eyed Boy
(Earth's End 1)

Lady Grace & the War for a New World
(Earth's End 2)

The Headman & the Assassin
(Earth's End 3)

The Earth's End Trilogy
(Earth's End 1 to 3 in a single eBook)

IN LOVE
BY CHRISTMAS

THE BLOODSONG SERIES 3
SANDY NATHAN

VILASA
PRESS

SANTA YNEZ, CA

ISBN-10: 1937927156
ISBN-13: 978-1-937927-15-8 (Trade paperback)
ISBN-13: 978-1-937927-16-5 (eBook)
Library of Congress Control Number: 2014907433

Editor: Melanie Rigney
Interior Design of Print & eBook Editions: Damonza.com
Book & eBook Cover Design: Book Cover Art, Clarissa Yeo

First Printing: 2014
Printed in the United States of America

May the love of Christmas blossom in our hearts,

today and every day.

"Leroy was always a good boy, destined for greatness.
He simply needed to discover it in himself,
and release it.
I suspect that Coyote, the Trickster,
loves him as much as I do."
Grandfather

TABLE OF CONTENTS

A NOTE FROM THE AUTHOR

I've written two books featuring Leroy Watches Jr., the grandson of the famous Native American shaman Grandfather. These were surprises—Leroy Watches Jr. snuck up on me. I was happily writing my Bloodsong Series, which starts with a trilogy about the richest man in the world meeting a great Native American shaman at a spiritual retreat in New Mexico.

When the second book in the series, *Mogollon: A Tale of Mysticism & Mayhem*, came out, I read it again and thought, *People will want more after they finish this. What can I do quickly so folks don't have to wait for a "big book"?*

I remembered some notes I'd written years before describing the zany transformation of a young rodeo participant into the FBI's Most Wanted Fugitive—all because of a *bull*. That young man was the shaman Grandfather's grandson, Leroy Watches Jr. I elaborated on that tale and *Leroy Watches Jr. & the Badass Bull* was born.

Those scribbled paragraphs were the beginning of The Bloodsong Novellas. I'm going to write more "shorter" books, featuring the "faces on Bloodsong's cutting room floor"—Doug Saunders, Janice Coto, Gil Canao, Delroy West, and Marina Selene.

But what about Leroy Watches Jr.? In writing the novella and working on the book cover, I'd fallen in love with him. I had to have more.

And I've always wanted to write a Christmas book. One of those warm, glowing things that make you feel good and have a sweet cover.

Aha! Why not combine Leroy and a Christmas book? This is that combo: *In Love by Christmas,* starring Leroy Watches Jr. and the love of his life. Unfortunately, I am constitutionally unable to write anything soft and fuzzy. *In Love by Christmas* is the most badass Christmas story ever written.

What genre is it? I describe myself as a writer of visionary fiction, which is a melding of mystical experience and the battle between good and evil. "This is *romance,*" my husband said. Yeah, it is. All of my writing has romantic elements, but *In Love by Christmas* piles it on. But this is more than *just* romance.

Leroy Watches Jr. has grown up with real hardship. I'll let the book tell you about it. Aside from everything else he faces, it's not easy being the grandson of probably the greatest Native American shaman in history. People have expectations. And then there's Coyote. Heard of him? Also known as the Trickster. This oddball Native American spiritual entity runs all over Leroy, making things turn out not just wrong, but absurdly wrong. Coyote has people *laughing* at a man as noble and honest as he is beautiful.

In Love by Christmas is about Leroy Watches coming into his own and claiming the power that is rightfully his.

This is truly a book about Christmas, the coming of the Christ to illuminate this world of sticks and dirt. This is not specifically a religious book; it treats spiritual experience and several religious traditions. But its focus is the coming of the divine.

So, *In Love by Christmas* is a romance about the coming of age of a marvelous man. It's about saving lives lost to evil, about social class and racism and their impact on human beings. It's a travelogue—ol' Leroy covers ground. It's a visionary, metaphysical, multi-religious, and Christian fantasy. And sexy as hell, but not too explicit. I'd give it PG-13, and that's for language.

This is a powerful book. For starters, *In Love by Christmas* shoved the final book in the trilogy set at the retreat in the New Mexico out of the way. *In Love by Christmas* is Bloodsong 3.

What about all those folks left out there in cactus and rattlesnakes? How does Grandfather's retreat end up? Jeez, they've already been run over by demons. What else could happen? Lots. That's in Bloodsong 4, tentatively titled *Eagle's Flight: A Tale of Mysticism & Miracles*, which will be out in 2015. Cheer the survivors as they claw their way home!

Is that all? I've already got about eight or nine more books in the Bloodsong Series on my hard drive. Given my brain's perpetual generation of *more* words, *more* stories, that trilogy will end up being a couple dozen books, assuming I live to write them all. (I say that not with the expectation of death, but knowing how much work it takes to get a book ready to present to you, my reader.)

I want to note that this work is fantasy. That means it's not real. This is particularly true when dealing with the Native American shaman, Grandfather, and his traditions and beliefs. What I say isn't intended to accurately represent any Native American culture or spirituality.

1

THE MAGNIFICENT MAN

ONE-TWO-THREE, *ONE*-TWO-THREE, *ONE*-TWO-THREE. Everyone in the amphitheater turned in the direction of the pounding noise. It came from outside the shallow crater where Will Duane sat—the Pit—to the northwest. Will craned his neck, but there were too many people between him and whatever it was to see.

A man's head appeared over the crater's edge, followed by a naked torso, and then a horse. The *one*-two-three was the sound of galloping hooves. As the animal grew closer, he could see the horse must have been running hard for a long time. Sweat covered it and dried foam collected around its neck and front legs. He could see the red interior of the animal's nostrils flamed as it gasped for breath.

Will jerked at the sight, eyes widening. The pair hurtled toward the front of the Pit where the shaman sat. The crowd stood as he approached. To protect the old man? Will could see that the newcomer was broad-chested; his height was obvious even mounted on a horse. His face and body were painted in black stripes. His face was contorted, agonized. He had a rawhide quirt on his right wrist. Lashes scored his back and sides. The horse was as flamboyant as the man, its coat wildly patterned in brown and white.

"Who is it?" Will whispered.

Someone in the row behind him bent over and said, "That's Leroy Watches, Grandfather's grandson. I guess he's upset on account of bein' late." The man chuckled. "He should be. If he was any later, he'd miss the whole Meeting." Will heard the snicker spreading throughout the crowd. The guy kept talking, "It's 1997. The retreat's been happening for eleven years. He's been late to every single one. Leroy beat his own record this year."

The horse slid to a stop in front of the stage. The rider swung off, leapt to the stage and ran at the old man on the platform as though he intended to kill him. Just before running into the shaman, he threw himself down, laying his head on the man's feet. Grandfather pulled him up and patted his forehead. "Leroy, Leroy, what is it, my grandson? What has happened?" Grandfather said with the weary air of one who'd heard it all before.

Leroy's life force was so powerful that it slapped Will like a hand. He and everyone else in the Pit could see what had happened to Leroy in images playing above the stage.

Will didn't get all of it; the man communicated his story in a Native language and pictures in the sky. His father had been hurt in a rodeo and Leroy was late because he'd saved him. The images showed blue beams coming from his eyes. It didn't make any sense.

When Leroy's communication centered upon him being pursued by the FBI, domestic Antiterrorism Force, cops and a bunch of cattlemen's associations, Will came to attention. He hadn't kept up with the news that week, being at the retreat in a bizarre geomagnetic site where nothing worked normally. Even his beyond-state-of-the-art satellite Internet connection didn't always work.

"They chased you *here*?" he said, leaping toward the shaman from the front row seats he and his corporate people occupied. "Where are they now?"

"Well …" Leroy looked at Grandfather before replying to the stranger. The old man nodded. "They're an hour behind me."

"Oh, shit." No matter what Will did in his business life—and it was an extensive life; he was the richest man in the world—he never messed with the feds. Any feds. All feds. They could take everything you had and demand change.

"This is reservation land. It's a sovereign nation. That should stop them."

"It never has before," the fellow who'd told him who Leroy was said wryly.

"That's true." Will ran his hand through his short white hair. "We have to develop a plan that will explain why we're here." He was in trouble. He and his people could not be found on an Indian reservation in the middle of a presumed plot against the United States Government.

Before he left for the retreat, Will had been informed by the Chief Justice of the United States Supreme Court that, because of his actions concerning a woman highly regarded by almost everyone at the higher levels of the government, the Attorney General's office was likely to indict him for thirty years of business behavior that he didn't think was so bad, but they might. They did, actually. Things were going to be bad enough once he got back to civilization without the FBI arresting him here.

He looked around the Pit, the shallow crater that had been their seminar room for almost a week. At the beginning of the retreat, more than four thousand people had jammed themselves into the amphitheater. Now only a third was there. All that remained looked like they'd gone through hell.

"OK. OK. I got it. I'm leading a Numenon management training seminar, a joint venture with Grandfather and the Nation." The crowd had been attacked by demons on Wednesday. It was Friday night. Even those who remained at the retreat showed they'd survived a battle. Will surveyed their pinched faces and hollow eyes. People at Numenon management trainings often looked the same way.

"We're having an employment fair. Gil," he shouted at one of his executives, "get those applications out. The rest of you," Will waved at his remaining staff, "get to work helping them fill them out. Make it real."

"Always have a plan B, and C, and D," Will had taught thousands of people at NumoFairs all over the globe. He implemented Plan B, dashing up the hill to their camp. He darted into the *Cass*, his multi-million dollar motor home. So many technological devices were incorporated into the vehicle that he could run his enterprises from it indefinitely. All he needed right now was a phone.

"Will Duane," he told the operator. He was patched through instantly and began his spiel. "Bill, it was a crazy man's delusion. No one can blow up a bull. That insane FBI agent Zemsky hallucinated the whole thing."

"What are you talking about? Wait a second. Let me get out of the pool."

"You're in the pool?"

"Yes, the White House has a pool under it." A slight pause. "Can you give us some privacy?" The down-home voice was directed at him again. "Had to get rid of the Secret Service. What are you talking about?"

Will convinced him that a crazy FBI agent hallucinated the whole story about an Indian blowing up a bull at a Las Vegas rodeo. "I'm here with the Indian now, on his reservation. These people are *militant*, Bill. If the FBI broke into a *sovereign* Indian nation, it could trigger the second Indian wars.

"Plus, I'm here with my staff. You remember Doug and Gil? And Melissa? A bunch of us are here on a spiritual retreat. *We* could get hurt. Who knows what our legal department would do …"

"*You're* on a spiritual retreat? An Indian blew up a bull ..." Bill sounded befuddled. "What do you want me to do, Will?"

"I'd like you to call off the FBI and ATF right away. A whacko agent caused the rumor."

"Well, if you're sure, I'll see the problem is put to bed immediately."

"That's great, Bill. I'm glad you understand.

"Oh, say hi to Hillary and Chelsea for me ..."

"Don't worry, everyone. We're fine. Bill called off the feds," he called to the crowd.

"Who's Bill?" echoed around.

The farewell dinner party was that night. So many things had happened at the retreat that Will found himself feeling exalted and pole-axed at the same time. Tomorrow, they'd pack up and go back to Palo Alto and the corporate headquarters. He would never be the same, and neither would Numenon, Inc.

As dusk deepened to night, he strolled around the camp watching Jon Walker, his chef; the three surviving drivers; and a few Indians prettying up the place. Will smiled at the transformation of their vehicles and encampment.

When they got there, the Numenon caravan had consisted of four matched motor homes and his rolling masterpiece, the *Cass*. They sported the corporate colors: pristine ivory, burgundy and gold. Their impact was tasteful and elegant. Jon had parked them in a circle like a wagon train, turning the central court into an outdoor living room.

Everything was different now. Two nights ago, demons had come screaming out of the earth and roared over the retreat site. They tore up everything, killing everyone they could. They painted pornographic graffiti on the Numenon RVs. The images were disgusting and insulting to his staff and him. And they couldn't get them off.

Indian kids had appeared out of nowhere and painted over the demons' porn with graffiti. Stampeding Day-Glo buffalo thundered across one side of the *Cass*. One of the RVs had the classic Japanese print of the wave by Hiroshige wrapped around the whole thing, with a crazy surfer using a Numenon Ranger laptop under the wave's rip curl. Every vehicle had a wild, hip, and very amusing motif.

In hours, the kids created the *new* Numenon Inc., giving the corporation an image update the best advertising agency couldn't pull off. The retreat remade Will's soul and updated his corporation, all at once. He might be able to save things back in Palo Alto. Maybe.

He heard music behind the camp in the Pit, which was directly behind the Numenon camp, and went over to listen. Over the week, a crazy half-Indian, half-hippie music had evolved. The Indians had their own instruments: drums, rattles, and shakers. Some of them played guitars and wooden flutes. And used their voices: they yodeled and yelped like mad. His drivers surprised him by bringing a small, international ensemble: guitar, mandolin, and every kind of drum you can think of. Turned out Mark Kenna had a band in Santa Cruz. He'd worked for him all these years, and Will didn't know.

The spectacular Leroy Watches was on the stage, straddling some kind of enormous wooden drum. Even seated, he looked tall. Broad back and shoulders, massive neck. Slim hips. Feathers bristled from the back of his neck. He looked like a throwback to a primitive age. When his huge hands hit the rawhide drumhead, the whole place seemed to shake. It wasn't that loud; it was just Leroy's playing. He played and all the other instruments seemed to fill in the cracks. Get vibrant. Come alive. Hold a beat.

He turned his head to his friends, smiling and laughing. Will could see his white teeth flash. Energy surged around him. The man was vividly alive. He was Grandfather's blood grandson and it showed.

Will began to feel that the answer Grandfather had suggested would work. His worry—the biggest worry—let up. Maybe he was just dreaming. Maybe the crazy vibe of this place had him fantasizing that things could turn out right.

The evening was as enchanting as his sweetest dreams. The Numenon crew had set the tables with embroidered cloths and the Numenon china and crystal. Every table had a candelabra. He sat at the most prominent table, having a pre-banquet meeting with Grandfather, Elizabeth Bright Eagle, and Leroy. They commandeered the courtyard before the guests arrived for the meal. Leroy had to drag himself way from his drum, amid the protestations of the other musicians and the crowd.

Across the table from Will, Elizabeth Bright Eagle sat, erect and powerful as a mountain in a black silk blouse with matching fringes. A Native American squash blossom necklace ringed her neck and silver bracelets adorned her wrists.

Elizabeth was everything he'd ever wanted in a woman: a beautiful professional who was at least as smart as him and had more advanced degrees. Dr. Bright Eagle was an internationally renowned physician and philanthropist. She'd been *People's* Woman of the Year.

Will would have married her in a heartbeat. She didn't want him. His running around most of his life repulsed her. But maybe it was possible. Maybe all sorts of things were possible.

He had a sweat lodge ceremony with Grandfather the day before and the old man had spent a great deal of time with him afterward. What the purification ceremony didn't drag out of him, being with the shaman did. Having shared the truth at long last liberated him.

Will told him of the things that hurt him most. His former wife had divorced him. Will deserved to be divorced; he'd stepped out on Kathryn from the first week they were married. He still loved her. He'd always loved her, but he couldn't be faithful. And she couldn't stay sober.

Enzo Donatore got her. The devil on Earth. Boy, did everyone at the retreat know who he was. Donatore was the cause of the monsters that overran the retreat, killing so many. He got Kathryn and that was the end of the woman he had known. Donatore ruined his daughter too. Kathryn had taken Ashley on her "summer vacations" with the devil.

Kathryn had somehow escaped with Ashley. He didn't know where either of them was. Kathryn seemed to have disappeared from the world. And Ashley was a nodded out junkie somewhere. A nodded out junkie who called herself Cass—from Cassandra, her middle name. Even she knew the sweet Ashley didn't fit the person she'd become.

The shaman had said he'd help him find his daughter and restore her to health. He said his grandson could help. Leroy was single and his father could handle their ranch alone. He could leave immediately.

Sitting at the table with him, Will studied Leroy. "You certainly can drum, Leroy."

He smiled shyly. "Thank you, sir. I been doin' it a long time. My mama said I banged on pots and pans from when I could sit up."

Leroy continued to listen carefully, making comments that showed he understood exactly what they were talking about. "You think we can get in and out without them knowin' and save her? I'd be interested in hearin' more about how you think you can do that."

Once the shock of Leroy's arrival diminished, Will found him to be a polite, soft-spoken and very nice young man. He was smart too, easily grasping their plans and their weak points.

As Will gazed at the stranger, a revelation burst upon him. It was like one of those explosive Native deities that kept popping out of the sky around Grandfather.

His daughter would *love* Leroy. Initially, she might love him because he was the opposite of every man he'd tried to set her up with—corporate suits, all of them. She might want Leroy because she thought a brown-skinned man would horrify her father. But she would love him for himself too.

Will was unable to keep his eyes off of the man. Leroy was Michelangelo's David, if the statue had come to life and turned into a person of color. His high cheekbones and aquiline nose said he was a Native

American. His wide lips and flared nostrils said African American. He had hazel-flecked light brown eyes. He'd seemed tall on the horse. In person, Leroy was taller than that. Perfectly formed and proportioned, the young man was almost slender, but for his shoulders and chest.

Leroy wore the spirit warriors' obligatory black shirt and jeans. Half a dozen unmatched earrings were spread over both ears. The brown and white feathers fastened at the nape of his neck said, "I am an American Indian."

Leroy had the same dignity and erect posture as Dr. Elizabeth Bright Eagle. Leroy was so presentable that his daughter would be able to go anywhere with him. Minus the feathers, in some places, but …

Stop it, Will! You do this all the time. You can't push her; she'll go the opposite direction. She has to see him, and then like him. He reined in his unrealistic thoughts. *Plus, you don't know where she is. Or if she's alive.*

But if Leroy found her and they married, I could have grandchildren. Will wanted grandkids as much as he had wanted his first billion dollars.

He forced himself to return to the conversation. Elizabeth was talking to Leroy, planning the rescue of the Indians' wild horses and their transport to Will's Montana ranch. Then she excused herself. Had her exodus been planned, Will wondered?

Grandfather coughed, and then said, "I told Leroy of your daughter, Will Duane. He wants to help her."

Will's eyes stung and swam with tears. The shaman was going to help him. Maybe it would be OK. "I worry about her every day. She's a heroin addict, Leroy, a very bad one. Before that, she was an alcoholic." His hands quivered.

"I don't know where she is. I want to find her and get her into treatment." His face tightened. "She's been hospitalized before. A lot of times. Nothing worked. See if you can find her and get her someplace where she can be treated. I can't say how much it would mean to me."

Will jumped up and returned minutes later, his nose blown and eyes wiped, clutching an album. Will flipped through it. It was mostly horse show pictures and a few from ballet recitals. Leroy turned the page and stopped at the only informal one in the book: an eight by ten of Cass galloping a cow pony across a creek. Cass was laughing, mouth wide open, head back. She had dark hair and pale skin.

"She was almost fourteen, just a young girl." Will's eyes filled again.

Leroy studied the photo. Will could see he was smitten. He hadn't breathed since he took the scrapbook. His eyes glistened as he picked the book up to examine the photo more closely.

Grandfather studied the photo and smiled. "You will find her, Leroy. No one else in the world can." The young man looked uncertainly at his grandfather. "You're soul mates, Leroy. I'm certain of it. The energy never lies. The Great One created you to be each other's perfect mates." He sat back with a satisfied grin.

"I'll help you," Leroy said. "When do you want me to start?"

"Right after dinner? I have a feeling that she's in terrible danger. She's in New York City somewhere. You'll need help finding her and getting her free."

"I can find her by myself."

"You may be able to find her, but I'm not sure you'll be able to get her away from whoever's got her." Will's mouth tightened. "I give her money. I know what they'll do to her if she can't pay. I can't *stand* thinking of that. She's a golden goose to them—guaranteed income. That's why they keep her alive and why they'll fight to keep her. Enzo Donatore is behind her condition. Did your grandfather tell you about him?"

Leroy nodded. "He is the devil in human form. He caused the massacre here."

"Never forget that. Donatore tried to kill me twice this week. Grandfather is the only reason I'm alive. Donatore wants to steal your soul and make you into his slave forever." Will stopped talking, ran his hand through his hair, and looked around wildly.

"You need to get going. I have some people at home who will be valuable in extracting her, wherever she is. Hannah Herhrman is my chief of security. She's a former Israeli commando. Hannah loves Cass. She was her unofficial babysitter. I'll send her and some of her operatives to New York. You should also take Doug Saunders. He's here at the Meeting. He has connections and knows how to get places you don't. Can you leave right away?"

Leroy nodded.

One of the warriors approached cautiously and said, "Leroy, want to drum?"

Leroy looked at his grandfather.

"Go ahead, Leroy. For a few minutes." Turning to Will, he said, "Leroy is the best drummer in all the Nations. He is the best drummer I have ever heard. Maybe the best in the world. Because of Leroy, we beat the Northern Salmon six years in a row."

Will thought Grandfather was exaggerating. He had no idea what he was talking about with the salmon. But very soon, he noticed a change in the music coming from the Pit. It had cohesion; it had rhythm, and power. The sound Leroy created was magnetic. Will had absolutely no musical abilities. He couldn't even clap in time. But he moved to Leroy's beat. Leroy's drumming was exciting, and that seemed to portend something changing in a good way.

Grandfather took the photo album Leroy had been examining, flipping a page. The shaman touched Will's hand. Energy flowed between them, joining them.

"Do you think Leroy can help Cass?"

The old man looked at the photo of Cass on the horse. "If anyone can. They are soul mates."

"He'll be able to save her, won't he?"

Grandfather shrugged and indicated the other side of the compound with his head. Elizabeth Bright Eagle chattered away with Larry Wolf and the other doctors. "Elizabeth is your soul mate. Both of you know it. But look at what she is doing. If they're sane, he'll be able to save her, but you never know."

Will saw Elizabeth pull out a chair and sit between Larry and an intern. She'd moved the place card with her name on it from his table over to Larry Wolf's.

Grandfather touched his hand again, "I know less as I get older, Will Duane. Leroy and your Cass, who knows?"

2

A MESSED-UP YOUNG WOMAN

WILL HAD WATCHED Leroy as he studied the images of Cass in the scrapbook. The young man's brows pulled together as he concentrated. The pages flipped: Cass smiling. Cass at a dance in a fancy dress at a ball. Cass riding a horse. Leroy's chest rose and fell with the photos as he turned the pages. He was captivated.

He's in love with her already, Will thought. *He would never play games with Cass as others had. He wouldn't hurt her, either. Not physically or mentally or in any way.*

Will heaved a sigh. Leroy was in big trouble.

After dinner, when they were making arrangements to go to New York, Will realized he needed to say something before letting the young man go off in total ignorance. He motioned to him. "Leroy, could you come with me into the *Cass*? I need to show you something."

Will got up from the banquet table and together they headed for the RV.

Leroy regarded the luxurious motor home, eyes widening.

"It's just fancy and expensive, Leroy. It won't bite," Will said.

He took him into the main cabin. "Take a seat, I'll be right back." Will went into his bedroom and brought out a thinner scrapbook than the one he'd shown at the table. He held it as though it were about to burst into flames.

"This is the real Cass, Leroy. I saved these pictures so I wouldn't forget who she is. I want you to find Cass and bring her back alive, but I don't want you hurt in the process. Take a look."

She was in a club, strobe lights cutting swaths in the darkness. Cass had her blouse off. Two men were sucking her tits, with more in the background waiting. Her head was tilted back. Her lips were parted and her eyes half closed in an expression of ecstasy.

"I've had investigators follow her at various times. They took the pictures, but some were sent to me anonymously. Cass or her friends were fooling … no, *fucking* with me. She does it to hurt me.

"I was a terrible father, Leroy. I didn't hurt her or abuse her sexually. I neglected her from the time she was born. And her mother too. Kathryn—Cass's mother and my former wife—got mixed up with Enzo Donatore. He has spies and slaves everywhere. They got my wife and daughter.

"I'm sure my daughter is worse than anyone you've seen. I don't know if you've had experience with mentally ill people, but some illnesses can be harmful to others. No, vicious and murderous toward others. That's Cass, Leroy.

"I want you to find her with all my heart. But I think a mental hospital is what she needs, not a husband. After a long time, maybe she could make someone a wife. But not you."

"Why not?"

"You're too good. She'll destroy you, and she'll do it deliberately. Keep looking at the pictures. They're my reality check."

Leroy worked his way through the album, pulling away from it, eyes narrowing. Will studied him. He sat forward, attentive, but not truly distressed. Will would have been happier if Leroy looked scared.

"She's a junkie. Heroin mostly, but she'll do whatever she can get. Cass will do anything to get drugs, and there's nothing she won't do when she's on them." Will looked down. "I give her money and she uses it for drugs. They call me an 'enabler' in recovery circles." He looked at Leroy. "I am. *I cannot stand* the thought of what they'd do to her if she couldn't pay.

"Of course, Donatore and his goons probably already have done it. She was fourteen when her mother started taking her to his castle in the summer. She was eighteen when her mother escaped and took Cass with her."

The last picture was Cass screaming at the camera. The hair on half of her head was done up in blue spikes, the other half was shaved. Her scalp bore a tattooed dragon that wound its way around, ending at her hairline, if she'd had hair. Her reddened, infected ears were pierced so many times that it was amazing that the earrings didn't tear through.

Cass's sweater hung off of her shoulder, exposing her skeletal collarbone and upper arm. In the background, a huge Christmas tree's lights shone cheerily. Garlands of evergreen branches, lights, and ornaments festooned a log room.

"That was last Christmas at my ranch in Montana, just three months ago. She cursed me, Leroy. She said the worst things that one person could say to another. I ran out of the house and took my jet back to Woodside. She was right! I was the things she said." Will's face was rigid. "Or she made me think I was. She took a thread that was true, and another one from somewhere else, and made it into a condemnation of me and everything I've done. She's so smart. She used her brains to crucify me. I don't want anyone else to go through that.

"Leroy, I don't want her to unleash her venom on *you*." Will moistened his lips and patted Leroy's hand. "You're my last hope. But know you're handling a vicious snake."

"I think I can heal her," Leroy said softly. "I can see her in there. She's not dead."

Will sighed heavily. "She'll destroy you if you try to have a relationship with her before she's healed."

Leroy nodded. "Yeah, maybe. But I want to try. I may be harder to destroy than you think." He set his chin.

"OK. I'll give you a chance. But we're going to do it my way. I've done this before, Leroy. I've gotten up a team and found her at death's door, and then put her in some nicey-nicey rehab center where she skipped out a couple of days later. To do it all again." Leroy tried to object, but Will cut him off. "It's my way or no way.

"First, she goes to the hospital to gain weight and get physically healthy, then a treatment center for mental illness. She's been in a bunch of those, by the way. Seven. Some have kicked her out before she was fully admitted. When they let her go from successful treatment, you can try to form a relationship with her."

"We're soul mates, Mr. Duane. I love her already, even seeing that." He indicated the photo with the dragon. "Even seeing all of those pictures." Tears gathered in Leroy's eyes. "I'll go get her and put her wherever you want. But I get a shot at healing her. I know that's what you want too."

"OK. Give it your best shot. But let's put some limits on this. It's the end of April. If you're not in love by Christmas, I want you to give up."

"I don't know that I can do that, sir."

"Well, I wanted you to know what you were getting into."

3

FINDING THE DRAGON LADY

"Bye, grandpa," Leroy said as he kissed the top of his grandfather's head, tears running down his face. "I'll never forget you." He bent down and hugged the old shaman standing in front of him, squeezing him to his belly. Leroy was 6' 8 ½" tall. Grandfather was not quite five feet. Hugging had always been a problem for them.

"Leroy, this old carcass is leaving this world, that's all. Just a pile of meat and shit. Would we love each other any less if you were here for my last gasp?" Leroy shook his head. "Find Cass Duane. She can have much time on this earth if you find her, or she can have none if you don't. Only you can save her. You are soul mates."

His grandfather paused a moment before letting him go. "You have been with me all your life, Leroy. You are a spirit warrior, *my* spirit warrior. We live a certain way, and you have lived that way better than any. Now, you may find it necessary to 'break the Rules.' Do you follow me?"

"No."

"To save Cass Duane, who has fallen to such a desperate low, you may have to do things that are counter to my teaching. For instance, my spirit warriors are faithful to their husbands and wives. If warriors are not married, they do not have sex at all."

Leroy blushed.

"You have lived this way perfectly, my grandson. I'm very proud of you. But because of where Cass is, you may have to lie to get to her. You may have to do other things too. You have my blessing, my dear one, to do what you need to do to save her."

Leroy sputtered. "You mean …"

"Yes, that is exactly what I mean."

He stood silent, glad they were alone. He didn't want any of the others to hear. He was a virgin at age twenty-four. The other warriors knew, of course. They respected him. But in the world … Would he have to betray the principles he'd held all his life?

Those were the last words he'd hear his grandfather say. He had made that crazy dash from the rodeo in Las Vegas to the Mogollon Bowl because his grandpa was dying. And now he had to cut their time short.

They bounced across the desert in a SUV. Will Duane had ordered a helicopter to pick them up at the main highway and take them to the Las Cruces airport. A Numenon jet waited for them there, ready to speed to New York City.

He was traveling with Doug Saunders. Leroy had barely spoken to him, but during the few minutes he'd spent drumming at the Meeting, he'd heard that Doug was Will's "fixer." He handled tricky situations, legal and illegal. Leroy couldn't see how Doug would be very useful. Doug's hair was messy and his shirttail hung out. He seemed stoned, but many participants in the Meeting did. He shambled when he walked, like a bear.

On the plane, Leroy clenched his teeth and grabbed the arms of the seat to keep from screaming. Two things got him on that plane: his grandpa told him to go and he wanted to save Cass. He'd never been on a plane; it was his greatest terror. Tumbling out of the sky, hitting the ground. The horrible noise the door would make when it closed. Thoughts like those had kept him from going near a plane. His breath exploded in short pants.

Doug looked him. "Your first time flying?"

Leroy nodded.

"If you get airsick, there's a bag in here." He pulled a flat bag out of a pouch in the back of the seat in front of Leroy and opened it up. "Puke in there, then close it with these tabs." Doug gave a pantomime demonstration.

Leroy left the bag in his lap. Hadn't occurred to him that he might throw up. His guts roiled at the possibility.

He didn't vomit and he did make it to New York.

"Hannah, would you stop doing that at the breakfast table?" Doug barked, his fork stuck into a gooey mass of sauce and egg yolk. "I can't eat my eggs Benedict with you flashing that, what? Vibrator? It's too big to be a shell. First you tore apart that *missile launcher,* now this. Don't you know how to act in a house?"

They had spent the night in a condo owned by Numenon, heading for bed the minute they arrived. The next morning, Leroy followed his nose and found himself in a very fancy living room. A compact woman in a black leather jumpsuit had a giant weapon torn apart at the far end of the dining table. Her face looked like his dad's when he took down his hunting rifle; touching the weapon thrilled him. The woman's face showed that joy she felt at reducing the massive apparatus to tiny pieces and reassembling them was greater than his dad's love of his gun.

A uniformed butler appeared and served them breakfast.

"I didn't know what you wanted, Leroy, so I ordered you eggs Benedict," Doug said. "That OK?"

He'd never heard of eggs Benedict, but they looked good. Like grits and gravy with fried eggs. That's when Hannah laid a long, cylindrical metal object with a pointed end across the back of her hand. Somehow, it ended up stuck vertically between her pointer and middle finger. She flipped it end to end, up and down, between the digits of her hand, one hand to the other.

"Hannah, stop that!" When Doug spoke the second time, she neatly caught the cylinder and stood it on end on the glossy tabletop.

"You will be happy with my dexterity when I save your life." she said. She had a heavy accent. "I practice so I can be ready. And I am ready. So are my people. They will be here when you finish your *eggs Benedict.*"

Leroy frowned. How did she do that? Why did she do that? She was playing with a very large caliber shell that went to a very big gun, a gun not seen outside the military.

"Eat! Eat your food!" she turned to Leroy. "Eggs taste terrible when they are cold." A broiled chicken breast sat in front of her, with a tall glass of green stuff. Hannah fastened her eyes on Leroy the way Kip, his border collie, laid eyes on a sheep. Like he could control it just with eye contact. Maybe kill it, too. "I am Hannah Hehrman. No one introduced us," she stuck out her hand and shot a dirty look at Doug. "He does not know how to live in a house.

"I am Mr. Duane's Chief of Security." She kept staring at him with those laser-eyes. She was a good-looking woman, compact and tough. She had shiny black hair cut straight all around. Her black jumpsuit clung to her trim and muscular figure, making her seem like a cartoon superhero. She had red lipstick and nails. But everything about her said she was a killer.

"Do you find me odd, Leroy?"

"Uh. No, ma'am." A fine strand of egg yolk dripped from his fork onto his chin.

She laughed. "I am very odd, Leroy, even for my country. I am from Israel. Do you know where that is?" He nodded. "In my country, people need to be tough. We need to be able to defend ourselves. We must make sure that the enemy knows we will retaliate, and our retaliation will be far harsher than what they meted out. I do not come from a peaceful place and I am not a peaceful person."

"Yes, ma'am." He couldn't eat. Sitting with Hannah was like hanging out with a shark and hoping it was in a good mood.

"I was in line to be a general in my country. Did you know that?"

"No, ma'am, though I can see how folks would want you to be a general."

"Here I sit, a woman raised with war all around her, whose home village had been blown to bits and all her family killed." She swept her tough, hard hand around the luxurious room; its perfectly manicured nails were as incongruous as her precisely cut hair and tailored suit.

Leroy's eyes followed her gesture. The condo in Manhattan was grander than anything Leroy had seen, including the buildings in the few movies he'd attended and all the TV he'd watched. One wall was glass, looking out over a river and a torrent of cars heading over a bridge. The furniture was gleaming white leather and straight lines with bright colored pillows and rugs thrown around. The tables had shiny chrome table legs and glass tops. The paintings looked like they'd been made with spray paint and masking tape.

"That's a Mondrian," Doug said, noticing Leroy gazing at one of the pieces of art. "He's a famous painter. I don't get him, but the experts say he's a genius. His stuff goes with the apartment."

Hannah looked at her watch, a space age monster that looked like a mini-computer on her wrist. "My operatives will be here in a moment and we will get to work finding Cass. You will see why Will Duane values me so much." A smirking smile. "If we can't do it, it can't be done."

"I don't think I'd get too jacked up about it, Hannah," Doug broke in. "You've found Cass a bunch of times before, and so have I. *This time* will be different because of *him*," Doug indicated Leroy with his fork. "He's the one who will straighten her out."

"Where is she?" Hannah asked. "Give me your ideas." Her team had arrived, seven of them, versions of Hannah, men and women dressed in low-key combat gear that didn't look much different than what people wore on the street. They wore the lean menace of professional killers. Hannah didn't introduce them.

"Yeah, where do you guys think she is?" Doug asked. They sat around the dining table sipping coffee.

One of the operatives said, "She's a junkie. She'll be where the junkies are. The city parks are our best bet. That and cheap hotels."

Hannah abruptly sat erect, face livid. Leroy had only seen top spirit warriors project so much directed fury. "Miss Duane is not a *junkie*. She is an addict and she is the daughter of the man who employs you. She will not be in some park or lying in a cellar." Her accent made her voice a growl. "Where will we find a young woman of enormous means whose father ensures that she will be 'cared for'? *That* is the problem." Hannah glared around the table.

"She tricking?" Doug asked.

Hannah bridled. "One would assume so, if she is well enough. She may not be presentable."

"She's hidden in a high-end whorehouse where they pay the cops up the kazoozie to keep things quiet." Doug seemed certain and almost nonchalant.

"I would assume that would be the case."

"You brought the arsenal?" Doug said.

"Yes, Doug. The whole package."

"They'll have metal sensors wherever she is. If you walk in armed, they'll kill her. We'll have to do a no-weapons, walk-in, walk-out. All friendly." Doug looked different to Leroy. Smarter, tougher. He'd done stuff like this before.

"All we have to do is find an upscale cat-house in a city of seven and a half million strangers without alerting the cops or bad guys. Send the kids home, Hannah. I need to think." Doug said. He meandered to a leather easy chair. "If I get any ideas, I'll tell you." He closed his eyes and appeared to sleep.

Leroy watched him for a moment. He seemed peaceful and far away. Doug was in the place shamans went to know the truth. Was Doug a shaman? No, not yet. But he would be one.

Hannah sent her operatives to their condo.

Hannah and Leroy stared at each other across the table.

"Where do you think she is?" Hannah asked him.

"Close," Leroy replied. "I can feel her here," he put a hand over his heart. "She's dried up like a dead flower before it turns to dust."

"I think, that, too. But how will we find her?" Hannah said. "I would normally reach out to the police, but Doug is right. This place will have purchased protection. Making an official inquiry would result in them killing her.

"And then we have Enzo Donatore. You have heard of him?"

"Yeah. Mr. Duane told me about him, and my grandpa told me, too. He was the one that attacked the Meeting and killed everyone."

"He is unstoppable, Leroy."

"My grandpa stopped him, the Great One and the Ancestors stopped him cold."

"Did your grandfather say he was stopped for good?"

Leroy shook his head. "No, ma'am. He just ran off to lick his wounds."

"He is back, perhaps not full strength, but growing. I can feel it. He has powers of his own and his own legions of monsters and spies. You need to know more: he can see all over the world with a crystal called the 'see-stone.' He can see anywhere. Will's technology can only slow him down." Hannah looked glum. They sat silently for a while.

Leroy didn't know how much time had passed when Hannah got up and poured them more coffee. "Do you know anything about torture, Leroy?" she said as though talking about turning on the news.

Leroy gulped. "Uh, no, ma'am."

"I know a great deal about torture, both from healing people who have been tortured, and inflicting it myself. It changes people. That is why I rebuked Charles for calling Miss Duane a junkie. She is a junkie, of course, but she is also a human being. And a torture victim. I know what she faces. Do you know what torture does, Leroy?"

"Huh. No, ma'am. Except maybe kill you."

"Dying is the easy way out. Torture does far worse than kill. Can you imagine being tied up and made available to hundreds of people? Being raped until your life is a succession of ramming thrusts and pain? Being flogged and screaming, or being shocked with a cattle prod in your body's depths and knowing that no one will ever help you? Learning tricks and ways of pleasing men that revolt you, but will buy another day's life?

"The mind breaks. Even if the person survives and gets away, it's not over. What happened repeats itself inside the brain, all the time. Faces leap out of nowhere, and the body shakes with remembered pain. Terror, always. Rage that it happened, that others allowed it to happen. Having known torture, you can never know peace.

"The survivor can look all right for a time, but then the vicious tide rises and she reacts, screaming and fighting for her life." Hannah grimaced. "That's what torture does, and that's what it's done to Cass Duane.

"I've known Cass since she was a child. When I came to California, I saw a disturbed family. Cass was a little girl, ignored by everyone. Her mother was often inebriated and unable to function. I cared for Cass like she was my daughter. I kept her safe. I loved the child the way no one else did. I will get her back, Leroy, and this time she will not be stolen again."

"No, ma'am."

"*Shit! I got it! I know how to find her.*" Doug jerked erect in his chair.

Leroy and Hannah turned to him.

"I can find her. But what time is it?"

"It's four p.m."

"Fuck."

"What?"

"It's too early. It's one in California. They won't be working yet. They'll just be getting up. Shit." He jumped up. "Your guys need to get ready!"

"For what?"

"Do you have the technology to look inside buildings? To get into government files? Like city or county offices?"

"Yes, of course. This is Numenon. We can look inside anything."

"Get your guys up here and ready for action. When it's dark in California, I'm going to make some calls. And we'll be ready.

"This is one reason I work for Will Duane," Hannah said, typing furiously on her keyboard. "He's got the technology to do *anything*. Prototypes of inventions that no one's even heard of."

She and her operatives had their laptops up on the dining room table. A screen that covered the wall had dropped from the ceiling across from the table. The agents' computers were hooked up to it. Each laptop's images circulated on the larger screen. A complicated metal structure like a pyramid about five feet tall was set up by the living room's large window. Leroy thought it must be an antenna of some sort.

It took them a long time to set it up, and more time to calibrate with their computers. The sun had fallen in the West. It was that dusky in-between time. The time of transitions and miracles.

"We're ready," Hannah said.

Doug looked at his watch. "It's seven here, that means four p.m. in California. Maybe someone will be around. I'll give it a try." He went into his bedroom and picked up a secure phone's receiver.

"Hey, babe! How you been? It's Doug Saunders, your old compadre. Yeah, been a while." Doug smiled broadly, leering. "Oh, yeah. I remember those days. I'd love to come by and see you. I never could leave you ladies alone. But I'm in New York, stranded high and dry." He lowered his voice. "Some poon would go great right now, but I don't know where to get it." He listened for a moment, grinning broadly.

"You got it. You know me—I want it top of the line and squeaky-clean. I'm not going to stick my dick someplace where it will rot off …

"If you could give me a couple of addresses in Manhattan, I'd be so grateful. You wouldn't even believe how grateful I'll be." Doug wrote something down. "Ah, thanks, sugar. You are the best. Now you get ready for a present, you hear? It will come in the mail. A nice present just for you." He dialed another number and went through the same routine.

"We've got five addresses." The minute he'd finished his calls, Doug dropped his drunken, lewd persona and went back into the main part of the condo. He pulled out his laptop, entering the addresses on a map of Manhattan. They appeared on the big wall screen. Most were close by. "Where do you think she is?"

"Wait," Leroy said. "What did you do? Where did you get those addresses?"

"I called up some old friends in the business and asked for help. Ladies back in California. They know where the best cathouses are here. They'd never tell the cops, but they would tell Doug Saunders, their biggest customer ever, outside Will Duane. Will and I fucked our way through life together for a long time. I was talking to mad-ams in California, Leroy. They spotted me the local, top-of-the-line establishments."

"I've got it," Hannah said. "I'll download it and then we'll get to work." She turned to her staff. "Keep going. Find the records for the other apart-ments. This may not be the one."

Hannah manipulated the file displayed on her screen, focusing and enlarging portions. "Leroy, this is the floor plan of the first of our poten-tial sites. I lifted it off of the building department records. Fortunately, the building is new enough to have digital records. And now I'm going to do this."

The image on the screen broke into sections. One displayed the floor plan of the apartment the California madam had targeted. Four other areas showed fuzzy views from inside the apartment. Hannah manip-ulated the images and they became clearer. They were views of rooms taken from inside the flat.

"This is the ultimate spy-ware," Hannah smiled. "A simple chip inside each Numenon device and we can snoop wherever it ends up. I convinced Mr. Duane to install the chips in all Numenon products. He complained about legality, but now we'll see how useful the chips are."

A fat man with a sandwich walked across the screen. "That's prob-ably his TV picking him up and broadcasting him." They couldn't hear what he said, but they could see everything in the room.

"The chip only works if a Numenon device is in a space. If one isn't in the room, but is in the apartment, we still can see patterns of hot and cold in the other areas." This wasn't the apartment where Cass was held. It was big, but there weren't enough warm bodies in the bedrooms. The screen in the living room showed a sole occupant, the fat, middle-aged man. Whatever Doug's contact said, this wasn't the foyer of a house of prostitution.

The operatives pulled down records and floor plans for the other addresses Doug had gotten.

"It's there," Leroy pointed to the map. He didn't need to look at the screen as the floor plan unfolded across it. The apartment was huge by New York standards. The plans showed at least seven bedrooms, but the patterns of warmth showed those had been bisected. The place was crawling with people.

"They must have Numenon products all over. TVs in every room. Probably showing porn," Hannah said. "Let's see." A large screen TV gave them a complete view of the living room. Another big TV on the opposite wall played a video of women doing *everything*. Women caressing their bared breasts. Women kissing each other. Women going down on men, and other women. Women's butts and thighs. Corsets and straps digging into soft flesh. The video's pictures intertwined and separated. New women appeared, coupled and left.

In the room, a slender blonde bound tightly in shiny black vinyl walked toward a hallway, an overweight man following her and grabbing at her breasts. Couples sat on sofas and lounges.

"It's a bordello, all right," Doug said. "Is it the right one?"

"She's right here," Leroy pointed to an area on the floor plan that was slightly paler than the background. It was at the far rear of the apartment.

"How do you know it's her?" Hannah asked.

"It's her," Doug said. "She's dying. The color of the screen shows there's almost no warmth."

"Let's go!" Leroy cried. "We have to save her!"

"How?" Doug said. "Way back where she is, they'll kill her before we can get to her. We can't shoot our way in." He thought, stroking his chin. Doug smiled radiantly and looked the others. "We have to buy our way in."

"With what?"

Doug's lascivious grin came back. "Ourselves. You and I are going to get laid, Leroy, my man."

4

CAPTURING THE DRAGON

HANNAH, DOUG, LEROY and five of the operatives huddled in the van near the apartment building. The other two operatives—the driver and a medic—cruised the area slowly in a service truck outfitted as an ambulance. This was a sober, very upscale, residential neighborhood, the last place you'd expect a bordello. Leroy comprehended immediately how rich their target must be and how much its management must pay the cops to stay away. And come fast, if they needed them.

He knew people who had been to New York City and came back to the reservation saying, "It's great! Everything's there! It's so cool." They loved it. It seemed like death to him, all moving so fast, nothing but huge buildings and machines. No life. The sun couldn't reach the sidewalk. He couldn't live there a day.

All the streets in Manhattan seemed to be permanently jammed and all the parking places filled. Leroy knew they'd never find parking on the street. He looked up, seemingly to the stars when they found the building they were looking for. It was huge and new, covering almost a block. It had underground parking. They turned into the opening and found a manned tollbooth. Doug's contacts had provided him with the passwords into the garage, through the lobby, and upstairs. Money was the most important password.

"Hey, buddy! Take your wife out to dinner." Slurring mightily, Doug stuck his head out the window past the driver, intoned the password, and threw a few hundred to the guard on duty. "We may be a while." He laughed crazily and the driver stepped on the gas. They shot into the basement garage.

Hannah did some typing on one of the computers. The van's interior looked like the high tech law enforcement vehicles Leroy had seen on TV; its walls were ringed with screens and equipment.

"OK. It's done. All the surveillance systems are down for blocks. We have about ten minutes."

Hannah and company held back while Doug and Leroy walked across the parking lot to the elevator and took it to a marble lobby at the street level. A big, tough-looking guy in a uniform was behind a desk.

"Everything's hunky dory this fine evening," Doug used the password he had procured from his California lady-friends.

The guard flashed Doug a look. His eyes made a fast circuit of the room, hitting on four wall-mounted screens giving impressive displays of static. He scowled and addressed Doug. "What's hunky about it?" The guy stood up, looking toward a door at the rear of the lobby for reinforcements. The door remained closed. His brows pulled together and his hand moved toward the handle of the desk's middle drawer, ready to pull a gun.

"Oh, Jeez. I guess I'm out of date." Doug pulled a wad of cash out of his pocket and fanned out some hundreds. "What will it take to get in?" His speech was slurred, but intelligible. "We just want to get laid. What's wrong with that?"

"Plenty, if you ain't right. And you ain't. You're not on the list for tonight." He waived at a clipboard on the desk.

"Wait a minute, tha's not fair. I been thinkin' about this all day." Leroy weaved forward and banged his fist on the reception table. He looked as drunk as Doug. "I can't wait no more. I never been to New York City an' I want to get *laid. Here. Now.*" He lurched forward.

When Leroy bumped into the security guard, he grasped his neck and the man collapsed, unconscious. Doug and Leroy dragged him behind the reception desk.

"You will sleep until I tell you to wake up," Leroy said to him.

"That's nifty, Leroy. I didn't know you could do that. It's on the seventy-fifth floor."

Leroy's stomach lurched.

"Don't worry, it's just like fear of flying. Do it once, and you'll be over it forever …"

Doug stepped out of the elevator, head turned back toward Leroy as he spoke. A thug in a fancy suit leaned around the door of the elevator, in his face.

"Who are you?" The thug had a New York accent, the most pronounced Leroy had heard. It sounded like, "Whoer uze?"

"Just here for a good ol' hunky dory time."

"Things ain't been hunky dory around here for a year." Leroy could understand what he said, but would not be able to repeat it to save his life. He grabbed Doug's jacket by the front and hauled him out of the doorway. "What is this? Did you do this?" The hood nodded at the screen mounted along the wall. It flashed black and white sparkles. "That happens and uze show up? Who sent you?"

Leroy swung out of the elevator box and grabbed New York City by the shoulder. He gasped and collapsed the way the man in the lobby had. They dragged him to an out of the way corner and Leroy ordered him to stay out until told otherwise.

They waited until Hannah and the others arrived in one of the other elevators.

"What now?" she said in that voice like a dozen cigarette rasps.

"No more 'hunky dory,' that's for sure," Doug said.

Doug took the floor plan out and they made their way to the condo. Hannah and the commandos followed closely, taking positions on each side of the door when they reached the suite. They had that fine Numenon tech gadgetry geared up, sensing everything. All they needed were the two starring actors. Leroy faltered, hanging back in the hallway.

"I know you don't want to do this," Doug said, "but you're the beef-cake. When they see you, they'll stampede. Whores aren't shy, Leroy. They'll grab you and want to fuck you. Go with it. If they want to kiss you, kiss them back. If they want to grab you *anywhere*, let them. If they drag you into the back, good. That's where Cass is. I know you're a spirit warrior and this is against what you believe. But if you end up fucking some girl and save Cass as a result, that's OK. Let's go."

Leroy lagged. This is what Grandfather had warned him about, and told him was all right. Maybe with his grandpa, but not with him. But he'd do it, if he had to. He and Doug wore cashmere sweaters with soft wool jackets over them, Italian shoes. Top of the line, all the way. Will had stocked their apartment with every conceivable thing they could need for *anything* they might do.

Doug grabbed his elbow and whispered viciously, "*Leroy*, smile. You're supposed to be out for a wild night with your old buddy."

Leroy heard the girls' intake of breath when he entered the living room. He hadn't known what Doug meant when he said, "You're the beefcake." Then he did. There were a bunch of them, but four focused on him. They were dressed in little bits of tight stuff like swimsuit material and undies so tiny he didn't know why they wore them at all. They had every color hair, curled, sticking out, straight. Eyebrows painted like hard semi-cir-cles sat above their eyes, which were circled with black paint.

After pulling in a hard breath all at the same time, they lunged. One of the women wiggled up to him and took hold of his privates through his pants. She pumped him a couple of times, and his body responded. It felt wonderful. Like something he should stop right now, that would definitely result in the Rules being broken. His cheeks flamed with embarrassment, but he didn't push her off. She kept handling him, so skilled that he was surprised he didn't let loose. She knew more about him than he did.

"Oh, baby, your dick is as big as the rest of you," she exclaimed, sounding awed. Hearing that, the others wiggled closer to look through his pants. "Look at him! That's what I call a *screwdriver!*"

"Let's get you in back so we can see you good." A redhead behind him put a hand on each of his buns and pushed him toward the hallway.

"When I get a hold of you, you're gonna remember me *forever.*" One of them whispered in his ear, kissing his cheek and running her hand down his chest inside of his sweater.

"Don't pay attention to her, sweetie. I'm the one who's gonna be your steady. You ever done a one-two-three-four? That's what *I* do."

"I do that, too," he said, while the pros kept stroking and whispering. Leroy remained fully clothed, but that didn't stop much. The girl who'd been handling his buns bit the cheeks of his ass and felt his balls between his legs. He struggled away.

"Come on, now. I got enough for all o' you. Let's go back there and let me make you happy." He headed up the hallway, four prostitutes in tow.

"Let's go in my room," one with blue-black hair said. That was the first door. Then it was "Mine! Mine! Mine!" A couple of big, muscly guys with bulges under their jackets indicating revolvers looked at him. They had baseball bats leaning against their legs. One smiled, then the other. Trying to keep from scaring the customers too much.

"Let's all go in the back. All of you. I can do you all."

"*All* of us?"

"Yeah, sure. Do it all the time." Since they were stuck to him, getting the bunch to move wasn't a problem. He smelled Cass's quarters before they got to them. "Let's go in here."

"No, we're not supposed to go in there."

Leroy stuck his head in. A huge, heart-shaped bed, made up with white satin and lace, sat in the middle of the room. "This is fine."

"We're not …"

"You want to do me, or not?" They entered the room, where he immediately laid them out on the bed and zapped them. Put them to sleep for a long time. "Except make noises like you're having …" He couldn't say the word. Even unconscious, they began moaning and crying out, then turned to each other and began kissing and caressing each other.

The smell drew him to the closet. It was a big walk-in. Something was in the back, a pile of clothes that had fallen off hangers. He turned on the light and pick them up. Leroy jumped back.

It didn't look human. It didn't look alive; face all jaundiced, eyelids stuck shut with yellow guck. Half-shaved head. The dragon Will had said was tattooed on the other side of her scalp peeked through a quarter-inch of stubbly hair. Cass had her arms and legs drawn up like a mummy they showed on the Adventure Channel. She looked like a mummy—dried out, joints twice the size of her limbs. She was wearing a bright-colored slip, that's all. The smell came from the mound behind her. Whatever shit she'd been able to make was stacked up there. A pool of half-dried golden liquid spread out in front of her. They didn't take her to the bathroom.

He looked at his soul mate for the first time. Her face was tawny rawhide glued to her bones. *Holy God in Heaven! O, Ancestors! O Great One. This is not possible. I cannot heal her.*

He would try. How to get her out of there? The girls were on the bed, moaning and carrying on. He smiled and went to the door.

"Hey, you guys want a freebee? They done me in, but they's still goin.' It's on me. I already paid for 'em. But I get to watch."

The guards came in warily, lighting up when they saw the girls on the bed, rolling in the throes of something.

"What'd you do to them?"

"Oh, jus' that ol' one-two-three-four. Go on. Have some. They'll never know. I'll go in this closet an' take a peek now 'n' then. Don't worry about me."

Leroy ducked in the closet, wrapped Cass in a coat hanging there. When he picked her up, she dripped and stinking clods fell off of her. *O God, Grandfather, help me.* How he could get out of there without sobbing, he didn't know. The smell, the way she looked. So unconscious that she had no idea he was there. She was so light in his arms. A child would be heavier. Her heels banged against him. Bones banging would have felt the same.

"Great One, protect me. Protect us. Save us." He ducked out of the closet and into the hallway. The guards were so deep into the hookers that they didn't notice him. He ran for the front door.

"Where did you say you got our address?" the madam said to Doug, scowling. She was a short, fat woman with a black wig and surgically enhanced boobs as big as her head. Doug almost took a step back. Angry, the bitch was scary. She nodded to one of the bouncers to get rid of Doug. "This is a private club. Only members are allowed here.

"Throw him out," she barked, then changed her mind. "No, wait a minute. How did you hear about us?"

"Oh, I don't know, sugar," Doug said. "We're here from California. I called up a friend back home. Charlene, maybe, or Karleene. She's got a real nice place in Hillsborough."

"I don't know anyone in Hillsborough." The bouncer moved closer.

"Well, they sure know you! Let's get this party going!" Doug beckoned to the guy at the bar. No one moved. "Come on! I came here for a party and I'm gonna have one."

"Who sent you here?" The madam's eyes were like recessed slits, sinking into her face. She crossed her pudgy arms. A tattoo of a snake ran down from one elbow.

"Who cares? My buddy's in there fucking four of your girls. Would you like to get paid? How 'bout that? Some cash put you in a better mood?" He pulled a roll out of his pocket and peeled off hundred dollar bills. "Say when." They didn't say when.

"Whoa, this is high-priced pussy. *He's got four of your best.* You outta give him a quantity discount." It took four thousand dollars, and they were still looking at him like road kill.

"Well, this is cheery. How about a drink?" Doug positioned himself a few steps from the entrance to the hallway where Leroy had disappeared, with the main entrance to his back. "Yoo-hoo! Can I get a drink? Some Scotch. You can bring it to me, sugar," he said to one of the three or four whores standing around looking scared. He made himself smile and act totally at ease. Doug began to look over the available talent. "Do I get to play, or just my friend?"

The madam and bouncers were silent, looking equally likely to beat the crap out of him as let him buy a woman.

"Hey! You got any more?" Doug shouted. "I want one with *big tits* and a *big ass.* How about back in there?" He headed toward the hallway and its multitude of bedrooms. A big guy with a baseball bat blocked his way.

"Pick one from the living room," he said.

"Sure, OK. Here I am, wanting a nice friendly screw and I get baseball bats. If you don't want me to go back there, I'll fuck her right here. You with the big ass, come over here." Doug began unzipping his pants. "Let's do it right here, honey. Bend over, baby. You're gonna love this."

Leroy walked out of the hallway and across the living room, carrying a scrap of flesh and rags wrapped in a big coat. "Let's go, Doug. I got her."

A couple of guys with bats and guns stumbled out of the hall after Leroy. Their pants were unzipped and hanging off their hips. They struggled to zip them as they ran.

The front door flew open. Hannah Hehrman and her operatives burst in, legs spread, and weapons drawn. "Lie face down on the floor. This is a raid."

Leroy stopped when he got to Hannah and opened the coat, letting Hannah see what they did to Cass. Leroy displayed all of her, from her jaundiced skull of a face to the reeking shreds at the back of her gown.

"Shut up, you stinking bitch," Hannah shouted at the madam. "Do you know who was in your closet?" Hannah had the madam shoved against the wall with a baseball bat jammed across her throat. The woman gagged as Hannah screamed, "*She was my baby!*

Hannah switched to a whisper, "No one hurts my baby. You will find that out. You and your people are going to tell me everything about yourselves. You are going to open your hearts and minds to me. If you do that, maybe you'll live. Do you understand?"

The madam spit in Hannah's face. Hannah laughed. "You think that scares me. Do you think I will not hurt you?" She jabbed the bat into the woman's throat, hard. The madam choked.

Her soldiers had assembled the bouncers and whores in the living room and secured them on chairs, taping their mouths. They arranged them in a circle so they could watch Hannah. Their eyes rolled, signaling their terror. The music was turned up high enough to muffle any noises the hostages might make, but not enough to bother the neighbors.

"You think you are as tough as me. Eh?" Hannah never wiped her face. "You should fear me, fatso. Because …" Hannah pulled the baseball bat away from the madam's throat and held it away for a long moment. The heavy woman remained frozen, and then lunged at Hannah.

Hannah pulled the bat back like a major league player and swung it the same way. It hit her target square across the face at the level of the nose. A thud filled the room. The woman dropped, dead, the center of her face caved in.

"You should be afraid of me." Hannah raised the bloody bat. She circled the room. "I really like using bats. The noise when you connect is so satisfying."

She casually walked up to one of the bouncers, tied in a chair. With that same lightning swing, Hannah drove the bat into his crotch, where his legs met his torso. He couldn't scream due to the duct tape over his mouth, but he tried. Several pops from deep in his body accompanied the swing. A wet stain began to spread from the point of impact.

"This type of blow breaks the pubic bone. I also cracked both of his hipbones, and of course, severed his urethra. I can't crush his genitals in this position. That requires a special type of chair."

She paced, "That girl you held captive means a great deal do me. When I saw what you did to her, it made me angry. It made me want to show you what pain is. And take my revenge."

Hannah went ape-shit, as only she could. She never made a sound, but she tore what was left of the bouncer to pieces. When she could do no more with a bat, one of her soldiers handed her a huge knife. The others put the subjects on tarps before she went to work on them. Hannah ran a very neat operation; no mess.

"You see, I have done this before," she turned to the terrorized hostages. "I love what I do, especially when it is for revenge. I deserve to take my revenge, don't you think? What you did to that girl was hideous. All of you were involved. No one helped her.

"I have not killed those of you who know something. For instance, you," she pointed to an innocuous bouncer, the smallest of the bunch, "are the accountant. You operate the computer systems and control the records. We will talk. Mostly, you will talk.

"That fat bitch was nothing. But you are," she leered into the face of one of the whores. "You know everything, don't you? You're the one who runs this place. Who was your contact? Who paid you to keep that girl here? Where did the money come from?"

A yellow puddle appeared and spread under the girl's chair. "You are smart. You should be afraid. However afraid you are of the one who paid you to keep my child, you should be twice as afraid of me." She taunted the girl. "Would you like some plastic surgery?" Hannah pulled sharp-nosed pliers from her belt and a small knife. "You want a nose job? Or I can put the basketballs from that piece of shit's chest in *yours*."

Hannah and her team did what she did best: data extraction. They left the apartment sparkling and clean with no evidence of anything untoward happening, Hannah and her team knew everything about everyone in the cathouse. Every name, every number, every contact. Hannah had all their accounting information, where they put their money. All the girls' names and where they came from.

And the name and address of the guy from Spain who kept track of Cass for Enzo Donatore. Hannah would kill him, and then go up the line to Enzo. No one would ever harm Cass again. She was sure that Enzo Donatore saw at least some of her revenge from his see-stone. "Hannah Hehrman declares war on you …" she said into the emptiness.

In her room much later, Hannah held on to the bathroom sink and sobbed. She slumped to the floor, her legs unable to hold her up. Her body convulsed as grief overwhelmed her.

"Oh, my sweet baby. What he did to you."

5

PASSING IN THE NIGHT

"LET'S GO, LEROY." Doug grabbed his arm and pulled him to the medic's vehicle, which was pulled up to the underground elevator in the condo's lot.

The medic approached, trying to put Cass on the gurney in the middle of the rear cabin. "No!" Leroy waved him off.

The van/ambulance started moving the instant Leroy slammed the door. The parking attendant barely looked up as they hurtled into the dark street.

Leroy held Cass across his lap like a baby, his breathing becoming ragged as her condition revealed itself. Her skin seemed glued to her bones; her face was a parchment-covered death's head. Black circles ringed her eyes. Her arms were bones full of needle marks. She seemed too light to be a grown woman. Her nightgown was filthy.

"They had her in a closet, Doug. With no heat or water. It stank." She stank. A cry escaped from him. "Oh, Cass. What did they do to you?" Her eyes were pasted shut with amber guck and she was so unconscious that his healing couldn't touch her.

"Oh, Cass. Wake up! I'm here. I've got you." Tears burst from Leroy's eyes. "She can't feel me, Doug, she's almost gone."

The van pulled into an alley and then into the opening of an underground parking lot. They stopped, the back opened and Doug led Leroy to an elevator. "This is a small clinic, Leroy. We can't take her to a public hospital. Enzo Donatore's spies will know instantly. This is a good place. They can stabilize her until we can take her somewhere where they can rebuild her physically."

They walked down a hall. Cass wasn't heavy enough to be a burden. Her bones poked into Leroy's arms. Her legs hung without control or sensation. She was dying, and he couldn't help her.

His ribs pumped. He couldn't stop crying.

Leroy had cured everyone who came to him, except for one person. He couldn't touch his mother's cancer and neither could his grandpa. The two of them sat by helplessly, unable to keep the woman they loved most on this earth from dying. He'd failed his mother.

And now he was failing Cass.

"In here, Leroy. Put her on the table."

It was a tidy intensive care unit. Machines ringed the table. A doctor was there, wearing green scrubs with a green cloth hat tied around his head. He nodded at Doug and went to work. He set up an IV in Cass's arm. Machines began to beep.

Finally, the doctor stopped and addressed them. "A few more hours and she'd have been dead. It's going to be touch and go as it is. I'm putting fluids in her. She needs a full-fledged hospital. She's yellow from kidney failure. She may have hepatitis, HIV, liver and kidney damage. I can't treat those. Her anorexia could cause her heart to quit at any time. I'll have her ready to travel in a few hours. Mr. Duane has ordered transportation."

The doctor turned to Leroy. "Are you her husband?" Leroy shook his head. "But you have a relationship?" Leroy nodded. "Well, she's in for a rough ride. What Mr. Duane proposes is the correct thing. She needs to be in a guarded medical facility until she gains weight and gets back on her feet. If that's possible."

Leroy sat next to her in the hospital, holding her hand. "Baby, it's me. Leroy. Can you feel me? Oh, baby, I'm here for you. I can heal, Cass. Did you know that? If you let me, I'll heal you. Sweetie, can you feel me?" He raised his head, despairing. "Baby, I been healin' since I was four. Almost nothing I can't heal."

But there was. He couldn't heal his own mother. He watched her die of cancer and wondered about how the Great One loved them and gave them abilities, but took them away when it mattered most? He'd failed before.

"Cass, honey, they're gonna take you to a hospital. It's a good place. They'll fix you up. Or, if you can, let me heal you. I can do it, baby. I can." He was lying to her. Not to himself though. All the time he sat next to her, praying and talking to her, he was there, six years old, talking to his mother as she faded away. Sitting next to his grandfather, the most powerful healer in the world, who couldn't heal his own daughter, either.

He'd done so much to save her, but he couldn't do this final thing that would make her well. He couldn't find a bit of consciousness in her. None existed; she was that close to death.

"Leroy, the ambulance is almost ready. We need to move her." Doug nudged him. "Donatore may find her. The hospital is a safer place. "

Leroy got up and bent over Cass. She was plumped up a little from the fluids, but still looked awful. He kissed her forehead over and over. "Cass, I love you. I want to marry you. Try and remember that while you're getting better."

When he raised himself, Cass's eyes were open. Their eyes locked for what seemed like hours. He felt her in his soul, his body. He thought she was going to speak, but then her eyes glazed and the pupils rolled back.

She began convulsing in long, slow rolls. Her mouth was flecked with foam.

"Get back," the doctor said. It took a while, but he stabilized her enough for the paramedics to take her.

Leroy's knees buckled. She had recognized him and gone into seizures. He had never felt so devastated.

The feeling lasted all the time they were in the ambulance, driving through the night through places he didn't know to a hospital he didn't know either. It was in the country; they drove through miles of forest. Different forest than the majestic mariposa trees he knew, the kings of the leafy world. These were skinny trees, jammed too close together. The headlights cut a tunnel through the darkness. Too green, even in the darkness. Too jammed together. Mist rose from the forest floor.

Cass was strapped in a gurney. He sat next to her, holding her hand, talking to her. Giving her all the energy he could.

"You're gonna make it through just fine. You're gonna get some weight on, get your heart going good. You're gonna be fine, Cass. When you see me next, you're going to crack open a big smile. You know who I am, don't you, baby? I'm Leroy. Your soul mate. When you see me next, we're gonna have a big wedding at your dad's house, or at my ranch. Your dad is going to buy you the most beautiful wedding dress ..."

He kept it up like that for three hours. Patter about them and how things were going to turn out. Their wedding. "I built a cabin on our ranch, Cass. I didn't know what I was doing, but it was for us. It's real big. Got high ceilings, all logs. It's got a bedroom, but I built it so I can add more easy. For our kids, we're going to have kids."

All the time he talked, he could feel the energy between them. Other spirit warriors had told him about the energy that flowed between soul mates. Nothing could have prepared him to experience it. Bliss. Golden bliss billowing through them.

She had to feel it. *Feel it, Cass,* he thought. *You'll know. We're meant for each other. You have to live.*

Cass lay on the bed in the ambulance, strapped down. Immobile. Eyes closed. They'd washed the sticky stuff that held her eyelids closed off, but the lids didn't flicker. Still, still as death. Only faint breathing that even he could barely hear said she was alive.

Oh, Grandpa, come and help me. Bring Mama and all the Ancestors. Bring the Great One and the eagles and Kachinas. Bring them, please. Save her, he prayed.

Nothing. No sustenance. No aid.

The driver spoke into a mic, asking for a gate they couldn't see to be opened. They pulled into an almost invisible lane and drove down it, leafy branches brushing the sides of the vehicle.

"It's an old estate," Doug said. Leroy was so glad Doug was there. He was a spirit warrior too, married to his soul mate. He knew what Leroy was feeling.

"Buddy," Doug said and laid a hand on Leroy's arm. "You can't save her. I don't even think your grandfather could. She's got a curse on her, Leroy. She's got to work her way through it herself. This is where she belongs. We have to leave her and leave her fast before Donatore knows what's going on. She's been here before. I brought her here. They got her better. We've got to get out of the way and let them do it."

They were at the emergency door of the hospital: an old mansion, shingled brown and three stories high. He could feel the place; it was a good place, old and well cared for.

They were in a white room. They had had to go through white corridors to get to it, fresh painted white and clean. Cass lay on the gurney, waxen.

"Please, baby, do something. Let me know you're alive. Let me know you know I'm here." Tears streamed down Leroy's cheeks. He didn't wipe them. Oh, if she didn't say something, do something ... His tears pelted down and he wanted to bend over and sob. He hovered at the edge.

"We've got to go. She can't hear you." Doug took his arm to lead him out, but he shrugged it away and ran to her.

Leaning over the bed, Leroy grabbed her arms and shoved his face close to hers. "Baby, it's *me*. Don't you know *me?*"

"Mr. Watches, I'm afraid I have to insist …" A doctor with a stethoscope around his neck and a clipboard entered the room. Two nurses followed. A big guy in a white suit was behind him.

Doug pulled on his shoulder. Leroy was ready to turn, ready to belt him, ready to go with him, when a movement stopped him. Cass was looking at him, eyes shiny in their sunken sockets. She just looked at him. Didn't say anything. Her soul pulled him into her; he inhabited her, just for a moment. Her eyes closed.

"I love you, Cass. Get well for me."

She couldn't die, could she? Not after their souls had touched.

6

TAKE A POWDER, KID

"SHE'S GOING TO be at the clinic about four months," Will Duane took Leroy into his study a few days after he had gotten back from rescuing Cass. Leroy was staying at Will's estate in Woodside, with the pack of warriors he had invited to his home after the Meeting.

Leroy glanced at him, and then looked away quickly.

"I'm sorry, son." Will knew how lousy he looked. "I'm stressed out. I've got a lot on my plate. What you did, finding Cass and getting her to safety, was heroic. I'm very grateful. Have a seat by my desk." Will moved to the gigantic desk in his personal quarters. "The most important problem in my life is solved. You'd think I'd be relieved. Maybe even *happy*." He chuckled.

"Turns out Cass was the most important problem *last* week. Now, the rest are screaming." He ran his hand through his hair, as he did when upset. Will was wired and angry and felt like snapping. At least Leroy didn't ask him why.

"Let's go over the game plan for Cass. When she's discharged from the hospital, I'll move her to the Havertin Institute for treatment of her addictions and mental illness." Leroy started to object, but Will shut him down.

"Havertin has an impeccable reputation. And they won't kick her out. They can't. It's a locked institution. I'm committing her involuntarily. She won't be able to get herself kicked out and go back to what she was. None of us want to go through that again."

"She's locked in an' can't get out?" Leroy said. "What if she *needs* to get out? What if that place isn't so good as you think? Can you visit her and see? Can I?"

"No. No visitors. I can talk to her shrink, but not her. By cutting the patients off from the outside world, the hospital becomes their universe and they learn how to live in it, something they didn't do in *this* world. Havertin is a good place."

"You don't know it's a good place. How many good places did you put her in before that didn't work?"

Leroy had challenged him. No one did that.

Will reared back in his chair, ready to blast the kid. But he smiled. "You care about her, I like that." He fiddled with a paperclip on his desk, thinking.

If Cass lives, this young man will most likely become my son-in-law. He won't make it at the level of the pond where I swim, but he's a damn sight better than all of the sleazy shit-heads Cass has brought home. He can do things that no one can. And he'll be good to her. Maybe I can clean him up a bit.

"Leroy, there's no sense you hanging around here for months. How would you like to take a vacation?"

"I'd rather see Cass."

"That's not going to happen until she completes treatment." Will shot a look at him. He'd been told people found his dark blue eyes intimidating. He didn't care. "Where have you been, Leroy? Have you been to Europe?"

"No."

"How'd you like to see Rome? And Venice? How about London?"

"No, I'm not interested."

"Everyone wants to see those places."

"That time I flew back to New York to get Cass with Doug was the only time I've been on a plane. I thought I'd die. I'd never have done it except for Cass. I never want to do it again."

Will smiled. "If we could handle your fear of flying, would you like to see London? Stay in a castle and go foxhunting in England? Eat pasta in Rome?"

"There is nothing that could make me not afraid of flying."

The phone rang. Will picked it up.

"Duane here," Will was silent maybe a minute. "What the fuck are you talking about?" He was out of his seat screaming into his receiver. *"No, Ric, it is not OK if you make 'a few adjustments' in the new NumoPhone.* Yes, I know it will increase our margins and market share—until our buyers discover that we've sold them crap.

"Numenon does not make crap, Ric, even if you and your friends want to. Numenon is what it is because it creates excellent products that you have to beat to death to break. We care about our customers." He listened a bit longer.

"Oh, yeah, Ric. You're right, we could toughen our exchange policies so if our stuff falls apart, our customers are stuck with it. But we're not going to, because we're honest and fair.

"You know the most important thing about Numenon as a corporation? We've never been whores for profit.

"No cheap crap. No lying. No screwing buyers. We pay our people living wages. That's how I've run this company for forty years." He slammed the phone down on the receiver, and stood over his desk, wanting to upend it. Will looked around, eyes settling on Leroy.

"I've got to get out of here." He pushed a button and some draperies opened, revealing a wall of glass with a pair of wide sliding doors going out to a huge deck. Fashionable teak furniture arranged in seating groups was spotted around the deck.

Will dashed out of the house like he was on fire. He walked to the far end of the patio, leaned on the railing, and raked his eyes across the view: rolling golden hills dotted with huge oaks. A freeway cut across the left corner of the scene. You couldn't hear the traffic from inside, but you could outside. Will looked at the rushing cars, laughing bitterly.

"I couldn't get CalTrans to build that son of a bitch one hill over thirty years ago when they did it. Look what they did. Ruined my view, but mostly raped the most beautiful valley on the planet. Assholes.

"I guess I shouldn't mind losing. I've lost before." He laughed again, a little hysterical. Will turned and took a step away from the railing. He stumbled and ended up sitting on one of the big lounge chairs. He swore again and slowly bent his body over his knees.

Leroy realized what was happening and ran over to him. "What's the matter, Mr. Duane?"

Will looked up, tears in his eyes. He took a moment to speak. "They're going to take Numenon from me. I thought it would happen when I got back from the Meeting, but I've held on." He flashed a glance at Leroy.

"They can take it from you?" Leroy looked mystified.

"Oh, yeah. All it takes is a vote of *my* Board of Directors and I'll be out. No matter that *I* founded Numenon and made it what it is for over forty years. Jackasses who couldn't keep a hamburger joint solvent are going to fire *me*." Will paused, hiding his face with his hands.

"I've known it was coming, I just didn't know how much it would *hurt* ..." Leroy handed him a handkerchief.

"I wrecked my marriage by running around with women, but I wasn't chasing my dick all the time. I gave every waking hour to Numenon. I gave it my soul, my heart." He made a pfft! and waved his hands. "And now, I'm going to lose it.

"What's happening?" Leroy said.

"The bad guys are going to win. You know about Sandy Sydney, don't you?" Leroy did. Doug had told him about the rogue super-secretary who was not only the most beautiful blonde in existence; she was a fiend and recruiter for the devil. "She fucked every one of my executives. If they weren't bastards before, they're demons now. That's what's taking over the company I founded. The spawn of the devil.

"Sandy Sydney would have gotten me, too, except I had a feeling about her. One thing screwing as many hookers as I have did for me—I can smell one coming." He chuckled. His face felt like a plaster casting.

"The Meeting was ..." he exhaled. "How can you describe the Meeting? Hell and heaven, back to back. I faced myself and saw what an asshole I had been. But I saw something else, too." Will raised his head, a little hope coming back. "I experienced the glory of the universe. I discovered that I was a man of God, and I had been all my life. I've had visions that guided me all my life. *They* are what made Numenon what it is."

"When I got back from the Meeting, I wanted to make Numenon into a corporation based on Love. Like your grandfather talks about. Love, respect. Caring for the people and the planet. I sound like a bleeding heart? Don't I? You know why? I *am*! I always have been. But I was too chicken to come out and be who I really was.

Will looked at him, face haggard again. "Ric Chao and Frank Sauvage will be monsters wearing human flesh by next year. They'll make my Numenon into an economic rape and pillage machine.

"They'll discredit everything I've done. That's what I'll get to live with in my golden years.

"And then Cass on top of it ..." He threw up his hands with a hopeless chuckle. "She's my only family."

Leroy moved forward. He was going to try to heal him, Will could see. But he wouldn't let him. He deserved to suffer. Will held up his hand, a stiff smile on his face.

"Hey. I'll have Doug or someone put an itinerary together for you. Go on a trip, Leroy. Have fun. Someone needs to. And who knows, next trip, maybe it will be you and me and Cass. A family."

"Go." Will waved him away before Leroy could lessen his pain.

"Will, dear," the raspy voice of one of his dearest and oldest—in every way—friends assailed Will's ears through his phone.

"You're always the harbinger of good news, Vanessa. What do you want to blame me for now?" She could not have chosen a worse time to call.

"Oh, my, aren't we touchy?"

"I just finished discussing the demise of my professional career with an almost stranger. A cowboy, or Indian. The man who saved Cass. All I needed was a vampire attack"

"I'm not a vampire, Will. My family has never had anything to do with *vampires*. But tell me about Cass. I heard that young man and your other people have found Cass. That's wonderful."

"It was nothing short of miraculous, Vanessa. She's in terrible condition. I've put her in a hospital to gain weight and stabilize her physical condition. When she's healthy enough, I'm moving her to the Havertin Institute in New York to handle her addiction and mental health problems."

"Why send her so far away, Will? My hospital is at your disposal, both for her physical and mental needs. Do you know how well our facility is rated? My hospital is top rated in every dimension. And we're thirty minutes from your house. I'll see that she gets well."

Will's jaws clenched. "Vanessa, I put her in your hospital years ago. You know what happened. I walked into your barn three days after she got there and found her fucking my horse trainer and doing coke.

"You can't handle her. You don't have the security and you don't have the experience to deal with someone like Cass. Your nicey-nicey staff, Rudy and the rest of them, don't know what to do with someone who attacks when she's threatened and can con you faster than shake your hand.

"What diseases do you treat, anyway?"

"You know what illnesses I treat at our clinic," Vanessa said stiffly. "My children are bipolar and schizophrenic. You know that. You also know that, in addition to caring for my family, I take other interesting psychiatric cases to keep my psychiatrists busy and myself alive intellectually."

"What's your cure rate?"

She bridled. "The diseases we treat are incurable. They are *treatable*. People with the disorders can live healthy, fully functioning lives."

"How many of your patients have jobs and marriages when you're done?"

"That's cruel, Will. You know how ill my family is. The other patients we take are the most difficult cases that exist. Other institutions have not been able to help them. When they leave here, they're better." The old lady's voice was tight with anger.

"Will, I think you're making a terrible mistake that you'll regret forever. Why a hospital so far away?

"I'm satisfied with my investigation and ..." He depressed the lever on his phone while he was speaking. He smiled. She'd never know he hung up on her.

Will sat at his desk in his home office. He stared at the fine wooden surface spreading out in front of him. The draperies were closed, but he wouldn't have been distracted by the priceless view of the rolling golden hills of Woodside, one of the most affluent towns in the world.

Why did Vanessa think she had the right to talk to him like that? Cass was his daughter. He had the right to decide what was best for her. He squirmed in his chair. He'd been uneasy since Leroy had come back. She would get well, and they would have the father-daughter relationship he'd dreamed of all of her life.

Leroy had found her, but *he* would save her. He and the hundreds of thousands it would cost to get her through the hospitals. He'd done it so many times before, and he would this time. He would save his daughter as long as she was alive. *He* would do that.

She would not run off with some penniless cowboy whose spelling didn't make fifth grade. Leroy had written him an email from New York. The man was barely literate. Cass was *his*. His muscles tensed: jaws, shoulders, arms. Thighs, feet. Will didn't notice.

He was back there again. What had happened last Christmas was live for a moment: his Montana ranch's log walls glowed. The lights on the pine garlands festooning the great hall twinkled. The tree touched the three story high ceiling, branches weighed down by ornaments.

Cass's head was half shaved. The dragon tattoo her hair had covered looked like it would come alive from her scalp. She screamed at him, "You are a *shit! You use people. You use me.* You want everyone to think you're such a good father, but you're not. People feel sorry for you because I'm such a *burden*, but they don't *know…*"

She'd gone on like that, cursing and screaming, her sweater's shoulder falling down to show her skeletal form.

He ran out of the house and called his pilots to take him back to the Bay Area. He'd cried all the way home, wiping away tears of pain and truth. She hurt him, almost mortally. He hated Cass. She was too smart and too sick and knew it was his fault. He hadn't kept her safe. He hated her for being so smart. She saw through anything. Deeper inside, some part wanted to get back at her for the pain she'd caused him.

This time, he'd do it right. Havertin was right. Will was sure of it. Fuck Vanessa, fuck Leroy. Maybe that clodhopper cowboy would learn something where he was sending him. If he didn't, see where he got with Cass. She wasn't the tender flower he thought she was.

Cass was as snobby as the best of them when she was clean and sober. Dressed like a model in a fashion magazine and spoke like an English professor. She didn't talk like a stevedore when she wasn't on drugs, but she wasn't a sweet thing that was so grateful, y'all. Leroy would get a big surprise, if her treatment worked.

Will picked up a crystal paperweight on his desk. For an instant, he wanted to throw it. He wouldn't. He didn't want Cass savaging Leroy over his manners. He wanted a family that worked. More than anything, Will wanted to do the right thing. This was it.

Two weeks later, when Leroy and Doug were flying across the Atlantic, Leroy had to admit that Mr. Duane was the most powerful and effective man he knew. He got a psychologist to hypnotize him. Leroy thought hypnosis would be like in the movies; he'd go to a creepy old house with cobwebs and spiders. A weird lady in robes would say, "Watch the shining ball."

It wasn't that way. A young man with a short beard had him sit down in a bright office. Then he gave him instructions. "Remember a time when you felt very strong." Leroy did. Somehow the guy added in an airplane, then imagining sitting in one. Imagining it taking off. Took a few sessions.

After hypnotizing him so he wasn't afraid *thinking* about getting on an airplane, the psychologist took Leroy to the San Jose airport. There, he had him climbing in and out of Will's planes, from really big ones to itty bitty ones.

7

JOLLY OLDE ENGLAND

OUTSIDE OF WILL'S home in Woodside, the condo in London was the most amazing place Leroy had seen, bigger and more luxurious than the one in New York. The apartment in New York had been all slick leather and straight lines, with artwork that looked like kids did it using duct tape and finger-paints.

This place was furnished with huge chairs and sofas covered with fabrics like the ones he'd seen on *Hermitage Estate: Upstairs and Down*. The pictures on the walls were of things you could recognize—people and horses and trees. Everything wooden was carved and polished and velvet draperies hung at the windows. Only the splendor of Will's house in Woodside surpassed this urban palace.

Leroy stalked around, looking in the rooms' doorways and peeking out the windows at the dark streets. They were shiny, wet with rain.

"You know what this trip is about?" Doug said, following him like a shadow.

"Oh, yeah. 'Welcome to Will's world.'" He couldn't stop pacing. The nervousness he'd felt since he set foot on that plane to rescue Cass had caught up with him. "Will's makin' sure that if Cass and me get married, I won't embarrass him."

Leroy went back to pacing. He would have sworn, if he had been a swearing man. What was so wrong with him? Back home, he felt just fine in his skin, and his world. Step into Will Duane's world and he had to be remodeled like a rundown house. Maybe get indoor plumbing for the first time. He kept moving, wanting to kick something.

He thought to himself, *Hold on, Leroy, if you want Cass, this is what you have to do. You have to fit into her world. Her world, not yours. Nothin' wrong with you that these folks won't find and make worse. Eat humble pie. Maybe you'll like it.*

Doug opened his mouth to say something, but the telephone rang. He grabbed it and scooted into his bedroom. Leroy could hear the strain in his voice through wooden panels.

"Baby, I will be home as soon as I can." Doug burst out of the bedroom. He held the phone against his ear with his shoulder, partially covering the mouthpiece with his hand. As though that kept Leroy from hearing everything. "You're OK. You're at Will's. Everyone cares about you. I'll be home in a week, tops. You're fine, sweetheart."

Leroy followed Doug's movements and words, becoming concerned.

"Don't worry, baby. I love you. Can I talk to Carl?" Doug turned around as though he was heading back into the bedroom then stopped. "Carl? Is she OK?" He listened. "I need to be there. I'll come home tomorrow." A deep voice resounded from the phone, but Leroy couldn't hear what he said, other than what the tone of his voice said, "No. You need to stay."

"Can you take care of her for me?" Tough, worldly Doug had tears in his eyes. "Thank you, man. I owe you big time."

He hung up the phone and looked at Leroy, desperate.

"Janice?"

"Yeah. She's freaking out. It's all too much," he waved his hand around the room. Will's world. "Do you know anything about Janice?"

Leroy knew all about Janice. He and Grandfather had rescued her from a situation similar to Cass's. Too similar. She'd become an exemplary warrior, recovering from what life had thrust on her and her alcoholism. But Leroy sensed that Janice needed Doug and needed him now. All the work she'd done since meeting Grandfather was in jeopardy.

"Go home. I can take care of myself. I'm a spirit warrior."

"No! You need me as much as Janice does. That's why Carl told me to stay. You don't know what you're in for. Sit down, Leroy. I'm going to tell you the facts of life." Doug indicated one of the overstuffed chairs. He sat on the adjoining sofa.

"You're in charm school." Doug's mouth tightened. "Will is giving you this trip because he needs to stash you somewhere until we see if Cass is going to make it. She's been hospitalized a bunch of times before. You know that. You don't know that I was there for her a couple of them." Leroy's jaw fell open.

"Yeah. I was in love with her. I fell out of love with her the first time she got mad at me. Have you heard about Will's temper?" Leroy shook his head. "No? If he blows up at you, you'll never forget it. Cass is *off* the scale. She *attacks*." He pulled up his sleeve and showed Leroy half-circle scars on his forearm, top and bottom. The scars bore tooth marks. "Cass. Thirty-six stitches.

"Most likely she won't make it out of rehab clean. But if she does, Will wants you ready to take her off his hands." Leroy slumped, brow furrowing. "If you asked Will what he was doing, he wouldn't say that, but it doesn't take a rocket scientist to figure it out.

"He wants you to fit in his world, which is also Cass's world. She was raised like this." He waved his hand, indicating the luxurious room.

"But what if she doesn't make it and you don't end up married? You're Grandfather's grandson. Whatever Grandfather has is in you too;

anybody can feel it. You're a valuable corporate asset. But Will needs a man he can send anywhere."

Leroy stood up. "I'm not good enough for him?"

"No, you're not. Not now."

"Why didn't he tell me that to my face?"

"Will doesn't work like that. You know some things about him. What does he do if he want's something fixed?"

Leroy was silent for a moment. "Sends a fixer."

"And what am I?"

"You're Will's fixer." Leroy wanted to head to his room and get his bags. "Are you fixing me?"

"What I can see that needs it. But there's fixing and there's fixing. There's what we did to save Cass, and there's me dealing with some lying motherfucker that needs his head kicked in. I don't do that, but I do the legal equivalent."

"What are you doing now?"

"I'm helping a friend. Will should have talked to you and said something like, 'I need to have you more polished if you're going to be going places with Cass or working for me.' He didn't; he sent me. Will's an asshole, Leroy. I knew that before the Meeting, and I really know it now. But that's not all of him. You've lived at his house. What do you notice about Will?"

Leroy was ready to leave. "He's rich. He gets his way. He's …"

"Not a bad guy. Sit down. What did you notice about the people he took to the Meeting? The people at his house?"

Leroy thought back to the retreat. He was only there a little while, but he remembered that the executives were an Asian guy, Melissa, and Doug. Some of the drivers died in the massacre, but they were white, Latino, and African American. His chef was gay. Living at his house now? Maybe fifteen people from the Meeting, Indians, all of them.

"Did he mind that Melissa, who everyone considers Will's real daughter, married Wesley, the most Indian Indian on the planet?"

Leroy shook his head.

"That's right. Will is *color blind*. Race does not matter to him. Neither does sex, sexual preference, or religion. He's a really good person in that respect. What he cares about is *performance*. Get the deal done. Win the prize, no matter who gets hurt. And he cares about his favorites. He will back them—us—up beyond what you can imagine. As long as we come through and don't betray him. The problem isn't Will. Do you understand?"

"No."

Doug blew out a breath. "Will wants you to fit in his world and make it with Cass. I want that too, Leroy, really a lot. I'm one of you; I'm a spirit warrior. I've never been around people like you. You love each other. And I feel you like me ... *love* me." Doug's face worked like he was trying to spit out a poison toad. "You deserve to be the man you could be—not just the really nice, country guy. You could be master of the universe." Doug seemed to be fighting with himself.

"What are you trying to say?"

"Oh, shit, Leroy. Some of the people you're going to meet would make hamburger out of you for the fun of it. They'll try to humiliate you. They'll break you if they can. Why?"

"To get back at Will?"

"Yeah. But mostly, because you're black."

Leroy jerked.

"Will's color blind, but some people you're going to meet and have to charm are just plain racist sons of bitches. Not just racist. They think they're descended from God because their ancestors got named Lord this or Earl that, most likely for doing shitty things to peasants living in the mud.

"If you don't get the stuff Will has lined up for you right, they'll keep you out of their world forever. And wreck your value to Will. They'll do it so slick, you won't know what happened.

"I know this, because they tried it with me. I was raised in Beverly Hills and my dad's a CEO. I can play their games. But you're a nice guy. They'll cut you to ribbons. That's why I need to stay here."

Leroy stared at Doug, speechless. "Where do you think I've been, Doug?" he finally choked out. "You think the neighbors love my dad and me because we're so nice? No. I heal every person and animal that can get to me for free. The neighbors *love* that. My dad's a famous rodeo clown. A celebrity. Neighbors like that too. But not *all* of them.

"Back when my long-ago grandpa got the place, they wanted to shoot us Watches back to Africa. We didn't get run off or killed because my daddy's people had always had a mojo going. Juju. I got an *African* juju *and Native* juju.

"You're so afraid for me that you won't go home to take care of Janice? That's crazy, man." Leroy shook his head. But Doug kept scratching at his head like Leroy was in terrible danger and couldn't see it.

"The Rez was worse. I lived there from when I was six 'til I was twenty. Do you think the reservation was *nice?*

"If we stepped one foot off the Rez, *nobody* liked us. *Everyone* wanted to humiliate us and ruin our chances. Especially *me*, because I was Grandfather's grandson *and* had African blood.

"You're afraid I can't handle people hatin' me because of my skin?" Leroy shook his head in amazement.

"Yes." Doug's eyes misted again.

Leroy didn't laugh. It was more of a convulsive chuckle. Doug's feelings were nice, and unusual, but only a white man would think he was such a flimsy piece of business. He was sweet and kind because of Grandfather and the Great One and his own Self, not because people hadn't noticed the color of his skin.

"You've never been where you're going now." Doug glared at him. "I know you think I'm stupid, but you don't know what you're in for." Leroy could almost hear a growl under Doug's breath. "We're up early tomorrow for breakfast instruction, by the way."

"Breakfast instruction?"

"Yes, sir. Breakfast and tableware. Do you know how many pieces of flatware there are in a formal place setting?"

"No."

"Nine on a skimpy service. With three crystal goblets and three plates. And a bowl. How many courses does a formal dinner have?"

"Why are you asking me this?"

"Because Leroy, you may end up dining with heads of state. You need to know that a formal dinner has eight courses, with a ninth optional."

"That's what I'm going to be doing here?"

"Some of it. Will has a lesson in table settings set up for you tomorrow morning, then for a little quiz on what you learned, a formal lunch with Peter Alexander Payton Faxmore, Lord of Ballentyne at his club. Then we play golf with him and a few pals."

"I've never played golf."

"I've played it all my life. I hope you're a fast learner. They're good here." Doug leaned toward him. "This is serious, Leroy. Your future hangs on mastering shit so stupid that if anyone ever told you that it mattered, you'd think they were joking.

"If you mess up with this shit, they'll fry your ass. Except you'll never know what you did. You'll break some rule and you'll never get invited anywhere in polite society again.

"That's why I need to stay with you. To cover your ass when you screw up. And you will screw up."

Doug's blue eyes bored into Leroy's like he was looking for the Titanic. "Anything else you want do before we turn in?"

"Yeah," Leroy said, as serious as Doug. "They're supposed to retire Jackie Robinson's number at the Mets/Dodgers game tonight. President Clinton's going to be there. Let's see if we can catch the ceremony on TV. It may make you feel better about what a black man can do."

Turned out they'd missed the presentation, so they channel-surfed the news. They stopped when the screen showed a couple of English newscasters standing in the dusty road leading to Leroy's reservation. The unmistakable loaf mountain poked up in the distance.

"Well, Clive, still no sign of the hundreds of people who disappeared only a few miles from here." The announcer looked like the raven-haired version of every newscaster Leroy had seen since news of what happened at the Meeting exploded around the planet. The camera panned the sky. Black military helicopters shot toward the Mogollon Bowl and the setting sun.

"Only a few miles up that road on reservation land, a mass murder as horrifying as the Jonestown/Guyana massacre occurred."

"That's right, Edmund. Thousands of Native Americans came here for a spiritual retreat led by a famous shaman." An artist's conception of Grandfather filled the screen.

"Thousands went, but thousands didn't return. We're going to cut to New York City and Paul Running, the head of the Running Way, a prominent Native American spiritual group. Paul is a shaman himself and witnessed the disaster."

"Paul Running Bird isn't a shaman!" Leroy cried. "He's a been my grandpa's student for twenty years and didn't learn a thing! He wasn't in the Mogollon Bowl when it happened."

"He's on every channel," Doug said. "He's the new face of Native American spirituality. The massacre is just what he needed."

Paul's sonorous voice quivered with emotion. "It was hideous …"

8

OUT OF THE BALLPARK

LORDS MARTINGALE, SURCINGLE, and Pontificate joined Lord Ballentyne, Doug, and Leroy at the Heritage course of the London Golf Club. He was introduced all around. They already knew Doug. *Everyone* knew Doug.

The English Lords were as polite as he'd seen them portrayed on *Hermitage Estate: Upstairs and Down.* He and his dad sat in front of their TV every Sunday night and discussed the plot for days after each episode. The people around him could have been in the show. The Lords looked him over without staring. One finally said, "How tall are you, Leroy?"

"I'm six foot, eight and a half inches tall. In my socks."

They tittered politely.

"You could be a basketball player," Lord Surcingle said.

"Yeah, if I knew how to play basketball, I could do that."

Leroy did fine at lunch. He'd grasped silverware well enough to make it through the meal in fine form. He grew more anxious as they approached the golf course. The London Golf Club—a private club—said ritzy in an exceptionally low-key way. Brilliant green grass swathed everything: green lawn mowed close. Mowed extremely close. Bushy. Sand patches nestled in, ringed by trees. Wide avenues of lawn turned abruptly around lakes that looked like they were there to swallow golf balls.

Leroy realized that this was probably a difficult sport, even if it was stupid. How much had the Lords paid for him to whack up the turf from his first step on the course to his last?

"I hope you all know that I've never played golf."

"Doug told us that. Give it your best shot, old fellow. We're playing for fun." That was Lord Pontificate.

"All right. I just don't want to have to replant this course at the end."

They laughed.

Leroy dropped into the inner state where he lived when he healed. Relaxed, vigilant without being tense … "What club do I use, Doug? The big wood one?"

The Lords tittered and then stared, open-mouthed. Leroy's ball soared past theirs, landing in the middle of the fairway.

"This is kind of fun," he loped after his ball, making the mistake of trying to carry his own clubs.

"The caddy does that, Leroy." Doug was plainly delighted. When they got to the green, Doug whispered, "Do *not* step on the green between anybody's ball and the hole. That's a no-no."

Leroy kept going, his balls soaring past the others'. "Yeah, I'm kinda getting the hang of this." Another fantastic swing and the ball shot through the air like a Winchester 223 Super Short Magnum, the fastest bullet in the world. Leroy loped ahead of the group from hole to hole, eschewing the carts.

"Oh, yeah, this one's hard. You got to be very careful here. I can see that. William, would you get me that one with the flat edge." He called his caddy by his first name. The Lords twitched every time he did it.

"Boy, this grass sure is short. I wonder how they get it this short." Leroy squatted on the green of the fourteenth hole and studied the distance between his ball and the hole. Someone pulled the flag out of the hole. "That's a good idea. Easier to get the ball in." He gave it the tiniest little tap, and the ball scooted into the hole.

"Good lord, you're on par," Lord Ballentyne. "The fourteenth hole is the hardest on the course. It has a stroke index of *one!*"

Leroy scored seventy-eight, probably the lowest of any first time player in history, on that course, certainly. The only place he didn't score was the 19th hole.

They went to a dark-paneled and very posh bar at the end of the course. Everyone ordered with gusto. Except Leroy.

"You don't imbibe?" one of the Lords asked. Maybe Lord Martingale.

"I don't drink. It's against my religion."

Drinking wasn't against their religion; the Lords drank freely, Scotch, mostly. They were very interested in his beliefs and spiritual life. He had to explain about shamans, spirit warriors, and his grandfather.

"Your grandfather is a shaman?"

"Was. He died a little while ago."

"Did he have supernatural powers?"

"Yes, he did. He could heal anything. Broken souls, mostly. And do all sorts of other things. Even blow things up."

Leroy could see it happen: with one mind, the Lords recalled the sensational reports of a bull that exploded at a Las Vegas rodeo not so long before. A very tall, African American cowboy had been implicated. Their collective eyes continued to widen as the coverage of a recent and horrific spiritual retreat led by a Native American shaman in New Mexico returned to their minds full force.

This was exactly what he and Doug had realized would happen as they watched the news the night before. Everyone—including the noblemen they were meeting the next day—knew about the massacre and the general descriptions of the parties involved. Will had been there: all the major networks had interviewed him. He was trying to do damage control for Grandfather. The Lords knew that Will employed Doug and that Leroy was connected to him. Was Leroy's grandfather the leader of a cult and a mass murderer? Was Leroy himself?

"This is your first big test," Doug had said after he turned off the news. "You have to convince them that you're a good guy, your Grandfather's a good guy, and neither of you were in on the massacre. If you don't convince them completely tomorrow, you won't have a future in England or anywhere. If they buy you and your story, they'll tell their friends and the upper classes will open to you. You'll never hear about it again. If they don't accept you, you might as well go home."

"How will I know if they've accepted me?"

"They'll invite you to their country houses."

"You were at the massacre?" Lord Ballentyne's features stiffened. Leroy learned that the British stiff upper lip included the whole body. "Did you see it? And what about the rodeo and the exploding bull?"

"I didn't blow up the bull. I don't know how he blew up," Leroy spoke carefully, using all the spiritual power he could muster. "The FBI said a crazy agent made up the story about the bull so he could get a promotion. President Clinton agreed. I got to the Meeting when it was almost over. I don't know anything about what happened, except that my grandfather is the best person I ever met."

Doug jumped in. "I was at the retreat the whole time and *I* don't know what happened. Everything was fine until a bunch of hoodlums brought out the booze. They had threatened to cause trouble every year, but this year they did it. They had mushrooms, psychedelics. I don't know what. *They* started a riot.

"Grandfather got us to a cave where nothing could get us." Doug nodded at Leroy. "His grandfather *is* the most wonderful person in the world. And Leroy got to the retreat the night before we came home. He didn't see anything."

"Good heavens," said Lord Ballentyne. "Drunken ruffians on drugs caused a riot? Is that what all the fuss is about? What about the monsters?"

"I didn't see any." Doug raised his hand. "Swear to God." Leroy was amazed by how easily Doug lied, and with such a convincing effect. But then *he* had lied. He'd told the Lords his first lie. He had blown up the bull to save his father.

"Were there monsters?" Lord Ballentyne's eyebrows rose so high that they nearly hit his hairline.

"I'm not supposed to say anything more. It's *classified.*" Doug's face was emotionless.

"Oh."

"Every federal agency you can think of interviewed everyone from Numenon. They've got a division that investigates paranormal experiences and UFOs. *That's* where the case ended up. In the division for fruits and nuts. And I'm not supposed to tell you that. It's *all* classified."

"But the news …"

"The news destroyed the feds' case, tromping all over any evidence. Everyone whose spouse ran off in the last ten years is saying it happened at the retreat. All the whackos in the world are swarming the desert and reservation." Doug shook his head, looking pained. "Your Lordships, we've known each other for years. You know I wouldn't lie to you."

"That's true," Ballentyne spoke for them all. "It's classified?"

"Extremely."

"Leroy wasn't implicated?"

"No. Tell them, Leroy."

He repeated the script he and Doug had worked out as sincerely as possible.

"Well, if Will Duane and Bill Clinton agreed, it must be true." Ballentyne nodded gravely and his noble compatriots nodded in sync. "Besides, Leroy has too much potential as a golfer to do wrong." He chuckled merrily.

"Where is your grandfather?" said Lord Martingale. Leroy's eyes filled instantly. The others turned to Martingale, scowling.

"I say, John, that's rather personal," Ballentyne added quickly.

Doug cut in again, which was a good thing, because Leroy's eyes swam with tears. Doug spoke barely above a whisper. "Every year after the retreat, Grandfather—that's what we all called him—went for a walk in the desert. This year he didn't come back." Leroy jumped to his feet and ran toward the men's room, stopping where he could hear what went on at the table, but not be seen. Doug continued. "They'll never find the body. Scavengers." The Lords gasped.

"What brings Leroy to England, if I may ask?" That was Martingale, who Leroy realized was a gadfly, but the one who asked all the questions that no one else would.

"Leroy did Will a personal favor," Doug's calm voice reassured them. "He's giving him a year on the continent to repay him."

"Oh," the Lords said collectively. All of them had had a year on the continent when growing up. It was a rite of passage. Martingale opened his mouth to ask about the nature of the favor, but Lord Ballentyne cut him off.

Leroy slipped back to his chair, shaky but composed.

"Is there anything you'd like to do while you're here, Leroy?" Ballentyne asked after a moment's silence.

"Yes, your Lordship. I'd like to play polo. I've never done that. And I'd like to go fox hunting. I've never done that either. Though I can't see any reason for hunting foxes. Wild boar. Elk. Deer. They're worth hunting." That earned him more smiles.

"Will has Leroy fully scheduled through December," Doug said. "But maybe we can cut him some free time. He goes to Rome soon."

"The hunt season starts in November. We could get you up an exhibition game of polo then too. Informally."

"Right on! Her Grace and I will expect you at our country house," said Lord Ballentyne.

"And then at my place."

"And mine!"

9

CHARM SCHOOL, WEEK ONE

"THAT WASN'T SO bad," Leroy said, basking in his triumph.

"That was baby stuff." Doug looked at him from under furrowed brows. "You hit a home run, but you're barely into the first inning."

"I still don't get why all this matters. Why don't I just travel around and see things?"

"Because you'd still be Leroy Watches Jr., cowboy rancher, when you're done. Will wants you to be his ambassador. Do you know why Will wants you to make it with these people? Or why he cares about them at all?"

"No."

"They're gatekeepers. They can open doors that pure money can't. Doors to bankers, more nobility, and *royalty*, plus the people who really make decisions. There's more to being at the top than just money.

"Will has wanted to expand into Britain and Europe in a big way for years. He wants to beat Donatore on his own turf. Europe is where Donatore is from and where he plays. And he plays; he's a social bigwig. Will wants a piece of the action."

"Will's the richest man on Earth. Why does he need 'in' on anything?"

"Will is in, but you need to know something else. There's rich, and there's rich. Among people who have been rich for four hundred years, Will's the new kid on the block. Did you know that he couldn't get invited *anywhere* when he first got to California? Couldn't get into a single top country club in San Francisco or the Peninsula, even for lunch?"

Leroy shook his head. "Why?"

"Will was raised with a lot of money, but it was from handling industrial waste or something; dirty and definitely not classy. His father was a thug. Will was too rough as a young Stanford grad for society to accept him, even though he was starting the tech industry and making a bundle, on top of his family's bundle. That was in the 50s and 60s. He had to do the same thing you're doing."

Leroy was dumbfounded. "Will had to learn knives and forks?"

"Yeah, Will Duane had to learn what people who are truly upper class care about. We've got an upper class in the US just as much as here. What got Will's career in the fast lane was meeting this crazy old lady, Dr. Vanessa Schierman. Her ancestors were the ones who took California from the Indians. Before that, they ruined the lives of peasant farmers back in Germany for a thousand years. That's *old* money.

"Dr. Schierman took a liking to Will and cleaned him up. And she got him in everywhere. They kowtow to her anywhere she goes. Breeding, money, and brains. She's a physicist. She views Will as a member of the family."

"Will got where he is because he had good manners?"

"No. The right people would talk to him and treat him as an equal when he got into their clubs because he has good manners, and connections to people with money and social power. He got where he is because he's a ruthless, driven competitor who was in the right place at the right time. Wait until you meet Dr. Schierman." Doug grinned ear to ear.

"Why?"

"You'll see." Doug smiled. "I know all this because Will and I were best friends once. I said we fucked our way around the world together; we also talked. I thought he was the best man on Earth once." Doug shrugged. "I found out he's OK. Not the best, not the worst.

"But—you're gonna be busy. The tailor is coming at one, followed by your hair stylist and manicurist." The doorbell rang. "That's your staff."

Doug admitted a group of people better groomed than the nobility Leroy had met, but dressed in plain black fabric. Doug led them into the kitchen and jerked his head at Leroy to get him to come. His staff?

"We're pleased that you are able to join Mr. Watches' household staff." Doug gave a formal spiel; picking his words as through he was born saying them. Maybe he was. "He's going to be coming and going from England, but you will remain in residence, ensuring that his London home is properly looked after, and that he meets his social obligations in good order."

Doug took Leroy's arm and pulled him toward the group. "This is Mr. Evan Ainsley, your butler." A tall man nodded. He had an enormous nose that pointed straight out, grey hair, and posture more rigid and upright than any of the Lords.

"How do you do, Mr. …" Leroy said, holding out his hand. Doug had gotten him that far with proper forms of address.

The butler bowed deeply. "*Ainsley* will do nicely, sir. This is …" Ainsley introduced the cook, housekeeper, the three maids, and Leroy's valet, Tom.

Leroy's face widened and opened. He started to speak.

"That will be all for now," Doug said. Leroy frantically gestured to Doug, but the cook cut in with great earnestness.

"What would sir being wanting for supper? An' what do ye like for tea at four?"

Leroy stood, mouth flapping.

"Show him a good English tea, Mrs. Elvers. Do you have time to prepare a beef roast for tonight? Mr. Watches will go over the weeks' menus with you after tea."

"Why do I need so many people? We've been doing fine, jus' us." Tension caused Leroy's voice to rise. "I'm not even going to be here most of the time."

"If you're going to have any of the people we met yesterday here, you *must* have an appropriate staff. If you are invited for polo or hunting at their country estates, you'd *better* have the best damn chauffeur and valet in the universe."

"I didn't meet a chauffeur."

"He's in the garage with the new car. It's a Jag. Will is going to send different cars when you need them. But do you know who's going to save your bacon when I'm gone? Tom Wyatt. Your valet."

"What does a valet do?"

"Buttons up your pants."

"Nobody's buttoning up my pants but me."

"Leroy, you're invited to Lord and Lady Ballentyne's London house for dinner in a week. You are no more ready for that than flying to the moon. You're *going* to be ready for it, and I am to make sure you are. Then I'm going home, to Janice.

"It's a simple family dinner, just thirty or forty of the Ballentyne's dearest and nearest. In town. That means it's the real thing. You're being auditioned for acceptance into their circle." The bell rang. "That's the tailor." Leroy ran to get the door. "No, Leroy. Ainsley does that. From now on, your servants do everything but wipe your ass."

The young valet Tom Wyatt watched carefully as the tailor went to work on Leroy. The tailor and a couple of assistants had cases of patterns and measuring tools, as well as fabric samples.

"I'm sorry, sir, I can't do bespoke clothing. I don't have time. Mr. Duane's man, Mr. Saunders, said you needed a formal wardrobe within a week. We'll have to do made-to measure." The tailor seemed genuinely ashamed.

They had measured every part of him to the quarter inch. He had learned that bespoke clothing was not made from a pattern; it was made to fit, entirely from scratch. What he was getting relied on a pattern that was altered to fit his measurements. Previously, Leroy had considered the Big and Tall Store the ultimate in fashion and fit.

"The invitation is to a semi-formal dinner in Lord Ballentyne's home." Leroy said to the tailor. "Slacks and a sport coat are fine."

Tom, the valet, cut in. "Sir, with all respect, that means it's black tie, not white tie." Tom looked horrified. "You *cannot* go to the Ballentyne residence without being properly dressed."

"The young gentleman is right, sir," the tailor said, practically shaking in his immaculately polished shoes. "Informal is black tie. Formal is white tie. But we'll be able to do bespoke for that. We've plenty of time before you'll need a tailcoat."

The late afternoon brought another horror: his tutor on matters of noble titles and court etiquette. Sir Glathering had a firm grasp on how to talk to the nobles he'd meet. "No, Mr. Watches, you do not call Lord Ballentyne's wife Lady Ballentyne," he said. "She is Her Grace Violetta, the Duchess of Radenberry and Cloudfill. She is a *Duchess*, while her husband is an *Earl*. Her title and ancestral lands are far superior to his. Address her informally as Your Grace." Sir Glathering's lips, nose and face pinched so hard Leroy was surprised he could breathe.

After the tailor and barber left—the only hair Leroy got to keep was the little tail in back where he tied his feathers—Sir Glathering had arrived to begin teaching him how to speak to his hosts. Leroy got right away that Glathering was not very high in the royal pecking order if he was giving Lord and Lady lessons to an unknown cattle rancher from America.

Continuing on the topic of Her Grace, the Duchess of Radenberry and Cloudfill, Sir Glathering explained, "It's not an unusual thing that a woman would marry lower than herself in the *new* England, but it would have been unheard of earlier. Now, what would you call Her Grace's mother? She will be in attendance at the dinner party."

"Ma'am?"

"No! She is the Dowager Duchess of Raddenbery and Cloudfill. She retains her titles even though her husband, the late Lord of Raddenbery and Cloudfill, has passed on. Her estates went to her daughter, Her Grace, with her titles also going to her daughter. She is the *Dowager* Duchess. She retains a small estate and lives independently." Sir Glathering brightened when the butler brought in a tray of food. "I must say your cook puts on a good tea."

"She has a *small* estate?"

"Yes. That's the way things are. When her husband died, her daughter inherited everything. Now, stand and pretend to greet the Dowager Duchess for the first time."

Leroy did. "How do you do, Your Royal Dowager …"

"No! You do not speak until spoken to. Do it again."

Leroy stood there until Doug put on a squeaky voice and said, "How do you do, Mr. Watches. I'm pleased to make your acquaintance." Then Leroy said, "How do you do, Your Grace."

Glathering was pleased. "Now, how do you greet Lord Ballentyne's mother, the Dowager Lady Ballentyne?"

"She'll be there too?"

"Oh, yes. And aunts and uncles. Cousins. Very eager to meet you. The massacre, you know. But they won't say anything about it."

The week was like that: Glathering and his friends harassed him every day, all day. They presented charts of people who would probably be at the party, with pictures so he'd recognize them. "I must comment, be careful of the Dowager Duchess. She's a bit of a bristler." That meant she was such a bitch that Glathering thought he should be warned ahead of time. More on knives and forks. He was trundled to a dance studio downtown for private dance lessons. They were exceptionally private: they shut the studio for him. A red-headed woman with no backbone slithered around with him while a guy in a toupee shouted orders.

"*Doug, I'm done.* I won't do this anymore."

"That's good, Leroy. Because the party's tomorrow night and I'm leaving in the morning. Will doesn't think you're ready to do this alone, but I do. I have to get back to Janice. You'll have to face the bristling dowagers yourself."

"The Dowager Duchess of Raddenberry and Cloudfill bristles, not the other one. She's nice." He was furious. "Why does Will tell *you* what he thinks about me? Why don't he talk to *me*? If I'm so stupid an' this matters so much, why don't he send someone else over who can do it better? Or send someone else to babysit me if you can't?"

"An' believe it or not, I *can* eat dinner with decent folks. Y'all seem to think I'm just a good ol' boy who's never done nothing ..."

"You seem to think that I'm a country boy who hasn't done anything," Doug corrected. They'd had the language police after him too. They had given up.

"I *don't care.* You think I'm can't walk across the street by myself. I've done *plenty.* Come in here. I want to show you something. You all just assume I can't do nothin'," Leroy stormed into the living room. He powered up the computer and hit the button to put it on the large screen. Half the wall lit up. Typing an address, he stood back. "What do you think of that?"

"Holy shit!" Doug walked to the front of the screen. "*What the fuck?*"

"Yeah, what the ..." Leroy didn't swear. "Dumb old can't-do-a-thing Leroy Watches did that. No education, no money, just a bunch of cows.

An' I did *that*. When I came home to the ranch, my daddy was goin' under. Four years later, this is what we are."

A brilliantly simple but stylish website filled the screen. Colors were black, red, white, with a couple of skin colored areas. The background was bright red. Watches Ranch was written across the top in huge black letters. Round, friendly-looking letters. Under the letters on the right side and moving down the screen was a simple, pen-and-ink sketch of Yosemite's half dome. Giant Sequoia trees were drawn on the other side. In the middle, a neat bulleted list said what they raised.

- Kosher beef.
- Grass fed beef.
- Our beef is organic pasture grass fed only.
- Certified no hormones, antibiotics, inoculations, or grain.

There was a menu going to other pages.

"You raise *Kosher* beef."

"Kosher and grass fed beef. All natural. We make four times what my pop was making before I got home."

"But *look* at this." Doug gawked at the rest of the web site covering the wall. The top half was spectacular enough, but the bottom part clenched the sale. A black, three-board fence ran across the red backdrop. The two very tall Watches men leaned against a fence, smiling at the viewer. Their cowboy hats were pushed back on their heads so their faces showed. Leaning against the fence next to them was a huge clock like an old-fashioned pocket watch. The clock face was white; its hands moved. The only flesh color in the composition was on the men's dark faces and hands.

"Watches Ranch." Doug continued staring at the clock. "That's California time. Jesus, Leroy, I'd buy *anything* from you."

"Yeah. Every animal we raise is sold before it hits the ground. Only reason money's so tight is we bought the trucks."

"Trucks?"

"Refrigerated trucks. We can't get our beef to those health food stores and yuppie markets fast enough. They'll pay for themselves. They are already"

Doug's shoulders sagged. He sagged and sat down, facing the screen. "How did you do that web site? That's as good as anything Will has."

"High school kids on the reservation. Those kids can do anything. They're so smart. They showed me some of what the other beef suppliers were doing for sites and then did up this for us. We gave 'em a side of beef for the job."

"I can't believe it, Leroy. All this time, I thought you were going to get creamed in this place, but you've got this major business going. Why didn't you tell me?"

"Why didn't you ask? I showed the website to you because I got sick of being treated like I needed diapers. Me an' my people don't flash what we got and brag about it. It's a *cultural* thing, Doug.

"An' we ain't the kings of kosher beef. We don't have big house and barn, but we do have refrigerated trucks. We got everything we need. An' money's coming easier."

Doug put his head in his hands. "I can't believe I didn't ask you about your ranch. Or guess. Or look you up online. I can't believe Will didn't either. I just assumed …"

"You just *assumed*. An' that's it, isn't it? Ol' Leroy can't be nothing if he looks like that. Or talks like that. Like *what*, Doug?

"You gave me a lecture on how people were gonna cut me because of my skin. How about you? And *color blind* Will? *You're* the only ones hurt my feelings so far."

Leroy stomped away from Doug, stopped, and stomped back. "If you'd have looked online, you'd 'a' found a lot more. You ever heard of cowboy poetry? My dad's been writing it since my mom died." Leroy's face ran through a half dozen feelings: sadness, pain, pride. "He wrote about everything that happened. Mama dyin', him beatin' me, and my grandpa taking me. All of it. And about rodeo. It's got all his feelin's in it. Rodeo isn't just a fun show. It's rough. And it hurts.

"He started reading at the rodeos. Almost every rodeo has a cowboy reading, an' he went to all of them. An' then the poetry competitions. My dad's a star! He sells his books on our site too. I should a brought you one."

"You raise Kosher beef and beef for yuppies. Your dad's a rodeo star and a cowboy poet."

"Yeah."

"Why didn't you tell me?"

"Why didn't you ask? Anyone else, you would have investigated before you met 'em. You, know," Leroy scratched his nose, "I think I'm lookin' at a situation of cultural and racial discrimination."

Leroy stood in the empty hall. Doug had gone home. He was alone in a terrifying world with massive expectations that meant his whole life piled on his head. He came from nothing. He didn't want to embarrass himself with the Sirs and Lords and Dowagers. He went back into the living room. The Watches Ranch website still covered the wall, clock hands moving reassuringly. The clock ticked, a nice sound.

Out the window, life pulsated on the street below. He had never had time off. Some animal always needed tending, or their hay crop was having a crisis. Or the house, tractor, truck. His father. Now all he had to do was go to dinner at palaces. The space of not having any real work felt almost too open.

And then it didn't. He'd do some things, and he wouldn't do others. He'd be true to Cass and he wouldn't drink. He'd be honorable. He was a spirit warrior. But that didn't mean he couldn't have a good time.

Mr. Duane had given him a whole closet of beautiful clothes.

Leroy slipped on a pair of slacks and sweater, grabbed his leather jacket and wallet and split. He was out on the town.

10

A CALL FROM DADDY

WILL SAT IN his study, staring at the phone. A week had passed since Leroy and Doug had deposited Cass in the hospital. He'd talked to her doctors; he'd talked to her nurses. They knew her; she'd been in there before.

"She's different this time," her doctor had said. "She's very ill, but she's more positive than I've seen her. I think she'll work with us and we'll have a chance to make some real progress. Let us have a bit more time. I'll have someone call you every day. I think you may be surprised."

He sat in front of the phone in his office, pondering. They'd told him Cass could talk to him briefly. He'd rehearsed this moment a thousand times. Cass would be somewhere safe, getting healthy. They'd talk. She'd say she was sorry for what she'd said to him at Christmas, and so many other times. He'd say he was sorry he'd let Enzo Donatore get her and her mother. He was sorry about everything.

Will knew he couldn't do all of that at once, it would take time. Skill. Patience. But maybe this time it would work. He would reach toward her—carefully, sensitively—and she would extend herself to him.

"Can you forgive me, Cass? Can we be friends? Can you love me?"

That's what sat on his chest at night, grabbed his throat during the day. Half killed him.

Will wasn't doing well. Exactly what he'd expected when he got back from the retreat had happened. Frank Sauvage and Ric Chao whirled around behind him like dervishes with razors, cutting away at his support in the Corporation. Hacking at his heels, not nipping at them.

But he had to call Cass. Nothing made sense if he didn't. If he didn't have Cass, keeping Numenon meant nothing.

He reached for the phone, the back of his hand tanned, his nails perfectly manicured.

"Cass?" His voice seemed to echo through a vast space, even though it was just the phone in his study. They said she was well enough to talk for a few minutes from her bed.

"Is that you, Daddy?" Her voice was tiny, a little girl's, not the dreadful dragon's. "Is that really you?"

"Yes, baby. It's me."

"Oh, Daddy, I'm so sorry." Broken sobs.

"Don't be sorry, baby."

"Yes, I have to be sorry. I am sorry. We had a fight. I don't remember what I said, but it was awful. I'm sorry."

He heard a voice in the background, a woman's voice, "Cass, if this is too much for you, you can try later. Doctor wants you to be calm."

"I'm OK. It's my *dad*." Her attention shifted back to him, "I wanted you to know how sorry I am. I've caused so much trouble." Frantic voice, unlike what he'd expected. "All my life. I'm sorry."

"Sweetie, that doesn't matter. You getting well matters. Are you OK?"

"I'm OK. I get tired. I sleep a lot."

"And eat too, I hope."

"Yes." A short silence. "Daddy, I remember someone. He brought me here. His face was dark, but I could see his eyes. They were funny colored. Do you …"

"No, I don't know who that was, sweetheart. There were ambulance drivers. Doctors. Doug was there."

"It wasn't Doug." She sounded wistful. "I wish you knew who he was. I keep remembering his eyes." She was crying. "I'm so sorry." Her soft snuffling didn't taper off.

"Honey, don't worry about it. I want you back on your feet, healthy, and we can talk about all that stuff."

He felt her faint; knew she had. The silence on the line told him, and the *thunk* when the phone hit the floor. A scuffle came through the receiver. Will shouted, "Hello! Hello! Is she all right? Hello! Talk to me!"

A woman's voice said, "Miss Duane fainted, Mr. Duane. She's *very* ill."

"She's going to make it, isn't she?"

"Doctor wishes to speak to you, sir. I'll transfer your call."

Clicks and canned music and then a voice.

"Mr. Duane? This is Vic Rankin, attending physician for your daughter."

"Is she all right?"

"A medical team is with her. I'll go to her momentarily."

"What happened?"

"She fainted because of low blood pressure. We've done more tests and have more information about her condition we can give you now, if you have time?"

"Yes. Tell me."

"You know some of this. Her internal organs—liver and kidneys, her heart—have been damaged by starvation. When the body doesn't get enough protein, it essentially eats its own muscle, including the heart.

"The drugs didn't damage her very much physically. Heroin actually doesn't cause that much bodily damage, unless you overdose. But the sexual abuse she's been subjected to has all but destroyed her reproductive system. That and VD. We're treating her, but she's massively infected and has been for a long time."

Will sat silently, clutching the phone. "Are you saying she still could die?"

A huge sigh. "Yes. I am. But I think she'll pull through. She won't be able to have children, however, except through transplanting her eggs to a surrogate. She can't maintain a pregnancy physically.

"She arrived here on death's door. The fact that she's alive is a miracle, and I don't use that word lightly." The doctor paused. He was stalling, hiding something more important.

"What else?"

"The latest tests have revealed that she's brain-damaged. She apparently died during her journey here, maybe several times. The scans show it. She was resuscitated, or came back, but not fast enough. She suffered brain damage from lack of oxygen."

"Will she be able to …" Look normal? Act normal? Will choked back a sob.

"We don't know the extent of it or how it will affect her daily functioning and personality. She could have rages. She could be childlike. She could forget everything that she's said or done fifteen minutes after doing it. Or, she might heal enough that you don't notice anything at all. Though she will be low functioning."

"*What do you mean?* She was top of her class when she got her MBA at Stanford. She's *brilliant!*"

"Not anymore, Mr. Duane. When she leaves here, if she leaves here—she's not out of the woods at all—she'll be a different person than you knew. You'll have to get to know each other again."

Will barked, a sound between a choke and a sob.

"I'm sorry to have to tell you that. We'll update you daily or more often as we have information. We're on red alert. I need to go now."

Leroy's face flashed before him. That stinking son of a bitch! He brings her back to life but doesn't *keep* her back. He let her die several times. Stinking bastard left her *brain-damaged.*

Will jumped up and began pacing in his office, then up and down the hall in his suite of rooms. Excluding the basement gym, Will's house was fifteen thousand square feet. Three guesthouses, the pool house, and the horse trainer's residence in the barn completed the estate. A village could live in style on his property.

His rooms were four thousand square feet, the size of a large normal house. They were complete with his colossal bedroom, an office, gym, kitchen, media room, and closets the size of most people's living rooms. He wanted to go to the basement and work out. His gym down there was as big as the footprint of the whole house. He had an indoor track. He could work this off. Figure out what to do.

But he couldn't go to the basement because he'd brought a dozen Indians back from the retreat with him. Staff, ostensibly, but a substitute family in fact. Or they were until he found out how much room Indians took up. They had their own quarters—the three guesthouses, the studio apartment in the pool house, and the apartment in the stables. But they came into his house to eat; Carl was a chef and cooked for all of them. They ate in the kitchen/family room.

Then they wandered around the house, looking at his art collection. He couldn't blame them for that. It was educational. They watched movies in the theater in the basement. Worked out in the underground gym all the time. They'd be there now, he knew. They played Frisbee on the lawn. And tennis. They swam. They laughed and talked. Carl cooked. He was as good a cook as Jon Walker had been, but he was huge and noisy and had tattoos all over and didn't look like his predecessor, the classy and stylish Jon.

Will was trapped in his suite of rooms in his own house. He didn't want to kick the Indians out, and he didn't want them there. All the camaraderie and love that had bound them at the Meeting seemed to have vanished. Between fighting for his life at work all day and Cass close to death, all he could do was draw a breath, and then the next, and figure out what he should say to whatever asshole was standing in front him.

Will sent Leroy Watches to save her. The bastard had saved her halfway. He'd left her brain-damaged. "You will never marry my daughter. If I have to kill you, you will never marry her." He shouldn't have sent Leroy. But he saved her. Leaving her brain-damaged.

Will stopped dead, clenching his hands. How did his life go so wrong? He was golden once, the man who couldn't be beaten, the hero of his age, the new age, the electronic age. Now, everything was dust.

Oh, Cass. I destroyed you. I should have seen. The silhouette of his ex-wife, the most beautiful woman he'd met, slim and graceful, standing with their tall, elegant little girl swam before him. He ruined them. It was all his fault. Everything was his fault.

He went into his bathroom and splashed cold water on his face. The universe did not contain enough cold water to hide the bags under his eyes or his anguish. Was life with Cass ever anything but a flood of pain? Would it ever be different?

Cassandra. Why had he named his daughter Cassandra, even as a middle name? The Greek prophetess that no one believed. She'd predicted the fall of Will Duane and his house since birth.

Will opened the door to his kingdom, dragging himself to work. He squared his shoulders.

Carl Redstone was there, in tattooed and gigantic majesty. He carried a breakfast tray.

"I don't have time to eat, Carl."

"Yes, you do. We need to talk. You need to know that Leroy always does the best he can. He don't leave nothin' undone. If he can't do it, it can't be done. You need to be healed, Will."

11

ANOTHER DEMON HEARD FROM

"*SEE*, YOU BASTARD puta! *See*! You are supposed to see and show me *everything*. You stinking fica! You ..." Enzo Donatore stood above his magical see-stone, screaming in frustration. When he was very upset, he cursed in Italian, his family's native tongue. He slammed his massive fists and forearms on the granite slab supporting the crystal. The table broke on each side of the triangular mass.

"Pezzo di merda! Piece of shit!" He tore the cracked end of the slab off and spun, slamming it against one of the stone pillars of his lair. The underground warren shuddered, and the hunk of granite broke into shards.

"Diego! Get in here!" Enzo screamed into the microphone. He continued to swear until his brother arrived. "Took you long enough." Diego arrived wild-eyed.

"It wasn't my fault ..."

"Look!" He indicated the fragmented desk. "The stinking piece of crap you got me two days ago broke, just like the last piece. Get me some *real* granite! Something strong." His eyes narrowed. "What do you know about this, Diego?"

"About what, Enzo?"

"The Duane bitch. She escaped from one of my business ventures in New York City. Except she was so weak, she couldn't escape. Have you seen these," he turned to the see-stone and commanded it. "Show him." He pulled back, trying not to threaten the stone. If it was afraid, the crystal didn't work. It was working: they watched Hannah Herhman, Doug, and some others break into the bordello and waft Cass away. He couldn't see who was carrying her, just a blur. And then she became a blur.

"Look! A sorcerer has taken her. He has disguised himself and the bitch so that the stone can't see them." Enzo threw his head back and howled; a screech of agony and frustration.

The next images thrown up by the all-seeing crystal were more disturbing: Hannah Hehrman taking apart the whorehouse and everyone in it. Enzo watched in disgust and admiration.

"She is so good, this Hehrman woman. Look at her work with a knife. And so neat. And listen to them, talk, stinking cowards, spilling my secrets. Cowards! Putas!" The crystal showed the empty apartment after Hannah's team left. No blood, no gore. Not a single living soul. "She is so good. Not even fingerprints. She will be charged with nothing. That woman should work for me!"

Enzo contemplated the image of the empty condo, and then abruptly recalled the problem "The Duane bitch has escaped me. You let him do it!"

Diego backed up, holding his hands out to his brother, trying to keep him away. "I didn't know anything about it, Enzo. I was assigned to …"

"I don't care what I told you to do. Cass Duane and her sow of a mother are my *top* priority. You should always be watching. You failed me, Diego, when I was injured and sick."

The Indian's "spiritual" retreat had left him not just chastened, but beaten to a shadow of himself. All those false deities the old man had called flapping around. That gigantic supernova that the old Indian called "the Great One" illuminating everything, eliminating darkness. It was nothing but an astronomic phenomenon, but a powerful one.

Being near it had almost killed him, though he wouldn't admit it to anyone in the castle. "I was wounded, and what do you do, quit on me. Lazy lay-about …"

"Enzo, I was in North Korea, taking care of our interests there. You told me to go there. I don't have a see-stone. I don't know what's happening on the other side of the world. And you didn't call me."

"Shut up! Look what you did!" Enzo turned his attention to the stone. The lovely crystal pyramid spun lights toward the cave's ceiling. They saw Cass's rescue again. This time, they couldn't see anything of her at all: a blur. Then the shadow of a blur, then a memory.

"Where did she go?" The man, he assumed it would have to be a man to carry her, didn't show up at all. "Play it again." Nothing. The event was gone from the stone's memory.

"Look at this. Play the following hours," he ordered the stone. Fuzzy images of a dark van traveling through the Manhattan streets. Turning in somewhere. All street signs were blank. None of the businesses had signage. The images became fuzzier. Finally, all the stone broadcast was shadow.

Enzo pulled himself up, holding his mouth shut. He couldn't rage at the stone. It wouldn't work. "Show me more. Show me everything. Where is she now?"

A map of Manhattan appeared, and then the state of New York, and finally surrounding states materialized as a hologram above the stone. The vision hovered, and dissolved, becoming a film with indistinguishable hallmarks and boundaries.

"Where is *she*?" Enzo bounced from foot to foot in front the fractured table that held the stone. "I don't want to see the fucking eastern seaboard. I want to see *her*." He grasped the edges of the slab with his fingers. It crumbled.

The vision disintegrated. He couldn't see the quarter of the *country* where she was. Nothing. Sure as the fact that he was the most powerful thing that existed, he couldn't search every stinking clinic and hospital in that area to find her.

"Something's blocking her," Diego said, peering at the mist above the stone. "Only something very powerful could do that. More powerful than …"

"Nothing is more powerful than *me! Nothing! That stupid old man, that shaman and his hocus-pocus is* not *more powerful than I.* This is *your* fault, Diego. You were asleep at the wheel."

He covered the step or two between him and his brother, his claws coming out unbidden. His human flesh, so fine and blond, lightly tanned with silver/gold hair dusting it, withdrew, revealing his shining black scales.

His teeth ripped through the flesh of Diego's throat before his brother's reptilian armor could protect him. Blood vessels ruptured and spurting, trachea standing out rigid-white, flesh torn open: Diego had no defense. Even if his demon form had emerged, he would have had no defense: Enzo was the king of demons, the essence of demonic nature personified. None of his kind could beat him.

"Clean up this place, you stinking stronzas," He roared as a knock on the door announced the housekeepers. "Turds like you don't deserve easy work like cleaning my office. You should be scrubbing the torture chambers."

The maids came in, long aprons over their shining snake-like skins. They carried buckets and mops and kept their heads averted.

"Clean it! All of it! And no licksies of the scraps or blood! He's mine. Not a bite for you. If you find something to eat, bring it to me." Enzo stalked from the main part of his quarters, a stone lair set under the castle. Its rock was warm buff color and should have given off a cheery feeling, but nothing in the castle or his chambers gave off anything but cold and dread.

Carrying one of Diego's legs and his torso, Enzo retreated to an upper level of the dungeon. What he had done to Diego was really too messy for his workspace. The see-stone had been very upset by it. He'd had to calm the stone down before covering it. He'd finish his snack here, and think about what was going on.

Sitting in a massive wooden chair upholstered with interwoven strips of leather, he daintily polished off Diego's thigh. Little prick had it coming. Always thought *he* was next-in-line. The Donatore dynasty had no next-in-line; Enzo would live forever, unless he met with terrible misfortune of the kind that only he could mete out. Usually.

He'd been at the receiving end because of that dreadful old man, that Indian charlatan. But the old man was right, even as he was driving away Enzo and his hordes; he had said that Enzo existed at the pleasure of the Great One. His superstition, known as *God* by idiots and sycophants far and wide, *did* keep Enzo alive because *it pleased him.*

Pleasure! Pleased! Nothing was pleased for very long in Enzo's world. But it was true; the old man had shown him. He was allowed to exist by a power larger than he because that power wanted it that way.

He ripped into the upper part of Diego's torso, lower jaw stuffed in the cavity of his ribs and upper jaw crunching down on his chest. Ripping and tearing his brother's flesh gave him some peace.

He'd been haunted by the defeat at the Indian's retreat. It could have been a great victory, but it wasn't. Only a few hundred of the thousands there had died, and none of those had joined his followers after death. Killed by a demon, they were supposed to become demons, his immortal servants. The shaman had stopped that.

What was going on with the see-stone? Delicately spreading Diego's ribs and stripping the meat from them, Enzo contemplated. Something—someone—had blocked the stone. Only a creature as strong as that shaman could do that. Was it the old shaman? It could have been. Enzo didn't know where he'd gone.

He tossed a stripped rib to the rats hiding in the shadows. Could the shaman have died and left someone as powerful in his place? The thought took Enzo's breath away. What if that person, atrocious though he or she might be, had picked the Duane bitch out of her filthy closet and taken her somewhere? What if that was what the fogginess of the stone meant? That person could block out the entire quarter of a country?

Enzo froze. What if that person had done something to the bitch that rendered her invisible to him? Changed her brain waves or identity to his sensors? How could he find something that couldn't be seen?

Easy! He ran his bloody hands through his hair. He'd turned back to his human form. He had to get to work. How to find what couldn't be seen? Look for what wasn't there. Look for people acting like they were doing/helping/healing someone–*her*, the bitch—that he couldn't see. How was he to find the new shaman, this very dangerous survivor/ usurper? Follow the blur. Use his assets to cover the globe. The bitch would be in a hospital. No one could heal her. He hadn't left the life force of a slug in her. Which hospital?

"Dr. Lanzing, I need to ask that favor that you promised so long ago. Yes, it has been a long time, but a promise is forever." He spoke into the telephone in his lair. In his human form, Enzo was as handsome a man as ever lived. Close to a giant, but beautifully formed in face and figure. Blond, blue eyed. Every inch a businessman. His voice was melodious and irresistible. "I need you to make some staff changes. I'll take care of all the details."

He smiled. Finding out what happened was too simple, really. That fake, Grandfather could evade the see-stone, as could the man he'd left in his place. But Will Duane couldn't, nor could his people. Enzo found out what had happened, directly from her father's mind. Cass Duane had been rescued by Grandfather's grandson, Leroy something. He had taken her to a hospital to gain weight and recover. After that, her loving father would transfer her to a very reputable mental hospital for treatment of her multitude of mental ills. Enzo thought that was smart. The bitch was a fruitcake, a very dangerous one.

As a reward, Will Duane was treating Leroy to a lavish vacation/makeover, to render him suitable as a spouse for the fair Cass. Talk about a match made in hell! Enzo belched, hitting himself in the chest with his fist. Diego didn't agree with him.

Leroy would be hobnobbing with royalty all over Europe. Riding to the hounds, making quite a splash. How to deflect that splash and destroy Will Duane's plan? And Leroy? And Cass?

He picked up the phone, "Ferguson, my man. I need you to deliver some horses. To your friends, the Ballentynes. Yes, *those* horses. I want them there."

He made another call, adopting a slight upper-class British accent. "Dash, my friend, how good it is to hear your voice!" He could feel the man on the other end of the line cringe.

Donatore's bonhomie was irresistible and unnecessary. Dashiell Pondichury, the ninth Duke of Lancature, had been in Enzo's pocket since that bacchanal four years ago. Not only was he Donatore's spiritual slave, he was terrified that his master would reveal the truth about what had happened to his three wives.

Dash had brought his first wife to a party at the castle four years ago. Enzo's parties were notorious; once they really got going, people lost control. They also lost other things: feet, hands. Heads. Dashiell had had a wonderful time; his first wife had not, alas. She lost her head and that was that. Didn't stop her husband from bringing his second and third wives to Enzo's galas in subsequent years.

Now Dashiell was worried sick that Enzo would reveal what he thought was buried out in his vineyard to the authorities. Dashiell needn't have been so concerned; his wives were fully resuscitated, "alive", and back in service at the castle. They made great whores. Indestructible. Dash should have worried about running into the three of them getting sued for bigamy! But he didn't know they were up and passing for alive.

"I need to you check on someone for me. His name is," the words burned Enzo's tongue. No, his whole mouth and throat, "Leroy Watches Jr. He's attempting to crash noble society in London. A pretender of the worst sort. I need you to destroy him …

"Of course not physically, Dash. I never do that. What happened to your wives was an accident. Stop blubbering, Dashiell, no one will ever know. Listen to me: I want you to shadow Mr. Watches and ruin him socially. You can do that, can't you?" Enzo grimaced while Dashiell groveled on the other end of the phone. Will Duane and his little errand boy, Leroy Watches *Jr.*, would find out what he had in mind soon enough.

"Yes, my man, I knew you could."

12

A FAMILY DINNER

LEROY STEPPED OUT of his car. The mansion loomed above him, five stories of pale stone. The entrance was a little half-circle canopy sticking out from the building with a few steps leading to it. Columns stood on each side of the steps. Other grand houses crowded up on each side. A shallow crescent, the road curved out of sight behind him.

Black iron fences ran along the sidewalk. The barely noticeable gate and steps to the basement were for the servants. He knew that from his favorite TV show. That program had prepared him for his jaunt on the high side better than anything he learned anywhere.

A butler opened the door. "Leroy Watches Jr." he said and placed his calling card on a tray the butler extended. The butler nodded, peeking out the door at Leroy's car. Will had set him up with a Bentley for the night, along with his chauffeur.

A guy in black livery helped him remove his overcoat and sleek top hat. The butler appraised his apparel with the slightest movement of his eyes. They registered approval. Leroy let some air out of his lungs. He hadn't been aware that he was holding his breath.

Leroy found himself in a three-story entry. His breathing stopped all the way for an instant. The hall was exactly like that of the London town house in *Hermitage Estate,* the season when World War I was on the horizon, but no one had been drafted. The marble floors, paintings of dead ancestors, tables, flowers; all of it could have been the program. The walls were even painted a shiny dark red.

The butler led him into a vast, high-ceilinged room with marble columns and carved wood-paneled walls. He looked up. The paintings up there were as big as the screen on the old drive-in on the Rez. PBS did not prepare him for the impact of actually being in that room. Scattered around on elegant chairs and divans were women in silk gauze and velvet, sparkling with jewels. They held their perfectly coifed heads just so. The men wore clothes identical to his, down to the black patent shoes. Voices were cultured murmurs; barely audible titters, all amused and interested.

He and his new valet almost had come to blows over this dinner. He did not need what Tom preached: the gospel of correct formal dress. When he walked the living room, Leroy saw that Tom was right. Leroy was set up properly: he wore a black tie and tuxedo, the junior players in the men's formal wear team. A white tie and tailcoat were the first string, but too formal for tonight.

His tuxedo was made of smooth black wool. The jacket's shawl collar was covered with subtly shining silk sateen that matched the stripes down the outside of his pants. Under his jacket, his black vest had the same silk sateen shawl collar. The shirt was painfully white; the collar, more painfully tight and high.

He was like every man in the room except for one thing: the color of his skin. No one had as much color as the olive complexion of an Italian.

He took a deep breath. So what? His life had been like that from the moment he toddled off of his family's ranch. Leroy stepped into the charade. Some part of him decided to pretend he was an actor in *Hermitage Estate.* It worked: no one noticed, including him.

Lord Ballentyne greeted him, smiling, hands outstretched. All heads went up at his entrance. Slowly, though. Heads pivoted to face him, looking above the doorway as though something amazing had materialized over his head. No one stared at him.

"How do you do, Your Grace," he said to Her Grace Violetta, Lord Ballentyne's wife. "How do you do, Your Lordship," And on and on, around the room.

The *bristling* Dowager Duchess was Lady Catherine, Dowager Duchess of Raddenbery and Cloudfill, the mother of his hostess. She sat in an alcove by herself, glowering. A silver-topped cane was propped against her knee. Lord Ballentyne led him to her, walking on the balls of his feet as though he was as afraid of his mother-in-law as anyone.

Leroy got it the instant he saw her: she was in extreme pain. Arthritis in both hands and down her spine. Her Grace glared at him from her seat, holding a crystal sherry glass in one clawed hand. She was in pain and grieving. Her husband had died not long before. The sherry was to numb the pain.

"Your Lordship, could you stand where you are for a moment?" And block the view from inquisitive eyes. Leroy gracefully lowered himself in the seat next to the older woman and took her free hand, smiling into her eyes. "I'm Leroy Watches, Your Grace. I'm so pleased to meet you."

He let healing energy run into her full on. He'd have an instant to do this. "I was so sorry to hear about His Grace." The scowling dreadnaught that had terrorized the nobility blinked twice. Tears filled her eyes, spilled over her lower lids, and rolled down her cheeks.

"That's kind of you, young man. Most people don't mention it."

"They're afraid of hurting you, Your Grace."

"Is that why? I thought they didn't care." Her stiff upper lip extended down her spine into her hands.

"They care very much. How do your hands feel now?" He leaned back, hoping that everyone in the room wasn't staring.

Her eyes widened. She dabbed at them with a lace hankie. "Why, they feel fine. What did you do?"

"Oh, it's nothing. Jus' somethin' I do. My daddy has the arthritis real bad, or he did 'til I treated it."

"You can *heal* it?" She'd stopped dabbing and stared at him with wonder.

"Yes. May take a couple of sessions."

"Good heavens, young man." That's when the full force of her grief hit her. Her mouth opened, chin dropping and quivering. "Oh, dear. I think I'm going to …"

"You need to be quiet now, but not alone. Are you here with anyone?"

"I have my maid, but she's useless."

"You may be surprised by her. She may turn out to be just the person you need, if you let her get close." Leroy surveyed the room. Everyone *was* staring at them in their polite fashion, but no one moved to comfort her. He wondered if they would have helped her had her Dowager Grace collapsed on the floor screaming.

On the other side of the room, he saw a group of younger people. A pretty, sad teenage girl with flyaway blond hair, a boy a few years younger who looked like a knock off of Lord Ballentyne.

And her. She would have stopped him dead wherever he was. Powder-blue eyes. Skin milkier than the palest rose petal, and so fine he could see her blue veins pulsing in her temples. Her hair was light brown, nougat colored, like the inside of a Milky Way bar. It curled in waves on each side of her face, ending at her chin. She was an angel. Her eyes were fixed on Her Grace, brows contracted. She shot across the room.

"Grandmamma, are you all right?" she ran to Her Grace, who was crying as openly as anyone in that group ever had.

"No, dear, I'm not all right. I need a bit of privacy and a lie-down."

"Arabella, take Mother to one of the spare rooms. Doctor will be here in a moment …" Lord Ballentyne said.

"No doctor. She don't need a doctor. She needs her family."

"And *you*, young man. I need *you*. Please don't leave. I must spend more time with you." The no-longer-bristling old lady clutched at Leroy's hands.

"I won't, Your Grace. I'll be here as long as you need me. I promise."

Arabella braced herself to help her grandmother stand. She didn't need to.

"Oh, my. I got up. Just like that." The old lady's eyes widened again. "Oh, my. My back doesn't hurt." And more tears came. "Arabella, help me. I can't be seen like this."

"Leroy, that was my daughter, Lady Arabella," his Lordship said to the angel's retreating back. "Sweetest child ever born." Yes, she was.

The pounding of his heart and the way his own eyes followed the young noblewoman disturbed Leroy. Cass was his soul mate. He was biding his time and learning until they could be together. Why was he so captivated by the young aristocrat?

Arabella had disappeared into the entry hall with her grandmother on her arm. Her dress was pale blue silk, straight and wispy. It hid her figure, while revealing it. Not a thing flashy about her, just beauty and quality.

He went into dinner, hoping he'd remember his silverware and dishes. Doug had been wrong about formal dinners. He said they were eight courses, with a ninth option. This one had twelve courses. He had a Your Ladyship on one side and a Your Grace on the other. He chatted with them, avoiding the topics that Sir Glathering had instructed him were forbidden in polite society.

Sir Glathering had been definite about what to say and not say at dinner: "Whatever you do, don't talk about politics, religion, or money.

Sex is a gray area, as long as you're extremely discrete. Assignations *have* been arranged over dinner." Leroy had looked bewildered at that word. "You know, sexual liaisons." He was still bewildered. "You know, *getting it on* with whomever you're seated next to." Leroy had blushed and Sir Glathering had continued, "Do not *ever* talk about work. As in physical labor. No one ever works."

That left: hunting. His people's customs, as long at *his* morays didn't forbid it. And what he knew about Will Duane. Leroy wouldn't talk about that, or Cass, or how he happened to be there.

Fortunately, he had been seated across from the younger people. The boy's face glowed. He was younger than Leroy had thought, eleven or twelve. "I'm Allie Paxton, Lord of Craexton. I'm His Lordship's son. My Christian name is Alexander." The names these aristocrats had.

They weren't as bad as Native names, though. Leroy had his American name, Leroy Watches Jr. He had his Indian names that everyone on the reservation called him. Then he had the name that Grandfather gave him, that just the two of them used, and his private name, known only to him and the Great One.

This boy was Alexander Paxton, currently the Lord of Craexton,, some minor estate the family owned. He'd be the Lord of Ballentyne and Crayton and whatever other estates the family held when his father passed.

"How do you do," Leroy replied perfectly.

"I'm very well, thank you. I say, I hope you don't mind, but I heard you rode in a rodeo." He looked thrilled. A bright, excited youngster in a tuxedo in his family's manor hall. No, that would be the country house. This was just the city house. "I would love to ride in a rodeo, but my father …" He shrugged hopelessly.

"Your father's right. You could get busted up for good in rodeo. Stick with polo."

"Do you play polo?"

"No, I never have. I'd like to. I've seen pictures of polo, and those are some great horses and riders."

"Could you play polo with us?"

"If I'm invited, I'd love to." Leroy didn't realize the effect his voice had on people. He was big, and his voice rumbled in his chest like a fine, stand-up bass. Conversations around them stopped.

"I'm sure my father can arrange something. You must come to the country and play." That was from the very unhappy teenage girl. Her hair was white-blond, silky and looked like it was wafting in the breeze, even without a breeze. She wore a pale lavender silk dress and long pearls.

"Nothing ever happens around here," she sulked. "*You* playing would be interesting." He thought she was alluding to his race, but she clarified what she meant. "Americans never come here. I am Lady Clarissa. I'm Allie and Arabella's cousin."

"Excuse me," Lady Arabella took one of the two empty chairs next to kids. She spoke to Leroy. "Grandmamma is ever so much better, Mr. Watches. She thanks you profusely. I left her with her maid. She hopes you'll stay the night so that you can speak with her in the morning." Blue eyes. Powder-blue, like they were painted on. He couldn't breathe.

"Um. Sure. I think that my valet packed my things."

"Oh, good! Do you shoot arrows?" Allie was adorable. He was enthusiastic, not cheeky. "I've never met an Indian before. Maybe you don't practice archery anymore."

"I hunt with a bow. I like bow-hunting very much."

"Oh, good. We can practice archery in the basement tomorrow morning." The boy's brows furrowed. "You aren't a regular Indian, are you?"

"I'm one kind of Indian. Native Americans mixed with African Americans pretty often in the old days. And now. My mom was half white and half Indian. My dad is like me. I'm all mixed up."

"But you're an Indian?"

"Yes, by tribal law, and my dad's got Indian blood too."

"Do you shoot arrows and go hunting and camping?"

"Yes. We do on our reservation. And we go to other Nations' lands and hunt there. But we only kill what we can use ourselves." Leroy smiled and nodded.

"Do you have secret ceremonies?" That was Allie.

"And magic powers?" said Clarissa. The room was silent, listening.

"Well, if we had secret ceremonies, I couldn't tell you about them. As for magic powers, the only thing I can do is heal people an' help them if they're sad. I've done that since I was little." The kids' eyebrows were bouncing up and down. Questions looked like they wanted to burst from them. "If that's magic, then I have powers. But I can only do it to help people. I can't do it for money."

"So you can't be a doctor? Though you could in England, where medicine is socialized," Clarissa's questions had an edge, fruit of her unhappiness.

"Allie! Clarissa! Let Mr. Watches eat his dinner." Arabella reined them in.

They were on course nine or ten. He was not really interested in dinner anymore. "No, I can't ..."

There was a stir at the entrance to the dining room. All heads turned as a tall man with reddish blond hair bounded into the room, beaming.

"Dashiell!" Lord Ballentyne jumped to his feet. "You made it after all."

Dashiell grasped his Lordship's hand. "So sorry, old chap. Worst thing in the world is being late for dinner, but it was this or nothing. The airports were jammed."

"So glad you made it. Come, we saved you a place." Ballentyne led Dashiell to the one empty seat at the table, next to Lady Arabella. "You know my daughter Arabella, of course."

Dashiell nodded, then turned and faced Leroy, who was seated directly across the table. His face was unreadable, except for his eyes. The devil had walked in the door. Leroy rocked back in his seat. Everything

Grandfather had told him about evil flamed in his mind: "Evil will never look the way you think it should. It will come when you are not prepared. It will hide from the eyes and minds of others. They will not see it or believe it is bad. They will defend it rather than you. And most of all, my grandson, remember that evil wants to destroy you. It wants to kill you and keep your soul for its own."

Lord Ballentyne introduced the newcomer to Leroy. "This is Dashiell Pondichury, the ninth Duke of Lancature, and our old family friend. We managed to persuade him to leave his vineyard in Spain to join us."

The word "Spain" caused Leroy to shudder.

"How do you do, Your Grace," Leroy spoke clearly and carefully. He couldn't remember if he was supposed to rise greeting a Duke, but it didn't matter. His Grace was being seated.

"I can have the staff bring …" Ballentyne was tending to Dashiell's dinner.

"Have Fulton make me up a plate. No fuss. I'm *terribly* late." He looked up and down the table, pseudo-abashed. All eyes, smiling eyes, were on Dashiell now.

Once the table settled down, Dashiell turned his attention to Leroy. Very intelligent eyes, a slate blue, knowing everything in the ways of the world, glittered across from him. The man was there to kill him, or if not, ruin his chances.

"What a great surprise to find an *Indian* in London. I thought the only Indians over here were those in the old Wild West shows. Not too healthy a place for them. Daresay, any that escaped from the shows died of the damp." Dashiell smiled, spreading his words to those seated beside them. "Hope *you* last, old fellow." He hoped Leroy died very soon.

Only Dashiell and Leroy seemed to realize a battle was being mounted.

"Oh. We Watches have a habit of lasting, Your Grace. We're hard to kill."

"I certainly bet you are!" A servant brought the nobleman a plate with samples of the various dishes that had been served. "Look at this piece of beef," rare, succulent roast, "I bet this is grass-fed." He raised his voice. "I had to wait in the airport. Bored, nothing to do. Looked up Leroy Watches on the Internet. Amazing what you find."

Brilliant smile, flashing teeth, his wispy blond hair curling a little. Such a handsome man. He leaned forward a little, drawing in everyone in the room. "Evil will never look the way you think it should," Grandfather had said.

"Did you know that our friend Leroy is not only a cattle rancher, he caters to *our friends of the* Jewish *persuasion.*"

If he had said, "Roasts babies for consumption in street cafes," the group's reaction could not have been greater. Leroy remembered what Doug had told him about prejudice. It was there; he hadn't run into it yet. But now it was directed, not against him, where it would have been gauche, but against his dear friends. Leroy jumped at the bait.

"Well, I expect the rabbis would like you to refer to them as rabbis and their people as Jewish people, or Jews, but you're right. I raise the best beef in the country and I see that it's made Kosher in the strictest ways. I'm not a rabbi, so I don't do the Shechita. But I'm there, making sure everything is done right. My customers know me. I know the value of religious ceremonies and how much doing them right matters."

Dashiell pursed his lips and sat back, making a joke. "*Well,* I stand corrected. There's such a problem these days, isn't there, with counterfeit Kosher foods? Beef that isn't slaughtered properly. Food being sold that isn't *really* Kosher. All the law suits being brought. Those poor *people*"—the word sounded like "idiots" in Dashiell's mouth—"whose *souls* depend upon the purity of their food not knowing if they've eaten *truly* Kosher foods." He was *mocking* Jewish people who ate Kosher, Leroy's friends and customers. Maybe mocking people who thought they had souls. But so smooth …

Leroy felt himself expand, felt the room grow smaller. "If you're say-ing, and I know you're not, because you're too much of a gentleman, that my beef isn't truly Kosher and I've been defrauding my customers, you'd be in a dueling situation in the old days. Back when my relatives used to jump ship from the Wild West shows. But I know that isn't what you're about."

He and Dashiell knew that what the latter wanted more than any-thing was for Leroy to lose his temper and pulverize the nobleman. He almost got his wish. Leroy was as angry as he had been in high school when Tommy Blunt Knife and his friends teased him about being the only virgin in eleventh grade. Tommy almost got to see what restrained sexual energy could do, martial-arts-abilities-wise. So did Dashiell. But Leroy pulled himself in, as he had then.

"What you're wondering is if I can shoot a bow and arrow better than you. That's it, isn't it?" Leroy challenged the Duke.

"Yes, certainly."

"You spendin' the night here? Good. We'll have a competition, first thing."

"I say, fellows, that sounds like a capital idea. First thing, about ten, after breakfast," Lord Ballentyne said, eyes glittering.

"I was thinking more about six, Your Lordship. I'm going to Italy tomorrow."

"Six? Well you won't have much of a gallery cheering you on. But some of us may make it. Capital. Right on. Competition!"

Lord Ballentyne rose at the head of the table. "We have a special treat tonight. Normally, we retire to brandy and cigars while the ladies ..." Ballentyne paused, looking puzzled, "do whatever they do.

"Tonight, we've arranged 'a little night music.' My daughter's favorite quartet is in the ballroom. We can't quite fill the ballroom with the pres-ent company, but I'd bet we can stir up a nice rhumba!"

Leroy might have enjoyed a spot of ballroom dancing after that massive pig-out of a dinner. Why these people didn't weigh four hundred pounds, he didn't know. But Dashiell attached himself to Lady Arabella like he was a barnacle. To her credit, her ladyship *did not like it.*

As she whirled by in Dashiell's strong, manly arms, her soul emitted little silent screams for help. All the while, she smiled like she was having a wonderful time.

"Excuse me, Your Grace, I'd love to dance with Lady Arabella, with your permission."

He cut in; the first and only time he'd exercised the privilege. She pulled away from Dashiell with a little force, like breaking some kind of membrane that had caught her. Arabella clutched his shoulder and pulled closer to him than might have been warranted, given the length of their acquaintance and her position. She was shaking.

"Oh, thank you," she whispered. "He wants to *marry* me. He said my father had consented. Oh, dear. What am I to do?"

He pulled her straight in front of him and held her a foot or so away from his body, staring at her. He spun her around a few times until they got to a couple of chairs and then indicated that she should sit.

"Don't you know how to say *no,* girl?" Her sweetness was a curse and a blessing. Arabella looked at him with those clear, innocent eyes, like Bambi's mother probably had before the fire burned her up. "Listen to me: tell him *NO.* Tell him no so hard it rattles his socks. And tell your father the same way. If that asshole climbs on you or tries to touch you, kick him in the balls as hard as you can."

Her shoulders rose and her head went forward. "Oh," she giggled. "Oh, my."

"I'm telling you the truth, girl. He is not the sort who will stop unless you hurt him and hurt him good. I'll talk to your father if you want, but you have to handle His Grace."

"You'd *help* me?" Wide eyes. Who wouldn't help her? What was wrong with these people?

"Yeah, I'll help you, but you gotta learn to do it yourself. I'm not always going to be here. Do you know that the women at my reservation carry knives a foot long? Start carrying them when they become women. A man messes with them is gonna loose his cojones."

Her eyes widened even more. "They castrate men for making advances?"

"That an' more. You better take a lesson, Your Ladyship ..."

"Call me Arabella."

"Arabella." Sounded so nice in his mouth. "Arabella. Whatever you do, do *not* marry that man. He's a bad man."

"I know that, Mr. Watches."

"Leroy."

"Leroy." She paused, as if thunderstruck. Leroy. "He's a bad man, but no one sees that. All they see is how he looks and his money and his title and his vineyards. But you saw that he's bad. And you saw that my Grandmamma really is nice ..."

"It's what I do, Arabella. I'm a healer. Now, would you like to dance?"

When he got on the dance floor with her that time, she wasn't scared. She held onto him, then pulled a little away, and gazed into his eyes. Her pretty face kept working and she looked at him a way he'd seen before. But he'd always walked away and not let the girl have her feelings about him. She looked at him as though he was the most beautiful man in the world. He didn't walk away.

He held her the way he'd just learned that week, smiling down on her. Something happened: the back of his tuxedo split open and the biggest rocket ship that NASA ever launched went up his back and out the top of his head. His eyes bugged out. So did hers. Pleasure flashed through him. He pulled her close, his belly a little lower than her chest. She wasn't very tall.

"What is it, Leroy?" Her voice was filled with alarm.

"I don't know, Arabella. It feels good, though." Did he have two soul mates? When he held Cass, it had been like NASA let loose with every rocket or even firecracker that they ever had. This wasn't as much, but this was big. She felt like heaven in his arms. She wasn't a skinny girl like the magazines showed. She was rounded and maybe a little chubby. It went with her softness and innocence. Arabella was a virgin, he knew that for sure. As virgin as he was. She'd saved herself for the right man.

Was he that man? How could that be?

"Oh, no," Arabella cried. Leroy looked across the ballroom. Dashiell was dancing with the pretty blond Lady Clarissa, Arabella's young cousin, holding her far too close for a teenaged girl. "He can't have her." Arabella cried, pulling away and darting across the floor. Leroy followed.

"Clary, I just got the best idea," she yanked her cousin from Dashiell's embrace. "Leroy said he'd be your escort when you make your debut in November. Won't that be wonderful?"

"Yes!" Clarissa jumped and clapped her hands as though she'd won the lottery. "Oh, thank you. My friends are going to go wild!"

Leroy was surprised that an African American/Native American purveyor of Kosher beef would be such a prize.

"But I thought you were going with *me*, Clary darling," Dashiell's words seem to ooze from his mouth. "I asked first." He looked directly into Leroy's eyes, a challenge.

"Well, I tell you what, Your Grace. If Lady Clarissa agrees, how about you and I have a little game of bow and arrow tomorrow morning? The winner escorts Her Ladyship." Leroy had neglected to say that his martial skills were far below his healing skills, but they were above any of the spirit warriors but Wesley Silverhorse. That was saying something.

"Of course, Mr. Watches. Though *competing* for a young lady's hand is rather déclassé … I'd be delighted to oblige if Lady Clarissa wants it."

Clarissa stood with her hands together with an expression of wild glee. Being used as a pawn was clearly the highlight of her life.

"Are you sure?" Arabella's knit brows said her idea had gone badly awry.

"I'm very sure," Leroy said. "But I'd better get my beauty sleep. After I beat His Grace, I'm off to Italy for Will."

He walked up the stairs to the main hall, leaving the whisper of Will Duane's name behind him. He hadn't mentioned Will all evening, wanting to impress people on his own. Leroy didn't want to play on Will's influence. *But why the hell not?* he thought. Let them wonder who he was and why he was there.

13

ONE MESSED UP WHITE MAN

THEY SAT IN the lounge area outside Will's steam room, having talked inside the steam room as long as they could without being poached. The two men wore towels wrapped around their middles. All of Carl's flamboyant tattoos showed on his dark skin.

Will scrunched up his nose and said, "That hurts, doesn't it? Getting tattoos?"

"Yeah." Carl scratched his jaw with his leonine hand.

"Why did you do it, Carl?"

"To keep me from doing what I'd done all my life. Grandfather told me to. He drew them on me, all of them. They're sacred."

"Sacred tattoos?"

"Yeah. Hard for a white boy to understand, eh?"

"Yes. You can't get them off."

"Oh, you can, all but these green-colored ones, but it costs a ton and hurts worse."

"Why did you do it?"

"So I looked tougher than anyone in the pen and didn't get gang raped every other day. An' have to kill however did it afterward." He nodded. "An' I did 'em for my sins. These are for my sins." He indicated his whole body. "I didn't do what they convicted me for, but I did plenty other stuff. I told Grandfather about it, and he told me to get the tats. Hurt plenty, I'll tell you. I got rid of lots of sins with these babies." He turned to Will so quickly that the older man pulled back.

"When are you going to get rid of your sins, Will?"

"What?"

"You told me that you were jealous of Leroy and your daughter. That you would never let him marry her because some doctor said she was brain-damaged. You never bothered to ask him what happened on the trip, if she died. If she was really brain-damaged or maybe he did something to protect her. You didn't check it out at all, just flipped out."

Will puffed up to explode.

"Don't pull that shit with me. You ain't God. Don't even come close. I've been with *God*, you ain't it. You are one messed up white man and that's all."

Will sat huffing. He couldn't pull anything with Carl. No Will Duane screamers, no power plays. No subtle, "I'm better than you." Carl wasn't afraid of him, knew what Will really needed, saw that he got it, and cared for him. Carl might have been a hula dancer from the North Pole; he was out of Will's reality. He loved Carl Redstone, and through Carl, he had remembered why he invited him and the others to live with him.

That morning he'd walked out looking so rough, Carl had taken him to the private eating area of his quarters, sat him down, fed him, and then did *something* that had him blubbering his brains out for hours. He told him everything. When he was empty, Carl cleaned him up, put on a suit and went with him to the Headquarters, where he sat next to Will all day. He'd kept it up since, home or at the office.

Carl scared the crap out of Frank Sauvage and everyone associated with him. Sauvage had asked Will to remove Carl from the premises. Since Carl was sitting in his office, he had to make his speech in front of Carl. Will watched Frank Sauvage's hands shake as he tried to make a case that Carl caused disruption in the offices.

"I c'n stop wearin' my feathers, if y' want," Carl's deep baritone rattled Sauvage further.

"That's not …"

"He stays. Personal security, Frank. It's in my contract. Do you have a reason for being in my office?"

They'd just had another soul-baring session in the steam room, when Carl hit him with, "When are you going to clean up your sins?"

Will had told him some questionable things he'd done in business that had fortunately made everyone involved, especially the stockholders, more money than anyone could conceive. So those weren't bad things. But they could have gone the other way. And *were* going that way now.

"I thought you said you wouldn't tell what I said."

"I didn't, did I? Just you and me are here. Hannah's got the security on this house so tight I can't whisper to Roxy in bed.

"When are you going to clean up your sins?"

"What are you talking about?"

"With Leroy? When are you going to talk to him about what happened with Cass and how he'll never marry her?"

Will blinked, and kept blinking.

"You're not going to be right until you clean that up. Do you know what he did for you? Why Enzo Donatore isn't all over that hospital now?"

Will scowled.

"Leroy and Cass's scrambled brain. Donatore can cut through Hannah's security like melted butter, and see you sitting on the can, if he wants. But not with me next to you."

Will's head fell forward as he gaped. "And not with us here, on your place. He can't see Leroy at all, only where he's been. An' he could never see Grandfather, or the Mogollon Bowl. What happened there was the result of human evil, which is what you're harboring for Leroy."

Carl was silent a minute, giving Will time to think.

"OK. I'll call him tomorrow." He looked at the multitude of clocks on the wall, set for different parts of the globe. "It's one a.m. in London."

"Good. Then I'll go to work with you tomorrow."

"You'd stop going with me?"

"Yes." Carl indicated the tattoos covering most of his body. "I didn't do this to repent so I could guard a sinner." Will thought about that some more. Carl continued, "Grandfather said there was something you told him after your sweat at the Meeting, something you wanted more than anything in the world."

"He talked about that? But he didn't tell you?" Will was appalled. "He wouldn't tell you?"

"Of course not. That's why I asked. What do you want more than anything in the world?"

Will shut down tight. Mouth clamped, shoulders dropped, eyebrows dropped and furrowed. The words leaked out, "I want to know my former wife is safe and well. I want her to be happy. I'd like to talk to her, and apologize for what I did."

"So find her." Will remained shut, clam-like. "You could die tonight. Donatore is having wet dreams over getting you. You may not get another chance at what you want."

"What do you mean?"

"Leroy's over there. He might be able to look around, inadvertent-like. He might be able to find her."

"Leroy?"

"Of course, Leroy. He saved Cass. He can probably find Mrs. Duane."

Will couldn't move. Of course he could, better than anyone. And Donatore couldn't see him. Leroy was *there*, in Europe, now.

Hannah had traced the international toll-free number he had, his only link to his ex-wife, to a place that would never yield the secret of

Kathryn's whereabouts to him. He could never send operatives there. He would always be suspected in that place. But the heir to a Native American spiritual dynasty would be welcomed.

The number originated in the Vatican.

"I'll call Leroy tomorrow and confess my sins."

14

BOWS AND ARROWS

H E GOT TO the archery range at 5:30 in the morning, before Dashiell Pondichury, the ninth Duke of Lancature. Arising so early wasn't hard; he'd barely slept. Arabella's pale blue eyes and sweet smile swam before him. The way her soft arms had felt, even through the wool of his tuxedo, never left. Thrills of pleasure swam up and down his spine. Love washed over him like the waves of the ocean he'd only seen from the airplane. Arabella. Who was she? What was happening?

He was somewhere, in total blackness, asleep, when she came to him. Leroy sat up, covered with sweat, and stared into space. Cass's dark blue eyes riveted him. She was screaming in terror. "Don't leave me! Don't forget me! Please, Leroy, don't forget me! I love you."

Cass felt what he felt, and knew what he knew. At the deep soul level where they were joined, no lies existed, no hiding. Nothing but truth.

He knew her truth. Her pain seared him. She loved him. She lived because of him and for him. Cass was his soul mate, not Arabella. What had happened earlier that night had terrified her. And she was getting better; she had much more energy than when he first saw her.

"Shh." he whispered to the phantom. "I'll never leave you. Arabella's nothin', Cass. Just something that happened. Don't worry about it, darlin'. I'll be back soon and we'll get married. We'll be so happy. No one will ever see two folks as happy as us. We're gonna have kids and dogs. Horses. You like horses, don't you?"

He cooed the way he never had until Cass relaxed and slept.

He didn't sleep after Cass drifted away. The horror of what Arabella was shook him like a 'coon in that ol' hound Rustler's jaws. A 'coon that wouldn't die or quit.

Arabella was a *spare*. His time for marriage had come. That decree, that turning of all existence, came from the Great One. Grandfather was gone and the lineage had to continue. He was supposed to marry Cass, but if she died ... if the evil one took her, the feelings he'd had for her would be transferred to Arabella without word or will. They'd be married in months as though Cass had never existed.

He couldn't let that happen. And he knew that Cass's mortal peril was greater than ever.

"Oh, you're *here*," His Lordship said, the corners of his mouth turning down when he entered the game room at 5:45. "Beating me to the equipment?"

"No. Did you have plans with the equipment?"

The shooting range was a marvel, occupying the southern half of the basement. It extended from the front of the house to the rear, one story below ground. His Lordship's armory—he apparently was an avid hunter with bow and arrow or any weapon—was a large room in the front of the cement-walled, shooting range.

Fulton, Lord Ballentyne's butler, had opened the armory/study for Leroy. The staff had been up since four a.m., getting the household moving. A few heads had poked into the open doorway while Leroy was waiting. The upstairs of the house slumbered on, but the servants were very interested in witnessing what was to happen. "A friendly archery contest," Fulton had described it. Like hell, everyone knew.

"Shall we wait for Lord Ballentyne?" Leroy asked Lord Dashiell.

"Hah! It will be noon by the time he gets here. Let's push on. What do you want to do?"

"Halloo!" Allie Paxton, Lord Ballentyne's son, popped in. "I had to be here. What are you fellows going to do?"

"We thought we'd start by killing each other," Dashiell said with a smile.

"Only *kill*? We won't scalp each other?" Leroy was deadpan.

"No! You're not going to do that!" Allie gasped.

"No. That was a joke. Let's see. We could do some target shooting with the long bows. Work our way from there."

Racks of bows of all kinds filled the walls. Leroy headed for a rack of long bows on one side of the room. They shared the wall with an extensive display of crossbows.

"I'll take this one," Dashiell said, lifting something that looked like it came from Star Wars, with levers and pulleys all over.

"That's a compound bow," Leroy said. "Not allowed in the Olympics or in polite company. It's high tech and easier to use than a recurve bow, like what Robin Hood used and all of these," his hand swept the rack of classic long bows. "Recurves are used in the Olympics, but we can use whatever you want."

"Don't say, old fellow. I just thought they were just more up to date."

Don't say, like the coyote didn't know the henhouse door was broken, Leroy thought. *Compounds are easier.*

A cabinet beneath the bows probably held arrows and bolts. The walls of the rest of the room—which was decorated like a study with Persian carpets, dark wood paneling, leather seating, and the ubiquitous tea tray crammed with alcoholic beverages—were covered with firearms, modern and antique. Mounted heads of game animals filled every spare inch.

"Sir," Tom Wyatt stood in the doorway. "As you do not have a bow-man, I will handle your equipment." He was dressed in tweeds, as though they were hunting in the country, not a basement.

"Thank you, Tom." Leroy was not worried. He knew he'd win, no matter what they used, though he had never shot a crossbow.

"I'll set up the targets," Tom trotted to the end of the range. Layers of foam designed to absorb the arrows' impact covered the back wall. Tom set up four targets—lighter foam board painted with concentric circles—two on top of two.

"Do you have preferences as to which side of the range you would like?"

"I'll take the left," Dashiell said. His smile matched his name: Dashing Dash.

They shot Leroy right, Dashiell left. Reversed it. Shot traditional recursive bows then switched to compound bows. Leroy won every time.

"I say, you're an expert. I suppose I should have known," Dash hid his sourness well. "How about we use the same target? Pierce-the-arrow thing?"

Nothing Lord Dashiell could do came near Leroy's skill. Even when his arrow pierced the very center of one of the targets at the end of the basement room, Leroy's arrow hit it dead center and shattered the shaft to the head. No matter how heavy the bow and the strength it demanded, Leroy shot better.

Tom glowed, as did Allie and Fulton. The butler made frequent trips to the basement to tend to their needs. "Lemonade, Mr. Watches?"

"Are you ready to concede, Your Lordship?" Leroy wanted it over. "I will gladly escort Lady Clarissa to the ball."

"Good heavens, no, man. We've barely begun. Let's try the cross-bows? Have you ever shot one?" Leroy shook his head. "See, you've been operating with a *Native* advantage." He laughed at his pun on native.

They went back into the armory. "So many of them. Which shall I choose?" The Lord's bow and crossbow collection was as varied as the firearms on the walls. The crossbows ranged from antique wooden beauties to deadly-looking modern models from the military. Dashiell lifted one of the latter off the wall. "I wonder where Peter got this bruiser?" It was a metal thing, very modern, looking more like a gun than a crossbow.

"That is a pistol crossbow, sir," Fulton intoned from the doorway. "From the Barnett International line. His Lordship obtained it as a gift from a friend in the Army. Said to have been used in Serbia."

Leroy followed Dashiell into the armory. Allie, Tom, and Fulton lingered in the doorway.

"The bolts are down here," Dashiell pulled a box of metal bolts from a drawer under the racks of weapons. He held the non-firing end of the crossbow against his belly, while fumbling with the bolts. They looked like missiles to Leroy, solid projectiles. "Anyone know how to load these? I've never used a crossbow."

The agile way His Lordship manipulated the piece told Leroy he was an expert with the crossbow. He held back, wondering what his opponent was up to.

"Tom, old fellow. I could use a hand," Dashiell whined. Tom moved forward instantly.

Leroy saw it immediately. Dashiell lifted the bow, business end pointed out, bolt in the slot. He seemed to be fumbling, but was in fact cocking the lever, aiming not at Leroy, but at Tom. Leroy did what Dashiell must have assumed he would, dashed forward faster than could be seen. He was a blur, extending his hand at the projectile.

The bolt bounced off of the force field Leroy emitted, ricocheting toward the doorway, where it lodged less than two inches from the eye of Allie Paxton, heir to the Ballentyne fortune and title.

"Oh," the boy said, feeling the side of his face. The bolt had clipped his face; it bled, not heavily, but enough.

"Oh, so sorry, Allie. I bumbled. I've never used a crossbow before." Dashiell lurched toward the child, the soul of remorse.

"You most certainly have," Lord Ballentyne filled the doorway. "You've used that very model shooting at the estate. What the *devil* are you up to, Dash? It's bad enough that you were pawing my daughter and niece last night. Are you attempting to kill our guest?"

"No, Peter. How can you say that? It would have hit his man."

"Oh, shooting a valet is all right? Not in my house, Peter. Leave." His Lordship turned his attention to his son. Leroy was already there. Tom had brought him cold water and a clean cloth. Leroy touched the scratch and it closed.

"Not even a scar, Allie," Leroy said, smiling.

"I wanted a scar. A dueling scar."

"This wasn't a duel."

"Yes, it was. I saw. That's why I had Bennet get Papa. Something was wrong."

"Something certainly was. My daughter showed me the right of it last night. Quite forcefully too." Lord Ballentyne made a disparaging, headshake. "That young woman speaks her mind.

"So, Mr. Watches, if you would like to escort my niece when she makes her debut in November, on behalf of her parents, I would be delighted to accept your services."

15

LEROY DOES THE VATICAN

EVEN WILL COULDN'T get him an audience with the Pope. He got him an audience with "The Archbishop." Leroy was supposed to find out who had the untraceable phone number, which was Will's only link to Kathryn. Having found out who had it, he was to pump him for information about Kathryn Duane's whereabouts. Then he was supposed to find her.

Leroy was having a hard time with Italy. It stuck in his craw. His apartment also stuck in his craw. This one was bigger and golder than anything he'd seen in England. Table legs weren't just carved, they were carved and beveled and loop-de-looped—then covered with gold. All the paintings had huge gilt frames, showing various levels of aging. The ceiling of his bedroom was blue, with wispy clouds over that, and fat angels with small wings flapping around. They *couldn't* fly with wings that small. His tutor, Sir Glathering, would call it "overdone." "But it is *Italy* ..." he would sniff, nose in the air.

Whoever "The Archbishop" was must have been important; they sent over a couple of priests the day before to teach him how to behave. Fortunately, he was pretty well schooled from his lessons on English royalty. Even so, they were there for hours. But if he learned all that for English noblemen, why not for Italian clergy?

He expected to be in Italy only a short while. The mission Will had given him meant he'd be traveling, he suspected. Sitting at a writing table so carved and rolled and pleated that it made the English versions look like they came from a prison woodshop, he looked around the equally excessive living room, missing his ranch. Missing his father. The reservation. Fry bread.

"Tom, you don't have to put all my stuff away." His stuff consisted of three trunks full of clothing, everything from a swimsuit to his tuxedo. He'd brought his valet, Tom Wyatt, with him for company. Given his druthers, Leroy would travel with a back-pack and a pair of jeans, but those days were over.

"Do you want me to lay out your clothes for tomorrow, sir?"

"Call me Leroy, Tom. And no. I want you to go shopping for me."

The audience was the next day. Leroy decided to be true to his traditions. His People's spirituality was older than anything in this gaudy place. That deserved acknowledgement.

The driver's head fell forward and his eyes bulged when he picked him up in the morning. "We're going to the Vatican, sir. To see the Archbishop," he said in accented English.

"Yes. Let's go."

They drove through the crazy Rome traffic, crossing a bridge over a river. They didn't have a sign that said, "This is the Vatican." There was a guardhouse, but that didn't mark the change, but something was different. The buildings seemed either very close together or far apart. They were more luxurious than anything he'd seen, Will's fabulous home and the place where he was staying included. Leroy spent the drive startling as he looked out the window, and trying to keep his teeth together and jaw shut.

The driver pulled up at another ornate building. "This is it, sir. I'll wait for you."

Leroy got out and ten men in red, blue and yellow pajamas with tin can armor like in the cartoons surrounded him. They didn't speak much English and he didn't speak any Italian. He gave them paperwork that Will had sent. They looked at it, mumbling, aiming an occasional dark look and exclamation at him.

"Why are you dressed like that? Were you not told what is acceptable?" one of them asked, bristling.

"I am dressed according to my culture and religion to honor a man of God."

He'd still be standing there, but someone wearing a black bathrobe and cape with red trim arrived in cart with two or three rows of seats, empty but for the driver and the man who got out.

The newcomer castigated the guys in stripped pajamas. The minute they saw the new guy, they bowed so low that they almost hit their metal visors on the ground.

Black bathrobe looked him up and down. "You are a Native American?" he said in very good English.

"Yes."

"A very tall Native American. Come with me. I am to give you a tour. I am Monsignor Abatangelo, secretary to His Eminence. We will take a little tour, have a little lunch, and talk."

"When do I get to see His Eminence?"

"Ah. That is what we are determining."

The Monsignor took him all over. Leroy appreciated the cart after the first set of museums. At first, Leroy's feelings about the hallways and wide rooms embellished with gold and jewels were the same as his feelings about Italy: too much. How many people had given all they had to make this place? It had taken centuries to amass all this. He was staggered. He kept his mouth shut.

The Monsignor took him to museums around the huge central square. He saw famous paintings and wonderful things. Hordes of tourists swarmed, but one look at the monsignor and the insignia on their carriage and they scattered.

They got to a vast hall with its curved arches. The space captivated him. "This place is wonderful."

"St. Peter's Basilica is one of the most beautiful buildings in the world."

Leroy was so confused. The man with him was a man of God. He felt God all around him. How could a religion have all these things, all this majestic stuff, when his grandfather brought God to people using eagle feathers and smoke?

He did not understand. And he didn't need to. He needed only appreciate what he was shown.

They went down a residential street with cobblestone paving. Stone buildings about five stories high were arranged around a square. The driver entered one through an arched driveway.

"Yes, Monsignor, it is very good." Leroy had found one thing he liked about Italy. The food. They ate delicious pasta and bread dripping with butter in a private courtyard with a small fountain. The sound of the water soothed him.

"Tell me why you are dressed this way," the Monsignor said.

Leroy wore a fringed buckskin shirt he'd brought for formal occasions, chaps and a breechclout, beaded moccasins laced up to his knees, and necklaces made of shell and beads and silver. The dozen eagle feathers woven into the tail of hair at the back of his neck bristled like a mace. Tom had to go to an upscale ladies' boutique to get the face paints. He had done a masterful job of selecting eye shadows and unguents in earth tones.

Spirit told him what to say. "I'm a member of the …" he named his tribe, where it was and how long it had been there. "I am here to pay my respects to a great leader and man of God." All well and good, but he said it in his language, which he could see the Monsignor didn't understand. So he translated it into English, putting his hands together in the prayer position, holding his string of eagle feathers, and bowing his head.

"I bear the well-wishes of my grandfather's lineage, which has existed since the beginning of time. Although he has passed, I bear his power and goodwill."

"You are a shaman of your people?" his companion said.

"Yes, I am a shaman, but a beginner shaman. My grandfather was a real shaman."

"Now tell me all about your grandfather. His Eminence wishes to know all about him."

Leroy told him everything he could think of.

The other man whispered, "Did he have magical powers? Could he bring people back from death?"

"He could do many things, heal people for sure. I don't know about making people live again. But the only power he recognized was the power to show people the Great One and who they really were inside. He *was* the power of love from the beginning of his life to the end."

As he spoke, Leroy felt his healing trance come over him. The splendid buildings around him took on a blue radiance. Everything looked beautiful. He wasn't awed by the splendor, or resentful that the work of peasants had paid for it. He saw what was around him as a prayer.

"That will be fine, my son," the monsignor said, standing abruptly. "I wish to present …"

Becoming aware that someone had entered, Leroy jumped to his feet. The newcomer was a tiny old man wearing a red dress. Leroy realized through his culture shock, that it wasn't a dress and cape and hat. The man's clothes were the insignia of his office. The man was bent, but very keen.

"My son. I am His Eminence, Agapito Agusto, Cardinal Bessagiori. If you will forgive me, I have taken the liberty of listening in on your conversation. I have also taken the place of my friend and colleague Archbishop Nunziata." Leroy realized he'd been "upgraded": the Cardinal was higher ranked than the Archbishop. The Cardinal shrugged. "It saves time. I always wonder what my friend Will Duane has sent me—I seem to be the one His Holiness selects to deal with Will's entreaties. You are certainly the most unusual.

"This time, someone from within the Vatican wants something from you. Come, I will take you to him. We have heard that you are a healer?" He glanced at Leroy, who nodded. "Let us go. It is a short distance from here."

They drove up a narrow street, faced with buildings of very plain stone. You wouldn't have thought it was part of the Vatican, but it was.

"My brother wishes to meet you. He is not well."

A black-clad servant opened the door for them. Lines of grief marked his face. He was bent over and almost sobbing.

"What happened, Luigi? He was fine when I left. Are we too late?"

The servant shook his head. "No, Your Eminence. He lives, but he is in great pain. I cannot stand to see him suffer."

"Take me to him," Leroy said, not realizing how his appearance would affect the houseman.

He jumped in front of Leroy, blocking the doorway and holding out his arms to clutch the door jamb on each side. Ready to die to protect his master, with all of his one hundred and forty pounds. "No! You will not touch him."

"Don't worry, I won't hurt him." Leroy stepped forward and the fellow in the door moved aside like a feather. "Take me to him."

The room was small and oval. Stone walls covered with white plaster rose high overhead. A window near the top cast light upon the man in the bed. He was ancient, dying, and in great pain, as his servant had said.

"Oh, Tomas. I am sorry that you must suffer so," the archbishop went to his brother, dropped to his knees and took his hand. The dying man flinched at the touch.

"Don't touch him yet," Leroy said. He dropped to the stone floor and began to chant, arms and hands spread over the shrunken form in the bed. "O Great One, this is a good man. Take his pain. If you wish to make him well, heal him now. If you don't wish to make him well, take his pain and let him leave in glory."

The archbishop and servant stood back, listening to Leroy singing in his tongue. He detached two of his eagle feathers and brushed them over the suffering man's body, touching his head and forehead, his lips, his throat, heart. Belly and all his internal organs, traveling down his legs and ending with his feet. Leroy continued to chant, traditional melodies and words that came to him.

"You belong to Jesus, you belong to Jesus. You have always belonged to Jesus, to Jesus you are going, from Jesus you came. Go in peace, good brother, go in peace and carry love from my People to Jesus. Tell him his son, Joseph Bishop, my grandfather, loves him. Tell him Joseph Bishop loves you and bids you good speed."

His voice rose, vibrating from the hard stone and plaster walls. When he said his grandfather's American name, a "crack!" rocked the room. The stone and plaster split, traveling down the wall from the high window to the top of the crucifix hanging above the sick man's head.

Leroy laughed, "See, my friend, Jesus is coming for you. Jesus knows you, and He will take you with Him and to my grandfather. There is no pain for those who know the Lord. No pain for those who know the Great One. No pain for those encircled by angels and lovers of God. Open your eyes, and see your dear brother."

The man on the bed opened his eyes wide in astonishment. "Aldo, what is this? Am I dead? What is this light?"

Light filled the room as though all the windows in the world had opened. Something ricocheted around. The man in the bed began to weep, as did his servant and brother Aldo. And Leroy.

Wings brushed them, angels brushed them; the golden radiance of God covered them. Someone else was there, unseen. A Someone that angels sang of throughout all time.

"You are here just for a moment longer, my friend. Glory awaits you. The reward of your life awaits you. And we are supposed to talk," Leroy said.

"Yes, that is true. Aldo, Luigi, wait outside, I must speak with my friend. I have waited for him all these years." He shooed the others out.

Leroy sat in a simple wooden chair next to Fr. Tomas's bed. He leaned forward, listening intently.

"I was a simple priest, not destined for greatness like my brother. I saw the people who had suffered most, at their own hands, and at the hands of the evil one." A faint smile touched the face of the prostrate priest.

"While my brother visited palaces and castles, I visited the homes of the poor, hospitals, places they took the wretched and cast off. I knew that evil existed. I saw terrible things." Tears misted his eyes. He wiped at one, and then looked astonished. "I can move this hand. I couldn't before you came. Hah! What they say of you is true."

Leroy didn't know what that was, but he wanted to make sure the padre understood. "I can't make you better. You are going to die."

"I know. We are granted this interval so I can tell you. This is between you and me, you understand. You may never repeat it." Leroy nodded. "Will Duane has called me so many times for so many years. He wanted to know where his wife is. He wanted to know if she was well."

Leroy about jumped out of his chair. This was the man on the other end of the telephone number!

"I would never tell him. I could never feel the hand of God on him, as I can on you. He would harm her, rather than help her. That is still true, you understand?" Leroy nodded. "In the beginning, Will Duane blustered and shouted. Demanded. He was the rich man with all the power. Not *all* the power. His wife gave him my telephone number, direct. How many times I wished she hadn't.

"But Kathryn Duane wanted to know if her daughter was well, or if not well, *alive*. Had she not pined for her daughter, she would have cut all ties.

"Will Duane would call and say Ashley was sick or had had an accident, but he couldn't lie well enough to fool me into passing the message on. I am a poor priest, but I have ways of getting information … I kept track of the girl." He sighed. "Poor lost soul." He coughed.

"I found Kathryn Duane in the worst of the hospitals for Rome's poor. Nothing more than a waiting room for death. She was the most beautiful woman I have ever seen, but broken. Physically maimed, ruined, diseased in body, but mostly in soul. I visited her and saw she had a light that the greatest evil could not extinguish.

"I had her moved to one of our hospitals." He raised his hand to the indicated crucifix over his bed. "She was protected there. The evil one could not enter. I visited her. She was so ill, but little by little, she began to talk to me and tell me what had happened. She was not Catholic then; it was not confession, but it was.

"She told me about her husband, a selfish, evil man who had never been faithful to her. She told me about her own faults, her drinking and addiction to tranquilizers. She told me of neglecting her daughter as a result. She told me about Enzo Donatore and all that happened to her at his hands.

"She told me these things when she could talk. When we found her, she was barely alive and barely human. She screamed in terror and pain.

Nothing was worse than hearing Kathryn Duane scream. That horror could make angels drop from heaven.

"Nothing could heal her. But Jesus planted an idea in my mind. I took her to the place where angels sing."

Music wafted into the room, becoming louder. Women's voices, chanting, "Glori Patri, et Filo, et Spiritui Sancto …" Chants in Latin. They reached the heights and flew upward from there. The man on the bed smiled. "My brother knows what I like." His cheek twitched and he touched his heart, and then began speaking again.

"She was terrified of Donatore finding her, more terrified of him finding the child. We brought her to a place where she was safe and protected. She gradually felt the love of God and the Holy Trinity. She released her daughter into the care of the Divine Protector and did what she needed to do for her own soul."

The bright old eyes twinkled a bit.

"What would Will Duane say if he knew his wife was a Catholic?" Leroy's eyes bulged. "He'd do more than that, my friend. Leroy, you must never tell a soul what I am going to say.

"Kathryn Duane is now Mother Kathryn. I won't tell you her order or her sacred name. She is safe where she is, cloistered from the world."

"She's a cloistered nun?" Leroy gasped.

"Yes, of course. What else could she be after being abused so badly? After hating her husband so much that she walked into the arms of the devil, knowing what he was, and what would happen to her? She is healed, she is forgiven, and she has forgiven the man she once loved."

Leroy was having trouble keeping his jaw shut.

"She will never leave her monastery. She is safe there. She does God's work, Leroy, praying day and night for the salvation of souls. The singing never stops in that place. It is a place for angels.

"She is the most beautiful woman I have ever seen. If ever a woman could cause me to break my vows, it was she. But I didn't and she didn't.

Still I have loved her all these years, keeping her safe from Donatore, and her husband."

"You've done a good job with that. Will's almost crazy wanting to know she's OK and wanting to say he's sorry. He's a changed man, Father, since he met my grandfather."

"But not changed all the way."

"No, that dog has some fleas to shed. But he cares about Mrs. Duane. And he cares about Cass, what Ashley calls herself now."

"How is the child?"

"Not a child anymore an' worked over by the devil about as much as her mother was. I think she's safe now. I'd make her safe if her father'd let me."

"Fleas, Leroy. He has fleas. And you don't." Dying eyes, filled with truth.

"I tried my best, sir."

"Do you intend to marry her?"

"If I can get my hands on her and get her well."

The priest was looking more shrunken by the minute. "I have a gift for you. Words from a saint, St. Louise de Marillac. She was co-founder of the Daughters of Charity of St. Vincent de Paul. Have you heard of her?" Leroy shook his head.

"Her life was filled with waiting and not getting what she wanted. About waiting, she said, 'I will tell you quite simply that we must wait peacefully for grace to produce true humility in us by revealing our powerlessness to us.'

"We are powerless, Leroy, until grace gives us the gift of that knowledge. And then we are *truly* powerless."

"An' the Great One comes and does it for you."

"Yes." He coughed and clutched his chest. "I must see my brother now, my friend. Everything is in God's hands and will work out as it should." He smiled. "I didn't get to meet your grandfather, but I got to meet you." The smile widened. "You will be greater than him, my son." He made the sign of the cross in Leroy's direction.

Archbishop Aldo entered, hands bearing a vial. A couple more priests were with him. They went right to work. The Last Rites, Leroy had heard it called. He stood in the hallway, until someone came.

"Your car is here, sir." He gave Leroy a parcel wrapped in brown paper and tied with string. "Father Tomas had this wrapped for you."

Leroy took it and walked into the blinding Roman light.

16

FINDING AN ANGEL

LEROY SAT SPRAWLED on the sofa of his villa. He held in his lap a framed black and white photograph, which was the content of the package the servant had given him the day before. The huge TV in the media room of his villa was on, the sound muted. Soundlessly wailing people filled the screen; short people in black keened. Talking-head announcers intoned dirges in Italian. He got Tom to turn off the sound and get the English subtitles up. Tom was very clever at things like that.

Ribbons along the bottom of the screen read, "Fr. Tomas Bessagiori died last night at about four a.m. after a long battle with cancer. Long considered a saint by Rome's poor and disadvantaged, the priest who devoted his life to the disenfranchised has gone home."

Leroy took in a huge gulp of air. His ribs heaved. He knew Tomas was dying. He could do nothing to stop it. He'd known him only a few minutes, yet he was devastated. As the announcements continued, his heaving ribs turned to uncontrolled sobs. His valet left the room discreetly.

"The streets are filled with mourners, people from all walks of life. They're converging on the little Vatican street where he breathed his last."

"Previously, Fr. Tomas was known for his charity to the poor, but now, as you can see from these shots from fashionable districts, he was loved by the rich as well." Chic faces lined with grief lit candles in front of a statue of the original St. Tomas in a wide plaza.

"He was able to heal the sick of heart and mind, as well as body. His charitable works are legendary. Hospitals, orphanages, and homes for those with incurable diseases."

"The Vatican has announced that one documented miracle has taken place since his death. That occurred in his death chamber, witnessed by five people, including his brother, His Eminence, Agapito Agusto, Cardinal Bessagiori. The process of canonization has thus begun for our beloved Father Tomas."

"Listen, Gianni, you can hear the people in the streets," the Italian news doll said.

Leroy turned up the sound for that one. The streets were flooded, and the crowds were heading to the Vatican. Shouts of, "Santo subito!" "Sainthood now!" filled the air. Black clad people, all ages, crawled toward the Vatican entrances on their hands and knees, striking their faces and tearing their clothes in grief.

The cameras moved around. Bundles of flowers five feet high piled around the little chapel where Tomas had preached. His home before his final illness, when he had been moved to the Vatican, was a little place at the back of the church no different than the shabby houses in the neighborhood. Now it was a shrine. Candles, flowers, crosses, wailing mourners. Grief poured from the screen.

Tears ran down Leroy's cheeks, both for Fr. Tomas and for his grandfather. This is what should have happened when his grandfather passed. He was a great saint, but Enzo Donatore and his black devils stole his glory. Now, grandpa was "the missing shaman," "a character so much like Jim Jones," "a cult leader."

What the people in the street were doing—expressing their anguish at losing a true man of God—is what should have happened for his grandfather, shaman, teacher, and healer. Piles of flowers and candles and placards lined the streets for Tomas, growing by the instant.

Leroy's eyes fell on the framed photo in his lap. It was bigger than 8" X 10" and matted. He had no idea what it was. It had hung in Tomas's bedchamber, his last place of rest. A black and white photo, it depicted the corner of a tiled roof, a three-quarters view so you could see both sides of the roof. The tiles were odd-shaped, not like the ones that sold in any of the building supply outlets he knew. Hand-made and old.

The shot was taken so you could see a funny little animal—carved in stone—under the tile's lip. It had a round hole for a mouth. A drain-spout. Behind the tiled corner, at some distance, a chimney stuck up. It was unusual too, with a notched, stair-step top. Each flat edge was tiled. The composition was nice; it was an artistic shot that no one would think anything about seeing in a priest's room.

Leroy jerked when he got it. Kathryn Duane was the Mother Superior of the monastery the shot depicted. If he found it, he would find her. But how? This clue was indecipherable. How many tile-roofed monasteries of cloistered nuns were there in Italy? Europe? The world? She could be anywhere. Tomas hadn't said she was in Europe. But Leroy's soul said she was. What was her name now? He didn't know.

He needed to find a cloistered monastery with singing nuns that had that weird tile and a gargoyle spout. He couldn't do it. Despite the impossibility of it, Leroy's mind immediately began to kick out plans to find Kathryn.

But should he, even if he could? Tomas had told him Will Duane was an evil man. Leroy had not known him when he chased women. He had stopped, but Leroy didn't know how sorry he was, or if he knew how he had hurt his wife and daughter. Even as a child, Cass knew her father was doing something hurtful to her mother and their family, even if she didn't know what. Now, she certainly knew what.

Leroy suspected Will wasn't being upfront with him about Cass. Was she getting better? Why wasn't he telling him the truth about his interactions with her? Will's *fleas* might be running the dog.

If that was so, knowing where his wife was would surely lead to her doom. Duane would go after her with Hannah and her troops and all of his computers and electronic powers. Kathryn's safe haven would be exposed, and Donatore would get her again. Leroy decided he would never tell Will even the bit he'd found: she was a nun in a cloistered monastery, and happy. She'd stay that way.

Why did *he* want to find Kathryn Duane? He did, absolutely. Leroy thought about what he'd say to her, if he found her. He'd tell her how sorry he was about all that had befallen her. She would tell him she did it to herself, and walked into the devil's arms on her own out of anger at her husband. But she didn't take her daughter; that was some hellish trick of Donatore's.

"How did you get free? Where did you find the strength and courage to get away? How can I help Cass do the same?" That's what Leroy wanted to ask.

The phone rang. *Oh, shit*, he thought. Will Duane. "Tom, would you get that. I'm out, unless it's God."

"Sir, I think it is God." Tom handed the receiver to him.

The voice belonged to an elderly, grief-stricken man. "Leroy, it is Aldo, Cardinal Aldo. The *important* son of the Bessagiori family." Aldo was weeping, out of control. "I need to confess a sin to you, Leroy. I have hidden something from you. I am the important one in my family, the Prince of the Holy Church. My brother was a mere priest, with a small parish. Oh, I knew he did good, but not to the extent he did. Stories are pouring in, thousands of stories of people he saved.

"Now, I want him to save me. And I want you to save me. I will tell you what happened after you left. You saw our Lord in his chamber, yes?"

"Yes."

"And angels, and holy beings. The Mother of God. You saw those?"

"Yes, I did."

"I administered the Last Rites. He lingered. We stayed and prayed; his retainer, Luigi, and his closest friends. The air was thick with holiness. I could barely breathe. When my brother's ribs stopped moving, a howl filled my ears. Not of pain, but of joy.

"The crack down the wall that started when you were here shot down the wall. The crucifix that was mounted there flew into the air, tumbling. It landed so that the holy heart of Jesus rested against my brother's heart. I fell on my knees, all of us did.

"The wall of the building exploded outward, a wall that was built nine-hundred years ago. Rocks and brick flew into the little street below, where people stood in vigil, having found out where my brother was. They could have been killed! No one was hurt! Not a soul! None of the rocks hit anyone.

"I saw what happened next, and so did Luigi and the others. Oh, Leroy, such a sight. I never dreamed. I didn't know it was *possible* ..." He was silent, then weeping, snuffling, and moaning.

"What did you see, Your Holiness?"

"Oh, Leroy, Our Lord came through the gaping hole in the wall, Jesus Christ our Lord in splendor. Surrounded by angels, with Holy Mary and the disciples. The light! Oh God!" He began speaking in Latin. "Our Lord held His hands over my brother's body, and his soul rose to the Savior's arms. He took my brother from his body and raised him to heaven! I cannot believe it! My brother!

"No one in the family thought anything of him, working with poor. With terrible people, a simple priest. No one. But *God* came for him, with all the ...

"I am a Cardinal of the Holy Catholic Church and I did not believe such things could happen. That is my confession, Leroy. I didn't believe in the power of the God I served."

Leroy was silent. He'd never had a Cardinal confess to him. "Now you know it's true. You can take the learning in it, all of it, and put it in your life. Live that lesson. That's what God told you."

Aldo wept silently, and then stammered, "You're right. I must make the lesson mine.

"My brother was a good man, and he will be a saint forever living with God and revered on Earth. For what all of us saw was a miracle; we will testify to it. And the people outside who had giant stones hurtle past them, but not touch them, will testify to that. It takes two documented miracles, plus much investigation, to make a saint.

"I'm going to follow what you say and give you a third miracle. I am a vain man, Leroy. A proud man. Proud of my position and the robes I wear. I have not always been gentle and righteous using my power.

"I was going to do something evil, Leroy. A sin. My brother told me to send you some things just before he breathed his last. I was going to keep one as a relic, and destroy the rest.

"I am going to trust my brother's soul, and send them to you. They are for you and you only." Leroy heard someone in the background calling the Cardinal. "I must go. These sad days are full of activities. You are welcome to come to my brother's funeral, but if I were you, I would not. You might attract attention and harm her. Everyone knows Will Duane sent you. They will be following you. A package will arrive for you, be content with that.

"And my life is transformed. I will live my brother's legacy on Earth and see that his projects are completed. I am changed, I swear to you."

"I believe it, Your Holiness. To have seen what you have and not follow its teaching would poison your soul worse than the devil could."

A gasp of fear, and the line went dead.

Four huge monsters with beat-up, scarred faces delivered it. They drove a black car with blacked-out windows.

Leroy met them at the door.

"This is for you," one said in guttural English. The package was large and square.

"Yeah, Aldo said he was havin' it sent," Leroy replied. "Thanks."

"It's for you, and no one else. No one's even supposed to know you've got it."

"If you'd give it to me and leave, then we'd be sure no one saw it." Leroy nodded up the street, where patrician Romans were presumably hanging at their front windows, enthralled by the spectacle.

"Y' better not let anyone see that."

"I already said I wouldn't." Get out, scum, he said in his language. Before something serious happens. A gust of wind blew one guy's straw hat off. They left.

Leroy opened it on the dining room table. The crucifix that had been hanging above Fr. Tomas was on top. He could feel the vibration of Fr. Tomas's heart and the heart of Jesus emanating from it. Leroy lifted it out, wondering why anyone would want a cross with a dead body hanging on it, even if the body was Jesus. His Grandfather was a staunch Christian, but he'd been raised in Protestant schools. The cross his Grandfather had given him was plain wood.

Now he had a fancy brass one with a dead Jesus, wounds graphically portrayed, and nails prominent. Next in the box was a large manila envelope holding a quarter-inch thick sheaf of paper with addresses printed on it. Forty-seven pages, twenty-five addresses typed in neat rows on each page. A total of 1,175 addresses. Of what?

Nunneries and monasteries. Kathryn Duane was at one of them, the one with the funny tile, gargoyle and chimney.

The rest of the box was full of old cassette tapes and CDs of—nuns singing in a dozen languages and Latin.

He had clues to finding her that no one else would be able to figure out. That *he* couldn't figure out. Leroy would have to know much more about computers and searching than he did. If he started looking up all those addresses on a computer, what would happen? Without being at the monastery, he couldn't tell if the tile came from there. He'd have to visit every one. Or search for them on a computer somehow.

Hannah said that Enzo Donatore had a crystal that allowed him to look anywhere. None of Will's technology could stop him. He probably could focus on Leroy, or Leroy's computer, and see what he was doing. Leroy didn't know a lot, but he knew that someone very skilled could figure out what he'd done on-line. If he found Kathryn Duane that way, he'd doom her as much as Hannah charging in with her soldiers.

Marco had said, "She is the most beautiful woman I have ever seen. If ever a woman could cause me to break my vows, it was she. But I didn't and she didn't. Still I have loved her all these years, keeping her safe from Donatore, and her husband."

A love story and a tale of enormous trust. One that could destroy Marco's chances for sainthood if it were known. "That whore of a nun was his lover." Leroy knew exactly what public opinion would do to them. This must never come out. He would not try to find Kathryn Duane. The phone rang.

Tom's voice came through the loudspeaker. "Leroy, sir, it's Will Duane."

"Oh, fuck!" Leroy never swore without grave provocation.

17

PROTECTING AN ANGEL

"WILL, YOU MUST have some news by now? How is she?" That raspy old voice again. Vanessa Schierman had taken to calling every few days. "How long has she been in that hospital? They must know if she's dead or *alive.*"

"She's alive, Vanessa. Very ill. In seclusion." Will was getting sick of being conciliatory. "It's a family matter, Vanessa. Private."

"*Pish. Family* pish. *I'm* family, Will. The child practically grew up on my estate when you were off gallivanting. I'm Cass's *grandmother* in all but blood. For years, I cared more about her than you did, *much* more."

"How dare you say that? I've supported her through *everything* she's done. This is the *eighth* hospitalization, Vanessa …"

"Necessitated because you were such a terrible parent and husband. You practically threw Kathryn at that monster so you could lally-lally around with your chippies. Except you sent her to a *real* monster, didn't you?"

He hung up. She called back and left a message. "Don't think I'll give up. I won't quit until Cass is sitting on my front porch, smiling. She belongs here, Will. I have resources too, my friend, and I'm not afraid to use them."

What did she mean by that? He poured a paper cup of water over his head and wiped his face with a towel. He was working out in his private gym again. The Indians were as annoying as ever. He'd taken to his quarters to escape. Carl did not consider his baring his soul to Leroy as being sufficient.

"You didn't tell him you were jealous of him. Or how you want to get back at her. You gotta let him talk to her. And you need to tell her she's doing bad. She's depressed and not eatin'. That's from not talking to her soul mate. *You're* making her sicker."

Should have fired the cheeky bastard.

Carl had stopped going to work with him. Stopped serving him dinner too. Damn bastards, costing him a fortune being there. Except they weren't: the guesthouses where they lived were already there. They cost him nothing. Those who could work got jobs right away, not depending on him for patronage. They didn't go on spending sprees. They even bought their own food.

Will felt so bad, he decided to call Leroy. He was one person who wouldn't disappoint him.

"You found the priest I've been talking to all these years? That's fantastic." Will was elated when he got Leroy on the phone. At least *one* person in his life wouldn't let him down. "Did he tell you where Kathryn is?"

"Have you been watching the news from Italy?"

"No. Why?"

"Fr. Tomas Bessagiori died last night. He was the man you've been talking to. He knew that you had sent me to find Kathryn. He had his brother take me to his room before he died."

"Yeah, *and* …"

"He died. He told me nothing. No clues. It's a dead end."

"How can it be a dead end?"

"Watch the news. The priest can't tell me where she is because he's dead."

"Those fucking Catholics got her! I should have known when I found out it was a Vatican number. God damn it! I gave her a hundred million dollars when we split. Fair and square—half what I was worth when we split. I bet they ..."

"Saved her life, healed her, and protected her all these years. I bet they're all that's standing between her and Donatore right now."

That calmed Will down a bit. "Who *is* protecting her now? This priest is dead. Did he name anyone else? You said he had a brother."

"His brother is His Imminence, Agapite Agusto, Cardinal Bessagiori."

"A *Cardinal?*"

"Yes."

"Great. Let's get him involved in this. I'm sure they got everything she had. They must know where she is."

"Will! Watch the news! They're rioting in the streets to get Fr. Thomas made a saint early. If people know about Kathryn, the press will be on it in a minute. If where she is becomes known, Donatore will be on her faster than that. He'll make sure that *everyone* knows what she did, especially the Church. She did *terrible* things. Aldo ..."

"Aldo?"

"His Eminence, the Cardinal, won't come to her aid. Anything that hooks a woman with a past like that to his brother will destroy Tomas's bid for sainthood. Twenty years of phone conversations definitely is a link."

Leroy got back on the phone the instant Will hung up. He called the only person he could think of who could help him.

"I cannot do that. I work for Mr. Duane," Hannah Herhman said.

"It's not lying, Hannah, it's not telling him everything. If he asks why you sent them out, tell him I was worried about security."

"But his regular people ..."

"I'm worried about *them*. I need really good people, Hannah. The best. The kind you know."

"You say if I don't do what you want, Cass could be in danger?"

"Yes. Worse danger. I got it when I was talking to Will. Kathryn has been protecting Cass all these years. Spiritually. She was friends with a saint, Hannah, a real one. Do you know what they say about holy people at the highest level?"

"No."

"'It takes one to know one.' All you've done to save Cass, and all Will's done has worked because of Kathryn's prayers. I bet that she's close to being a saint herself."

"This is crazy."

"This is not crazy. This is how spirit works. Like attracts like. Fr. Tomas loved and cared for Kathryn because she was like him. She was interested in one worldly thing: her daughter. If Donatore gets Kathryn, he gets Cass. Nothing we can do about it. There's no one on Earth to protect Kathryn now."

"But me," Leroy said softly.

"You." Hannah was thoughtful. "Yes, this is true. You stand between her and hell."

"Yes. I'm going to find Kathryn and see that she is protected the rest of her life."

"Isn't her prayer and vocation enough?"

"Maybe. But in wars, they always kill the holy people first. Will you do what I say, and do it fast?"

Less than an hour later, Leroy got a beep on his cell.

"Open your kitchen door." He let them in.

The three of them were clad in black, completely. Not an inch of skin showed. No words, no introductions. They covered the villa, studying and testing. They unearthed bugs in every room, despite Will's stringent security.

"Could anyone see in a box if I was sitting here?" On the sofa, where he'd opened the box and taken out its contents? A nod, yes. The crucifix. The papers. The tapes. And the black and white photo. "Can they blow the images up and know what they were? Or said?" Maybe.

Maybe. He had to get rid of everything permanently. "You brought the incinerator?" They set it up in his room.

The high tech and tiny furnace was easy to use. It rendered anything put inside to unanalyzable powder. The noise blockers they left were also easy to use. Tom could not hear him even in the same villa. The surveillance experts would stay nearby until he summoned them to take everything away.

"Tom, I trust you. I need to really trust you now. I need to do something; it's a ceremony from my people. I need to make sure someone is safe. To do that, I have to go to a place where I go for a few days. It's where a shaman goes.

"I'll need you to take care of me, to feed me; bring me food, but feed me too. I'll look drunk, Tom, but I'm not. Can I trust you to help me and not tell anyone about it, ever? Lives depend upon it. Can you do that?"

"Certainly, sir ..."

"*Please Tom,* call me Leroy."

"All right, Leroy, sir." Leroy rolled his eyes. "I'm sorry, sir, Leroy."

"Forget it. Cover the phones for me. I'm sick or ... no, I'm in a Native American ceremony. A quest. Goes on for days ..."

Leroy went to his room and rearranged his altar. It was set up on a wide chest of drawers. He carried it with him everywhere, packing the objects in a specially made case. A fine woven rug made by one of the women of his Nation ran down the middle. A small buffalo skull sat in the very middle. Hard to explain at the airport, but he wouldn't be without it.

Arrayed on each side of the buffalo skull were his pipe, a fan of eagle feathers, bundles of cedar, sage, sweet grass: smudges. An abalone shell for the ashes of smudging.

A small painting of the crystal eagle sat behind everything, leaning against the mirror. Depicting the eagle was impossible, but this artist had made a good stab. He and his grandfather shared the same totem. Not a regular eagle, this was the being that covered the thin membrane between birth and death. She guarded the Western gate that led from this life to the next. A totem of immeasurable power, the eagle appeared as a neon strip in the sky whose coming released brilliant light and all of God's power. She came with a terrifying shriek. Those were all in the center.

He looked to each side of his People's sacred objects. Did they know what they did to him, his dear friends of other faiths? They branded him; they separated him from his own with their sacred gifts and symbols. And their knowledge of God.

On the left side, he'd placed the Menorah given him by his grandfather's dear friend, the rabbi who got them going with the Kosher beef. Next to it were three Stars of David, a yarmulke—skullcap—of white with gold embroidery, a flat symbol of a hand—the *hamsa*—with an eye in the middle to symbolize God's protection and watchful eye. His prayer shawl was draped over his shoulders.

The rabbis wanted to convert him so much; they didn't realize that they *had* converted him. They were his people. He loved them and their religion. It was his religion. "I'm an Indian," Leroy whispered. "They don't know we don't toe the line. We don't convert same as others."

Leroy touched the ritual objects with his fingers, working his way to the other side of his chest of drawers. He wasn't a Christian. His Grandfather had been a Christian. Jesus had come to him the first night he had been stolen from his family and band so many years ago.

Jesus had saved him and kept him from being so raped and abused that his light could not shine and he could not be the gift of God he was. Jesus stayed with his grandfather every day of the shaman's life. Leroy knew of Christianity through Christ himself, who was visible in Grandfather's every smile and move. But Jesus wasn't the center of Leroy's soul.

The lemongrass and sage owned his soul, as did the buffalo skull and the shrieking eagle that covered the horizon. His People's ways and legends and ceremonies owned Leroy Watches. He was traditional, despite it all.

Leroy did not know why words of Jesus had poured from him as Fr. Tomas lay dying. He did not know why he prayed to the man who needed to be nailed to a cross to save the world. He didn't know why Jesus and his multitudes had flooded in as the holy name came from his mouth. Leroy didn't understand that.

But he had been branded by the soul of Jesus, the man Grandfather had loved as much as life. Grandfather was a soul that held all religions as equal because he *knew them as equal.* Leroy's fingers ran to the end of the bureau. On the other side of his People's totems was the smooth wood cross his grandfather left him, a Protestant cross with no ornamentation. Next to it was the crucifix left him by Fr. Tomas. The nailed God. The cross with Jesus's ruined body hanging on it. It stood on a base, so he couldn't escape seeing it wherever he was in the room.

As did the Menorah and Star of David and cross and this new thing, this nailed and naked God. He held them all and understood them all to their depths and heights.

Did his loved ones, the holy men and women of God who had gifted him so, know what they had done? They had converted him, all of them, even with this horrifying new cross. He was *all* of them.

He was like his Grandfather. A shudder ran through him.

Grandfather was 100% Native from an ancient lineage of holy men. A great holy man had picked him as a toddler to be the next Great One to save his People. And then he was stolen by the whites and locked in

Indian schools, a lot of them. He was so smart; they wanted to show him off. And they did.

They made him into a preacher. He taught the Christian Gospel to his mangled People who stared at him through depression and alcohol, unable to understand how the benevolent Savior he preached about was supposed to appear and fix their ruined world. Grandfather was a perfectly trained white-man's Indian, until he found out what had happened to his family and band and left the white man's world.

He walked into the desert, intending to die, but was found by the greatest shaman of all, Great-grandfather. Great-grandfather nurtured him, taught him, healed his soul, and gave him his secrets. When the old shaman died, he turned the power of his lineage over to the master shaman Grandfather, the Christian Joseph Bishop, the hybrid who loved God in all forms.

Very nice for a sermon on ecumenical Sunday, but that wasn't reality. Leroy had heard his Grandfather reviled—screamed at, hated—by traditional People because he loved Jesus.

Where was he to go in this world? It didn't matter. He needed to do his work.

Leroy turned on the sound-masking device Hannah's people had left and spread out the pages with the names of the monasteries and spread them on the bed. He took one of the tapes out of the box and inserted it in the player. Leroy leaned back in a chair and closed his eyes. A smile came over his face, then rapture. He began to chant with the tape, a phrase or two. And with the next tape, and the next, until they were gone and he started with the CDs.

When he was finished, he incinerated everything, leaving not a trace of evidence that would lead to Kathryn Duane's location. No trace of the desire to find her in his heart either.

She was protected. Legions of angels protected her. And all of God's warriors stood between her and evil. The life she lived in her stone lair was sufficient to keep her safe. Kathryn Duane didn't need him or any-one to guard her. The chanting of ages permeated her bones. That's why Donatore couldn't find her, and never would.

Leroy saw her as he chanted with the nuns in all those recordings. She sat in a stone garden wearing a simple black dress. Her hair was trimmed very short, an inch or so. Kathryn looked at him directly, blue eyes of amazing depth. Her beauty, even as an old woman, was astonish-ing. She spoke to him wordlessly. He was to give up the search and leave her alone. She needed nothing.

What about Cass, he'd cried back wordlessly.

Cass is in God's hands, she always has been. When the time comes you will save her. The vision disappeared.

He was so elevated that he couldn't muster questions. *How can I handle your husband?* He won't let me near Cass.

Leroy knew that question would be handled, too. In time.

When Leroy came out, he felt as though he could see to the end of the universe. He knew that his eyes had the bottomless look of his Grandfather's to others.

"Are you all right, Mr. Watches?"

"Sure, Tom, do you have any more of that beef roast?"

"Oh, good, sir. I was so worried about you. I have food in the kitchen."

While Leroy ate, Tom filled him in on what had happened while he was indisposed.

"Mr. Duane called six times."

"Did he say anything about Cass?" Tom shook his head.

Leroy snorted. "I knew he wouldn't." He called for the cleaners and they came and debugged the place again. No new bugs; no one had been in there. They took away the portable incinerator. That was that.

"What do we do now, sir?"

"I don't know."

18

WHAT'S GOING ON HERE?

"HONEY, DO YOU want me to come back there and stay with you?" Will had Cass on the line. She was both stronger and weaker each time he called. Her doctor said she was gaining weight and doing well. That meant not attacking anyone or having screaming fits—they'd had her there before.

"No, Daddy. I'm just blue. I keep having bad dreams and remembering things." She sniffled. Weeping. She sounded broken. He was glad he couldn't see it. "I'm so sorry, daddy. I ..."

"Honey, you have to put all that behind you. No one holds what happened against you, certainly not me. That was another lifetime. What you've got now is new. You'll get through this. We'll get you through this."

"I wish I had someone to hold me. To make me feel safe. Someone who loved me."

"*I* love you. I'm there for you. Don't you know that, sweetie? I'm your dad."

"I know, Daddy. Not like that ..."

Leroy didn't trust Will. Something was off. He had spoken to his pop, who told him to "milk that cow for everything he could get." Pop was mad at Will too, but he was up to something himself. He wasn't telling Leroy everything, but his secret wasn't about Cass.

Wasn't there anyone in the world he could talk to and trust? Who would tell him the truth?

"Carl. It's Leroy."

"I know it's you, Leroy. You're the only person in the world who's got a voice lower than Barry White."

"Who's that?"

"You wouldn't know him, Leroy. He's a sexy singer. Outside your universe."

At least Carl still had a sense of humor. "What does that mean?"

"I'm jus' bein' as crabby as everyone else around here. Why are we speaking our own language? Are we code talkers?" The Diné—Navajo—code talkers played a major part in WWII. The Germans were never able to break their code: the Diné language.

"We are code talkers," Leroy said. "None of Hannah's bugs can figure out what we're saying. You know she's got someone listening. What is going on there? Will says Cass is fine, gaining weight, and doesn't remember me. I don't believe it. I feel like every second with her got branded into my hide. Into eyes, my skin …"

"Hold that, buddy. I'm married to my soul mate, I know all about that. You must be burnin' up, it's been so long since you held her."

"Yes, Carl, I am. I feel …"

"You're a spirit warrior and you're going to stay one. You're not going to go out an' rub on some little," he said a word meaning 'loose woman,' "just to scratch an itch. If it gets too bad, brother, take matters into your own hands."

"What?"

"You got hands, use 'em."

Leroy blushed. He didn't have a big brother; Carl was as close as it came. Carl kept talking, "I'll tell you what's going on and turning Will Duane into a lying asshole, which I think he's been for a long time. First off, Numenon is at war. They want to get rid of Will, who has tried to put some of the ideas from the Meeting into place. It's just that the Meeting turning into a massacre shot his mojo. He can't say where he got the new ideas. They're a little radical for corporate America. He's fighting hard, but he's in trouble." Leroy knew all this. "Didn't help that I stopped going to work with him."

"Why?"

"'Cuz of what he was doing to you, little brother. Lying. I can't stand a liar. I told him to level with you or I'd quit helping him. Me an' everyone here are about to pack up and get out."

"Then he'd be alone."

"Like he wants. Don't you want to know what he's not telling you?"

"Yeah."

"He's jealous of you."

"What!?"

"I told you he's crazy. He wants Cass to love him most. He wants a big father/daughter reunion like in the movies—the ones that would never happen. All pink clouds and 'I love Daddy best.' He thinks if she forgets about you, she'll love him. Then, he'll tell her about you. By that time, you will be transformed into the Stanford MBA that he thinks is the man of her dreams. He always tried to push guys like that on her."

"How do you know all this?"

"Hannah. We're good buds. She saw me working out and tried to recruit me to work for her. The woman *likes* warriors. She bugs everything, Leroy. Even Will's phones and email. Good thing we're code talkers!" Carl laughed. "She listens in on Will's talks with Cass. She was around when he was trying to push all these suits on her. Cass got her MBA to make Will happy."

"She has an MBA?" Leroy barely made it out of high school.

"Yeah. She's really smart. Maybe she has some brain cells left to think with. Did you put the brain damage on her so Donatore couldn't find her?"

"What? She's brain-damaged?"

"Oh, shit. I thought you knew. Yeah, but she can talk to Will, so it can't be too bad."

Leroy was in free-fall.

"Leroy!"

"Yeah."

"Remember this: Cass has touched you too. There'll come a time when she'll break out of the hospital and find you if she has to walk across the ocean. Until then, they'll feed her and get her healthy. You need to get what you can for yourself.

"She's here and Will is not going to let you near her, even if you could find her," Carl added. "The name of the hospital's secret, even in this house. Hannah isn't divulging that.

"Stay there and do everything Will wants like it's what you've wanted your whole life. Happy face, bro! Get what you can for yourself, Leroy. Nobody's gonna give you what he's givin' you, ever. Take it. Know that whatever you're turning into, the Great One wants.

"Know something else. Leroy, you weren't at the Meeting to see Will in action. He's a warrior's warrior. He ran out to face Donatore and all of his monsters by himself, trying to get them to take *him* instead of killin' us. I saw him stand out in the desert all alone, with the sky full of black demons and fire, screaming at Donatore.

"It was stupid, of course. Donatore would have killed him without Grandfather and the Great One, but he's got balls, Leroy. More than that, he's got a heart. He's a good man, Leroy, just got lost somehow since the Meeting. If you can bring who he really is out, the whole world will benefit.

"We'll stay here at his house, all of us, and try to keep Will from wrecking everything. I won't leave, buddy, until he orders me out. That's a promise.

"Hannah's on the job, Leroy. She knows where the hospital is and Will's plans for Cass. She won't tell anyone, 'cuz she's loyal to Will. In love with him, if you ask me. But she's *really* in love with Cass. Cass is the baby she'll never have. Hannah's got people workin' in the hospital kitchen, and laundry. With the nurses. She's got that hospital covered. Cass is safe there. As long as she's there, you can do whatever you want.

"Go fox huntin'. Go to parties. Do what you want. For you. An' remember, no matter what happens, I'm behind you. Your People are behind you. Also remember that you got hands."

19

THE HOME RUN TRAIL

"NO, I WILL not go after her, Mr. Duane," Leroy said. "The guy you been talkin' to all these years is *dead*. There's nothing to track her by. If I started pokin' around, Donatore would be on me in a minute. Maybe *he'll* find her. You don't want that, I know." Will didn't reply.

"How's Cass? You must be talkin' to her. I never heard of a hospital tellin' someone's *father* he can't talk to his daughter. How is she? Did you tell her about me?" Leroy couldn't keep the edge out of his voice as he talked to Will on the phone.

"No, I didn't, Leroy, and no, she didn't ask. She's fine, regaining what she lost in physical condition and in weight. They're letting her work out a little, with a physical therapist."

"What's your plans for her, Mr. Duane?"

"Same plan as always …" Mr. Duane's voice quit in the middle of a sentence. Line must have died. Leroy's chest heaved up and down a few times. He couldn't remember being so angry. If Cass was *alive*, she'd remember him. Sleeping was all he could do every night, her eyes never left his, once he got in bed and tried to sleep.

Now what was he supposed to do? He felt like going home. To the ranch, not Will's fancy summer camp for Indian warriors.

"You ready to jump ship?" Doug phoned him unexpectedly.

"Yeah." Hearing Doug's voice unleashed him enough that he talked about his conversation with Will. "How's Cass?"

"Mum's the word, Leroy. I'm sure she hasn't died. We would have heard about that. Will ain't talkin' and no one's asking. I'm assuming he's doing his 'Daddy of the year' deal. He wants Cass to love him and see him as her savior, not just the one who put her in harm's way. So he won't let anyone near her.

"If you still want to play 'Leroy Watches as *My Fair Lady* …?'"

"What?"

"It's an old movie that Audrey Hepburn starred in, *My Fair Lady.* A snotty professor claimed a person's accent and manners determine their social position. He trained up a pretty flower seller to take over London society. Which she did. That's what we've been doing, but you're not a pretty flower seller.

"Will loved your website, by the way. Ordered all your dad's books."

"Really?"

"Yeah. He said, 'Why didn't *you* know about this, Doug? This is significant.' I told him I was a racist pig fooled by your skin color and the way you talk, so I didn't look online, thinking you weren't up to it."

"You did?"

"Yeah. And I still work for him, but more as an advisor. You ready for your next job?"

"What is it?"

"Take over Italian society. I've got a tour of Italy planned. Good work at the Vatican: Leroy Watches walks in and the missing priest croaks."

Leroy laughed. "OK. I'll do it, what was that? *My Fair Lady* goes to Italy. What should I do …?"

"You're going to spend a little more time in Rome, but the game plan is changing. You're going to host dinner parties wherever you are from now on. That means people will be coming to your house and you'll feed them." Leroy felt his gut clench at the prospect of entertaining big wigs. "Don't sweat it," Doug said. "Use your staff."

Doug provided him the guest lists and he let his staff do their thing. "I'm going to let you handle the table settings, Gianni. You know all that," he said to the butler in his Roman mega-condo. "What do people like to eat here? In English."

Gianni gave him a formal dinner menu with all eight courses.

"You know, that sounds good, but I'm American. How about if we give them a barbecue? Ribs and potato salad? Baked beans? I've got my dad's recipes. He's the king of barbecue. An' we can have some straw-berry short cake for dessert. Let me get in the kitchen with you all and we'll cook up somethin' people won't forget. Be sure and have those little water bowls for your washin' your fingers on the table. And extra napkins."

His guests were shocked at first, putting plastic aprons over their designer clothes.

"Consider yourself guests at my ranch. My dad's in the yard, cookin' on the barbecue. It's been under that oak for over a hundred years. You can look out the window and see the giant sequoias right over there." Leroy pointed. "It's the prettiest place in the world. Makes you feel like takin' a ride. We've got some fine horses. Yep, we're in California, the California of the buffalo soldiers."

Leroy wasn't aware of the change in his voice and how he used it to move people. The dinner could have been a disaster if the VIPs and nobility didn't buy into his California theme and took offense at the plastic bibs and messy sauce. But they didn't. They loved it.

"I'm so glad you could come," Leroy looked into their eyes and shook their hands as they came and went. As his butler introduced his guests, Leroy remembered everyone's name and who they were effortlessly. He'd always been able to do that. Word got around. After that first dinner, his guests requested barbecue in advance. He served like an impresario and his father's recipes typed up so the guests could take them home.

Something disturbing came up. He was escorting a very high style and attractive young woman to the door. She was pretty well lit. Leroy didn't drink, but he knew his guests would want alcohol. He went skimpy on that, providing wine and beer, but nothing harder.

The girl took his hand and caressed it, running her lips along the palm. To his dismay, his body responded to her. She leaned into him, drunkenly, but maybe not so drunkenly. After rubbing against him, she looked into his eyes and said, "I don't have to leave."

Leroy jumped away. He was going to be faithful to Cass, no matter if he had to lock himself in his room. "That's so nice, Signorina. I'm leaving for Venice tomorrow at five a.m." He bent over and kissed to top of her head, prying her torso off his person and pointing her out the door. Shoving, maybe.

That sort of thing had started happening all the time. Something had changed. He put on his beautiful new clothes and walked down the street as though he wasn't an impostor. The clothes fit and he fit. His step was firm and sure. He looked people in the eye and met the companions Will had arranged without being nervous or feeling like a hick. He was a different person than the rancher who had arrived in Europe. Or he appeared to be, anyway.

Everywhere he went, Will set him up in beyond luxurious accommodations. Numenon condos in Naples and Florence. His condos and houses were fully staffed. He had felt bad sending Tom back to England, but he was so busy he didn't need the young man's company or a valet.

Will hired guides and teachers for him, so he learned about the painters and history of art. He saw more cathedrals than he knew existed and more museums. Leroy loved them. The paintings took his breath away. Originally, Leroy had forced himself to stay in Italy and not go home, but it turned out he liked everything, especially the food. And the sights. The people on the street. The art. Buildings. Museums. The women.

The stone monasteries with tile roofs. Monasteries where the nuns sang. He asked his guides to point them out. Nothing existed that could point to Kathryn Duane's whereabouts—except in Leroy's brain. He recalled every detail of the photo of the tile roof and its odd little gargoyle. Kathryn's soul had absolved him from searching for her, but if he ran across that monastery, he'd know. She was Cass's mother. She might need help.

He stayed at a villa in Venice. The front end of it was open to the canal. Carved stone furniture and luxurious pillows furnished the wide veranda. Silk draperies billowed with the wind. The place was beautiful and old and ornate. He liked Venice the best of everywhere he'd gone. A town without streets. The sun went down and the water and stone buildings glowed gold. The light was like opals and milk. He had a guide, as usual. They walked all over the city.

"Venice does not smell, as some say," said his guide. Leroy hadn't known that Venice was supposed to smell.

He hit a low ebb, surrounded by the splendor of Venice. He wanted to share it with Cass. He wanted to glide along a canal with her and feel the magic of gondoliers and moonlight. He'd looked into her eyes for a few seconds, but they had branded him forever. Will said she was doing fine, gaining weight. No, she hadn't asked for him. He knew that was a lie. She remembered him. She wanted to be there with him. But Cass wasn't the only one haunting him.

At night, he felt soft arms around him, smoothly covered with white flesh. He saw light blue eyes and nougat-colored hair. Lady Arabella. He buried his lips into her hair, only to have Cass's tortured face leap at him, terrified. *Don't leave me, Leroy. Don't forget me.* He could hear her silent voice.

In the day, dark eyes caught his. Dark eyes and glossy black tresses. He couldn't get away from the Italian women. The content of his dreams seemed to be broadcasting from his forehead: come to me.

His clothes became a problem. Silk boxers sliding across his buttocks. Fine cotton shirts slipping over his arms, touching his back. When he brushed his trousers, the feel of their fabric clung to his hands and lingered. Touches, sights, sensations.

Women. Leroy had never been bothered by sexual urges. Oh, maybe once in a while, but not like this. He felt like his body might set his clothes on fire. Or worse, he might throw off his clothes and go after one of the lovely signorinas that were *everywhere.*

He had no dinner parties in Venice. A few luncheons, mostly with businessmen, occasionally a woman. The women dazzled him. He wanted to run. The beauty of Venice was a temptress wanting to coil around him.

Leroy was delighted when Will sent him to Milan. Maybe the fire that Venice stoked would simmer down.

"It's where Italian fashion begins," Will said, "Go shopping Leroy, get the best."

Milan was having a week of fashion shows. Leroy got ready for them without thought, putting on an easy-fitting, slubbed silk jacket with a finer black silk shirt under it.

He walked loosely, as though his joints weren't quite jelled. His walk had changed since England. There he watched men move like they were holding a raw egg between their butt cheeks, very different from his rangy lope. That lope got him from his barn to the house efficiently when he was at his ranch. It didn't work here.

In a sudden burst, he figured out how to walk like the elegant men around him. He slunk along on the balls of his feet as though he was trying to catch a spooky horse out in the pasture. Worked perfectly. He put an eagle feather in his ponytail for the fashion show.

"Oh, trés chic," said the Fashion Woman Will hired to escort him, looking him up and down. His gut said she was as old as the Elders at the Meeting, but she had utterly smooth skin and teeth so white they glowed. She dressed like a teenager in shocking pink and shiny black shoes.

"We are going to the shows of ..." she reeled off a bunch Italian names he'd never heard of. "We were lucky to get tickets."

Leroy was glad he was wearing his eagle feather. Fashion Woman turned out to be the most normal person he saw, but one. Every place they went was an auditorium with a raised walkway. Every single one had a backdrop going up to the ceiling behind the stage. Movies were projected on the backdrop. They ranged from a multi-color waterfall to men wearing suits rolling around on the floor shoving their butts in the air. Loud rock music blared.

He couldn't imagine anyone wearing the clothes anywhere. One show was built around women wearing tight-fitted pink panties with see-through pink jackets hanging open with no blouse underneath. People applauded. Some cried.

Leroy ended it by jumping to his feet and bolting for the door. Fashion Woman stood up, bewildered. The models were so thin; they were dying. They reminded him of Cass. Where was she? Was she dying?

He made it out to the executives' parking and signaled their driver. Photographers were everywhere. They took pictures of him; they seemed to think he was famous. He waved his hand and shook his head, saying, "No". Didn't stop them.

Then he saw her getting into her limousine. She was older now, but she looked wonderful. Her hair was smoother and not bushy the way it had been. Her fine Creole skin glowed. She wore a skirt above her knees, showing off those great legs. Everything about her was beautiful. Not thinking, he walked over.

"Ma'am, I admire you more than any woman on Earth. I have been your fan as long as I've been alive." Her bodyguard started to push him away, but she stopped him.

She looked Leroy up and down, the way almost every woman seemed to those days, smiling broadly. "Oh, my. You are *something fine*. Come over here, my young man." She held his hand to her cheek through the car window. About twelve paparazzi jumped them, shooting wildly.

Her driver moved the limousine out of the lot.

Leroy wanted to invite her for dinner. The woman from Nutbush, Tennessee, would love his father's barbecue sauce, no matter how high and far she had flown.

20

OUT OF THE BALLPARK

"LEROY, YOU HIT it out of the ballpark!" Will Duane sounded delighted. Leroy had called him to check on Cass. "I got calls from three CEOs and a duke telling me how much you impressed them. Everybody loves your barbecues. And Tina Turner's agent called wanting to sign you as a model. Or an actor. He *wanted* you. Did you see the *Enquirer* and every other rag? You and Tina are front and center. You are on a roll."

"Oh."

"You've still got France, then Germany and Scandinavia to visit. How do you like being a world traveler?"

"After I stopped screaming when I got on a plane, it wasn't so bad." Will was silent, not appreciating Leroy's joke. "No. I love it, Mr. Duane. I appreciate everything you've done for me and all the money you've spent. And the stipend you been sendin' …"

"Don't worry about it, son. I consider it an investment. We have a future, you and I."

"OK. Yeah. Mr. Duane, how is Cass?"

"Doing as well as you are. She's gained twenty pounds and is adjusting to life at the hospital. No incidents of any kind."

"That's really good. Can I talk to her?"

"Not advised at this point, Leroy."

"Does she know who I am?"

"No, Leroy. The doctors said it was best to keep things simple. She almost died. While you're waiting, I have a job for you. It will be a departure from the trip we had planned, but it will be interesting for you. I'll pay you a good salary."

"You've been doing all this for me. I don't need to get paid."

Will chuckled. "Never say no to money, Leroy. That's the first law of getting rich. You can never have too much money. How much are you worth?"

Affronted, Leroy barked, "More than you could ever count."

Will laughed. "That's what I like. Chutzpah."

Leroy knew what chutzpah was from his rabbi friends, but he didn't like the feel of the conversation. "What do you want, Mr. Duane?"

"I'm never going to get you to call me Will, am I?" He didn't wait for an answer. "What we've seen from you so far is super-fast learning of everything we've put in front of you. You get an A+ in everything."

The fact that all he did was being graded galled Leroy. As did the feeling he was an animal being tested. Was he good enough for Cass? Was he good enough for Numenon? Mostly, was he good enough for Will?

"What I'd like to do is enroll you in a language school in Switzerland. I'll be in France for the Economic Summit meetings in a couple of months. It's a conference for the top industrialists from all over the world. The Summit meetings are private, unlike the G8 Summit, which is for governments. Bill Clinton goes to those.

"At the Economic Summits, a few of the most influential guys in the world get together and kick the can about world economic problems. We talk about how we can iron out tensions between us. I don't need an interpreter; I've got several. I want someone to tell me if what the interpreter tells me is what was actually said. Billions of dollars hang on those meetings, Leroy. I want someone to cover my back."

Leroy frowned. This was big, not just learning about tableware and how to say hello properly. "What do you want me to learn?"

"All the Romance languages—French, Italian, Spanish, Portuguese. And as many Eastern European languages as possible. German, the Slavic dialects. Russian. As many as you can. My next meeting is in mid-October, the eighteenth and nineteenth. You can study until then, and then sit with me at the meeting. It usually averages about twenty hours over two days."

"I can't do that. No one could do that. You should get different people who have studied all those languages."

"That's the beauty of it, Leroy. No one will suspect that you're doing what you're doing. They'll see you as a stranger, a country boy. You can blindside them. And I think you *can* do what I ask, or give it a pretty good shot."

"What makes you think that?"

"Your golf score. No one could score like you did the first time on the range. My informant was thrilled."

"Are you having me followed?"

"Not exactly. I know the people who have entertained you. They've given me feedback on their experience of you." His tone was cool and level. Something about it told Leroy that he was being followed everywhere he went *and* evaluated. This clenched what he'd felt every time he left a guide or instructor: Will would get a blow-by-blow account of his performance. He was a rat in a maze, being graded before being let loose.

"You know, I'm really homesick," Leroy said. "I'd like to go home tomorrow."

"What!? I'm giving you the chance of a lifetime."

"No, you're not. You're seeing if you can turn me into a trick poodle you can control the rest of my life. You can't. If I stay here, you won't get another one of those 'feedback' reports. You will tell people *not* to tell you how I'm doing. If I feel any of that's going on, I'll take the next plane home."

"Do you have the money for an international flight?" Will's voice sounded innocent.

"Mr. Duane, if I want to get home, I'll do it if I have to sit on a stewardess's lap. Don't you worry." Leroy could not remember being so angry. This man would destroy him if he allowed him. What was it like for Cass, growing up with Will as a father?

"We need to get straight on some things. I appreciate what you've done for me—every minute of it and every penny you've spent. But I am not a monkey, or a parrot, or a trained dog. I will never be any of those for you. If you'd like me to pay you back everything you've put into me, I'll do it."

Will sighed. "Leroy, it would take you a lifetime to pay me back."

"If that's what it takes, then that's what I'll do."

There was a long silence on the other end of the line. Will sounded chastened when he spoke. "Leroy, I don't know how this conversation got so sidetracked. I didn't mean for us to fight. I need your help. How do I get it?"

Another long silence. "Well, Mr. Duane, you could call me back tomorrow and ask me what you want in a nice way. And tell me what I have to do to get it done."

21

FOREIGN LANGUAGE

Turned out, it wasn't so hard. He'd never tried to learn a language, but he did know Spanish fluently from the hired hands on the ranch. Nobody taught him; he just spoke the language. When he started studying, turned out that Italian and Portuguese were very similar and just as easy to learn. And so was French. He left his teachers applauding.

"Oh, my goodness, Mr. Watches, you are a prodigy."

He was not so much a prodigy as a shaman who had the power of bending language so he could understand and be understood. Didn't seem to matter what language was involved. That probably came from all the languages his People spoke at the Meeting and whenever he was with Grandfather. He knew them all, but he couldn't remember learning them.

The language school did something else. He could understand, remember, and speak languages very easily. He could never read or write very well. His handwriting embarrassed him. All through school on the reservation, his teachers had chided him, given him terrible grades, and never helped him one single bit.

"Oh, Monsieur, you are dyslexic." The instructor was kind. "Do you know what that means?"

He knew that letters and numbers seemed to arrange themselves differently on the page for him. He knew that what he saw must be different than what others saw.

His teacher said, "We cannot believe that no one diagnosed you. We will help you."

They fitted him with a special computer. He spoke into it, and *it* spelled for him. They gave him a recorder that he could talk to and then play into the computer. It wrote up whatever he said. He could read and write without having to figure out which way the letters went.

"Almost makes me cry. School was so hard. I *tried*," he said to his instructor, moved by the help the school had given him. His teacher was a late-middle-aged, large-breasted Swiss woman who wore grey suits almost to the floor. She reminded him of the English dowagers.

"It almost makes *me* cry that you were not diagnosed all your life," she replied. "So much needless suffering."

"Please, let me pay for the computer and recorder myself." He didn't want Will to add "handicapped" to his score.

"These things are part of your program, Mr. Watches. Now, you must practice what we teach."

And he did, moving from language to language. German and the Eastern European languages were harder. Russian almost killed him.

So did his ass. He hadn't *ever* sat that long. He finally got the lessons on CDs and walked around town listening to them and talking into his recorder, then studying what the computer did with his words. His chest swelled. Finally, what was on the page made sense. After that, Leroy spent as little time as possible in the classroom. He was learning faster than he imagined he could.

He sat at a few favorite cafés, listening to people talk and sipping a latté, a habit he'd never cultivated before. He'd never before been anywhere that had pastries and strudels and all manners of irresistible sweets. Leroy kept walking so he didn't end up a caffeine addict and a lard-butt.

"Oh, monsieur, all of the tables are taken. Do you mind if I sit with you?" A pretty face and big eyes, eyelashes flapping like fly swatters. That happened all over. All kinds of girls approached him, blond, brunette and everything in between. He could have gotten laid ten times a day. But he didn't. He kept his eye on the scenery, the kind with mountains and buildings.

Switzerland was as tidy and crisp as Venice had been romantic and lush. He liked them both. Switzerland reminded him of Yosemite. They thought their mountains were grand, but he thought Yosemite's grander.

On weekends, he traveled, taking his language lessons, laptop, CD player and recorder, being a tourist and doing his own research projects. Special maps of monasteries existed; he hadn't known that. Tourists liked to make pilgrimages to them. He did a lot of walking those weekends, passing by untold numbers of stone monasteries and nunneries. None of them had the distinctive tiles or the funny gargoyle. Lots of walking and looking. He didn't get fat.

Austria, Germany, Belgium, the Netherlands, and Denmark. He saw many of the places Will had originally scheduled him to see, just faster. Turned out that many of the monasteries were renting out rooms, or acting almost like hotels, to make ends meet. He stayed at the convent of St. Birgitta in Denmark, in Abbaye Notre-Dam des Niges in France. So many monasteries, none of them right.

By that time, Leroy felt like he was running, not walking. He was making himself obvious by touring monasteries. He knew he should stop his "casual" search, but kept on. Kathryn's soul had warned him off. Why didn't he heed it?

And then it was time for that economic meeting. He shared a three-bedroom penthouse in Paris with Will Duane. Will called for him and Leroy climbed on a plane as ordered. A car met him at the airport and took him to the apartment building, if you could call it that. Set on a street slightly better-groomed than the English royals he'd met, the edifice had carved stone pillars, a canopy and two doormen in front. He entered the building, flanked by Will's guards. The floor was inset with pieces of different colored marble. One of Will's black-clad strong men carried his bags to the apartment. When the door opened, the entrance hall and living room beyond were as extraordinary as the palaces he'd visited. Home, sweet home, Numenon style.

Will was there, bouncing on the balls of his feet. He swung his fists in arcs; he pulled them in front of him and then swung them out to the sides. He was scared, Leroy knew it the instant he saw him.

"Ah, Leroy. I'm glad you're here." He took Leroy's hand and patted him on the shoulder. "I took that room," he pointed in the direction of what was undoubtedly the largest bedroom. "You can pick which you want of the other two." He kept talking rapidly, acting wired.

"How's Cass?" Leroy was determined not to let Will dodge his questions. *This* time, Will would put out, or Leroy … Well, he'd make him spill the beans.

"I'll tell you when we get where we're going. Have you eaten yet? Good. I'd like to show you the place we're having the meeting before the action starts. Le Hotel Meurice is a real grande dame, built in the nineteenth century. It's luxurious. Be prepared for your mind to be blown. We'll walk; it's only a block."

They were strolling down a posh Parisian street as the evening dimmed to night. "The Tuileries Gardens are across the street. Catherine de Medici put the garden in during the 1500s. They've held up pretty well, don't you think? The Arc de triomphe du Carrousel is over there." Will jerked his head in its direction.

Leroy noted that Will had a tolerable French accent, but not as good as his. Turning to follow Will's gesture, he noticed two black clad men following them.

"A couple of guys are following us," he whispered.

"Six actually. I rented the apartments above, below, and all around us. Hannah's European staff is on duty. She'll be here in a few hours."

"Is this conference dangerous?"

"To my pride, mostly. But I'm exposed. The guys at this meeting aren't friends. If someone wants to kill me, now's the time."

"Should you be walking on the street like this?"

"No. But I like Paris. I've got to do stupid things once in a while. Most of the time, I feel like a fucking French poodle, locked up in a cage."

They had reached an elaborate building, not too tall with kind of a loaf shape on top. The roof "loaf" looked like it was glass. A colonnade of arcs ran along the street for a whole block.

Leroy sucked in a deep breath as they walked through the very large revolving door, thankful for every English country house, palace and museum he'd visited. This hotel would be intolerable if he had hadn't gone to all those places.

"It's a world-class hotel, Leroy. Royalty stays here, and heads of state. Everyone from the composer Tchaikovsky to Queen Elizabeth has camped out at Le Meurice.

"We're holding the meeting here so we can demonstrate *we're* world-class. We have our annual meetings all over the globe, but it's hard to top this."

They walked down a wide gallery that ran the length of the hotel. The check-in desks were to his left, as elegant as the rest of the vast space. The arched windows to the outside were to his right. The hotel was gorgeous. High, high ceilings, big stripes of marble running up the walls. Everything that could be gold-trimmed was. The designs on some of the rugs were pretty weird, like drunken amoebas. Some light fixtures were like that too.

"Salvador Dali used to hang out here for a month every summer. A lot of the hotel's design relates to his work. Do you know Dali?"

"Yeah. Melting clocks." Leroy felt like he was being quizzed, but not so that it bothered him.

"I expect my people have drilled you up the wazoo." They made their way across the marble-floored expanse. The window arches that ran down the hall looked out on the Tuileries garden. You couldn't see much now, but it must be beautiful in the daytime.

"This is Le Dali, one of the hotel's restaurants," Will walked to a wide opening. Beyond it was a big open space adjoining the promenade. The restaurant was furnished with sculptured metal chairs and tables with dazzling white tablecloths.

"This is their informal restaurant. I'd take you here, but I can't." Will looked a little wistful, gazing at the open room. They walked on. "I can't take you here, either." Will stuck his head into a room as fancy as any Leroy had seen. More marble and paintings of pastel-clothed people in a garden, swinging and playing like adults never would. The white linen tablecloths fell to the floor. The tables were set farther apart than a regular restaurant; the place would never be crowded.

"This is their formal restaurant. All the art work is original to the building, which was built in the late 1800s, I think." Will patted Leroy's shoulder. "We're going this way."

A tuxedo-clad man, too grand and formal to be a waiter, led them through a passage and into an elegant room at the end. A single dining table was set for them. "I trust this will do, Mr. Duane."

"Certainly," Will tried to speak French, but his accent was lousy.

A waiter in black livery seated them. Will spread his napkin on his lap and Leroy followed suit.

"I can't tell you how much I'd like to go to MacDonald's," Will confided. "I can't. Some jerk with the only Numo Ranger in the world that doesn't work would corral me. Or someone who thinks I should have solved the problems of the world instead of living like I do will start screaming. Or worse …"

Leroy listened to Will. He hadn't thought of any of this. "You've been attacked?"

"Oh, yeah. Hassled, shoved around. They almost got me a couple of times." He pointed at his ribs. "Hannah makes me wear Kevlar when I'm in public. She's right. I've gotten a couple of bullet holes from not following her advice."

Will's eyes made a fast circuit around the room, obviously a habit, before boring into Leroy's. "They tried to kidnap Kathryn and Cass. My security men were following them, thank God. But they weren't good enough. The bad guys already had Cass into the van. She was a little kid. They lured her with a box of kittens. The other one was manhandling Kathryn. She was drunk, as usual. A perfect patsy.

"That's when I hired Hannah and gave her free rein. She runs her missions her way. Easier for me, I don't know anything I shouldn't." He indicated the sumptuous room. "We get to eat in a private dining room instead of with everyone else. Hannah will have a fit when she finds out. But she's not here yet."

The food was delicious, perhaps the best he'd had on his trip. Will tried to order in French, but Leroy spoke the language better than his boss. He ordered for them. They ate their way forward, course after course.

Finally, a full belly slowed Will down enough so that Leroy could get him to talk about what he wanted. "How's Cass?" Every time he'd spoken to Will, he'd asked about Cass, but Leroy never got the full picture. Just, "She's doing fine. No problems." Now, he wanted to know everything.

Will sat back, heaved a huge sigh and wiped his mouth with his napkin. "We've hit a snafu. Her bulimia kicked in." Leroy didn't know what that was.

"It's an eating disorder. The person with the disorder feels ugly and fat, so she—it's almost always a she—throws up after she gets a decent meal. Or maybe, any kind of a meal. The minute she started looking like a semi-normal woman, Cass made herself throw up. The hospital won't let her go until she's got her eating under control. She thinks she looks like a pig.

"Cass is 5' 9". She could weigh 160 pounds and not be overweight. Do you know how much she weighed when she got to the hospital?" Leroy shook his head.

"Eighty-seven pounds. She was barely alive. They got her up to 120 and all hell broke loose. They want to keep her until she stops throwing up and weighs 130. So—we've got a couple of months to wait. She was doing so well until all this came up, I don't think she'll be in the mental hospital for more than a month or two."

"You're still going to put her there?"

"Oh, yes. Leroy, you are a newcomer to our lives. You don't know what Cass is capable of. I'm not going to let a few months of good behavior fool me into thinking she's healed."

Leroy kept his mouth shut. He knew he could heal her, but he'd have to ride rough-shod over her father to get to her. Carl had said that Cass was burning for him too. In a while, she'd bust loose from the hospital and come after him. That wasn't a good idea. In the hospital, she was safe. Hannah's soldiers would watch out for her. He needed to trust the Great One and all of *Its* soldiers to make this work out right.

"What do you want to do for a couple of months, Leroy? I think you should plan on coming home for Christmas, but you've got some time to kill. My meeting will be over on October 20th. You've got two months to fill. Do you want more language school?"

Leroy raised his hand in defense. "Please, no."

Will smiled. "What do you want to do?"

Leroy leaned forward and whispered. "What's a *debutante ball*? I got invited to one."

"Which one?"

"The Queen Charlotte's Ball in London. It's next weekend, October 25th."

"Boy, you scored a big one." Will shook his head ruefully, smiling enigmatically. "I can remember escorting the debs. Those were the days. Who are you escorting?"

"Lord Martingale's daughter, Lady Clarissa. I met him golfing. She's Lord Ballentyne's niece, too. He asked me to escort her, and I said I would." Leroy felt embarrassed to be going to such an event. He had no idea why Lady Arabella had wanted him to help her cousin "come out." He was also embarrassed for another reason.

"Will, what's a debutante ball?" Leroy leaned forward, whispering furtively.

Will rocked back in his chair and chuckled. "A debutante ball is part of an elaborate, upper class, puberty ritual. It's when a young woman makes her début in society—when her parents chuck her out into their rarified world, signaling that she's ripe for marriage.

"It's as archaic as horses and buggies, yet 'coming out' endures. Everyone knows if a family can afford to 'bring out' their daughter in style—the whole spectacle costs a bundle—she's got the chops to make her worth marrying. Financial chops, anyway."

A look Leroy hadn't seen on Will before crept onto his face. A smirk. A bad boy grin.

"I've been to so many debutante balls. I was the most desirable escort in the world for years. Even now I get asked once in a while." The grin blossomed. "Some of the mothers wanted me to escort *them*. I did, and their daughters too. You'd be surprised at how attractive being the richest man on the planet makes you."

Will's grin effervesced. "God, those were the days. I did 'em all. Lined 'em up and fucked my way down the line." He leaned toward Leroy as though imparting a secret. "When they see *you*, there's going to be a stampede. You are *prime* beefcake, Leroy. Top of the line dick. It's time for you to cash in on what you've got." Leroy's nostrils flared and he pulled away from his host, eyes growing wider with Will's every word.

"Son, if you want to sample a few of those rich little tarts, go ahead. It won't bother me at all. You and Cass can get together when the time comes, and you'll have some delicious memories."

Leroy pushed his chair away from the table and jumped up.

"It's *not* OK with *me*," he said to his prospective father-in-law. Leroy could feel his cheeks redden and his heart pound. He'd heard about how Will was with women, but never like this. If what Will said was true, and Leroy knew it was, he was disgusting.

Will registered his loathing. "Sit down, Leroy. I don't know why I say things like that. People, the *men* at Numenon, and everywhere, thought I was the coolest thing in the world when I was running around. But I don't think it's cool now and I don't do it any more either.

"I did fuck all those pop-tarts all those years. I'm not proud of myself." He looked down, putting his hands in his lap to hide their shaking. "I haven't been like that for years. I met a friend of Elizabeth Bright Eagle's, a healer, and she didn't allow 'acting out.' Long story. She dumped me.

"But that's how I ended up at the Meeting and met your grandfather. And fell in love with Elizabeth." He made a little huffing noise. "I'm lucky with money, but not with love." Will's face seemed carved from granite. Lines spelling sadness dropped from his nose to the corners of his mouth.

Leroy looked up as Hannah Hehrman *stormed* into the room. She wore a black sequined jacket that dropped below her hips, a short black skirt and high heels. She still walked like a commando. Leroy saw the bulge of her pistol at her waist.

"*What are you doing here, Will? Are you out of your mind?*" She leaned over the table and skewered Will with her eyes. Her voice was low. Hearing it was like being hit with bullets from a silenced weapon. "*Do you know who's here? Diego Donatore.*"

"Enzo's brother? Donatore Industrial isn't supposed to be at the conference."

"It is now. One of the South Americans 'got sick' and your friends drafted Donatore to come. He'll fight every word you have to say tomorrow, if he doesn't kill you on the way back to the apartment.

"My men are outside, as are Donatore's. But Donatore's soldiers are not men. You know what they are: scaled monsters with acid venom and claws who can look human when they want. You saw them at the Meeting. You know all about them.

"It's dark; they can take their reptilian forms. Conveniently, there's a park across the street where they can hide." Hannah grabbed Will's elbow and dragged him out of his seat. "How could you be so foolish?"

Hannah kept spitting her bullets as she dragged Will toward the hotel entrance. "Now all we need to do is get back to our hotel with monsters chasing us. Monsters that can't be killed."

22

A WALK BY THE PARK

LEROY WATCHED HANNAH carefully as she crossed the lobby in front of him. She stalked with her knees bent, covering ground like a tracking cat. She scanned the gigantic hall, head moving from side to side in barely perceptible arcs. Her hands moved repeatedly to the bulge on her waist as though they were out of her control. She wanted to pull her weapon out. Not here. Not in the vast promenade that was the entrance to the Hotel Le Meurice.

The main entrance, a very large rotating door, was exactly in the middle of the foyer. If they left from there, they'd have to walk an additional half block on Rue de Rivoli, the street fronting Le Meurice, exposed to whatever lurked in the park across the boulevard.

The three of them made for the far end of the esplanade. Another entrance was there, but something had changed while Will and Leroy had been eating dinner. A shiny black concert grand piano sat in front of the door. Someone very good was playing it.

The hotel had put chairs out, arranged in rows like a small concert. Every chair was taken. Le Meurice was known for the comforts it provided guests. Cushy chairs and seating areas were arranged from one end of the hall to the other. They were packed with people, especially the groupings closest to the recital. Waiters served drinks and appetizers.

Leroy saw a red dot flash on the wall behind the check-in area. Someone outside was using an automatic scope, sighting on Will's white hair. His head was a bright target.

"Will, we must run," Hannah said, turning around to grab his hand.

"Did you see it?"

"Yes."

"We can't go out the door at the end," Leroy said. "If they start shooting, the bullets will come right through the glass. Those people will be killed."

Hannah sucked in a breath and looked around. "Where can we go?"

"They must have an exit on the side of the building. For employees." Leroy said, walking toward the end of the check-in desk.

Hannah beat him, dragging Will by the wrist. She barked at the attendant, "We must leave the hotel very fast. Is very important." Leroy smiled. With her Israeli accent, Hannah murdered French worse than Will did.

Will tried next. "Is there an exit to the street back there?" He pointed at the doorway at the end of the long registration desk. "What's over there? Can we get out there?"

The clerk's French was impeccable. Leroy could see that Will understood it, but could not reproduce it. "Guests are not allowed through that door. Only staff." Will was about to offer a small fortune if the guy let them out. The clerk anticipated that. "Even if you were to give me all the money in the world, I could not let you through that door. See," he pointed to a camera above the doorframe, aimed in their direction. "Things have been stolen ..."

Leroy leaned against the registration desk. He spoke to the clerk in his very good French, grinning with a close approximation of Will's bad-boy grin. He drawled, "They need to get out of here because her husband just walked into Le Dali. He was with his mistress, of course. But husbands never take this sort of thing well." Leroy nodded his head to Hannah and Will. Hannah continued to clutch Will's arm. "Her husband carries a firearm, from his time in the Legion. I would get them out of here so that none of those good people are hurt."

The clerk's eyes widened. "Why didn't you tell me?"

"I just did. They don't speak French well enough to explain. Or maybe they don't want to."

The whites of the fellow's eyes flashed. "Come with me." He raised the wooden counter top and they slipped through. He took them to the door with the camera over it and opened the elaborate lock. "Go there. Follow the hallway. There's a freight receiving area. The metal door opens to the outside."

The passageway ended in a bay that must have been used to receive guests' luggage and packages, as well as small hotel necessities. It was too small to be a general freight access. They lifted the metal roll-up door and found themselves on Rue de Castiglione, the street that ran at ninety degrees to Rue de Rivoli.

"Stay back," Hannah barked at Will.

He had no intention of lagging. "No. We're in danger because of me." He pushed forward, jogging even with her.

Hannah looked up and down the street. "Where are my soldiers? They should be here."

"We'll come upon them bye and bye," Leroy said. "The problem is—which way should we go?" The door had dumped them out half-way down the block from the Rue di Rivoli where the Le Meurice's front entrance was located. To get back to their apartment, they'd have to go back that half block toward the front of the Le Meurice, and then turn right for another block, exposed to the shooters in the garden.

"Maybe we should go to the end of this block, and then get home around the back," Leroy offered.

"I don't know what's back there. The monsters could be there too," Hannah said. "Where are my soldiers?"

"Let's try the back way, Hannah," Will offered. "It can't be as dangerous as walking down Rue de Rivoli."

They turned right, heading away from the front of the hotel. Less than thirty feet down the street, Hannah pulled her pistol. "What's that?"

"What?"

"On the ground, on the other side of the street." They started to follow her. "No! Do not follow me." She crept across the street, holding her gun in both hands, moving with her stalking cat's slink.

"Oh, no," she cried, dropping to her knees over the body of one of her soldiers.

"Don't touch him," Leroy shouted. "If a demon killed him, he'll become a demon. You can become one from his infected blood."

Anguish bathed Hannah's face. "We are both from Israel. He was very good. How could this happen?"

"Don't touch him, Hannah." Leroy crossed the street and took over. "You take Will back to the hotel. Go that way, the way we know. I'll handle the demons."

"What about my warrior?"

"I'll handle him too. Go!"

Will had heard speech like Leroy's from Grandfather. Whatever Leroy was doing with his voice was compelling. He had to do what he said, as did Hannah. He put his arm around Hannah and dragged her off. "We need to get home fast." They left Leroy by himself.

When they rounded the corner to Rue de Rivoli, Will saw a flashing red dot on the stone building on the corner.

"Run," he cried. There was hardly any noise at all. A Poof! and a chunk of the building's corner exploded. "Oh!" Will dropped to his knees, grabbing at his shoulder where it met his neck. Blood blossomed, covering his shirt and jacket. "Shit," he said. "They got me. Oh, shit." He dropped to the sidewalk, clutching his neck.

Hannah pulled his hands from the wound and examined it. "It's not a stone fragment. The bullet must have ricocheted. You're bleeding. We must take you to a hospital."

Hannah looked back in the direction they had come. Leroy was running up the street toward them. A fire flamed on the sidewalk where the body had been. Hannah wailed, leaning toward her fallen soldier.

"Get Will to the apartment, Hannah," Leroy bellowed. "I'll handle everything."

Leroy walked out to Rue de Rivoli, looking to his right. Hannah and Will were scuttling toward the apartment. He could feel the demons rustling in the garden, and see their red eyes glowing. They were converging on Hannah and Will. He had to do something, fast.

Stepping forward to the edge of the sidewalk, Leroy raised his arms, palms pointed toward the garden in a gesture of peace.

"Hello, good demons! You are very good demons!" He sang in his language, a few words bringing goodwill. "Good demons! Stand where you are and listen to me." He put the greatest power he could into his voice. "You are so good. All you can do is think good thoughts and do good things.

"You are very sleepy, so sleepy that you must sit down on the ground. You cannot keep your eyes open. You feel very good and happy. Think good thoughts and listen to me.

"You are good. You are kind and loving. You are kind to your husbands and wives and children. You never fight. You came to this life to make the world a better place. Everything you do is to make the world better.

"You hear my words and know they are true. You will never be the way you were. You will never need to show your scales and teeth and claws. You are so good that you'll only need your human selves. Nothing could make you hate and hurt others. Nothing anyone can do, even the strongest demon, Enzo Donatore, can make you hateful and bad again. You no longer fear him and you no longer obey him."

He sang a few more words in his language. "Now, you cannot stay awake. You will find places in the garden where no one can see you. You will go to sleep there, sleeping very deeply. You will sleep for a week. No one will be able to awaken you.

"*Diego Donatore*, you are the best of all. The most loving of all. You are good. No one can make you be anything but good. You are the leader, Diego, of the new demons, the demons of love and goodness. Diego, you will find the most hidden spot in all the garden. You will go there and sleep so deeply that nothing can wake you for *two* weeks. In two weeks, you can arise. You will be kind and good to your soldiers for the rest of your life. You will love them, and they will love you."

He clapped his hands. "Go now, and sleep. Take your clothes and put them near you so you can put them on when you turn back to your human form. Go! Go to sleep now."

Leroy heard scuffling in the bushes and saw the bushes moving as the monsters found their sleeping areas. Lots of them rustled. When he was sure they were asleep, Leroy called out again.

"Hannah's commandos. Come forward to me. I will protect you."

Four walked out of the Tuileries and crossed the street. Hannah had said she had six soldiers. One was dead. Four were in front of him. That left one wounded or dead.

"Where is the other one?" he asked.

"Monsters bit off his head. He's dead."

"Where is he? Point." They did. "Go to the apartment. Hannah needs help. Go fast."

Leroy went into the garden and found the dead body. He did exactly what he had done to the first soldier. Pointing the palm of his hand at the corpse, he sent a jolt of white-hot fire to the body, burning it to ash instantly. The man would rise as demon if his remains were not obliterated.

He jogged home. He could feel Will calling him.

23

ONE THING AFTER ANOTHER

"HANNAH? WILL?" LEROY marched down the passageway to Will's room. He was lying on the bed, pale and obviously in pain. Hannah seemed to have used every towel in the place to stop the bleeding. White terry cloth rags, splotched with red, *lots* of red, were tossed all over.

Hannah sat by Will's side, holding his hand. "Oh, Leroy. Can you heal him? The wound is so bad."

"I'll take care of him," Leroy said. "You go out and see what's wrong with your commandos. They're in that hallway. I think they got too close to the demons. Watch yourself. You may have to kill them."

Will's mouth gaped a bit. He panted in fear and pain. Leroy could see the bullet's path, a tunnel in Will's neck emerging out the back. Bone splinters from his collarbone gleamed white. He could see an artery throbbing deep inside the wound. The demons had almost killed him.

"I can handle this, Will. I've been healin' since I was four." Leroy moved closer to the wounded billionaire, humming. Will's eyes drooped and then closed. "Sleep, Will. OK, let's see what I can do."

Wasn't any harder than curing a foundering horse—though that was pretty hard. Leroy waved his hands over the bullet hole, humming and finally singing. He touched the raw flesh, and eventually inserted his finger into the hole.

"Come now, bones and flesh, heal up. This man's givin' a big speech tomorrow, he's got to be tip top."

The bone chips pulled together, making Will's collarbone twice as hard as it had been. The open hole in his neck filled with new tissue. Leroy withdrew his finger as flesh filled the hole. He ran his hand along Will's neck and shoulder. The outer damage became a round scar. Another swipe with his hand and no scar existed. He took what pain remained away, and then shook out his hands.

"Will, wake up, you're fine. Oh, wait a minute, I forgot all the blood you lost." He passed his hands over Will's body. "OK, that should be enough. You can wake up now. You're healed."

When Will opened his eyes, Leroy saw he wasn't healed. Physically, he was all right, but he was a jellyfish inside. His real healing hadn't begun.

"Will, can you get up and take a shower?" He'd heard the muffled Pops! of silenced gunshots in the hall. He couldn't leave Hannah to face four semi-demons. "Put some clothes on. I'll be right back and we'll talk."

Leroy slunk down the hallway and looked out the peephole in the front door. Hannah had her back to the door and was firing at her erstwhile soldiers. They were more than semi-demons. Leroy could see their fangs and claws. They didn't have coats of black scales, but those would be next.

"Hannah, I'm coming out," he said.

Two of the four lay dead in the hallway. The other two ranged around Hannah. They had weapons, but seemed intent on tearing her apart. They snarled and leapt back when they saw him.

"Who's he?" they snapped at Hannah.

"I'm jus' nobody. I work here. Why are you doin' what your doin'? Hannah's your boss."

"Not anymore. Diego is our boss." The erstwhile commando's canine teeth were growing longer and longer, slobber running down his chin.

"Well, I'm sorry to say, but Diego and his friends have had a change of heart. They're good now and never will do anyone harm. Does that sound like a good idea to you?"

It didn't. They leapt at Hannah and him. She managed to hit pay dirt with a couple of rounds, but it wasn't enough.

"I'm sorry to have to do this." Leroy pointed the palms of his hands at the two of them. White flames shot out, not just killing them, but burning them to cinders instantly. Leroy didn't stop there; he did the same thing to the bodies on the floor.

"You can't let them go without burning them up; they'll become demons quicker than that." He snapped his fingers. "Sorry to leave you to clean up this mess, Hannah. We don't want anyone to see this. I've got to get back to Will."

Hannah stared at her former colleagues. "They look like piles of kitty litter. What should I do with them?"

"I'd find the janitor's closet and get a broom and dustpan. Put them in a garbage can and dump them down the chute."

"What if someone comes?"

"I can take care of that." He inhaled and said in his power voice. "People, you will not come home for three hours. You are having a wonderful time. If you must come home, you will see nothing in the hall. Nothing and no one. You will sleep until noon tomorrow. You will feel wonderful.

"That should do it." Leroy went back to Will.

Will lay propped up in bed, his hands clutching the quilt covering his body. He wore navy blue silk pajamas. Deep lines ran from his nose to his mouth. His skin was grey and his eyes darted from side to side. Leroy had never seen him so afraid.

"What's the matter, Will?" Leroy sat next to him on a fine upholstered chair.

"It's over, Leroy. I can't do it anymore. I told you that my enemies are going to take Numenon from me.

"I can't hold out much longer. By February, the greatest corporation in history will be a rape and pillage machine run by demons. And I'm the only one who will know it. They'll blame everything that's ever gone wrong on me ...

"I may have been an asshole in lots of ways, Leroy, but I got some of it right. My visions showed me the way to go with Numenon." Will looked at him, face haggard. "I'm lying, here, *shot*. I can't speak at that conference.

"Next year, Frank Sauvage or Ric Chao will be here in my place. My shoulder hurts like shit, but it doesn't hurt as much as knowing they won. That *hurts*." He ran his hand through his hair, trying to wipe something out. Leroy had seen him do that before.

"This is my last chance to make an impact on the world at the top level. I have so much to say. We need to clean up our acts, *especially* at the top. *We're* the ones who own the world's assets—and squander them. Or hoard them." He paused a while, gasping. Will grabbed Leroy's forearm.

"I don't know if I can do it. Did you hear about the Meeting? What I did?"

"You ran out into the desert in your bare feet, screaming at Donatore? Carl told me."

"He told you?"

"Yeah. He said it was stupid, but amazing and you were a warrior of warriors."

"Really?"

"Yeah. All my People know about it. You're a hero: what you did was like one of our war chiefs standing up to the white man in the old days. He knew he wouldn't win and would be killed, but he did it anyway."

Will cracked a little smile. "Thanks for telling me that. Yeah, it was stupid, but I had to do it." He held on to Leroy's arm. "I'm scared, Leroy. I don't remember being scared then. I ran out of the cave because I couldn't let him kill any more people, or hurt them. I had to stop it.

"But he hurt me, Leroy. Your Grandfather healed me and I went on. But I'm hurt. I don't know what's wrong with me." Shiny wet lines tracked down his cheeks.

"If it weren't for your grandfather, I'd be dead. And if it weren't for *you* ..." Will wept, the dry sobs of an old man. "I'm so glad you're here. I don't know how to repay you."

Leroy got it. Demons' claws had raked Will's soul. His grandfather had healed the gashes for then, but the gouges had festered. *That* was why Will had been so crazy about Cass and everything else. He was tainted by a demon's curse and unable to fight it.

If a grizzly had come along and bashed him upside his skull, Leroy couldn't have been more surprised. Will was damned by the work of demons. Struggling to do right. He was grateful to Leroy and his grandfather. And a lost, scared old man. Power surged through the healer, up from his boots to the top of his skull.

"Let me work on you inside. What the Great One showed you in that vision was the truth. There's not a thing a demon or anyone else can do against the truth. Tomorrow, you're going to tell the truth as hard as you can. You *are* able to go to that meeting." Will's eyelids fluttered.

"Go ahead and sleep, Will. Take long breaths. Let all this fade away." Leroy did his work in silence while Will slept. He smiled when he was done. The Great One wanted Will to succeed.

"You're going to knock 'em dead tomorrow. I'll be right next to you, watchin' your back. You'll be safe every moment, from now until then. Now go to sleep and stay asleep until it's time to wake up."

Leroy got up to leave, surprising himself by kissing Will's forehead.

Before going to his room, Leroy picked up all the bloody towels and threw them in the bathtub. He torched them with a white-hot flame from his palm. Didn't even smoke.

24

TRYING TO SLEEP

LEROY COULDN'T SLEEP; his body shuddered. Everything that happened that crazy day swam around his head. In his heart and body. How did he do that stuff? Put demons to sleep and make them good? Kill men who were becoming demons easily and with no remorse.

How would he help Will tomorrow? Did Will really believe that someone with three months of language lessons could tell him when an interpreter was misinterpreting what he said? No, he didn't and never had. Will wanted Leroy's presence. He wanted Leroy's personal support, but he was beset by demons and couldn't say what he needed. And he'd never been good at asking for help.

The healing that had just come through him gave Leroy that understanding. All he had to do was what he could. The chants of his People reverberated in his brain. Other chants, in Latin, the chants of the people who worshiped the cross with the nailed Jesus, wove in and out. Kathryn Duane was with him, Mother Whoever-she-was, wanting him to help her flawed husband get straight with the universe

He clutched his eagle feathers, sat up in his bed and sang of love to the Great One. "Oh, please Great Mystery, stay with me tomorrow. Keep Will safe. He's got some important things to say and he's shook up. Stay with me and keep us safe. And Hannah. An' Cass."

What he wanted more than anything was his grandpa. No one had seen him since the Meeting; everyone said that he had died. Leroy thought that was true; he had felt death all around him when they said goodbye.

Holding the feathers in the air before him, Leroy prayed, "Oh, Grandfather, if you could just come to me. I need you so much. I know you never thought much of me when you were alive. I know you thought I was dumb and everything, but I loved you and followed your teachings as well as I could. Oh, please Grandfather, come to me."

Quick as that, his grandfather appeared over his bed, a little old Indian man with white braids, feet dangling from the chaps covering his legs, golden clouds of bliss surrounding him. The only difference from the last time they met was that Leroy could see through him.

"Why did you think I didn't think much of you?" Grandfather asked.

"Because as hard as I tried, I messed up everything. I couldn't remember what you taught. I missed half the Meetings, even though I wanted to be there real bad."

Grandfather floated down so he was standing on Leroy's bed. Then he was in it, slipped between the sheets.

"Ah," the shaman said, wiggling to get comfortable. "I have never had such a bed. I should travel with rich people more often." He seemed oblivious to Leroy's distress, until he turned his million-watt, strobe-light eyes on him.

"Leroy, I have always known you would lead the lineage when I died. I had no doubt."

"But why did you look at me like I was a joke? Why did the People laugh at me, even your shaman friends?"

"You do funny things. What you said, and other things. You didn't follow my directions. You couldn't leave the scorpions and rattlesnakes alone, for instance.

"But they liked me ..."

"I know that, but how many of the other young warriors were stung or bitten because they copied you?

"Leroy, you have always had the greatest potential of all my students. From the very beginning, I knew you would be the greatest shaman and continue my line."

"What about Wesley? Everyone said Wesley was better than me. He was the next leader."

"Wesley is Wesley. I knew his darkness could one day claim him. I knew he was flawed. You are not. You are perfect inside, Leroy, a perfect warrior. My successor."

Leroy felt like a tornado had picked him up and slammed him in the river head first. "You didn't tell *me* anything like that. You looked at me like this," Leroy pulled his brows together and scowled. "You never said I was perfect and would be your successor. It was all Wesley. Wesley. From *everyone.*

"You sent *me* back to my father and the ranch. I thought you hated me and I'd failed."

"I sent you to your father so that you two could make peace. That needed to happen. You needed to leave the reservation to become what you are. You needed to know more of the world than I could teach you. Your father's ranch was the best I could think of. I asked you to leave to promote you, not punish you."

Leroy sat, bewildered past any hope of comprehension. "You sent me back to my daddy's ranch to *promote* me?"

"Yes. But you could never become the person you were meant to be on the ranch, either, talking to cows. You needed schooling and finishing in the ways of the world. You needed Will Duane to take over and give what only he could.

"You're doing *so well*, Leroy. Our Ancestors look down on you from heaven and cheer. You're learning the white-man's languages. The proper use of knives and forks. How to play golf, which is almost impossible."

The old man sighed and touched Leroy's shoulder. "I won't say that I won't have other successors one day, Leroy. But you are the first among them, and the one I always knew would follow me."

"You'll have other shamans leading our lineage *in addition* to me?"

"Not *I'll*, Leroy. The Great One will. These are complicated times. Great-grandfather had a handful of disciples as his flock. Times were easier; just one successor was needed. Great-grandfather picked me to lead the lineage when he died. I have had many good students and disciples—hundreds that were truly fine.

"Let's face it—the world is a mess. It's not enough for our People to stay in the desert and teach each other. We have to—*reach new markets*—if we are to keep the world going. So, I have you as my first successor. I'm telling you this so that you aren't surprised when you meet one of the others. But there aren't any now."

"That's nice. Thanks for tellin' me, like tellin' me all the other. I grew up thinkin' I was a freak, when I was just a gigantic African-Native-American dyslexic person who could drum."

"I should talk more, Leroy. I don't explain well enough."

"I'll say. 'Use your words' is something they teach kindergarteners where I've been. Maybe you should try it."

"Will Duane is healing you, my grandson. You are learning to speak your mind. You need to ask for what you need more."

"I need to sleep and I need help tomorrow."

Grandfather didn't leave him that night. After healing his feelings of inferiority, the shaman led him into his Power. The glory that went with it filled the room.

"Sleep, my Leroy. I will be with you in the big powwow tomorrow. You will be safe, and Will and Hannah will be safe. Will will say what he needs to. Now, sleep, my grandson and my darling."

The shaman was amazed that Leroy hadn't known that he was his successor all along. "Use your words." What an amazing concept.

25

THE SPEECH

L E MEURICE WAS as elegant and impressive as it had been the
night before. The menace posed by the demons was gone, replaced
by the menace of the richest men in the world.

Leroy stalked down the hotel's wide foyer with Will and Hannah.
Hannah looked nervous, stripped of her soldiers. He felt loose and
relaxed; a predator who was afraid of *nothing*. Will seemed the same.

The meeting used all three of the hotel's conference rooms. The
main room was set up with tables with pristine white cloths to the floor
arranged in a circle. They held pitchers of water and baskets of snacks.
Each chair was equipped with a microphone and speaker. The mics and
recording equipment fed into the neighboring hall, the tech's kingdom.

Hannah may have lost her troops, but Numenon/Europe supported
Will to the max. There were more techs in that room than fleas on a
hound dog. Will barely had time to walk around the room shaking
hands with his employees.

"This is a situation where nuclear-sized hanky-panky may
occur," Will said. "Guard those recordings with your lives. We'll need
documentation."

The third banquet space was a dining room set with lovely tables seating eight waiting for the lunch break.

A gong rang and the meeting was on.

"As the old man here, I've been elected to give the keynote speech." Will had elected himself, but he was so senior no one would dispute it. "This big guy," he indicated Leroy with his head, "isn't my bodyguard. He's my language coach. You know how handy those are."

Will spoke into the mic with the practiced modulation of a professional actor. "What are we going to talk about today? What we do we talk about every year? How to make ourselves richer than we are? Not this year." He said it in a joking tone, but a ripple went through the crowd.

"I'm going to teach some economics. A little economics doesn't scare us, right? We're grown-ups and can stand thinking a bit." He raised his eyebrows, posing a mock question. "A long time ago, a gloomy preacher named Parson Malthus looked around his world. In 1798, England didn't offer much of a life for the average man. It offered *death* by starvation to the average man.

"Malthus made what he saw into a doctrine: if the masses had more to eat, they'd have more children, eating up the surplus food, and putting themselves back to the edge of starvation. The common man would live in misery and famine, forever.

"It didn't turn out that way, exactly. Malthus didn't realize how much the engine of capitalism could raise the standard of living. How much the free market could raise incomes, for *those who fit into society*.

"Everything that Malthus predicted didn't happen for the First World, but it certainly did for the Third World and anyone disadvantaged in the market. The disabled and ill, those with low IQs." Slides appeared on a screen on the wall opposite Will. "This map shows annual per capita income by country. A lot of the world doesn't have enough to eat.

"Liberals have boo-hoo fits over this, thinking about the *poor* poor people and how to save them. But we don't. We're capitalists. We hold the reins and keep the engine going. We're so good at what we do that we control most of the wealth on the planet. Who cares about losers?

"There's *no limit* on what we can earn. The more we produce, the less it costs to produce, forever. That's the learning curve, documented by the BCG, the Boston Consulting Group, one of the best in the world.

"Our techs and engineers can figure out how to make more stuff, better and cheaper, with no limit. If the price stays sort of steady, what does that mean? More profit. What does that mean? *We* get to keep the change—*forever*."

Will reached up plucking something invisible from the air. He put it in his jacket pocket. "Who gets the profit of the colossal engine of capitalism?" He kept pulling invisible money from the air and putting it in his pocket.

"*Who gets the profit?*" Will half-shouted. "*We* do, the owners of the companies making the goods.

"What do we do with the money that keeps piling up around our feet? Do we share it with the poor? Build things that people need that the government doesn't have the chops to do? Give it to our employees? Fix things like the health care system?

"Hell, no! We're capitalists. We put everything into our own pockets. I sure do. You know how I live. I *think* I've got sixteen houses all over the world. I'm not just *one* of you, *I'm the richest*." He smiled and held out his hands, as if offering jewels. "Not only am I rich, I intend to get richer.

"What I've talked about isn't the whole story. The things people say crack me up. Conservatives in my country get infuriated about poor people feeling *entitled* to the miserable dregs our welfare system gives them. But that's barely enough to keep us from having dead bodies lying in the streets. Some people throw fits because the poor feel *entitled to the worst shit of the richest country on Earth*."

Will slammed his fist on the table. "They aren't the ones who feel entitled, *we are.* I know am entitled to *everything.* And you do too." He looked around the table, making eye contact. "Don't you think you deserve it all? That you should get it all?" He raised his eyebrows and nodded like crazy, grinning. Some of the others did too.

"Malthus was wrong about what capitalism could do. And he was wrong about where the wealth it produced would go: not to make babies. *It goes to us."*

Will looked around. "I'm not saying it shouldn't. Maybe yachts and show horses are the highest and best use of wealth. Private islands. Private armies. Dresses that cost fifty grand." The crowd sat; a group of almost all men, still and silent, with their mouths hanging open. Will felt like laughing.

"What is the point of this?"

"Every year, we come here and talk about cooperative ventures that will make us even richer. Us. Not our societies, and sure as hell not the people who work for us. We talk about cooperation, but the talk doesn't get as far as that door." He pointed at the exit. "We can't cooperate enough to deliver a carton of eggs to a single poor family.

"This year we're going to talk about *really* making the world better. We've got the money to do it. If I gave tenth of a thousandth of what I've got to help people, it could change the world. A friend of mine, Elizabeth Bright Eagle, spends her extra salary helping her People on the reservations. She's a doctor; they don't really make that much. Elizabeth has saved lives with the little she can give. Her People treat her like she was Mother Teresa.

"How would you like people worshiping you because you gave them a chunk of change so they could survive, instead of buying another airplane? How would you like to do something that mattered while you're on this planet?"

A surge went around the room as the attendees scrambled to leave. Leroy stopped them and settled them down, singing a few syllables in his language and casting energy to the people in the room.

Oh, good people, he thought, you are so good. You can see the wisdom of what Will is saying. You have known him so long. *He is just like you: rich.* He has great ideas. Accept them and do what he says.

His energy surged around, just as it had touched the demons the night before and changed them.

"How are we going to change things? Let's talk about it after lunch."

"Why you don't like rich people? We do not create the bad in the world, as you say we do. We make jobs and good lives." The follow-up discussion didn't wait for lunch. As they were leaving the room, an Asian potentate whose name was known and feared around the globe bustled up to Will, pointing a finger and speaking very accented English.

Leroy realized that most of them spoke English in at least a rudimentary way and could probably participate in the meeting without translation. Why the interpreters? So their employers couldn't be blamed for mistakes if things shook out badly. The interpreters might have an agenda too. From their bosses in the room, and forces outside it. This was a complicated game.

"Sir," Leroy said in almost perfect Mandarin, "If you will forgive me, Mr. Duane did not say he hated rich people. He said, '*I'm one of you.* Not only am I rich, I am the richest and I intend to get richer.'" He gave a few other examples of Will identifying with the rich, all in Mandarin.

"But my interpreter said that he said he hated rich people."

"Did your interpreter tell you what he said about his houses all over and the way he lived? Listen to our interpreter's recording. We'll translate it right."

The potentate glared and walked out of the room, presumably to castigate, or kill, his interpreter.

Leroy didn't know Mandarin. What happened made him catch his breath. Grandfather said he would be with him and protect him. He didn't realize that included teaching him an exotic foreign language.

After that, Leroy was besieged with questions about what people had heard, or what their interpreter had said. Often the differences between what Will said and the interpreter reported were subtle twists of meaning and shading. Just enough to distort what Will said so it meant something else.

Grandfather and the ancestors didn't let up; he could speak any language that was thrown at him. More than that, he heard strains of Latin chanting and knew God, *all* of God, loved him. At the end of the questioning period, the meeting participants looked at Leroy with awe.

"It's amazing what can be lost in translation," Will quipped. "Are we going to eat lunch, or what?"

With all the triumph, Leroy could feel the withering hand of Donatore all over the meeting. In angry glances and whisperings between hostile people.

"Say Will, we heard that you're going to step down." An English Lord approached, his face a mask of sophistication that didn't quite hide his enmity. Leroy gasped when he saw who it was. Dashiell Pondichury, the ninth Duke of Lancature, the man who'd tried to kill him with a crossbow at Lord Ballentyne's home and wounded little Allie, the Lord's son. Tall, handsome, ruddy as ever. Evil through and through. How had he gotten invited?

"I'm not going to step down, Dashiell, I'm going to get fired," Will shot back, raising his voice so everyone could hear. "The Feds may come after me too. But I'd say that's a rather personal question from a man of your stature." The crowd spun to follow Will's words. "What are you doing here, anyway? You aren't a member of the group."

"A friend pulled up sick. I'm sitting in." Leroy knew who it was. Diego Donatore was sleeping under some bush in the Tuileries Garden.

"But I'm concerned about you, Will. The rumors are true? You're about to be …"

"I just told you that, Dashiell. I'm getting fired." Everyone in the place was listening. "I'm sure you're wondering if I'm going to be ruined by leaving Numenon. No. I've got so much money that I could lose half of it and have more than all of you. I'm thinking of starting a new corporation. *Really* high tech. It will shake up the world.

"Let's get to work." He led the others into the meeting room.

"More than one third of children who die under five die within the first month of life," Will took up speaking as though he hadn't stopped. "About seventy percent of those deaths could be avoided by simple, cheap programs. Water, maternal care … Sleeping nets treated with insecticide …" He pulled out one proposal after another that would bring food and water to hungry people, vaccinate kids, build dams; provide projects for every level of involvement.

"Here's a list. Pick a project and take it home. Tomorrow we'll work on actualization plans. And then we'll go home and do them."

He had specially prepared packets for each participant, outlining projects appropriate to their country, cost estimates, plans to stage phases of the projects.

"You guys know you can set up these programs so they give you ten times the PR value of the program itself. And when they pay off, with more crops, less disease, and fewer deaths, you'll have workers who will bring every dollar you spent back to you."

Rather than start a riot as he had feared, Will's plan was a success. He picked ventures that were big enough to have an impact, but not too big to change the balance of power. They didn't change anything, and they did. He looked at Leroy, sitting next to him and realized why everything worked. Leroy's jacket was sweat through and he trembled as though he'd used a pick and shovel all afternoon.

"Leroy, that was fantastic," Will said as Leroy dropped him off at the private international terminal outside Paris. "What you did was beyond amazing."

Leroy hadn't realized what it meant to come into his own. He was a powerful warrior, not a joke. He was going to be a great person. The realization was terrifying. He jerked as he realized Will was talking to him.

"Well, plan on coming home for Christmas. Can you amuse yourself for two months?"

"Yeah, I've got that debutante party next week. Some folks in England want me to visit their estates and go hunting, play polo."

"There's your agenda. Keep in touch, Leroy. If you need anything, call me."

"Wait a minute! The debutante party is next week. I could go to it and fly home afterward. I could visit Cass and come back if you needed me here."

Leroy once saw someone throw a bucket of water on a cat. It ran out of there as fast as Will's amiability took off. "We've talked about this before, Leroy. The Institute doesn't allow visitors. Not me. Not you. Not Santa Claus. I've got to get back to war at Numenon. It's not a good time to be in Woodside.

"Have a good time. Go foxhunting. Play with the debutantes." Will patted Leroy's shoulder. All of his good will wasn't gone.

Leroy wanted to say something about the debutantes. *I'll be true to her. I won't be the way you were.*

Will looked back, seeming to read Leroy's mind. "We talked about what went on at those balls when *I* went to them, Leroy. I've come around to Grandfather's point of view about intercourse, but you're a big boy. You're on your own."

They stood there, the air vibrating between them. If Leroy could have listened to Will's heart, he would have heard it say: *I love you. You're everything I want a son to be. Everything I wish I could be.* Will's deeper heart would say, *I want you and Cass to marry and be happy and give me grandchildren. I want a truly rich life.* And Leroy did hear it.

Will didn't have Leroy's abilities, but he had enough intuition to read what was written on the young man's face, *I love you. I want to be close to you and marry your daughter. But you can be great, and you can be a jerk. You scare me.*

When Will left for Palo Alto, Leroy felt empty, and yet full. He'd discovered he was a supremely powerful shaman. In that bright moment, everything seemed possible, even certain.

Cass would get well. They would marry and be very happy. He would *love* having Will for a father-in-law. Maybe. He would work for Will and earn money so he didn't need to have things given to him.

He wasn't going back to his dad and their ranch. The last few months had made him a different person. Leroy felt for a moment that he'd slipped on someone else's skin. But then he realized that the skin was his, polished and tailored and ready for a new life.

26

DEBUTANTES

L EROY STOOD IN front of a tall mirror, wearing his complete ensemble for the first time. The Ball was a white-tie affair, very different than the simple tuxedo/cummerbund/black tie getup that passed for formal dress almost everywhere. Leroy's tailcoat and trousers were bespoke clothing, along with his shirt and white pique vest. And his white tie, of course.

Tom, the valet, and the tailor stood by, breathless. Leroy looked at himself. The jacket flowed over his shoulders and chest perfectly. Not a bulge or any other imperfection marred any part of his regalia. His patent leather shoes shone from underneath his trousers, which broke at exactly the right spot above his instep. White tie, white vest, black tail-coat: all perfect. Slick and tight as the gloves on his hands.

"Does it please you, sir?"

"It's good. Excellent. Thank you very much." Leroy then studied the only part of his presentation he hadn't taken in: himself. He considered his face in the mirror. Brown eyes with hazel splotches. Long, curling black eyelashes. Flaring nostrils and wide lips. A high-bridged nose. High cheekbones, smooth cheeks and brow.

He was beautiful. Leroy had to acknowledge that. Usually, he brushed off compliments about his appearance, but he couldn't this time. His cheeks flamed. Leroy felt profoundly embarrassed.

"Sir, your car is ready. It's time to meet Lady Clarissa at the hotel."

He was escorting a sixteen-year-old little girl that he'd met once to a gigantic farce. Regardless of that, he knew how much it meant to her and he was committed to seeing that she had a good time. Melancholy and hopelessness had radiated from her when he met her at Lord Ballentyne's home. He wanted that to go away, at least for the night.

His driver pulled up to the hotel. The Debutante Ball had been held there for years. He waited more than fifteen minutes for Lady Clarissa and her parents, Lord and Lady Martingale, to pull up behind him in their Bentley.

He got out of his limousine and smiled in the direction of Clarissa's car. He liked her. She and her cousin, Lady Arabella, had roped him into taking her to this silly thing. Sad and lonely and whatever else she'd been at the Ballentyne's party where he'd met her, she was a sweet child making her début to society at one of the fanciest balls on the planet.

When she got out of the Bentley, Clarissa's face was white and pinched. She grabbed his arm, dashing toward the hotel. Leroy looked back and found out why. His Lordship and Ladybird were fighting, falling out of their vehicle in a drunken rage.

Lady Clarissa's blond hair was styled in tousled curls. A veil dropped from the top of her head, almost obscuring her bright blue eyes. The veil didn't hide the tears swimming in them.

"Why do they have to do this now? This is the most important day of my life. They *always* do this. They did this the night of auntie and uncle's dinner party. That's why I was by myself." The tears poured over her lower lid. "Oh, no. I'm *crying*."

Leroy noticed two things: she had that classy voice even when upset, and she thought this party was the most important event of her life. Why? It seemed stupid to him from the get go. Will had spent a fortune on him. Clarissa's gown made it two fortunes. How many more fortunes in silk organza did that hotel ballroom hold?

"Hold on, girl. Let me help you." He put his hand on her shoulder and gave her his handkerchief. "Breathe slow a couple of times. I'll help you." He let a little energy flow.

She relaxed and looked at him. "What did you do?"

"Oh, jus' something I can do."

He squired Lady Clarissa to an area in the hotel where all the girls and their mothers waited, preparing to be presented. Presented to what? Queen Elizabeth had called off the royal participation in the debutante tradition in 1958. Her husband, Prince Philip, called the whole thing "bloody daft."

In the old days, the debutantes were presented to Her Majesty, giving a regal stamp to the proceedings and making the participants true nobility, if only for an evening. The royals backing out didn't do a thing to stop the ball. The tradition was reincarnated with a different focus. Girls wearing enough silk to make a thousand parachutes stood around, picking at invisible flaws in their gowns.

He felt angry. The excess of it. Girls who would never work in their lives wearing million dollar dresses, almost levitating about how exciting the evening was. *Wasn't this great?* Spending more money than most folks would ever see for a party? Except they said those words in those high-toned voices that made it sound like being presented *was really* great.

The snobbery wasn't below the surface. By the angles of those pedigreed noses and the way they looked at him, some of those ... *girls* would be asking him to bus their tables by the end of the evening. The only thing that kept him in that hotel was little Lady Clarissa, who was sniffling softly.

"Hey, you want to split? We could go to a movie."

She looked at him in amazement. "I couldn't possibly leave. They're not going to have a debutante ball anymore—this is the last year. 1997. This is my only chance to come out."

They began moving forward, the girls in their frothy white dresses walking beside their mothers, who wore beaded, sequined, less-frothy white gowns. The excitement became almost frenzied as mothers and daughters approached the area where they were to be presented. The closer they got, the more upset Clarissa became. Leroy was about to go out in that Bentley and bust some aristocratic ass, when an angel appeared, with her mother.

"Clary, I'm so sorry," Lady Arabella was a vision in that pale blue that accentuated her eyes. They were of a powdery hue impossible in the human species. She put her arm around her cousin. "If this had happened to me during my début, I don't know what I would have done. We would have come over sooner, but we didn't realize …"

"Darling, I'll stand in for your mother." That was her aunt, Arabella's mother, Her Grace Violetta, the Duchess of Raddenbery and Cloudfill appearing in a suitably overdone dress.

"Oh, Auntie, I can't believe they …"

"I can, my dear. Your parents need to be curbed. Now, wipe your eyes and I will present you." She moved forward with the other pairs of moms and debs, but Clarissa held back.

"Stay with me," Clarissa whispered to Leroy.

"I ain't left yet and I don' intend to."

"Mr. Watches, this is most unusual. A man co-presenting a debutante," said Her Grace.

"It is, indeed, Your Grace, most girls Clarissa's age don't have to deal with their parents fightin' in Bentleys an' lettin' them down all the time. 'Specially now. Lady Arabella, why don' you come along too?" He couldn't take his eyes off of Arabella. She made him forget *everything*.

"All right, Mr. Watches. They aren't having the Ball next year. Who can say what's proper? Let's give it a good last go." The two young ladies hooked arms with Leroy. Her Grace preceded them and the four made their way to Clarissa's presentation.

Leroy practically guffawed when he saw what they were presented to—a giant cake. Mothers and daughters approached the cake with reverence. Someone called out their names and pedigrees as the crowd oohed and ahhed. Then they bowed to the cake. Wasn't just a bow, either. The girls leaned over so far he thought they were doing a nose-dive into the floor.

Their foursome went up, the only such group in history. Lady Clarissa did her swan dive and they left, followed by astonished glances and muttering.

Leroy could barely contain his laughter. Why were they bowing to a *cake?* He sure could see why Queen Elizabeth shut this deal down. He'd bow to Queen Elizabeth—she did a great job. But a *cake?*

After that it was just a standard formal dinner in a palace with tons of really rich people and girls in white dresses. And their mothers, wearing white sequined corsets. Leroy's sense of humor was going to get him into trouble. He didn't see another brown face, including the waiters.

I ain't seen so much white outside the Good Ol' Boys Club back home. Come to think of it, I've never seen so much white, anywhere. Lord, I hope they don't get a drunk up and ask me to wash the dishes.

They were getting a drunk up, fast. He noticed the English were good at many things. Drinking was one of them. The kids were drinking too. Somebody reached over to fill Lady Clarissa's glass. He put his hand over it.

"You don't want to get messed up with that, Your Ladyship. You'll go the way of your parents. Don't drink now, or ever again," Leroy said in the voice that had tamed demons and made them good. "All of you," he spoke to the table and those around him. "Don't drink. That's the devil in a glass."

Clary looked at the crystal glass, squaring her jaw. "You're right. Grandpapa was the same as Mum and Da. He died from it." She turned to Leroy. "Help me, I don't want to be like them."

He put his huge hand on her tiny one. "I will, Your Ladyship."

"Clary."

The dancing was as white as everything else. Fortunately, Leroy could waltz and rhumba and paso doble with the best of them. Other debutantes wanted to cut in on him and Clarissa. That reminded him some of what Will had said, but he couldn't call it a stampede.

He stuck with Clarissa. She was upset and he wouldn't leave her. He wanted her to have the enchanted night she had dreamed of. Her parents never showed. Clary's cheeks flamed hotter the longer her parents *didn't* appear.

"You OK, Clary?"

She nodded vigorously. "Yes. If my parents came now, they'd fall all over and start screaming and clawing each other even at the party." She looked up at Leroy, baring her soul. "Do you know what my father did once?" Leroy shook his head. "He took his trousers off at the Polo Ball. And his … *Everyone* saw. No one stopped him. Only the servants. I never want to go anywhere with them again."

"Folks do stuff like that, Clary, blacked out-drunk. Run down the street naked. Stuff like that. It's his …"

"Do you know what they're doing, Leroy?" she whispered as they danced. He shook his head. "They're at our country estate, throwing things at each other, drinking everything in the house—and having sex all over. Even with the servants there." She elevated her head, with its pretty sculpted nose and elegant features.

"Oh, Clarissa, I'm so sorry." He hummed to her a bit. "You can have a life of your own. You don't have to do what they do. You are a very good person."

Arabella stood next to them, a pale blue vision. "Well, cousin Clarissa, may I dance with the handsome prince?" Clary looked up with a preternaturally knowing little smile.

"Of course, cousin Arabella."

He took Arabella in his arms. They glided away to some sugary tune. Her smile dazzled him. In seconds, the shock came. Energy rushed up his spine, pleasure swirling around it. She grabbed his shoulder, having to reach high to get it; her right hand clutched his left.

"Leroy, what's happening to us? It's not a mistake. It's *something*." She moaned and her head tilted back.

"Shh. Not here, girl." Not ever if Cass lived. He piloted her to a quiet corner, aware that everyone in the room followed them with their eyes. "It's somethin' in my culture and in my religion. If a man and woman are perfect for each other, they're called soul mates. When they touch, it's like with us."

"*We're* soul mates?" Her eyes were misty.

"I'd say so, but my grandfather isn't here. He'd know for sure." Leroy had realized that the old chieftains and warriors had often more than one wife. Maybe the Great One had sent him Arabella to be his second wife, not a spare in case Cass died. That was *really* impossible. So many nights, he'd dreamt he was rolling in Arabella's plump arms, only to have Cass's anguished eyes make Arabella disappear.

She stood before him, with those eyes yearning. "Do soul mates marry?"

"As soon as possible, yes."

Her head fell forward and her forehead touched his chest. She was silent, and then her shaking shoulders told him what was happening. He pushed her away, so he could see her face. Silvery tracks ran down her cheeks.

"Father will never let me marry you. I want to marry you, but he won't let me. I'm twenty-three years old, Leroy. I made my début seven years ago. I would have married a dozen times, but for my father. No one's good enough for me. He has to have a better title than mine. Be richer than us and have more land. He has to have been to university." All of those let him out. "But most of all …" She looked up at his face.

He knew what she was seeing. His nose was twice as wide as hers and didn't end with a sharp point. His hair was short, but very curly. Most of all, his skin was brown.

"He won't let you marry a black man." Leroy's jaw clenched. There it was; what Doug had said so long ago. Cut him to the core. He turned and walked toward the main door, intending to leave. Good old Lord Ballentyne who loved him and his ability to play golf. Invited him to his country house to play polo and go fox hunting. Leroy was good enough for anything, but marrying his daughter.

Leroy *would* have married Arabella if Cass died. He'd have come right back to England and married her. Not now. Oh. If he did, he'd have to go to war with her family and kin. And he might do that, anyway.

Enraged, he stormed past the bandstand. He looked up and gasped.

The band's trap drum set was a miracle, especially compared to the crappy drums Leroy had played at high school dances. It contained not just the standard four piece kit of music schools: a snare drum, bass drum, hi-hat stand and cymbals, a tom tom drum and more cymbals. The drum kit on the podium had *double* bass drums, and enough cymbals, cowbells, tambourines to arm a major rock 'n' roll band.

Leroy had been a drummer since he first struck a wooden spoon to a pot as a baby. His rhythm was the beating heart of his high school. He was the pride of his Nation, causing them to nail the marching band competitions year after year. Leroy graduated from high school because of his ability to drum. He was not a scholar, tending to trance out during most of his classes. And bliss out when he wasn't tranced out. That was part of becoming a shaman; the Rez understood that.

Almost single-handedly, he kept the inter-tribal political situation peaceful for many years. His Nation had an on-going (several centuries) beef with the Northern Salmon Nation, whose reservation was at the Northern end of New Mexico.

The advent of freeways, airplanes, buses, and cars would have made it easy for Leroy's People to go up north and wipe out the Salmon, ending their vendetta. Essentially peaceful People, the two Nations worked out their differences without violence, through their high school marching bands. Every year, rotating the host Nation, the marching bands would carry out a competition that proved the cultural and metaphysical superiority of the winner.

It was always Leroy's Nation, until he graduated from high school. The elders kept him in school a couple of extra years, until the Salmon figured out what they were doing. He was ejected from high school, though they called it "graduation."

Leroy's reaction to the trap drums at the Debutante Ball was understandable. It was a beautiful set of drums; drums anyone would love. And Leroy did, especially when enraged after realizing the truth of the oh-so-polite-Ballentynes.

After using his voice and four £100 notes to get the limp-wristed, pasty-faced white boy out of the throne, he took over. He used his voice to limber up the rest of the band. He felt that they might be able to kick it pretty good, if they didn't act like they were dead.

Leroy commenced to beat out rhythms never heard outside of his reservation. His band followed him.

Soon, no one was dead. The drummer that beat the Northern Salmon Nation got the debs, their escorts, parents, and the serving staff rockin'.

They rocked and kept on rocking. The usual debutante party might end in the wee hours with everyone snookered and lying in the corners, often on top of each other. At this Ball, no one stopped dancing until his or her carbuncles gave out (the older generation) or Leroy got sick of playing. That's what finally happened.

"OK. That's it, everyone. Time to get home so you can groom your polo ponies tomorrow."

He jumped off the dais onto the dance floor. "You need a ride home, Clarissa?" She followed him to the exit. Leroy paid no more mind to the tribal customs of these people. Maybe they were supposed to bow to the cake again, who knows. He left, Clarissa in tow. She wasn't Lady Clarissa anymore either. He pretended not to notice Arabella's stricken face. And failed.

"Clarissa, wait one second. I'll be right back." Turning on his heel, he returned to Arabella. "I can't leave without sayin' something. I'd like to see you again, even just for tea. I don't know where I'm goin' next. Will might want me to tour Fiji or something." He pulled his card out of his jacket. It was a traditional visiting card, containing only his name. Useless.

"Here," Leroy turned it over, wondering what to put on the back. He didn't know what his number would be; he was given a new phone in each place. He scribbled on the back.

"If you want to contact me, you can reach me through this number. That's Will Duane's direct number. He'll know where I am." Leroy smiled. "Tell him I told you to call him." He chuckled, remembering what Will said all the time. "If you need a lawyer, ask him. Will's got the best in the world."

"Better than our family barrister?"

"Better than anyone's. Will likes to help people." Pretty girls especially. "Good-bye, Arabella. I hope to see you again."

No one waited for Clarissa in front of the hotel. Her family's driver had chauffeured her parents to their country estate and stayed there. Clarissa made the tiniest squeak of agony, realizing she was abandoned.

"Do you have someone to stay with?" he asked. He finally had realized what a big deal it was for parents to miss their daughter's debutante party and leave her standing at the front of the ballroom at the end. An almost-fatal car crash would be an acceptable excuse not to show, but not what the Lord and Lady did.

"Can I go home with you?" Her eyes were huge, wet lashes clumped together. She was heartbroken, and in love with him.

"No, you may not. Do you have any relatives nearby who will take care of you?"

"Grandmama and Papa."

"Your grandparents. Do they drink?"

"No."

"Where do they live?"

"In St. George's Hill, in Weybridge. About forty five minutes from here."

"OK. Let's go. Tell Ralph the address."

"Ralph?"

"My driver."

"Oh." Wide eyes, big O of a mouth. Calling a servant by his first name was almost as revolutionary as Leroy's playing the drums. "It's on Wood Lane."

He pulled a cell phone out of a compartment in the side of the car door. Her eyes opened wide when she saw the brick of a phone. Not everyone had such an advanced device in 1997 and *very* few had them connected to satellite networks so they could use them anywhere. Numenon offered a lot.

"What's your home phone number, Clarissa?" Leroy said, dialing quickly. The butler answered instantly. Leroy had the feeling that, having seen the Lord and Lady leave for the Ball soused and knowing their drunken proclivities, the entire staff waited in frenzy, wondering how the Ball went. He explained what happened, making no attempt to sugar-coat anything. "I'm taking Lady Clarissa to her grandparents' for the night. I didn't want you to worry."

Clarissa cuddled up to him as they drove, stroking his body in a tentative fashion and raising her lips to him at one point.

"Clarissa, do you think if you have sex with me, what your parents did won't hurt so much?"

She froze, and then started really crying for the first time. She didn't stop, finally leaning on him in a different way.

Leroy stroked her head. "It's all right. I understand. Nothing went right tonight. If you had me, you'd have gotten something at least.

"Are you a virgin, Clarissa?" She nodded miserably. "Good. Stay that way. You're holy. You're the most valuable thing in the universe. You don't want to give yourself to anybody, someone you don't know. Someone who isn't right for you and doesn't want you for the right reasons. Do you understand?

"When you meet the right man, when you both love each other, all of that will be perfect. In the meantime, stay as you are."

She clutched him all the way to her grandparents, messing up his fancy suit with her tears. He figured that was the best thing that could happen to it.

Dawn was nowhere in evidence, but he could see the tall trees and mansions of Clarissa's grandparents' neighborhood. This was as fancy as his place in London, it just had trees and space. Clarissa would never lack for anything, even if she left her parents cold. But that wasn't enough for a life.

"You need to start thinking about the future, Clarissa. You need to go to school so you can get a job."

"A job?!" She pulled away from him, horrified. "For *money?*"

"Nothin' wrong with working for wages, girl. But if you don't want to work for money, you need a job on Earth. You need to take care of poor people, or get sick people medical care. Take care of the environment. Work for world peace. You're smart; you could be in Parliament or an Ambassador. You could do anything." He said it all in his voice. Every word was a command she couldn't ignore.

He took her to her grandmother's house, calling ahead to alert the butler so everyone could be presentable when they arrived at four a.m.

The mansion had big columns in front and miles of grass. Her grandparents were standing on the front porch.

"You need to take care of her," he said. "You know what goes on in her house. She shouldn't be living with her parents." More commands.

"Well, Lady Clarissa, it was a delight accompanying you to the Ball." He kissed her hand and let her go. He could see the stars twinkling in her eyes as she went to her grandparents.

27

MAKING IT THROUGH THE NIGHT

SITTING IN HIS grand living room the evening after the Ball, Leroy stared out the window at the lights and beauty of London at night. After what Arabella had revealed, everything seemed pointless. Learning stuff that didn't matter and he'd never use again. Impressing people who had nothing to them and would *never* truly accept him. He didn't want to give any more parties or visit cathedrals or museums.

He wanted his ranch. He wanted Grandfather and he wanted his father. Seeing his dad's warm, wrinkled brown face and curly grey hair would have put some reality in the crazy life he was living.

It was nine p.m. London time, one in the afternoon in California. He wouldn't make the mistake he had when he called home and it was three a.m. in California. He picked up the phone, "Daddy, it's me. Leroy. Give me a call when you get in. I'd really like to talk to you."

That was the third call where he talked to the answering machine. His dad hadn't called back once. Something was going on. His father never left the ranch. But he *did* call back this time.

"Hi, son! I've been out of town. Sorry I missed your calls." His father sounded happier than he'd heard him.

"Where have you been?"

"We just got back from San Diego. Figure on heading up to San Francisco in a few days."

"Who's 'we', dad?"

"The new neighbor. Real friendly."

Those stuck up rich people who turned a nice ranch house into a fake Western monument? "*They're* friendly?"

"Yes, very friendly and fun to be around. What are you up to?"

I'm about to die of homesickness. "I just wanted to hear your voice and see that you were OK."

"I'm more than OK. Ever since you healed my arthritis, I've had a new life. I can't tell you how grateful I am, son.

"When are you coming home?"

Leroy sighed. "By Christmas, Will says."

"Ah, you're homesick. Well, traveling like you been would do that. Come on home, son. I can get you a plane ticket if you need it. Come home tomorrow."

Where the hell did his father get the money to buy a plane ticket for the next *day*, not using bonus miles and buying a year ahead to get the cheapest rate?

"Son, I have a big surprise for you. I was going to save it until you got home, but you sound so down that I'll tell you. Your cabin is done!" Leroy could see his father's smile through the phone.

"It's all done? What do you mean?"

"Remember all the stuff those rich people gave me when they were remodeling?"

"Yeah. All the cabinets and everything."

"Way more than what you saw last Christmas. Toilets and tubs. Doors, wood ones with panels. A whole pile of tile and granite. You wouldn't believe what they gave me. They were goin' to throw it away. So I had 'em bring it over. Those people were so rich that they had carpenters and electricians and plumbers standing around doing nothing."

"What?!" Nobody did that.

"It's true. If that rich lady didn't like what came in, she'd refuse it, even with the crew waiting to install it. Craziest thing you ever saw.

"They fixed your whole cabin in their spare time, son. Installed everything from the front door to the back porch. Will Duane could live there, the way it came out."

Rage erupted in Leroy. "That was *my* cabin. I built it and I was going to finish it. That was for *me* and my *wife*. I wanted to do that for *us*. *By myself*."

His father made a little snort and backpedaled fast. "Son, you've been gone almost a year. I didn't know when you were coming back. I thought, 'Better grab what I can.' I thought you'd *love* that it was done."

"I don't, Dad, that was my own place, that I built by myself. It was private. For me and my wife."

"Leroy, that's crazy. Everyone in this valley came over to raise those logs. Other people have been in on it from the start. I just was trying to help. Don't be mad at me."

Leroy sat, breathing hard and wiping his eyes. Why did the cabin matter so much? Why was he crying? Why did Cass and him getting married seem so far away? Why should Arabella saying her father would never accept him matter? She wasn't even his real soul mate. She was a spare or a number two. But why did it feel like his happiness with Cass or anyone was being snatched away?

Would he ever get what he really wanted? What did he deserve— a gigantic half-breed black/red/white person who only got out of high school because the Salmon caught on?

Nothing he'd done since he left home meant anything. Learning silverware. Bespoke clothing. Was he really just a grown up "cute pickaninny" like some lady visiting the ranch had said so many years before? He had to ask his daddy what that meant.

Who was he? He wasn't the rancher who left to see his Grandfather at the last Meeting. Nowhere near. He'd been to all those places; he was different. But going where he'd been and doing what he'd done meant he didn't belong *anywhere.*

He didn't belong at home. The ranch and their valley and everyone he'd called friends all his life seemed different from him.

How could he go home after this year? He couldn't be a multi-lingual ranch hand who knew formal dress code. And he couldn't forget that he knew it, and the parties and dancing with the debutantes. What was he, who was he? What was he going to do when it was over?

All along, he'd figured that he'd do something with Will after this year. Help him somehow. He didn't know how he'd make a living without Will. His new lifestyle was far above anything he could have imagined before.

Will was pissing him off. He was screwing around, not telling what he knew about Cass. Just, "I'm getting good reports." She must have been moved to that other hospital, but why didn't Will tell him right out? Will was hiding something. Why?

What was his dad doing hanging around with the rich people? They were awful. Were they giving him money so he could buy a plane ticket? Why would they give him money? Had he done something with the ranch? Sold it to them? Crazy things were happening everywhere. His life was out of control.

28

OK. SO HE DIDN'T MAKE IT THROUGH THE NIGHT

"WILL? I WANT to know where Cass is and how she's doing." The words shot out of Leroy's mouth. His interaction with his father had wound him up enough to take Will on.

"She's fine, Leroy." Will's voice was too smooth.

"Fine, like fine, or fine, like not dead?"

"I'm getting good reports from the Institute. She's settling in and adjusting to their regimen."

"She's at that Institute? Why didn't you tell me you'd moved her?"

"I wasn't aware that I *had* to tell you anything."

"Have you talked to her?"

"I have not talked to her. I've talked to the director and her psychiatrist. The Institute has a very effective treatment program.

"The patients are denied access to the outside world. They have to learn to cope inside the hospital culture and learn healthy ways of living. Remember, they're addicts with severe mental disorders and criminals. It's the only way they can heal, Leroy."

"That is not the only way they can heal. My grandfather could have healed her in two days. It might take me three. She doesn't have to be there. She's there because you don't trust me."

"I haven't seen her since we rescued her on March 23rd. It's October 26th. That's *seven* months. I figured you'd moved her to that other place. But when? Why didn't you tell me?"

"That's none of your business."

"That is my business as much as yours." Leroy could feel himself lean into it. "I am going to marry her. Cass matters to me. And you're lying. There's something you're not telling me.

The moment he said "lying," he could feel Will change, like popping a grenade.

"You're calling me a liar*? You're a two-bit pretty boy. All you can do is drum and spend my money."*

"I thought you didn't care what you spent on me. You were bringing me into the family. *I'm Cass's soul mate.*" Leroy had had enough. Sarcasm permeated his words. "Tell me what you're keeping from me or I'll fly home *now* and drag it out of you."

Big pause on Will's end. The grenade was ticking. "She's brain-damaged. Apparently when you *saved* her, you let her die a few times too. And waited too long to bring her back. She's brain-damaged. Now are you happy?"

Leroy couldn't move. Speak. Breathe. "She's brain-damaged?"

"Yes. Fruit of your healing. If you …"

"I can't bring anyone back from the dead. If she came back, she did it herself. Are those doctors sure? Half the time their tests are wrong …"

"They're sure." Will's voice was clipped.

"How bad is it? Can she talk?"

"She sounds fine when I talk to her on the phone. They say her IQ has dropped significantly, but that will just make you a better couple."

"*What?*"

"I've had you investigated. You barely got out of high school. I saw your records, Leroy. Six years to graduate from a lousy reservation high school with a D average."

"You think I let Cass die and get brain-damaged? But that doesn't matter because I'm so dumb, we'll make a better match now?" Will meant that exactly; Leroy felt him breathing it in and breathing it out.

"I saved your life in Paris. I prayed for you all night. I watched your back and covered your ass in that meeting.

"And you lie to me, and blame me, and hold all this shit about me for months and months and never say a thing. You really are an asshole." Leroy quivered as he spoke.

Leroy could feel Will suck in air, maybe all the air in the universe. "YOU UNGRATEFUL SON OF A BITCH!" Will exploded. "All you're good for is playing drums and dancing with little girls. I know about you. I had you *investigated. Watched, Leroy! I've had you watched every minute you've been over there!*

"WHAT DO YOU HAVE TO OFFER ME *FOR WHAT I'VE DONE FOR YOU?*" Will stopped. Leroy could hear him breathing, panting as he thought up more insults. Time seemed to pause and then Leroy fired back.

"Never speak to me like that. Never speak to *anyone* like that." Leroy's voice was low and very intense. He hung up. The fury he'd felt after talking to his dad was not even a fly-speck on the surface of the cosmos to what he felt then.

He took off into the night, running along the deserted sidewalk. He wanted thugs to show up so he could kill them. Demons. Will. He could disembowel Will a dozen times before feeling satisfied. Two dozen.

Another man would have gone to a bar and gotten drunk. Leroy kept running and hoping Enzo *and* Diego Donatore would show up so he could tear them apart.

Asshole. What Will had said hurt. He didn't know what Leroy was in training to be. *My grandpa was in a trance for twenty years when he was becoming a holy man. I did it in six.*

His ribs heaved in and out. Cass wasn't safe. She was in a very bad place. Her father was an asshole. No wonder she was so sick. What did Will say to Cass about *her* grades?

29

DADDY'S LITTLE GIRL

WILL DROPPED THE smoking shards of his phone, backing away from his desk. The phone had exploded when Leroy spoke those quiet but charged words. The part that didn't explode melted. Electrical energy surged out of the telephone, fried the line, went into the wall, and kept going. He could see charred lines along the floor where the phone's power went. It probably burned all the way out of the house to the telephone pole.

"Are you all right, Mr. Duane?" One of his operatives was at his door. They were back in force. When he moved Cass to the Institute and didn't tell Leroy, Carl refused to work for him. He cooked, that was it. Hannah's people were the top dogs in security again, crawling all over in their black clothes. "We lost the power in the house for a second. Are you OK?"

"I'm fine. Don't worry."

Jesus Christ, Will gasped. That kid blew up a bull. He kills demons. He'd saved Will's life. *What the fuck are you screwing with him for?*

"Don't talk to me that way. Don't talk to anyone that way." Remembering Leroy's words made Will's guts shiver. The remains of the phone wiggled too.

He *was* a foul-mouthed, bad-tempered old man with no sense of propriety when he was angry. How did he know what Leroy's high school was like? Out on a reservation? Maybe they'd didn't have books. Maybe he was dyslexic or had an attention deficit. He'd proven he could outperform anybody, anywhere. What he'd said to Leroy was *so* rude.

Oh, shit. He cleared the rubble of the phone away and leaned his forehead on his hand. Something *was fi*shy about that Havertin Institute. Why did he defend it so? Because of a corporate buddy who wasn't even a good friend? Because he didn't think Cass could be saved? Because he wanted to punish her for what she'd said to him last Christmas and for years before?

Or was it what Leroy said, he didn't trust him? Will didn't trust anyone. If something awful happened and he needed help, would Leroy come after what he said?

His cell phone rang—he could hear it in his bedroom. He ran to get it, thinking it was Leroy calling back.

"I'm sorry ..."

"Well, good Will. I'm sure that you have lots to be sorry about." The dry old voice was like a rasp on his already shredded nerves. It was Vanessa Schierman. Dr. Vanessa Schierman. "Do you want to tell me what it is?"

"No."

"I figured not. Probably would be good for your soul if you did."

"I lost my temper and mouthed off at Ashley's fiancé." The words came out: Ashley, fiancé.

"I didn't know she was engaged. I thought you put her in jail."

"Vanessa, she is not in jail, she is in a very fine mental hospital."

"*I* run a fine mental hospital. *Cass*—or does she like Ashley now?— is in jail. Probably a medieval type one where they torture people."

"Why do you say that?"

"Months ago, when Cass was rescued and you announced your plans for her, I looked up the Havertin Institute on my Numenon Ranger. That new Internet is handy. They have a very nice website laying out their treatment program and introducing their staff.

"I talked to Rudy about the place. Have you met him, my Chief of Psychiatry? Brilliant and with the credentials of God. He knew the director and key staff personally and felt they were highly qualified. Rudy didn't like their prohibition of family and patient contact, but he said it fit with their therapeutic modality and wasn't bad for a mid-term program. He said that the hospital should try to reintegrate the patient with the family and rebuild the family structure, but that was a long-term goal.

"Rudy was satisfied, so I was satisfied, for the moment.

"I looked up Havertin again today and couldn't believe my eyes. New director, almost all new staff. Rudy's never heard of any of them. He's investigating them now. Same treatment program, though it looked as though they simply hadn't changed that portion of their website. Did they contact you to tell you this?"

"Yes, Vanessa, they did. It was a corporate buy-out. A larger medical group now owns Havertin. The director of the overarching corporation is also a friend of mine. Cass has her existing psychiatrist and counseling team, though they have changed some players at the administrative level. And I've talked with her psychiatrist. Cass is fine. Does that satisfy you?"

"No, Will, it doesn't. Given Cass's propensity to attract demons, I'd be very suspicious of any staff changes, anywhere in the organization. Why don't you have your famous lawyers check them out? I'll let Rudy continue researching their shrinks. Why don't you hop on a plane and demand to see her and meet her doctors? I know you're assertive enough to manage that." He was silent. Why *didn't* he do that?

"Will, I don't understand why any hospital would prohibit the patients from contact with their families? If their families are also their drug dealers, I can see it, but you? Have they involved you in any of her therapy?"

"No."

"There's a big mistake. You're at least as crazy as she is. I'm sure half of what's wrong with her is due to you."

"Did you call to insult me, Vanessa, or was something on your mind?"

"I called to invite you to Christmas dinner."

"Christmas dinner. Just like that? Out of the blue?"

"Yes. I had to find out about Cass first. The dinner is on Christmas Day. In a couple of months. I know I'm early, but I forget everything even with my staff to help. I'll probably call and invite you again. I wanted to make sure I got on your busy social calendar. Three o'clock sharp. You're coming, yes?"

"Yes."

"Good. Do you need Driver to pick you up?"

"No. I have my own driver."

He shivered when he hung up. God, that old woman scared him. She was a witch, he knew it. Her house was way up on the top of Skyline Boulevard in the middle of the redwoods. Looked like a haunted house. It had to be a haunted house. The stone gargoyles on the walls moved. The carvings on the wood paneling winked. Ancestor portraits circled the staircase, going up four stories. They winked, and waved.

Why did he say he'd go? The mental hospital portion of her property was so much more normal than the rest of the estate. What could Christmas be like up there? Why did she even celebrate Christmas? She couldn't possibly believe in it.

But it was months away. Plenty of time to think of an excuse. Plenty of time to calm down from Leroy's attack. Plenty of time to forget what he had said. All the time he needed to adjust to the fact that the Native

Americans he had brought home from the Meeting had announced that they would be leaving. Leroy hadn't called them and told them about their fight and what Will had said; Carl made the announcement before he and Leroy fought.

He'd asked Carl why they were leaving. "'Ain't workin' for us here. We can't help you anymore."

This Christmas, he'd be alone in his luxurious mansion on his expansive estate that could hold all those people without much fuss, really. Once he got used to being around people everything was fine. The children would be gone and the baby. Bud and Bert let him hold the baby whenever he wanted. He had bright brown eyes and glossy black hair. Four new teeth! And the two little ones would be gone. He was going to get Junior a puppy for Christmas. He was having a hard time adjusting to Woodside. Tore at Will's heart to see Junior's sad brown eyes.

They would all be gone. The estate would be silent. He would be alone. He'd been alone most of his life. What was the problem? If he was lonely, he could go to the ranch in Montana and have his cook make a fabulous spread for him and the ranch hands. Or dig up some corporate party. How about having Frank Sauvage and his family over? Hysteria tinged his short laugh.

Will struggled, chest heaving. He would go to Vanessa's for Christmas and he knew it. Why? Because she was more a mother to him than his real mother could have been if she'd gone to therapy every day of her life. Vanessa knew everything about him and accepted him.

Her voice was gruff and so was she, but that was a front, just like her crazy mansion. She made him feel good, and safe, and at home. She loved him. He'd go to Christmas at her house when the day came. If it came.

30

WAR CHIEF

WILL WOULDN'T LET Leroy see Cass or know where she was, but he wasn't done in England, anyway. His royal marmalade, Lord Ballentyne, had invited him to play polo and go fox hunting at his country estate in two months, right before Christmas.

"That's when you wanted to come, wasn't it, Leroy?" Ballentyne called to reconfirm his invitation. He was polite as ever, but Leroy could feel that every door to his heart was closed. "We're redoing the grounds and house 'til then. Redecorating. Won't be presentable until December, old fellow, so we can't have guests. We can get up an exhibition match once we're done.

"If the weather holds. Could be a monsoon then. Or snowing like the North Pole. But if we can get decent weather, we should have a good game. Private game, of course. The club will be finished for the season. But we'll get you a horse to ride."

"Thank you, Your Lordship." He had no intention of playing a part in Ballentyne's show on a borrowed horse.

Leroy called Tom into the room. "Tom, why are you working as a valet? You're smart and can do anything. I heard you had a university degree."

Tom blushed to the roots of his dark red hair. "Uh. I …"

"Tell me the truth, Tom."

"Well, Leroy," he dropped the "Sir" that once, "I'm Catholic and I'm from Scotland. There's a bit of tension between Scotland and the English. Has been for ever. I have a Scots' accent." Leroy had noticed his accent was different from the other Brits, but they all had accents.

"That keeps you from getting a good job?"

"Sir, I like working for Numenon at the London manse. I like working for you. I'm not complaining."

"I got that. Would you like to come to the United States with me, some day?"

"Oh, yes. What would I do?"

"Don't know yet, Tom. I've got a ranch, but maybe I'll start a company too, something like that. That may take time. But I've got something that needs doing real fast. Any of your Scottish friends play polo?"

"Oh, yes, sir. Like demons." Leroy blanched at the word. "We love polo. Only ones like it more than us are the Irish."

"You have any friends in Ireland?"

"Yes, sir."

"They feel about the English like the Scots do, don't they?"

"Yes. Worse, most likely."

"Tell me about polo. How many players on a team, Tom?"

"Four, sir."

"How many horses do they need to play a game?"

"Six or more each, sir."

"Do you know any Irish and Scottish polo players who'd like to beat the shit out of Lord Ballentyne's team just before Christmas?"

"I know dozens who'd like to do that, but you can't play then."

"Why?"

"The estate will be frozen tight."

"Don't worry about the weather. I'll take care of that. Call your friends. And get grooms for the horses. Whatever they need. I'll get the horses. We have two months to become a champion team. Also, we're moving. Can you find me a place up in Scotland where we can all stay? With a polo field and stables? Cheap?"

Leroy would have made the kindest and most conciliatory war chief in history, until something happened that pushed his buttons. Finding out that Arabella's father would reject him because of the color of his skin pushed almost all of his buttons. What Will had said pushed the rest.

He thought he'd push back—as hard as he could. There were two more things he wanted to do in England; he'd do them and leave. He didn't need his dad to buy a plane ticket for him. He'd buy his own. He had enough money to buy pretty near anything, even though it was Will Duane's money. He hadn't spent but the tiniest fraction of his stipend. He could finance the polo team himself. He wouldn't fly back in Will's stinking jet, nor would he have anything to do with the man.

"It's great, Tom. You did *good.*" Leroy knew he was messing with the English language, just like he was messing with everything else. They had just arrived at Glamisdale Castle in Scotland, his new headquarters.

"It's been on the market for ages. I got it for a super price for the two months. Polo field is in great shape, and so is the hunt field. Castle's pretty good, except for the part where the roof fell in. Rains back in '93 nearly did the place in. Snow on the roof froze and then melted. Flooded the galleries.

"His Lordship—he's a Scottish laird, not an English one—fixed what he cared about and lived with the rest. He died just a month ago. Plenty of room for the team to stay. Sir Glamis's cook an' housekeeper 'r' here, but that's all."

"Let's see the stables."

Leroy nodded as they walked around the U-shaped stone building that was the main barn. "He cared about his horses. This is kept up nice. I never liked box stalls, 'cept in winter. Looks like it's winter here a lot."

They walked out behind the barns. Flat polo fields spread out, with rolling hunt fields beyond that. They were well-kept, but not summer green. The fall cold had burned the grass. It wasn't optimal and would only get worse in the next two months.

"Do you think the weather will hold, sir, *Leroy*, sir, so we can practice?"

"I expect it will hold fine, Tom." Leroy chuckled. "Yeah, the laird did take care of what mattered to him. Now, it matters to us.

"When does the team arrive, Tom?"

"About supper time. I got 'em a lorry to get up here. It's only a mile from the train, but with the saddles and all."

"That's the Rules. Nothin' alcoholic on this place or at that game or near me 'til this is over." Leroy held forth in the large dining hall. He made sure he'd have enough riders and grooms for the rigorous training schedule he set out, plus Tom and himself. All Scottish nationalists cruising for a way to beat the British.

"No drinking? But man, this is *Scotland*," one of them howled. His new team, their backups, and the associated grooms and barn boys, were horrified when he announced the Rules. They were the same as Grandfather's Rules for the spirit warriors.

"No. This is *not* Scotland. This is …" He said the name of his tribal lands in his language. "This is Indian country and will be until I leave. I am the boss. We're going to find out which of you are warriors and which of you are drunken cry-babies. I don't think *any* of you, except Tom, could last a day under the rules I grew up with. Now eat your stew and get to bed. We start at dawn."

"Start what, man? An' where are the horses? Are none in the barns."

"We're going to begin getting them tomorrow. We'll visit the local farms for prospects. I'll start their training, and you'll finish them." He was a little short, budget-wise.

"Anybody breed race horses around here?" Leroy asked in the morning.

"Everyone who can afford a horse has a race horse, mate. Might be a racehorse only in the eyes of the ol' codger who's got him, but it's a Derby winner, sure." The evening's lack of libation had not improved his crew's temper.

"Then we'd better start looking everywhere …"

"Man, ninety percent of the game is the horse," a rider said. "I could ride a mule, but it would still be a mule. I came up here to win."

"I got a higher opinion of mules. What's that grey horse out there in the pasture?"

"That's Sir Glammis's polo pony. Good horse, but seventeen years old and lame."

Leroy continued to study the animal as it grazed. "I think that's *my* polo pony." He walked out to the field without a halter or a backward glance.

"The man's daft. We're wasting our time." Three of them left right then, riders and grooms alike. Those that left didn't get to see Leroy ride the old horse up to the castle without a saddle or bridle. The animal was sound and strong, pricking its ears like lances, and strutting like a warhorse.

"Holy Mother! What did you do to him?"

"I told him he'd get to kick some English butt if he let me ride him. Now, the rest of you are going to get around to the farms and tell folks what we got going here. We need horses. I can pay up to £1,000 pounds to rent or buy horses I approve. You go out and look, bring the good ones here."

They went through a few more riders as the training progressed. Leroy ended up importing some from Ireland. They weren't happy about the no-drinking clause, but when they saw Leroy lead out a rank, crabby Thoroughbred that had been standing in some old lady's paddock for five years and turn it into a horse that could win in any reined stock horse class in the planet, they were impressed.

"Sure'n he can ride like St. Eligius, the patron saint of horses and horsemen. But how're we gonna play polo with that horse?"

"I don't know how to play polo, but I can set a horse up to work cows. *You* have to make polo ponies out of them." Leroy said. He swung off and approached another unbroken horse about sixteen and a half hands high.

"Too big."

"If this horse has the heart I think he does, he wouldn't be too big if he was an elephant."

Scotland was a strange place, and they were discovering that Leroy was a stranger man.

"Ah, feel hooched," He heard one of his team say. "Jus' being near him, I feel like I did on St. Bride's day four years past, when I slept for three days after. But no headache w' Leroy."

"Aye. An' ye noticed it hasn't rained here more 'n' necessary to wet the lawns? Nor has it gotten cold?"

31

DAMSELS IN DISTRESS

WILL PICKED UP the receiver. The English codes on the incoming call made him think it was Leroy. He could apologize; they could clean things up. "It's Will." Silence. "Hello? This is Will Duane. May I help you?"

"Oh, I was disconcerted when you answered, Mr. Duane. Leroy said that it was your personal number but I thought …"

"I'd have a secretary. Not when I'm home."

"Oh, dear. I'm sorry to disturb you …"

"Don't hang up." The voice was that of a young, supremely upper class Englishwoman. That was enough to hook Will. "Leroy gave you my number?"

"Yes, at the Ball. He said that he didn't know where he would be going and couldn't give me his phone number, but he wanted me to be able to contact him."

"He's in Scotland somewhere, getting a polo team together." Will had kept an eye on Leroy.

"Oh, yes. Everyone knows that. He's got Scots and Irish getting ready to tear our team apart. I think he'd like to tear my father apart." And me, thought Will. She sounded sweet and troubled. "But it's you I'd like to talk to, if you have time. I'm in a bit of a pickle."

Oh, shit. Leroy didn't get her pregnant?

"You see, since Leroy left, things have changed terribly in our family. I didn't introduce myself. I'm Arabella Faxmore, Lady Arabella. My father is Lord Ballentyne."

Will recalled that Leroy had stayed with them. Lord Ballentyne had raved about him. Will had visited the family in London, but not when Arabella was there.

"It seems years ago since Leroy was with us. May I confide in you? Leroy said you were a very nice person and liked to help people. He spoke so highly of you, and, well, I'm in the most dreadful difficulty."

"Certainly. Go ahead."

"Well, when Leroy was here, my father saw what a rotter Dash— Dashiell Pondichury, the ninth Duke of Lancature—was. He almost hit my brother in the eye with a bolt from a crossbow. Papa threw him out. I thought all was well. Father has wanted me to marry Dash forever, but he saw the man's true colors that day.

"Leroy went away, and Dash came slinking back. One evening, he and my father went into Papa's study. When they came out, they were smoking cigars and smiling at each other. Papa wants me to marry Dash again, most insistently." Her voice broke.

"I can't marry him. He's a really bad person. I can tell, and Leroy could tell too, but no one else. Since that evening, Dash practically has lived with us. He's replaced most of the staff. He wanted to sack Fulton, our butler, but I said that the village would talk. Fulton has been with us forever. They're already talking about all the Spaniards …"

"Spaniards?"

"Yes. Dash has vineyards in Spain. He's been bringing staff in from there. His best friend is a nob who has a castle …"

"Is his name Enzo Donatore?" Will sat bolt upright at his desk. This was way worse than he thought.

"Yes, he lives in a castle and has parties all the time. We're supposed to go there, all of us, Mama, Papa, my brother, and myself, as soon as the polo match is over. I don't want to go. I have very bad feeling about it."

"You should have the worst feeling you can possibly have, Lady Arabella. Do *not* go there." Will's body went to full alert.

"What am I to do? I'm watched day and night. I'm calling you from the coach house of my friend's estate. I'm here to play bridge, supposedly, but it was really to call you on the way home. I said I had to use the loo in order to get the driver to stop. The phones at home are monitored. I'm not allowed to go anywhere.

"What I wanted to say is I think Dashiell is taking money from my parents. More than that—properties. Estates we own. I think he's swindling them. It's as though they're bewitched. Whatever he wants is fine.

"I think Dash is taking everything. And then he'll take me. Papa says I have to marry him. Papa grabbed my arm last night. He *hurt* me. I have bruises." Will heard her voice tremble: a woman whose breeding would only allow her to sound composed was unraveling.

"He doesn't have *all* our money. I have my own, gifted from my Grandmamma, in my own name. I'm afraid Papa and Dashiell will make me sign it over. I have quite a bit, Mr. Duane. It may be all that's left."

"He's not getting it. You need a very good lawyer and right now." Will was enraged. Hurting a girl to make her marry a demon. Her father should be horsewhipped. Taking her money.

"Yes. Leroy said you had the best lawyers and liked to help people. Mr. Duane, I need help *so* badly. Would you please help me?"

"Yes. I'm going to call my London legal team now. Is there a way for you to get to London without suspicion?"

"Yes. I have a doctor appointment in the village tomorrow. I could go and tell everyone at home that I need to have a procedure in London. They wouldn't suspect, if I made out it was serious."

"All right. Give me your doctor's number. My people will work through him. You'll see a new doctor in his office, Dr. ... *Beckham.*"

Will made up a name. "Do you have your financial documents in your possession?"

"They're in the bank."

"Can you get to the bank safely?"

"No."

"Then Dr. Beckham will need some signatures and permissions for the procedure. We'll work it out.

"Lady Arabella ..."

"Call me Arabella."

"Arabella. You are in the worst danger you have ever faced. Is there any way of getting Leroy back to your estate?"

"Oh, no. Papa hates him now. Can't say enough bad things about him. I don't know why. He'll be back for the polo match and then—I'll never see him again." Her voice caught.

She's in love with him, Will thought. Shit. Where does this leave Cass? No matter.

"Arabella. We'll get this done. Do *not* marry Dashiell or be alone with him and especially don't have sex with him." She gasped. "He's a monster. You already know that.

"Dr. Beckham will be in touch."

Will got off the phone trembling. He wouldn't allow Enzo Donatore to ruin another young girl's life. But what if Leroy loved her now, not Cass? What if he'd been such a jerk that he'd ruined Cass's chances? No. First things first.

"She's going to need airtight protection of her assets," Will dialed his London legal team. "If it was here, I'd set up an untraceable trust and park it in the Caymans, but you know what to do on your side of the pond. She's watched at home and can't go out. Have a fake Dr. Beckham set up at the address of her current doctor." Will gave his London legal team the doctor's contact information. "All contact through him. She's in physical danger—I'd have the cops or our Numenon guys, or one of Hannah's English teams, ready to bust in."

"Hey, Chet. Will Duane here." Helping Arabella had warmed Will up to handle a problem closer to home. He dialed his friend Chester MacKay, the Chairman of the Board of the firm that had just acquired Havertin. "Just shooting the breeze. Actually, more than that. What do you know about the staff changes at the Havertin Institute that your group just acquired?"

"Normal in a takeover, Will. Our team can't work with the old team. You know about that." Will did. "We have to set up our guys and our culture as top dogs for the buy out to work." Also true.

"What do you think of Havertin's policy of not allowing family to speak with the patients?"

"I'm not a psychiatrist, but I understand that is one way of doing things, in the medium term at least. Parents and family are entitled to progress reports, but they want the patients to learn to toe the line. They can't do that if the patients get to run to mommy and skip out."

"What about emergencies?"

"I'm sure that in emergencies, the families would be allowed to speak to the patients and the patients can phone home. Why, Will?"

Will's throat closed down a little. "Well, my daughter's in Havertin now. You know that she's had troubles before." Cass had made national headlines when she stabbed a psych tech she said was making advances. The event became a women's cause rather than a simple attack.

"Yes, I recall."

"I admitted her to Havertin because I heard it was the best for very hard cases like hers. But I'm troubled by not being able to see or talk to her. I've always been able to do both, before. In other places."

Chet's voice was compassionate. "I understand. Maybe her not being able to talk to you is what will make the difference between successful treatment and failure. It may force her to get to work and face her problems." Will couldn't speak.

"I tell you what. I'm going to a meeting with the directors of the hospitals we own next week. What's your daughter's psychiatrist's name? I'll have him …"

"Her."

"… put on the meeting list and talk to her. Get a clear picture of how Cass is doing. I'm not saying that the psychiatrist will let you have access to her, but we'll get some personal interest going."

"OK. Thank you so much. I'll look forward to your call."

"Absolutely, Will. I'm sorry about Cass."

"Well, as you say, this may be the hospital stay that does it." Will heaved a huge sigh when he got off the phone. Maybe of relief.

32

THEY WERE A TEAM

DAYS AND WEEKS passed and they were a team. It took just under two months, the amount of time they had. The strange collection of over the hill, broken down polo ponies, untrained racehorses of dubious pedigrees, and rank youngsters with no particular breeding but the bodies of athletes it took someone like Leroy to see melted into a phalanx of equine conquerors. And the riders no longer needed liquid fixes; they needed Leroy, and their own souls.

"The uniforms are here!" Leroy announced, pulling a helmet out of a big carton. The black helmet had a stylized red buffalo skull emblazoned on the front. Black knit polo shirts and traditional white pants completed the ensemble. "Watches Ranch" was embroidered in red across the shirts' backs, up by the collar. Each had a red, old-fashioned pocket watch embossed on the heart. Their scarlet numbers covered most of the shirts' backs.

"We are the Watches Ranch Wild Buffalo!" Leroy made war cries while the men took their uniforms and added Scottish and Irish clan war screams.

One of the grooms came running out. "Stop! Stop! Y're makin' the horses crazy!"

Two days before they were to pile on the train to go to the match—horses and men alike—Leroy took Lightning out for a ride. He'd dubbed the laird's horse that. He was his favorite horse; he'd last into this thirties, with any care. Leroy needed to clear his mind.

He'd done this crazy thing and gotten an anti-British team together. He'd somehow thought word of what they were doing wouldn't spread. It had spread *everywhere*. Tom reported through the valet information network that if the Ballentyne estate had been a hotel, they would have reached record occupancies with people coming for the match. As it was, everyone in England with a drop of even potentially noble blood was packing into the mansion. Commoners of all stripes had jammed the local hotels and inns. They were hoping to see the polo match on closed circuit TV, and maybe a bit of the hunt the next day.

Leroy was ready for polo game and the hunt. He had trained himself a jumping horse with the help of the polo players. He thought jumping was great fun, but stupid. What horse didn't know that a fence was something to keep cows in, not jump over?

He couldn't understand what was going on in Ballentyne Manor. Why the crowds? Why the hype? It was an informal match, as was the hunt the next day, both out of season and on a private estate.

"Someone's spreadin' the word, sir, Leroy," Tom said. "Someone important. Lord Lancature's moved into the Ballentyne estate, sir. And they're all to go off to his friend's place in Spain after the match." Leroy felt like Tom had slugged him in the gut. "It's bad, sir, isn't it? This is real war." He could only nod. He needed to be alone.

The forest was deep out in the folds of the mountains. Not many trees out in the open in Scotland, but the mists and rains grew trees where the soil would support them. They weren't the majestic sequoias of his home, but the trees comforted him.

He took a trail he'd not traveled before. Leroy had tried to keep up his inspection of local monasteries, but had fallen away during his stay at the castle. Scotland had so many old ruins and holy places, cloisters and priories; looking at them all was impossible. Besides, Kathryn Duane's spirit had told him to give up time and again.

He pushed a leafy branch out of the way and headed down a steep incline into a fairly wide valley, and then into the uplands of Scotland. Pretty. Taking a new way was worthwhile. A brook gurgled by Lightning's feet. The place was hushed; a hum of insects, the little creek … just what he needed. He needed quiet solitude to search for an answer.

Last March, he had left his ranch to help his dad bullfight at one final rodeo. That resulted in the FBI chasing him to the Meeting in New Mexico. Where he met Will Duane, who called up the President of the United States and got him to call off the feds. Since then, his life had been crazy. Nuts. Insane.

He'd found and rescued his soul mate, only to lose her to her own father. He'd been turned into *My Fair Leroy*, charmed society, danced with debutantes, found and lost his other soul mate, met a living saint, who died on him, helped at an economic summit, searched for a mystical lady, and gotten a mongrel polo team together.

Why? That's what he was trying to figure out on this ride. Getting out in the woods on a horse was often the way to hear the voice of Spirit. "I don't understand, Great One. Why have you sent me on this strange pilgrimage?" He'd heard stories of the spirit journeys of many famous shamans. None had included Le Hotel Meurice or Hannah Hehrman.

What was it about him that attracted such bizarre occurrences? Leroy realized that maybe that's why all Grandfather's friends, and his Grandpa himself, looked at him askance and laughed. His was a crazy passage, uncharted with a big hint of Coyote, the Trickster. Where was he going? What was the next step after the polo match? He wouldn't go back to Will. What craziness was up ahead?

He sent his horse down the path, wherever it was taking him. Green, leafy, brook burbling, insects humming. He crossed a stream, pebbles lining its bottom.

Lightning stopped dead, raised his head and let out a monster-sized whiney.

Why? Horses whinnied to acknowledge other horses. He didn't see any. Riding around a bend showed why the old horse had opened its mouth. A farm with stone-walled pens was nestled into a hollow. He rode up; no one came out, so he rode around the animal enclosures. A few shaggy Highland cattle. He loved them.

A grey-white mare raised her head to answer Lightning's call. She stopped him in his tracks. "Come on, Princess. Come over here." She was in a rock-walled paddock.

The mare approached, ears pricked, showing as nice a disposition as anyone could want in a horse. He watched her. Perfect chunky conformation. What was she? Not a Thoroughbred, a hot and speedy racehorse. She was some kind of a pony. A big pony.

She reminded him of the horse Cass had been riding in that picture Will had shown him so long ago. She once had liked to ride. When she was well, she'd want to again, he was sure of it. He had not forgotten her for one minute as he struggled to build his polo team.

Longing gripped him. He had enough money to buy this horse at any fair price. He would ride her and make sure she was right. If she was, he'd buy her for Cass and ship her home.

"Hello!" he rode around the farm calling out. "Is anyone here?" He found the farm's occupants out in a field digging something. They were women, all dressed in natural homespun dresses to the ground with long sleeves. Their heads were bound with cloths. Seemed like particularly inefficient clothes for working a field.

"Excuse me, ladies. My name is Leroy Watches Jr. I've been living hereabouts for a couple of months. I'm getting ready to leave, but I wonder ... Who owns that mare? She's lovely."

All of them but one turned her back to him like he was something forbidden.

"You'll have to forgive my sisters, Mr. Watches," said an Irish-tinged voice. "Our order has very little to do with the outside world and we have nothing to do with men at all."

"Oh. I didn't realize there was a cloister near here."

"Very few do. That's the point, you see. But the Priory is an ancient refuge for those who find the outside world intolerable. This is our land." The nun had a plain, good-tempered face and coloring that blended in with the homespun of her kerchief and clothes.

"I see, well, I'll bid you good day in that case." He reined Lightning away.

"Wait, you asked about the mare. Mother is keeping her for her real owner. But I believe she said that she's given up waiting for her owner to claim her. She wishes to find a home for the mare with someone who will appreciate her. She's very fine, as you can see."

"How do I get to see your Mother Superior so I can discuss the mare with her?"

The nuns tittered. "She is not our Mother Superior, Mr. Watches. We call her Mother, because she is a mother to us all, and a mother of our faith. She is really our Anchoress. Her position is seated with her faith and holiness, not the Church. She stays within our cloisters and is in deep contemplation most of the time."

"I'd like to buy the mare for the woman I'm going to marry. I'd import her to the United States." He looked down. "My fiancée's name is Cass."

"I will send a messenger. Wait." The young woman went into what he had thought was the farmhouse. It was a medium-sized stone house with a big coop attached. When he was listening for them, he could hear the pigeons inside. A pigeon flew out the back and up the mountain, out of sight. The nun returned. "We'll know what Mother says in a moment."

"Can I ride that mare? She needs to be gentle for my fiancée."

"Yes. You do need to know if she will be suitable. She hasn't been ridden in years."

Leroy got on her with a halter and lead rope for guidance, after touching every inch of her body. Healthy, sound, no physical ailments. She was *beautiful*. Big black eyes rimmed with black. Her white eyelashes said she was a true grey; she'd once been darker but turned white with age. She was about eight, he thought, looking at her teeth. The perfect age for a riding horse.

They had a flat area beyond the mare's paddock. He took her over there. He put her into a walk, jog and lope, in both directions, and did some circles and figure eights. She was as good as he thought she'd be. Well trained with no vices. She was perfect for Cass.

When he got back to where he'd tied Lightning, he was ready to get on the gelding and storm the monastery's gate. Proved unnecessary. Another pigeon had returned.

The nun took the message off of its leg. "Oh. Mother wants to find a home for the mare. You may ride to the monastery gates." She pointed at a small rut in the grass, that led to a track barely visible through the trees. Not a high traffic route. He followed the trail. The monastery was out of sight.

He rode Lightning up the pathway and around the corner. The nuns disappeared behind him. His heart began to beat, banging away in his chest. His breath quickened when he rode around a bend and the convent was above him, halfway up a sheer mountain face.

The three-quarter angle of the tile roof with the odd little gargoyle beneath it was just above him as he rode in. You'd have to be at the height of a person on horseback to notice it; it would be invisible from any other angle. The tall chimney stood in the background, with stair-steps on each side, the flat parts tiled. He'd never seen that kind of handmade tile anywhere before, except on Fr. Marco's photo.

Kathryn Duane was here. Tears streaked his cheeks.

He kicked Lighting into a gallop and rode for the abbey's door.

All this traveling, all his visiting monasteries, had not prepared him for the stone jewel before him. It rose up the side of a steep rock, a mountain, really, cleaving to it as though emerging from it. Moss covered the building, the rock it sprang from, and the trees. Bright stillness surrounded him, but for the trilling birds. The abbey was the purest place he had been, apart from anywhere Grandfather lived. He could hear angels' voices. Leroy shook his head. Was he hearing nuns singing or angels' voices ringing the ancient stone? Protecting it? Kathryn was protected here.

The trees accompanied him almost to the door, but fell back to reveal the ancient wooden portal with the half-round top. The whole was bound by iron. Hand-wrought hinges reached from one side of the heavy wood, almost to the other. The building had a single-wide entrance; portals were not thrown wide here.

"Hello," he said. "I'm here to see the …" What did they call her? … "the Anchoress. About a horse."

"Come in, Mr. Watches. You may tie your horse to the ring by the entrance," a middle-aged voice said through a grate in the door.

Six stout, hand-forged rings were set into the stone of the walls. Once, the abbey had had more visitors. He tied Lightning by his lead rope, glad he'd left the halter over his bridle. "Lightning, you stay here. If I get lucky, we may be able to bring a present home to Cass."

When he turned around, a nun was standing by the open door. She wore the oatmeal homespun the others had and her hair was covered with something like a scarf.

"I'll take you to Mother."

He walked through the entrance and into a wide hall. Bigger than he thought it would be, the walls were stone, but the beamed ceiling was wood. Very old tapestries hung on a few of the walls, but the place wasn't like one of those royal palaces on TV. It was like a medieval hall, all stone and very plain. Just what he thought an ancient abbey should look like.

The nun took him to the chapel. Its walls were plastered, the wooden ceiling high and peaked. Little boxes were arranged around the sides.

"Mother will talk to you in that confessional." She indicated which one and left.

Leroy crept toward it. Kathryn Duane was the Anchoress, he knew it.

The confessional was made for medieval nuns, not late-twentieth century Watches. Leroy jammed himself in. When she saw what trouble he was having, the Anchoress laughed.

"Oh, Mr. Watches, I didn't realize what a trial this would be for you. We could meet elsewhere, if there was anywhere else that my vows would permit."

"No problem, ma'am. I'll just pretend I'm getting into my coffin."

She laughed again, honest and full of mirth. "You *are* funny. I've gotten reports from the castle that you are funny indeed."

"Where we're practicin'?"

"Yes. I am in seclusion, but I know what's happening in my district. Tell me about my daughter." Melodious voice, cultured, and fine. Seldom used, indicated by a bit of hesitation and huskiness, as though she was learning how to form words again. Kathryn Duane was a lady.

He told her about Cass's rescue and current hospitalization, including the brain damage and Will not being able to speak to her or visit her. "No one can."

She drew in a breath at that. "I see my former husband hasn't changed."

"He has changed, ma'am, just not all the way."

All he could see of the Anchoress was through tiny holes drilled in the wood between the two sides of the confessional. He saw hands with fine, long fingers. Oatmeal-colored cloth draped her form, like the other nuns' habits. He saw the side of her head where the cloth wrapped her face, revealing none of her hair. A refined profile and sculptured nose. He saw scattered images, moving as she did.

"You saved her, didn't you?"

"Yes, ma'am. An' I'd do it again in a minute. I aim to marry her, if I can. I'm thinkin' about bustin' in to that place when I get back and takin' her."

"I'd think carefully about that, Mr. Watches. Our friend Enzo is in play again. At the hospital, and here."

And then she blew his mind, telling him more than Tom had about what was going on at Ballentyne Manor.

"Should I go get Arabella now?"

"They would kill her. You must wait until the Holy Spirit gives you a sign. To move prematurely would cause death to both Arabella and Cass. You will know when, and you will know what to do."

"Oh, ma'am."

"Play the game, Mr. Watches. Play the hand that's been dealt you. That's all we can do. Play it perfectly and with intent to win. The Lord's grace will arise and give you strength when you need it. God bless you, Mr. Watches.

"You may have the mare. I bought her for Cass, hoping one day we'd be able to reunite. I see that is not possible. Take her, with my blessing and God's. Tell Cass her mother sends her with love.

"I'll take her down to where we're stayin' to ship her."

"No. I'll have her shipped. What about that marvelous horse you're on? Do you want him?"

"Yeah, I do, but I'm playin' polo on him."

"After the game, someone will come for him."

"All right. I gotta ask, Ma'am. Are you safe?

"Safer than anyone on Earth, Leroy."

He told her to call him if she needed him, he'd come from anywhere.

"I know, my dear.

"Thank you for what you've done for my daughter, Leroy. If she were to marry you, twenty years of my prayers would be answered. You have my blessing on your marriage, and all the love in my heart, my dear sir."

The interview was ended.

He rode back to the castle. Mrs. Duane was everything he thought she'd be. Elegant. Serene. Loving. Holy. Healed. His tears fell on Lightning's withers.

33

ARABELLA ABIDES

A T CLARY'S DEBUTANTE Ball, she'd told Leroy that she couldn't, or wouldn't, marry him. Without words, hardly with gestures. She hurt him, and she'd hurt herself. Why things had to be the way they were? Arabella didn't understand.

Leroy had told her to fight her father and Dash, and she was determined to do that. Leroy had told her about Indian women carrying knives for protection. The story moved her deeply. If they could fight, so could she.

She went to her doctor appointment the next day as she and Will had discussed. It was on the calendar; had been for ages. Her gynaecologist. No problem getting the new driver to take her to that and he certainly wasn't snoopy about following her in.

The new doctor helping her old practitioner was Clarence Beckham. He was a real doctor. From what Mr. Duane said, she thought it would all be play acting, but it wasn't. He examined her and said that she had a growth that needed to be removed and biopsied immediately. His main practice was in London; he'd make the arrangements.

"In two days, then?" he said. "Don't worry, we've caught it in time. You'll be able to have children, if we act."

Scared her to death. She had no trouble mustering tears when she told her mother. "I'm so afraid, Mama. What if I can't have children?"

Mama was running around, balmy, eyes bulging and twitching, jittery because of whatever Dash was giving her, but she got that right away. Arabella had better be able to produce children or Dash wouldn't want her. "You *must* be fertile. And we mustn't let your father or Dash know. Do you want me to go with you?"

"No, Mummy, I've got Compton. That's what a lady's maid is for." She could barely sit still in her mother's day room, Arabella was so upset. "The doctor is sending the papers for me to sign at home so I can get in quicker. I can have it done while Dash is in Spain."

"Good show, dear. No need for Dash to know at all. And Peter is hunting this week. He doesn't need to know, either."

Two nurses wearing uniforms and navy-blue capes came to the door with the hospital admission papers early the next morning. They were accompanied by a chirpy social worker in a poorly-fitting navy blue suit.

"Just wanted to make sure things were fine at home, Lady Arabella. Doctor noticed the bruises on your arm yesterday. There's been talk in the village of changes in the household. Might I speak to your mother?"

Good Lord, did everyone know? Dash was going wild firing staff and changing tenancies on the properties. He had the gardens torn up now, claiming he hated roses.

She went into her father's library with the nurses while the social worker cornered her mother and asked about Arabella's bruises. She heard a bit of the interchange.

"The girl has always been clumsy, ask anyone on the staff. Come here …" Her mother couldn't remember the names of the new staff. "*Fulton*, come in here. Arabella's always been a danger to herself, hasn't she?"

"I am absorbed in my duties, Your Grace. I see *nothing*." One nurse closed the door so Arabella couldn't hear anymore. She would always remember how Fulton's upright stance and compressed mouth voiced his condemnation without words.

"Your Ladyship," the taller nurse spoke to her as she sat at her father's desk, ready to sign. The other got out a notary's kit. "Here are the papers. Sign on the pages with the tags. Yes, the entire set." One nurse witnessed the signatures and then the other nurse notarized them. She had to sign in quite a few places. "We'll take a set with us, and leave one for you. We'll leave this set of documents here. No need to worry. We've done this sort of thing before. The procedure is tomorrow."

"That's awfully fast, isn't it?"

"In this case, it needs to be fast. Don't worry. Doctor is very experienced." She gave her the map to the hospital and check-in instructions. "You may be in the hospital more than one night."

You would have thought the cancer was real, the ruse was so well done. The papers for the bank, empowering the solicitors to act for her and remove her assets from the depository and stock brokers, giving them free rein, really, were interlaced with a real-seeming medical report, with printouts of ultrasounds, and everything. Lab results. The results said she had cancer. Even knowing it was a sham, her hands shook. The taller nurse took the version that had all the legal permissions, and left a copy of a real-looking medical admission document with all the reports.

Arabella wobbled back into the sitting room after the three women left. "Mother, are you all right?"

Her mother was as rattled as a goose chased by hounds.

"It's communist," Mama said. "How can they know everything that goes on? Doesn't a person have the right to change staff in her own house? The village people are jealous, that's it. They don't live like we do. Jealous little bastards." She gulped at a drink of what looked like straight Scotch.

"Arabella, you know that your father and I only want the best for you. Papa would never harm you. The other night, when he grasped your arm, he had simply imbibed a bit too much. He's been worried lately, with the rents declining, and taxes soaring. Your skin is so fair and delicate, it marks easily. He didn't mean ... a thing."

"As long as it never happens again, Mama. What might others say, who didn't know Papa the way we do?" Those words registered with her mother, even through the pills and Scotch.

Their driver took her to the hospital the next morning. Two nurses took her directly to her room, where she left some things so it would look like she was staying there. They escorted her straight out the back, disguised as an Arab woman in one of those things like a blue shroud that covered all of her. She got into a chauffeured Rolls and went straight to the underground garage of a legal firm in the best professional address in London.

She was escorted to a very posh office and talked to three barristers who made their family fellow look a fool.

The barristers posed difficult questions. "Your parents and Lord Dashiell are committing serious crimes in keeping you enclosed in your house. Your confinement is willful on their parts, without your consent, and its intent is to make you do something against your will, marry the Duke of Lancature.

"Unlawful confinement, Your Ladyship, is a crime and a civil wrong. We can move against all of them in court."

Her brows pulled together and she began to have trouble breathing, which she did when terribly upset. But she stammered out, "It will take too long. They're taking me to Spain after the polo game."

"That would be kidnapping, if you didn't wish to go. The authorities can stop that. We can stop that." Arabella was horrified. Coppers at the Manor? Accosting them at the airport?

"Oh, no. I couldn't."

"There's another tack to take. Deprivation of liberty is a serious offense, applied to those giving care to mentally-impaired individuals. We can act on knowledge that someone *might* be confined. We can act now."

"But I'm not mentally incapacitated."

"I'm not talking about you. Your parents are not behaving normally. Dashiell Pondichury is influencing them somehow, restricting their behavior. We could have people look at their mental soundness. Think about it, Your Ladyship. You need help."

The second barrister spoke, "The other issue concerns your family's wealth. Do you know if your parents have accepted money from Dashiell Pondichury?"

"I think they have, but I don't know."

"Have they sold or mortgaged any of your estates to him or anyone else?"

"I don't know." Her silly eyes filled with tears. "I'm sorry to be such a fool, but I don't know anything about our family's finances."

"That's all right, Lady Arabella, you've done the right thing with your own. You should know that mortgaging properties on the National Heritage List to foreign nationals is regulated. Dashiell Pondichury is a citizen of Spain, having given up his English citizenship several years ago. Has Pondichury registered the mortgages?"

"I don't know." Her voice became tiny. She didn't know Dash wasn't English anymore. How could she be so ignorant? And how could she charge Mama and Papa with serious crimes? Or with being mentally incompetent? She could have Dash charged, but if she moved against him, her parents would be implicated. And he had so many terrifying men around him. The servants. His polo team. Her cheeks flushed and she began to feel faint.

"Your Ladyship, you need to know how serious your situation is."

She did faint. They brought smelling salts.

"I think we should inform the authorities on your behalf. Now."

Mummy and Daddy kidnappers? "I can't accuse my parents. They can't go to prison."

"As you wish. If you don't wish the police to be involved, Mr. Duane suggested a private security force be in place at the polo match."

Did she blink? Nod? 'Bella couldn't remember. Everything was so awful.

When she went home two days later, her money was safe. Arabella didn't know where her money was. The solicitors had created a corporation to hold it and placed it where no one could find it. Her father or Dash could beat her to death, and she couldn't tell them where it was. She didn't know. She knew what she was worth. She had enough money to support them in some style, not the way they had lived with the London house and the Manor, but well.

Except for the disturbing issues the barristers brought up, the trip to London was a huge success. However, Dash sacked Compton when they got home. Dash found out somehow. His agents went to the Gynaecological Hospital and checked that she had been there and that her "procedure" was scheduled and completed. It was; records existed. But they saw through them somehow. Or suspected her of something else. An assignation? Meeting Leroy?

Esmeralda was her new maid, one of those odd, dark people from Dash's vineyards in Spain. Esmeralda eyed her with the most peculiar expression as she helped her dress. Frightening and somehow reptilian.

They had replaced most of the staff. One of the new people stopped her whenever she tried to leave the house. They didn't say anything, just barred her way. When she picked up a phone, she could hear talking and breathing on the line. Arabella was truly a prisoner. She should have told the barristers to act; they were right. She needed help. But it was too late.

She wanted to tell Leroy that she didn't care what her father said or did; she would marry him, if he would have her. If. Nothing had ever felt like dancing in Leroy's arms. She couldn't give it up because her father was a … bigot.

But Leroy had disappeared. Someone said he'd gone to Scotland to get up a polo team. She didn't know if that was true. Arabella thought of trying to find him, but everything changed too fast. Dash moved into the estate. Her father seemed positively enamored with him, letting him run the estate and all concerned with it.

In a home with almost one hundred bedrooms, dodging the attentions of an unwanted suitor wouldn't have been hard. But Dash was persistent and good at cornering her in odd places. Sniffing her out in wings of the mansion she hadn't visited in years. At first, he was quite circumspect with her. Tender, even. But that changed.

"You'll come to love me, Arabella. You'll love me and do anything I ask. Things you can't imagine, darling." He stroked her hair. "So fine. Your hair and skin. The perfect Englishwoman. As soon as we get some of the chub off of you, you'll be a heartbreaker." He reached out, so fast, and pinched the flesh of her side, hard. He laughed.

Her side hurt like blazes. She felt dirty and ugly. He thought she was fat. Arabella had *always* thought she was fat. Only Leroy had made her feel lovely.

Tears gathering in her eyes, she ran down to the armory in the basement. The Native American women carried foot-long knives. But they knew how to use them. What would she do with a knife? The police said that carrying a pistol did not increase the safety of the person carrying it; a lawbreaker could take it from them.

What could she do? She knew nothing about self-defense. "Oh, Leroy, I wish you were here. I'm so afraid. How can I protect myself?" She wasn't safe in her home. Arabella knew that Dash would have no compunctions about assaulting her if she crossed him. Or raping her either, marriage or none.

They lived like that, Arabella sneaking and hiding and trying to keep her little brother with her. He marched around, eyes fever-bright, swaggering like Dash. When the Spanish horses came, she knew she'd lost. Her brother stayed at the barn, worshipping the animals and the men who brought them. Out of anyone's control—but Dash's.

Her mother was the same. Wide-eyed, wild-eyed, she insisted on music and dancing every night. Sometimes she stamped wildly into the night with the Spanish riff-raff Dash brought, shrieking in her rendition of Flamenco singing. She insisted that Arabella sit with Dash at dinner and keep company with him in the drawing room afterward.

Papa sat with Dash for hours, telling him stories of hunts he'd ridden thirty years ago, living in the glowing past and letting the present crumble around them. The crazy burlesque grew more heated as the date of the polo match approached.

They had "the family discussion," just the three of them, and Papa finally told the truth. "Arabella, darling, we've been living a lie. I've known it for years, but couldn't face it. We can't afford our way of life. And now we're done in. Bankrupt. Belly up.

"Dash has saved us. He's paid our debts and allowed me to sign notes to him. He's paid for everything. We could not be living here were it not for Dashielle."

"We're going to be so much richer, 'Bella. Dash will reestablish us." Her mother added with joy.

"Did you sell him everything, Papa?"

"No, dearest, mortgaged everything to him. He holds the reins; we get the life we've always had. It's a miracle. His friend in Spain came up with the idea."

"Where are the mortgages, Papa?"

"Dunno. Expect Dash has them. He might have left them in the village bank until we go to Spain after he trounces that rotter Leroy. That, probably. When we get them, we'll pick up your papers too."

"My papers?"

"Of course, the deeds to your properties and securities that you grandmother gave you."

"Those are mine, Papa."

His face grew red and his brows dropped. His hands clenched and he was out of his chair, at her, screaming. "Listen, you spoiled little tart, you are part of this family. You will benefit from Dash's generosity more than anyone. He wants to marry you, 'Bella, make you an honest woman after that black …"

"What?"

"Dash told me what Leroy did to you. Good that you got rid of it, 'Bella, no one would expect you to carry that man's bastard."

She couldn't speak. They thought her trip to London was to abort Leroy's child?

"You thought I wouldn't find out. But I did. Dash told me. Good job, girl. And now you're going to do another good job, you're marrying Dash as soon as we get to Spain. He loves you 'Bella; he'll take you even after that black monster defiled you."

"Leroy didn't …"

"Yes, he did," her mother barked. "I saw him."

"What? Where, Mama?"

"In your room, of course. But I'll never tell." She dropped her voice and tried another tack. "'Bella, we're ruined. Dash has saved us. He wants to marry you so much. It's part of the mortgages, 'Bella. You marry him or he calls all the notes. It's such a little thing. You'll find it quite pleasurable. Dash will make it that way. It won't be like what Leroy did."

Tears burst from her and she ran from the room. On the way to her bedroom, Dash caught her, pawing her body with his reptilian hands, licking her with his long tongue. He ran his hands over her breasts, gasping with pleasure.

"I may leave you fat. These are so jolly," he pulled at the opening of her blouse, but she bent and pulled something from her low boot.

Pressing the barrel of the little pistol against his neck, Arabella said, "I will never marry you. Stay away from me or I'll kill you."

Dash jumped back, grinning wildly. "Oh, the bunny has some spirit. Breaking you will be delicious, Arabella. I can hardly wait."

Arabella hid. A person who lives in a house with a hundred bedrooms *can* hide, and Arabella did. She had one chance and one chance only. The polo game.

34

HORSEFLESH

THE WIND WHISTLED past Leroy's ears as he rode Lightning from the stable onto the polo field. He'd never been to the Ballentyne country house and had hardly spoken to His Lordship since the debutante ball. Ballentyne seemed angry with him for something Leroy couldn't fathom.

No matter, he'd been in warrior training with his Scots and Irish horsemen for the last two months. To them, the great mansions and castles were created from the blood of their countrymen. The nobility's rents and taxes and levies were used to build ostentatious masterpieces from their ancestors' impoverished bones.

Leroy kept that in mind as he rode toward the five-story block of stone, the grandest country mansion in England. Surrounded by a thousand park-like acres, the rock of the great house was streaked with age and mossy. Carvings and gargoyles covered its surfaces.

Statues ran across the top edge all the way around. Knights, they looked like, with mounted cavaliers on each corner. The statues must have been three times the size of normal people to look so big up there.

Flags flew from all of them, standards with the Ballentyne colors and the British flag. They'd gone all out, preparing for this day of triumph.

A month before, Tom had called a friend, one of the footmen at the Ballentyne's estate. "You won't believe it, Tom," his friend had said. "His Lordship's gone crazy, firing and hiring. Fulton's lucky he's still the butler. Some toff in Spain sent his Lordship all new horses for the match. An' riders too. They're here, skulking about the castle and scaring the housemaids.

"The worst is His Lordship's given Lady Arabella's hand to Lord Dashiell." Tom looked searchingly at Leroy when he told him. "Everyone knows that she doesn't like him, but His Lordship's set on the match. He's going to announce it after the game. Everyone at the castle's going crazy, sir ... Leroy, sir. The press will be at the match. His Lordship called them in. That isn't like him." Tom had paused before kicking out the last bit. "Dashiell Pondichury is the other team's captain. They're all professionals, Leroy. His Lordship let him hire *professionals*."

"Don't worry, Tom, they haven't beaten us yet." He'd spent his two months practicing polo and getting his mounts and riders working as a team. Working as warriors. And they were warriors. They'd find out how good in the next few hours. He'd told his team to expect the roughest, dirtiest game they'd played. His warriors replied that the Scots and Irish knew a thing or two about that.

Riding onto the field on the big grey gelding, Leroy could see the insanity the game had generated all over the estate. It was just a country polo match on a day that promised a downpour.

Wet clouds hung all around the polo field, yet the elite spectators were decked out for a summer picnic. Hundreds were seated on the mansion's rear terrace; so many portable chairs were stuffed onto it that those on the edges looked in danger of falling off. Below that, running dangerously close to the field, were more chairs, shielded by flapping white canvas tents.

On the driveways and creeping across the great lawns in the back were the common people, covered in waterproof mackintoshes and carrying umbrellas. They had some sense. He saw a van or two parked discreetly: TV stations.

What had prompted the elitist and publicity shy Lord Ballentyne to have media coverage? Leroy smiled. The reason was riding toward him. Dashiell Pondichury, the ninth Duke of Lancature, sat on an enormous black stallion. The creature had its neck arched and chin set as hard and tight as a horse could. He was covered with foam and sweat, and strands of saliva drifted from his mouth. Prancing like a locomotive, the stud looked like it might explode. Dashiell had been "working him down" somewhere out of sight. Didn't seem to have done much good.

Dash waved like they were best friends. "Look what I get to ride!" he called. "My friend Enzo sent them for the game. For all of us." He nodded toward the other three horses and riders on his team. All the animals had the arched necks and vicious intensity, plus the hindquarters and muscling to carry out whatever their riders might intend. Devil's horses ridden by the devil's men. Leroy had expected something like this.

The officials—two mounted umpires and a referee, all Brits—had another thought. They pulled Leroy and Lord Dashiell in before the game, but questioned only Dashiell. "That's not a polo pony. What is he?"

"Andalusian mix." Dashiell scowled, not happy to be questioned. "Polo ponies don't have to be purebred." Unlike the sleek and mostly Thoroughbred horses normally used for polo, these steeds had rounded hindquarters and arched necks. Their manes weren't roached—clipped flat with the horse's neck—as most of the polo horses were. Their manes were braided, the braids bunched up and tied so they stood erect, looking like big pegs sticking out from the animals' necks. Their tails, like Leroy's horses's, were clubbed, bound up around the bones of the horses's tails and wrapped with bandages so that only a hairless stump showed. The effect was feudal rather than sporting.

"But can he play polo? He looks too hot to do anything but huff around a parade ground," an umpire commented.

"Can you control him?" said the other umpire.

"I can control him." Dashiell snapped.

Leroy looked at the shanks of the bit hanging from horse's mouth. If the mouthpiece was anything like the sides, he'd seen instruments in the dungeon of the castle where he'd stayed that looked kinder. Medieval torture instruments. Dash's spurs must have come from the same place.

"You have to use those on them to make him pay attention?" Leroy asked.

"Ride your own horse, Watches. Is that old nag going to make it through the game?" Dashiell barked. The umpires turned their attention to Leroy's mount.

"Ah, yes, Mr. Watches, that was Sir Glamis's horse. Brilliant animal— in his day. Will playing today kill him?"

"He's sound and fit," Leroy said. "He'll do for a chukker." Lightning had a tendency to nod off when he wasn't in action. His head had dropped toward the turf. Leroy gently moved his fingers on the reins. The horse startled awake, ears pricked, looking for combat.

The game began. The two teams lined up midfield, facing each other. Lord Dashiell Pondichury; dashing, fair-haired and riding a horse that could have come from a fairy tale. With him were three professionals, unknown in the British Isles, but all had his Lordship's noble and handsome mien. And his fair looks. They rode black horses that could have been siblings of Dashiell's stallion. Their uniforms were pale blue polo shirts with purple clumps of grapes embroidered over the heart. Their white numbers covered their backs. White britches, of course. Those were traditional.

Against them rode Leroy and his team in red and black, a black buffalo skull outlined on his red helmet and red shirt front, and traditional white britches. His teammates were: an aging, Scottish pro polo player who had been out of the game since a horse fell on him two years earlier. A brilliant young Scottish rider, his game diminished just a bit by alcohol for a few years, but now very sober. And old Laurie, who said he had severed all association with the Irish Republican Army. They rode a mismatched set of horses: a gigantic draft-horse-looking thing with a wild pinto coat. A rangy roan with a bald face and a Roman nose. Laurie brought his own horse from Ireland, a fine Irish polo pony. It was probably older than Lightning.

The umpire tossed the ball between the two teams and the game was on. About two hours from then, something would have been proven. Leroy wasn't sure what. The game was six chukkers, each seven minutes long. A bell would announce the completion of each chukker. Three minute break between chukkers; five minutes at half-time. A neat, tidy schedule with timeouts only for mayhem or injury.

35

LADY ARABELLA

LADY ARABELLA SAT in an open tent at the edge of the field with her mother and the most prestigious women. They were arranged around an enormous table upon which a startlingly gaudy silver trophy was displayed. The trophy was totally unnecessary. This was an informal match, out of season. No league championship was involved; yet her father had commissioned it. She knew to whom he hoped to present it later. The staff moved around, serving them drinks. Arabella could neither eat nor drink.

She wore her signature pale blue, this time in a wool dress with matching coat; her shoulders were wrapped in a woolen shawl that was crewel-embroidered in her blue. It was cold on the field, though she felt the ice in her veins and her frozen hands and feet most acutely. On her head was an enormous hat of the type beloved by upper class Englishwomen.

It looked like a flying saucer wrapped in net with little pale lavender grape sprigs stuck all over. Dash had bought it for her; a present for what everyone assumed would be his glorious day. The hat was hellishly expensive; it was meant to highlight the wonderful announcement to be made after the hunt tomorrow. Or possibly tonight, if Dash won well enough.

Her stomach lurched and she stood unsteadily. "Be right back, Mama," she said, heading for the house. Her mother's eyes were unnaturally bright. The Duchess waved as though her daughter was embarking for the Orient rather than heading for the loo. "Tally ho, 'Bella!"

Arabella had to thread her way across the terrace through every parvenu and major greengrocer in the county to get inside her own house.

"Everything all right, Your Ladyship?" Fulton looked at her with worried eyes, which matched his worried demeanor. He was as distraught as she. Two months in the new Ballentyne estate had shrunk him. "I'm keeping an eye out for you," he'd said. They both knew why.

Arabella went back to her seat at the polo match. Mama's bright eyes followed her across the rear patio. Mama was watching her too. Seeing that she didn't bolt.

She was still a virgin. For how long? She knew something deep inside, in that place that knows everything. If she married Dashiell, she would also marry those three riders on his team. They sniffed at her as though she was already theirs. Arabella searched the field for Leroy, so anxious she could barely see.

The game was violent, the worst she'd attended. Dash charged into Leroy's grey gelding, hitting him with his stallion's shoulder behind Leroy's leg. It wasn't a foul, because Dash hit him at less than forty-five degrees. The gelding staggered, but didn't go down and Leroy drove the ball home. Leroy's team was ahead.

The score went back and forth: one to nothing, Leroy's team ahead. One to one, one to two. One to three, Dash's team ahead. Every chukker they changed mounts. Dash's blond team with their fiery black horses; Leroy's motley crew on a bunch of mutts. Leroy's team's mismatched mounts obviously changed each chukker. Dash's team went off to their corner between chukkers and milled about. More black horses were there. Arabella couldn't tell if they changed them. The horses acted as energized as fresh horses.

"Oh, my goodness, did you see that?" Lady Humphington gasped. One of Leroy's Scots had the ball, riding a rangy chestnut Thoroughbred. Two of Dash's gigantic blacks came up from the rear. One bumped him from the left, but within the rules. The horse missed a stride in the rear, but kept going. The other black horse bumped him from the other side, also within the regulations, but before it could get its feet totally under itself. The chestnut's hindquarters flew out from under it and it was down on the turf. Athletic, it leaped up in an instant, but the rider didn't. Screaming obscenities in *Gaelic*, Arabella assumed, the rider grabbed his leg. The horse had fallen on it.

"Stop play," umpire bellowed and whistled. The other riders turned to look at the fallen man.

"Oh, terrible luck, old man," Dash cried with false sympathy.

Leroy jumped off his horse, which stood as though planted to the spot he'd left it, and ran to the fallen Scot and began singing in a foreign language. Arabella could barely hear it. His language. He laid his hands on the fallen man's leg, stroking it. After the shortest time, the man sat up, and then gingerly stood. Grinning, he clapped Leroy on the back. "Where's my horse?"

The game raged over the field, the umpires galloping to keep up. Unable to move as fast as the ball. Unable to see what was really happening. The horses on both sides seemed super-charged. "Look! He did it again!"

The horses Leroy's team rode did strange things. One of Dash's men was after a squinty old Irishman Arabella remembered playing years before. The man on the black horse swung his mallet back, aiming not at the ball, but at the back of the Irishman's horse's knee.

"No! Everyone stood up." The scrappy horse stopped so fast that it slid across the turf. The viciously wielded mallet whizzed past its legs.

The horse spun on its rear and tore off, leaving the Spaniard looking bewildered.

"Not fair!" Dash shouted, riding to the umpire. "Those are cowboy tricks!"

"Not so, young sir. The original polo ponies were often ranch horses skilled in moving cattle. Nothing wrong at all, though had your man connected with that horse's knee, I would have called unfair, indeed. The clock is running."

They were on the third chukker; each side had scored three goals. Both teams looked ragged. However mismatched Leroy's team was, they were good at the sport. Arabella dug into her oversized handbag and pulled out tennis shoes.

"*What* are you doing, 'Bella?" Her mother's eyes widened more than the drug already had made them. She could see a vein pulsating at her mother's temple.

"I'm not going to wear £600 shoes on the field." She slipped her dagger pointed, high-heeled designer shoes in her bag. "It's almost halftime. I must do my part."

"Divot *stamping*," the matron refused the common term "stomping", "isn't for us, 'Bella; it's for *them*." She indicated the hordes behind them.

"Mother, Dash gave me this hat so he could see me out there at halftime, cheering him on." False smile, shaking lips, trembling hands.

"Oh. Well, if that's what *Dash* wants, you'd better do it." She smiled as though Arabella had invoked the name of God.

Arabella shot onto the field the moment the half-time bell rang. Once on the greensward, she pulled off the ridiculous hat and sailed it back toward her mother. It flew like one of those Frisbee toys. She ran toward Leroy, who was off of his horse, picking up divots and stomping them down like everyone else.

Dashiell's men took off after her, but Dash whistled shrilly. They came back and surrounded him.

36

LET'S PLAY POLO

"*PLEASE HELP ME.*" Leroy jumped when Arabella ran up to him and grabbed his hands. Her face was frost white and pinched, her hands like ice sculptures. "Please don't let him get me. Father told me I had to marry Dash. He'll kill me." Breathless, she tried to explain what had been happening at Ballentyne Manor. He looked up to where she'd been sitting. Ten liveried servants grouped around her mother, all on their feet, leaning in Leroy's direction. They'd be after her in seconds.

"We're all going to Spain after the hunt tomorrow. Something terrible is going to happen there … Oh please, I'm so sorry …" She was begging, terrified.

The half-time was five minutes. In American football, you could put on a whole concert between the halves of the game. Not in polo.

"Girl, he will *never* have you." Leroy grabbed her elbows and looked into her eyes. "I've got you." He pulled her to him, where her terror released. She grabbed Leroy around the waist, sobbing.

"Oh, Leroy, I've been so afraid," she looked at him, skin blotchy and tear stained, as beautiful as she'd ever been.

272 | In Love by Christmas

"Arabella, don't worry. My men are going to take you back to our stable area. They're going to guard you. We'll finish this game and then figure out what's happening. You are not marrying him. He will never hurt you. We'll sort all this out after the game." He waved at the huge mansion and the crowds.

Leroy climbed on his horse and went back to the game. He knew what he had to do. He'd conquered demons when he and Will were in Paris. "Tom, get the TV crews. I want one here," he pointed, "and one here. Bring in as many as you can get. Tell them to look sharp and they'll make their careers."

If the first three chukkers were rough, these were deadly. Dash's team did their "attack from both sides" routine again, staying barely within the rules. The umpires seemed disinclined to enforcing the rulebook, or noticing that fouls were being committed by Dash's team. This time they aimed the one-two punch at Leroy, who was riding a gigantic pinto that had to be mostly draft horse.

The horse took the blows from the black animals as though they were flies on its flanks. It swatted its tail and kept flying. Dash shot to block Leroy, crossing the line of the ball, the direct line between the ball and the goal. A definite foul.

"You've got to be blind!" Leroy screamed at the referee. "He was across the line of the ball on that play!"

"This is not America, Mr. Watches. Team captains do not argue with the officials on the field. Free hit for Lord Dashiell's team, thirty yards from the goal."

Leroy and his team backed off so that the goal would be undefended, as specified by the rules.

Dashiell made the goal. He'd have to be a blind toddler not to.

The umpires and referee were being coopted by Dashiell and his monsters. Some demonic magic was changing everything while he stood by. The blue team gloated and panted, riding by Leroy and his men. They were two, hard-fought goals ahead. The score was three to five.

"They aren't playing by the rules," Leroy whispered to himself. So why should *he*? How had he beaten them in Paris? With words. There, he wanted them to go away and not hurt anyone. Now he wanted them to show themselves for what they were and not hurt anyone. He wanted everyone to see.

In the fifth chukker, Leroy rode a high-strung bay mare, fastest of all of them. A failed racehorse, but a very good polo pony. He rode her in a Pelham bit, holding the double reins from each side of the bit crossed over her withers in his left hand. Clasping his mallet in his right hand, Leroy did a pantomime with that hand, pretending to release his lariat and shake out his loop. He swung his arm around like he was getting ready to throw. The mare didn't like the unaccustomed movement.

"Steady, mare. In a moment, you will be able to fly," he said in his language. The demons were watching from the corners of their eyes as they moved down the field, wondering what Leroy was doing. In his own language, he said, "Stupid demons. You will now show us how stupid you are. Umpires! Referee! You will wake up and see." He pretend-tossed the loop in the direction of one of the blue team riders, as though hauling him in.

The demon immediately crossed the line of the ball to go after old Laurie, formerly of the IRA and a damned good polo player, who was steering the ball toward the goal competently. The demon rider was not over the line to bump Laurie; he intended to ram him.

Laurie saw the black devil coming and let out a ferocious Irish war cry, "*Cromadh-abu! Cromadh-abuuuuuuuu!*" He spun his animal, which responded with the adroitness of a stock horse. Leroy had taught all the horses on his team how to stop and spin and back like blazes. Laurie charged the approaching rider, keeping his mallet low, not intending to do anything with it, obviously—to everyone, especially the TV crews, which Tom had placed exactly where they needed to be to film the field.

"You are a stupid demon," Leroy shouted.

He did not reckon on how stupid. The blue team rider, grimacing and screaming in some satanic dialect, swung his mallet at Laurie's head. Dodging the English had undoubtedly sharpened Laurie, who saw what was coming and ducked behind his horse's neck. The pointed end of the mallet hit the horse squarely in the middle of the forehead, where the mechanical bolt would have landed, had one been employed to put the horse down. The horse dropped stone-fast. Laurie was able to scramble off before the dead horse rolled over on its side and pinned his leg.

"Oh, ye stinkin' bastard. Ye killed ma Liam." Laurie threw himself on his horse as it lay in the field, "Oh, Liam. They killed ye dead. Oh, lad." Laurie howled in anguish, TV cameras recording. When he saw them, he leapt to his feet, screaming, "Ye saw that, bonnie lads! Make sure every man, woman, and child in the world sees what that," the phrase he used to describe the demon must have been Gaelic, "did to ma horse. Oh, ma Liam."

Leroy's mare got to use her speed as he raced to Laurie. This was not what he'd hoped the demon would do. And Laurie was distraught. He hugged the older man, blessing him in his language, stroking him, and alleviating his grief. "Liam is in a better place, Laurie. He'll always be sound with lots to eat."

"Really, Leroy?"

Leroy had his eyes closed, praying. "I see him, Laurie. He's in a bright pasture, waitin' for *you*, Laurie. I see him, true."

Leroy stood up and faced the officials. "You did see that foul? If you didn't, *they* did," he pointed to the cameras. "The game's over. I will not play with those cheating"—an extremely unflattering Native American word. Leroy took the mare's reins and started off the field when noise erupted.

His entire Irish and Scottish team, back-ups, and barn staff rushed onto the field, screaming, "Kill the bastards" in Gaelic. Leroy had that in mind, but it wasn't peaceable, and therefore outside his repertoire.

Lord Dashiell rode over, not even affecting crocodile tears. "So sorry, old fellow. Polo is dangerous. If you haven't the heart for it, I'd be glad to accept your admission of defeat." He swept his arm, indicating the entire castle, its grounds, and Arabella, wherever she was. What he would win.

"Sir, Leroy, if you wish to stop, we will finish the game," one of the Scots said.

Leroy smiled grimly. "No, let's finish it." He would destroy Dashiell Pondichury and he would do it on the field with everyone watching.

First, the knacker had to come, attach chains to the murdered horse's hocks, and drag poor Liam up a ramp into the bed of a high-walled truck. Laurie cried, but then turned toward the demons with his "*Cromadh-abu!*" The spectators moaned, but remained where they were, transfixed by the horror of death.

Leroy rode yet another horse in the fifth chukker, a straight up roan with wild eyes and the heart of a panther. Dodging the black beasts, Leroy drove through, flanked by his men, and made another goal hand-ily. The score was four to five. The team lagged, but not irremediably.

"You are stupid demons. You will show us what you are," Leroy sat his horse between chukkers, half-yelling at Dash and the blue team. He was riding a dangerous horse this last chukker. A good horse, an elegant and beautiful dark bay, but with a fatal vice. Which he hoped she would employ, if the situation arose, which he suspected it would.

"Stupid demons. You will show us what you are. You will not hurt anyone or any horses. You will create your own downfall by your vicious greed."

Leroy had the ball and was driving it toward the goal, square and true. Dashiell and one of his riders came up on him from the rear, one on each side, getting ready to execute their double bumping maneuver. Their horses moved at preternatural speed, faster than normal horses could move. They closed the ground inexorably. Leroy's mare was flat out.

The black demons rode up on each side of him, planning what? Murder? The mare grew increasingly nervous. Her ears flicked and she rolled her eyes. Sweat flew from her. The closer the demons got, the greater her distress. The instant the horse on her left moved in to bump her, she did exactly what Leroy thought she would. He just didn't know how *hard* she'd do it.

She leapt to the right in a way only the most athletic horse could, executing a jump that a stadium jumper would be hard-pressed to match. She vaulted up and to the right, rearing high and leaping far.

She landed on top of Dash and his horse. Her front hooves struck Dashiell's stallion's head immediately behind the ears. That spot, the poll, is the most sensitive part of the horse. It is the kill spot. Carnivores know it from birth. They instinctively bite right behind the skull, crushing the brain stem and spinal cord and producing instant death. When the mare's steel-shod hooves struck its poll, Dash's devil-horse dropped stone dead.

Blood rushed from the stallion, creating a vile-smelling stench. The mare's eyes seemed to double in size as greater terror took her. She thrashed and attempted to leap again and again, but she was unable to raise her belly off of Dash and the dead stud to jump free.

She panicked, repeatedly leaping and rolling from side to side, pulling her hind feet under her, trying to get enough traction for one great leap. Leroy was able to jump free early in her struggle. He flipped her reins over her head and attempted to calm her.

"Quiet, mare, calm down. You are all right." He sang in his language, but it did no good. Dash's eyes were wide open; he struggled to extract himself to no avail. Dash made guttural sounds of distress, but didn't scream in pain. Every time she moved, her body crushed Pondichury into the dead stallion.

Leroy had found out during his two-month-long training session in Scotland that the reason this fine mare had been so cheap was that two riders had bumped her and thrown her to the ground in a rough game years before. He thought he'd healed her; but her reaction had been much more intense than what he'd wanted.

"Quiet mare, be still," he said over and over. He tried to calm her and get her off of Dash, but he couldn't. The Lord remained underneath the mare, taking blow after blow from her belly and legs. He should have been crushed; the mare weighed over a thousand pounds, plenty to kill a fallen rider.

Finally, the horse heaved herself onto her feet and jumped hard, shoving with all her strength to clear the dead horse and Dash. Her front end provided most of the initial lift, but her rear end propelled her over the downed stud. Her rear hooves landed just on the other side of his corpse.

Dash's skull crunched like a raw coconut when her left rear hoof settled on it. Everyone heard it. The cameras rushed in, as did much of the crowd. Everyone (except for some of the aristocrats who thought it in bad taste) had been filming the match all day.

Leroy turned to Dash and tried to pull his body away. He screamed for help from the crowd. An ambulance. Doctors. Someone to save Lord Dashiell. He couldn't heal him; Dashiell wasn't human.

The dark blue ambulance drove onto the field, along with the knacker's truck, again. All those of strong stomach saw it. The dead horse lay there, black with a satiny, shiny coat ruffled by the wind. As the knacker set up his chains around the animal's hocks, the skin of the horse's face thinned and then fell away, revealing a complex electronic mechanism attached to metal pieces matching a horse's anatomy. The flesh quickly pulled from the *robot's* bones. It did have bones, long bones of metal, perhaps stainless steel.

A glass eye rolled in its metallic socket, revealing gears and electronic sparks inside. The once-beautiful animal, now a shiny, complex, and chillingly beautiful metal sculpture, rolled up on its breastbone, stuck its front legs in front of it, and heaved itself erect. Blood flowed from its trailing veins, along with scraps of flesh that hadn't fallen entirely away. Blood, streaming intestines, metal rods, and electronic flashes. A horse from a horror movie. The crowd panicked, clawing its way from the field. Only the TV crews stood their ground. This *was* a career maker, as that chap who let them on the field had said.

The metal head turned, and the thing opened its mouth. A roaring sound filled the field. The other "horses" responded. Their riders had already piled off and stood gaping. The animal—or something—trotted toward its mates. They nickered, ghoulish imitations of horse sounds. As one, they ran for the main road faster than Maseratis.

After filming their retreat, the cameras turned back to Dash, who looked as bad as a human being could, or at least his head did. Leroy stood by in anguish; he had not wanted him killed, just revealed.

The white mush, bone fragments, and blood that were his brain and broken skull quickly reformed, and black, scaled skin covered his wounds. His human flesh dropped away as the horse's artificial hair and hide had, revealing Dashiell Pondichury, the ninth Duke of Lancature, in his true form: a scaled demon, venom dripping from his jagged teeth, erect scales marching down his back to the end of his barbed tail. He saw Leroy and turned toward him, claws extending. Then he saw all the cameras. Crews from more stations had been arriving. All the big networks were there.

Enzo would not like this exposure.

"Leave here," Leroy said in his language. "Leave here and take all your spells and deviltry with you. Get away from me, Evil One!" He used a few more sacred words to drive away the satanic. Also to seal the images in the cameras permanently, so that Enzo Donatore couldn't corrupt them. So that the world could see.

Calling to his teammates in his rasping language, which replicated the sounds of the stones in the bowels of the earth grating, Dashiell headed for the treed park beyond the field, his "men" followed him. Tails and scales burst through their polo garb. They were exposed, and filmed by all the media in Britain.

Leroy was exhausted and at wits end. Crowds from the mansion were heading across the playing field, while the more timid guests ran for their cars. Camera teams and announcers with microphones approached. His team stood on the edge of the sward close to the barns.

"Great One, Ancestors, tell me what to do. I pray to you. What do I do now?" He raised his hands toward the heavens. The winter weather had been holding back for months so that Leroy could complete his errand in Switzerland for Will and get to Ballentyne Manor for his day of polo. Clouds had piled up around the estate as if waiting for a command. Leroy's prayer was that command.

The deluge was fast and utter. Nothing could describe it: the heavens opened and all the rain that existed fell. All the ladies in their stupid hats, the local gentry, including the owner of the new upscale market with the escalator from the first to second floor "just like in California," and everyone else who did not belong on the estate ran like chickens pursued by the most vicious weasel ever to draw breath.

The rain was part of their desire to vacate Ballentyne Manor, but the police cars blocking the drive told them that it was *really* time to leave. Officers of the law and crowd of ominous men in black raincoats poured out of their vehicles toward the mansion. The news people stayed where they were, putting longer lenses on their cameras.

What was left was Leroy, the Ballentyne family, most of their original servants, a whole bunch of Irish and Scottish polo players, and a small herd of horses of dubious merit, who could really kick butt like crazy. Or at least play polo.

And more kinds of cops than any of them knew existed.

37

SORTING THINGS OUT

LEROY TOOK CONTROL. He turned to his team, "Put the horses away an' see 'em fed. Then come to the house. I'll need you. Tom, bring Arabella out. Let's go back."

Arabella clung to him and Tom walked on her other side. They threaded their way along paths that were mostly puddles, soon to be small lakes. Rain whipped them and made talking hard.

"You're not going anywhere, 'Bella. You didn't see what happened when you were hidden in the barn, but Dash and his team, even the horses, showed themselves for the monsters they are. Let's go. Some things need sorting."

He put his arm around her and led her toward the house through the downpour. An umbrella'd crowd was milling around the rear patio—the press. Dozens of microphones were shoved in their faces, rain and all.

"What were those horses, Mr. Watches? Robots?"

"Did you know they were robots?"

"Lord Dashiell …" The rain slashed at them, almost blowing them over.

"Why is Interpol here? That's their van ..."

"You better get out of the rain before you electrocute yourselves," Leroy said. "Let us through. Lady Arabella needs to get inside."

Another crowd was inside, milling around the vast entry hall. He shoved his way through a troop of serious men and women in black raincoats. Behind them, toward the servants' stairs to the kitchen, the former staff of Ballentyne Manor clustered, goggle-eyed. Leroy decided to dodge the raincoats and get Arabella settled. He headed for the servants.

"Fulton, everyone." When he got them gathered round, he asked, "Why are you here?"

Fulton answered for all of them, "We were terribly afraid of Lady Arabella coming to harm. Everyone came to the polo match hoping to keep *them* from carrying her off. It was our only chance." The staff nodded agreement.

"Good. You're all hired again." He pointed at a young woman. "You're Lady Arabella's maid."

"Yes, sir."

"Take Arabella upstairs and get her out of her wet clothes. We'll need her in a bit, but she should get warm."

He gave 'Bella a little hug, "Go on, now. You're shivering." To the rest of them. "That goes for the rest of you too. Get dried off and cleaned up. Then get ready to work.

"Fulton. I'm sure Dashiell was planning a victory banquet. We'll eat it. No one can leave tonight." A gust of wind rocked the building. A loud crack followed by a crash indicated that trees were falling along the drive.

"Yes, sir."

The powwow was on in Lord Ballentyne's library. Ballentyne sat in his big wing chair, eyes bulging, cheeks going in and out like a blow-fish. "Jolly show, today, I'll tell you! Dash and his boys can really play." He scowled when Leroy walked in.

"What is he doing here? Arrest him! He assaulted my daughter. Dash told me all about it."

"No, he told *me* all about it and I told *you* about it," said Her Grace. "Terrible thing. I could almost see it the way Dash described it. Forced himself on her brutally."

"I never touched Arabella!" Leroy cried. "That's a lie."

"Yes, it is a lie," Arabella said, slipping into the room. "Nothing but lies in this place. Leroy never touched me, but I lived in terror of Dashiell Pontichury and his men day and night."

"As well you might, Lady Arabella," an odd-looking little man with a bald head held a bowler hat in his hands. "We're with Interpol." He turned to Lord Ballentyne and his wife. "We suspect Dashiell Pontichury of murdering his previous three wives."

"Oh, Dash wouldn't do that. He's never been married." The puffer fish's cheeks bulged and shrank. Bulged, deflated.

"Dash has *never* been married. He wouldn't hurt a fly," said Her Grace. "Let's stop this dismal talk. It's bad enough that the rain cancelled the polo match. Why don't we have a little drink? Cheer us up.

"Does anyone tango? I absolutely *love* it! Dash has transformed my life! We're going to Spain with him tomorrow!" Her eyes bulged. A fleck of saliva escaped her mouth, shooting past the shocking pink, smeared lipstick on her mouth. "A little tango, and then some din-din? Fulton? Where is that man?"

A mousy woman in a rumpled tweed suit came forward, gesturing for the others to be quiet. "Let me handle this. I'm from National Health." She knelt by Her Grace. "Are you aware that the polo match ended when Dashiell Pontechury's horses were exposed as robots and he and his men as monsters?"

"That's impossible. Monsters aren't real. The rain. The match was called off. Peter ..." Lord Peter Ballentyne kept opening and closing his mouth.

"You don't know what happened?" said National Health quietly. "Where were you sitting?"

"In the front row of the gallery, with everyone. Everything is quite straightforward; we're going to Spain tomorrow. Dash saved us." Her Grace craned her neck, looking for approval.

The guy with the bowler hat stepped forward, "Lord Ballentyne and Your Grace, Dashiell Pondichury, under a number of aliases, is suspected of the murder of three of his spouses and their families, as well as the unlawful appropriation of their assets. The situations involved wealthy families with income shortfalls but substantial assets who were lured by him into thinking he could save them. He married their daughters, as a condition of the financial assistance, and then they all disappeared.

"What do you think of that?" The woman from National Health stepped back, searching the faces of the two older people.

"It's impossible. Dash showed us pictures of his vineyards, his castle. Of his friend's castle. We're going there," His Lordship blinked and shook his head, denying everything. "They were very real, I assure you. Dash *is* the ninth Duke of Lancature."

"The dukedom of Lancature doesn't exist. Dashiell Pondichury, also known as Evan Niell, Nylan Jones-Schmitt and a few other aliases, owns nothing. His friend," said the fellow from Interpol, "is a major industrialist, Enzo Donatore. He currently owns the properties of Pontichury's missing wives' families. He obtained them through legal, but suspicious means. Donatore is being investigated for a number of international crimes, which I cannot discuss."

"He is also being scrutinized by MI15, domestic intelligence, which I represent," a tall, thin fellow way in the back bowed. "I can't say what's being investigated, just that you're in deep and muddy water, Your Lordship and Your Grace.

"The word 'treason' has often been used with respect to Dashiell and his associates. Including you. MI16, international counterterrorism, suspects that you've been laundering money for illegal enterprises globally.

Flows of cash leave your accounts and go to various countries. You're an intelligent man; you should have seen the impropriety of this."

His Lordship sputtered, "No. Those transfers were perfectly legal. Dash said so. Just setting up the financial arrangements …"

"*Your daughter would have been murdered* if you had gone to Spain. Murdered, but *brutalized* first." A good-looking, middle-aged man in a black suit almost shouted. "She came to my firm in utmost distress, terrified for her life. We were able to save her assets. But her *life* would have been forfeited if we didn't protect her from *you*. Don't you understand *that*?

"We *did* protect her, calling in interested agencies," he waved his hand, indicating the crowd in the room. "I am Lucien Craig, Queens' Counsel, of Freinheim, Tarne, Craig, et. al., representing Lady Arabella."

"Solicitors and barristers, cabbages and kings," Arabella's mother waived her index finger, grinning foolishly.

"Her Grace is intoxicated," Leroy said. "Dashiell hooked her on something. Look at her."

The woman from National Health pulled a pen-light out and peered Arabella's mother's eyes. "Her pupils are pinpoints."

"She wasn't like this," Arabella's eyes misted. "Mama has had problems at times, but not like this."

"Oh, you're such a piker, 'Bella. No fun at all." Her Grace looked around the room as though in the middle of a party. "I'm not inebriated. I just feel good. Is that a crime?"

His Lordship sat silently, puffing, not appearing to understand anything. "Dash *saved* us. He paid our bills and taxes. He saved the Manor. We gave him mortgages; that's only fair, but at very low interest rates. Our solicitor said it was a great idea."

"Where is your solicitor now? I represent Lady Arabella. My colleagues and I are here to assure her rights. Where's your boy?"

"Don't know. Suppose he couldn't make the polo match with the rain. Pelting down, isn't it?" The lights flickered. The rain lashed the windows of the old mansion. "Who would come out on a night like this?"

"We'll need to do more thorough clinical interviews, but as far as I am concerned, neither of them is mentally competent," the National Health lady said.

Arabella made a little bleat, but Leroy touched her arm and soothed her.

"Since they are not mentally competent, they cannot enter enforceable contracts, including the mortgages they signed on their properties." That was Arabella's lawyer. "Have those mortgages been registered to Dashiell Pontechury?"

Someone else answered. "I'm from the Royal Bank of England, Sensitive Investigations Unit. We found the documents in Pontechury's safe deposit box at the bank in the village. They have not been registered in any name but that yours, Lord Ballentyne, though they do bear His Lordship's signature. Cagey bastard, … excuse me, ladies. Dashiell was so lazy and sure of himself, he thought he could let them lie around and not even move them to a more secure bank."

"So we still have the estates and the Manor?" Arabella looked delighted.

"No. Not quite. I'm from the National Trust," a dour gentleman spoke for the first time.

"And I'm from Her Majesty's Revenue and Customs," said another. "The taxes on these properties are in arrears. You'll have to pay them or forfeit the estates. They'd make great additions to the public …"

"My firm represents Lady Arabella. We cannot discuss this further. Lady Arabella needs informed counsel. I suggest that we meet with members of HMRC after a study of the matter."

Leroy smiled. Arabella's lawyer was on the ball. Maybe Will Duane did have the best lawyers in the world.

Thunder shook the house, volleying first on one side of the mansion and then the other. The lights flickered again.

"We need to wrap this up while we still have light," Leroy said.

"I need to have some papers signed, Lord Ballentyne and Your Grace," the National Health lady moved forward toward the old couple. She had a folder of forms, already filled out. "We're going to put you in a hospital for evaluation. That will determine your mental competence officially. If you are incompetent, then the mortgages you signed are invalid."

"Do we have to give the money back? I spent some of it," said the old "Lord Blowfish."

"Yes, you will."

"Then we're not signing anything and we're not going anywhere. Where's Dash? We need to talk to him." He crossed his arms in an expression of defiance.

"If you are mentally *competent*, Lord Ballentyne," said Arabella's solicitor, "then the Crown will raise more criminal charges against you than you can imagine, plus the issue of human trafficking." The lawyer and everyone in the room glared at the old man.

"Human trafficking?"

"Yes, the condition of Dashiell Pontichury's giving you the mortgages was your daughter, was it not?"

"Yes, of course. He wanted her as part of the package. How's that ...?"

"Ask those missing women and their families. I'd sign the papers and go for a nice rest, Your Lordship."

"Do you think I should set a formal table for the people from Interpol and the others, Mr. Watches?" Fulton asked Leroy.

"No. I'd make it easy for them. Just five or six pieces of silver. Make up rooms for everyone too. Trees are down on the road. No one will leave tonight."

38

DIFFERENT THAN
ANYONE IMAGINED

DINNER WAS A little different than the aristocratic, formal banquet Dashiell Pondichury had planned to celebrate his victory. The rough Scots and Irish polo players sat at the grand banquet table, thrilled to see the tables turned, quite literally. Lady Arabella, Leroy, and more representatives of Her Majesty's various investigative and enforcement agencies than most people knew existed completed the company in the dining room.

Peter Faxmore, Lord of Ballentyne, and his wife, Her Grace Violetta, the Duchess of Raddenbery and Cloudfill, sat in the morning room, eating at the breakfast table, surrounded by people from National Health. Their son Allie joined them. He had made the mistake of trying to bite the woman in the rumpled suit.

Leroy sat at the head of the "grown-ups table" in his tailcoat and white tie. Why not? The table resembled the runway for a small jet, if one could be set with blazing candelabras, flowers, and sterling silver. The staff served the grand dinner Dash's culinary crew had been working on for days. Leroy blessed the food, getting rid of any demonic residue.

Fulton had seated him at the head of the table, with Arabella to his right. The arrangement caused Leroy great discomfort. He had once liked His Lordship and Her Grace. He had no desire to usurp their places. He could repair them partially, but given that their staying out of jail depended upon their dementia, he thought the Ancestors would forgive him passing up a healing this one time.

He knew his silverware and glasses, and how to make polite conversation better than anyone but the Ballentyne family, but etiquette wasn't the problem at this get-together. It was Arabella and his clothes. He had heard that men who had been in battle often wanted sex desperately. They raped women because of their overwhelming desire. Leroy had been embattled all day. He would never rape, but his skin screamed for her touch. His lips throbbed and fingers pulsed. He wanted her to rip off his clothing and do the same to her.

Something had become very clear to him: whatever he once had thought was going to happen with Cass was off. The world had tilted.

Arabella leaned toward him, her pretty face and tinted lips smiling. She was sad, but the soft silk dress she wore rippled and revealed. But never revealed too much. She was a lady.

Everyone accepted Leroy at the head of the table and family. His unfortunate skin color was forgiven, or unnoticed.

"I've never seen it rain like this. Like it's been holding off for months." The group kept looking out the windows at the downpour. The wind was blowing so hard that the rain flew sideways. The shutters shook and the ceiling moaned. Lightning flickered and the thunder seemed as though it was coming from inside the house. Dashiell had hired a quartet to play after dinner, one that specialized in tangos. That was out. No one was in the mood.

Leroy went to his room, but not to rest. He couldn't leave Arabella and her tattered family like it was. He pulled out his case with the crosses and menorah, buffalo skull and painting of the great eagle, the brilliant line that marked the divide between life and death.

Arranging the holy objects where he could see them, Leroy sat cross-legged on the floor before the fireplace and lit his pipe, raising it high and low and to the four directions. Leroy slipped into the world of Power.

"Ballentyne family—Peter and Violetta, Arabella and Allie—come to me, here." They came, as spirits detached from their bodies. They sat cross-legged around him, looking as they always did, except see-through. "You have been through a great trial and need healing. You have been in contact with a demon and damaged.

"Peter and Violetta, I allow you to understand the errors you have made. You will feel them. I do not heal you." He smiled. "Mostly because, if I healed you, you'd go to jail. You need to be as crazy as you are now. You will have to find your way out of the maze the way ordinary people do. But know that you will be whole when you have righted yourselves. Young Allie, I remove the taint of the demon from you. I free you to make your own choices and go your way in peace.

"Peter and Violetta, you commanded great wealth and wasted it on things that didn't matter. You had power and gave it to a false god. You put Arabella and Allie's lives and souls in danger, and your own.

"You have been stupid, and you will pay for it. I absolve you nothing. I take your personal power, Peter and Violetta. You have no more power. Young Allie, I take your power until you show me you deserve it.

"Arabella, you are the only one strong enough to see the demon as he was. You were the only one brave and smart enough to fight and save yourself and what you had. Arabella, I heal you of fear and damage. I give you all the spiritual power of your family and ancestors back to the dawn of days. You will use that power for good for yourself and all of the world."

He sat with them a while and told them to leave.

Leroy knew he wouldn't sleep that night. The day swam in his mind. Monsters and mechanical horses. Laurie's brave horse killed. Every kind of cop in the world. Lord Ballentyne and his wife totally nuts. What now?

What about Arabella? What about Cass?

Was Cass in his life at all? Since he'd left for Scotland to get ready for the polo game, he'd left two messages on Will Duane's phone. Will's phone was the highest tech ever made and backed up many times. He knew his message wasn't lost. Two months before, Leroy left his first message. He'd said, "I'm going to Scotland for a couple of months to train a polo team. You've got my number if you need me. How's Cass?" Not too friendly, but complete.

Will had screamed at him in a way that no one ever had. Time passed. He sent him another message, reflecting other feelings, which were closer to forgiveness. "We're playing Lord Ballentyne's team in an exhibition match right before Christmas. If you'd like to come, let me know. They'll make up a suite for you. How's Cass?"

No answer. Will must have seen that afternoon's TV coverage where Dashiell Pondichury turned into a demon and ran off the field with his robot horses. The broadcasts from every major station had covered the world. That would wake up *anyone.* Will had not called. Leroy's phone was a monster portable phone with a satellite antenna. He could use it anywhere in the world.

The relationship was dead.

What did he owe Will, aside from the cost of the extravagant trip? He'd looked into Cass's tormented eyes for seconds and held her unconscious body for a few hours in an ambulance. Was she still alive? She zoomed in on his dreams like a banshee-in-distress, but was she even alive? No one had told him.

Could she be healed? Will had maintained that she couldn't, which was why Leroy couldn't see her. Made no sense, but maybe it did. Maybe Cass hadn't gotten any better. Maybe she was a raving maniac ready to jump into the first addiction she could find? Did he want her if she was incurable?

No.

He wanted his father's advice. That rascal was taking the Will Duane route. They'd played phone tag for a few weeks, and then Leroy gave up.

"Grandfather?" he prayed. "Could you pay me a little visit like in that hotel in Paris? I need help." He didn't think the shaman would come; everyone else deserted him.

His Grandfather obliged. Leroy could see his shadowy outline in front of the fireplace in front of his bed.

"Grandfather, you're here!"

"Of course I'm here. I love you. And your life is so exciting. I've never had a spirit warrior have to choose between an English noblewoman and the daughter of the richest man in the world." Grandfather would have clapped his back, if he weren't a specter. "Good job, my grandson."

Leroy slumped, miserable. "Yeah. Great."

"Not only did you find *two* of your soul mates, you …"

"Does everyone have more than one?"

The old ghost shrugged. "I don't know, but the Great One *is* big-heartedness, Leroy. Not stingy at all. Everyone probably has many soul mates. That's efficient too. The Great One wants soul mates to marry and have children so the world is a better place. What if you had just one? Say one soul mate was in Asia and the other was in South America. How would they ever meet?"

"Then why do people get so excited when they meet their soul mate?"

"They always look in the wrong places. Bars and places like that. They should go to church. Where did you find Cass?"

"She was in a whorehouse. And Arabella was in a giant mansion where they wouldn't let me in except because I was Will Duane's … *boy*.

"Grandfather! What should I do?"

"Arabella is really something, Leroy. Her room is very easy to find. You go back to the main landing, turn left and down the other big hall. Her room is the third on the right. Facing the front of the house."

"What are you doing? You're supposed to be helping me."

"I am. She looks so soft, but she outwitted the demon. Smart. And strong. Doesn't she look pretty in blue?"

"What are you doing?" Grandfather had disappeared. Shit. His grandpa had gone, leaving his tip of the day: the location of Arabella's room.

He wanted to hug and kiss her until her hands lost that terrible chill he'd felt and her face returned to its normal sweet self.

But he was afraid of what would happen if he walked into her room. What if he took her in his arms, and laid next to her? What if he saw that fine, pale skin, and her cloud blue eyes up close? If she lifted her lips to him, what would he do? She was his soul mate, as much as Cass, but differently.

Cass, even if she hadn't been ruined, would never be as sweet and willing as Arabella. Cass would always be a handful like that racehorse he'd ridden on the polo field. Fast, and quick, and exciting.

Arabella would make him happy.

"Arabella?" he knocked at her door. The lady's maid opened it.

"Her Ladyship is sleeping, sir."

"I'll just peek in. I wanted to see that she is all right."

"Yes, sir." The maid left.

Arabella's face made the palest ivory and the most lustrous pearls look coarse. She lay on her back, one hand drawn up by her cheek. Quilts of finest silk, sheets of embroidered cotton covered her to her chin. Her eyelashes were a soft brown next to the glow of her skin. He brushed the fine, pale hair from her forehead with his fingertips. He leaned over and brushed her cheek with his lips. He leaned over and fell in love.

When he lifted his head, her eyes were open. "Leroy." She couldn't say more. Her arms pulled him down. She buried her face in his neck, shuddering. "I was so afraid, Leroy. Dash was going to marry me, and they were all going to …"

"But they didn't, and they never will. I'm here."

"Leroy, Papa … And Mama … Allie …"

"I've helped them, 'Bella, as much as I can."

"Please, don't leave. I think I'd die if you left." A hand shot out and drew him closer. He could feel her soft breath on his face and neck. She didn't smell like anything, except sweetness. His lips drifted downward. He drifted downward, until he was lying next to her on the bed. She was kind and sweet, with a soft chubbiness that wasn't quite fashionable, but he loved.

Fire ran through him, through her, all over them. Soul mates. She grabbed him, plastering her body against him. He could feel her breasts, soft hips, the roundness of her. She seemed to be suspended in the air. She pulled his face to her and kissed him, holding the back of his head.

He responded like a bass to an expertly fished Zara Spook lure. Leroy's mouth grabbed hers and held on. She kept touching and petting, with both hands. Leroy was on a losing course.

She moaned, moving without guile. "Oh, Leroy, I want something …" She didn't know any more than he did what she wanted.

"Me too, 'Bella." His spirit warrior's virginity was going to be lost in the bed of a beautiful English noblewoman and he didn't care.

And why should he? He felt something real and true for her, the soul energy that would bond them for a lifetime. She was lovely and had a title. She still had her money. He didn't care about that, but he had some ideas about what they could do. They could make this place a better hotel that Le Meurice. Leroy stopped fighting her and began kissing and touching in earnest.

Cass's eyes burst into his mind, wild, and frantic. She needed him desperately. Leroy couldn't stop. He fought with himself. Fumbling and mumbling, he dragged himself from Arabella's arms. "I'm so sorry, 'Bella. I can't."

"Oh, I didn't mean to force myself on you. I've never behaved like this, but …" She frowned, studying him and realizing she wasn't the problem. "There's someone else?"

"Yes."

"Who?" Pale fire lit her eyes.

"Cass Duane."

Her eyes widened in horror. "*Really*?"

"Yes."

Arabella pulled away. "Oh, Leroy, you can't be interested in her. She's awful. Is that why Will's giving you this trip? So you'll marry her?"

"There's not enough money in the world to force me to marry someone I don't love. We're soul mates." He wanted to shut up, but couldn't. "Just like you 'n' me are soul mates. I've got to leave." He spun and left the room.

When he slept, he dreamt of a soft woman in blue who loved him in her dreamy way, giving him everything he wanted, mostly herself. He could see them on the mansion's rear patio, laughing as Fulton and a gang of maids waited on them and their kids. Softness surrounded him. That skin. Those eyes. Her sweetness. A good, gentle life.

Cass burst through those dreams, a Molotov cocktail tossed into a polite drawing room. "Help me!" she screamed in his mind, real screams from the girl who didn't get away. "Don't leave me, Leroy. Don't forget me! I love you." He sat up in bed sweating, feeling his heart pound. He got up and got a drink of water, wiped himself down with a damp cloth. He paced around his room a bit, stoked the fire.

He needed to marry Arabella in the next twenty-four hours or go back to California and make Will tell him where Cass was. Shit, he could take some of the warriors and find her himself.

A faint knock that might have been his imagination sounded at his door. He didn't answer. It occurred again. Maybe there was a problem somewhere. He put on his robe and went to the door.

"Yes?"

Arabella pulled him into the hallway. She threw herself at him, grabbing and kissing. She didn't ask, and she didn't stop. "Leroy," she gasped.

He lunged, spinning and shoving her back against the wall outside his door. He lifted her up so that her legs could reach around him. Neither of them knew what they were doing, and yet they knew, because every creature knows what they were about.

He let her kiss him again and again. He let her do more than that. He liked her soft flesh and warmth, her probing tongue. He'd like everything she offered. She certainly wanted to give him more. He felt her body and let her touch him until he was groaning. Sweat covered him.

He wanted to rear up on her like one of his stud horses on a mare. He wanted to do it again and again, as he heard the little noises she was making. She moaned for him. He wanted to roll with her all night …

He opened her robe and searched under her gown. She was wearing panties, just a wisp between her legs. His fingers slipped along their elastic, seeking an edge.

Everything, all the Ancestors, Kachinas, Supernaturals, the nailed Jesus and the plain cross reared up all around him. Inside him. They said: NO! He stiffened and let her feet gently drop to the floor.

"I can't, Your Ladyship, not until I've sorted it out with Cass."

"How can you do that? How can you leave me like this?" Her hair was messed and her features swollen. Her lips parted. "Please. Help me."

He did something he'd not done before. Placing his hand in front of her belly, he let some energy go through it. Pulsing. Warming. Pleasuring. She convulsed and fell against him, limp.

"Oh, Leroy. What did you do? Oh, my God." She wasn't frantic anymore. She shuddered and wilted, clutching him. "I love you, Leroy."

He did it again, stretching it out. She shuddered harder and longer. He watched her, fascinated. He wanted to see her full out, no stops. He wanted to see her spread for him, all night, not just twice.

NO! said all the sacred ones around him.

"I like you like that, Arabella. I want to make you feel good and know how much I like you." He stopped. "No. I *love* you. I do. But I'm not free."

He heard his cell phone ringing in his room. Only one person would be calling. He went in and pulled the antenna out of the boxy brick.

"Will?"

"She's in bad trouble. Leroy. She may be dead. It's my fault. I was wrong about everything; I need you. Please ..." The old man could barely talk. He sobbed and hiccoughed. "Please. I'm sorry."

"You got me."

"You've got to get to New York, fast. Doug and Hannah are already on the way. Havertin ... They're killing Cass. Can a plane pick you up?'

"A helicopter could land in the front lawn, if you fixed the lawn afterward. There's a big storm here. Fifteen minutes? I'll be ready."

Arabella was standing in the doorway. She straightened her robe. "What's happening?"

"Darlin', I have to leave." She looked stricken. A row of velvet pulls hung on the wall by his bed. "Which one of these do I pull to get Tom?"

"The servant's rooms are here." She pulled the correct velvet rope.

"You'd better go. You shouldn't be in my room."

"I don't want to go."

"Then stand out in the hallway so no one thinks you and I ... I have to change my clothes." He shut the door. A few minutes passed.

"Sir. What's happening?" Tom dashed up and Leroy opened the door.

Arabella gasped when he came out into the hall. Leroy wore a black shirt and black jeans. Earrings studded his ears and a black scarf was tied tightly around his head. Brilliant marks flared on his skin. They looked like glowing brands. The feathers on the back of his neck glowed as though they were on fire.

"Tom. I need you to pack my stuff. You and Rich drive the car back to London. Pack up my clothes and send them here," he handed over a piece of the Manor stationery that was stocked in each room. He had debated on where to have his things sent. The ranch? Will's? He was too pissed at Will and his dad to use either address. He gave the Numenon headquarters, care of Doug Saunders.

"I'll leave," He looked at his watch, "in a couple of minutes." The rain had stopped. "Will is sending a helicopter. Arabella, gardeners will be out tomorrow to repair the damage to the lawn.

"Things will straighten out, Arabella. Use your lawyers, and use Fulton. And use Tom." He turned to his valet, "You'll help her, won't you?"

"Yes."

"I will never forget *you,* Arabella." He kissed the soft flesh inside her forearm, his lips lingering the tiniest bit.

Then he gave up fighting and pulled her to him, lips melting together, bodies all but fusing. He showed her the tiniest bit of the passion he felt for her. But he broke it off.

"Is it Cass?" Arabella's cheeks were streaked with moisture. She grabbed at his arm.

"Yes. They're killing her."

39

PSYCHO THERAPY

TIME WAS FUZZY for Cass. She didn't know when she'd been brought to the hospital, and didn't remember much of her life before it. She'd have bursts of memories like fireworks, and then time went back to being like pudding. Mushy. You could squish it through your hands, but you couldn't see anything in it.

The hospital where she gained weight had been nice. She'd been there before. She knew a couple of the nurses. They understood. She didn't know what she had looked like when she got there. Who wanted to see herself dying with guck pasting her eyes shut? The nurses let her know how close to death she had been, but they didn't lecture her or show her pictures of herself.

"Cass, do you want some more tapioca? It's on your diet?" the night nurse dropped by, smiling. Her diet was *everything*. She could stuff herself all day. Cass took the tapioca. She *loved* tapioca pudding.

The nurses let her lay around eating and doing what she wanted. They listened if she wanted to talk, and didn't want to know more than what she could talk about. If they knew anything about her past, they didn't bring it up.

"Was there a man with me when they brought me in?" she asked her favorite nurse.

"A couple. Doug Saunders." Cass knew him very well. They had been a couple at one time, until she bit him and he needed thirty-six stiches. She felt sorry about that. The nurse kept talking, "And a black guy. African American. He seemed to be a doctor or something. He was with you a long time. They practically had to pry him off of you to get him to leave."

The most amazing thing about the hospital was her daddy called. She hadn't talked to him since last Christmas when she screamed at him. Before that must have been a year. Or years. He called one day, and he kept calling. For the first time ever, maybe, she felt like things might work out. Like she might really get better.

"Daddy, I remember someone when I was brought here." She described the man with funny colored eyes. "Who was he?"

"There wasn't anyone like that, Cass."

She asked the nurse again. Yes, he had been there. He was very tall. She asked her father again, adding the part about him being tall. "No, Cass. It was just Doug and the paramedic crew."

Why would her daddy not tell her about him? Maybe he was "the help." If daddy considered him inconsequential, he would disappear in his eyes. If he was, like, an orderly or something, he'd go poof! to her father. Would having brown skin be a problem? A brown-skinned PhD candidate, no. A brown-skinned orderly? Big problem.

She decided that was it and stopped asking about the guy. She'd track him down when she got out. The ambulance company would know.

As soon as she could, Cass started back running. They let her, *if* she followed the doctors' orders. She did exactly what they said. And they let her do more. She had to be in shape. Cass knew that she always had to be able to escape and fight her way out.

They had a punching bag in the hospital gym. For releasing hostility. She made it sing. She broke the connection of the little speed bag to its mooring, she hit it so hard. Cass Duane never went down easy. Or for free, she smiled sadly. Once, it had been for free.

She weighed one hundred and forty pounds when she left the hospital. She had gained fifty-five pounds and looked like a pig. The head doctor called her into her office when she hit a chubby one hundred and thirty and told her she would be "moving on to a more advanced level of treatment" in a while. She thought they moved her in September, except that the pudding filled her head and she forgot.

Big time pudding when they moved her to the Havertin Institute. They moved her at night, sedated, she thought, because her memories were so garbled. Her memories were normally garbled, but not as screwed up as they were that night. She remembered glimpses of a white colonial building with floodlights around the roof. A white marble entry hall. That was all she knew of the place, except for the day room, her room, and some corridors.

This was where she was supposed to have a "more advanced level of treatment." Cass had been in eight mental hospitals, counting this one. She knew something about mental hospitals. This place was shit. How her dad stuck her in there, she'd never know.

She also found out that she had been branded brain-damaged by the hospital. She was *not* brain-damaged. She just couldn't remember things very well and had big holes in her life. Like years were gone. That wasn't brain-damage. That was fucked up. And given what she *could* remember, the more years missing, the better.

After two weeks, Cass hated the Havertin Institute with every molecule of her body and every wisp of her soul. She hated it from the moment she woke up to the time she fell exhausted into her bed. She hated all the staff and admins and patients and everything she did and they did and even the walls. Everything. Why not? Who heard of a schedule like Havertin's? None of the other places she'd been in had been like it.

6:30 AM	Get up and get dressed. Cass had never gotten up at 6:30. Even at summer camp when she was twelve, she got up at 10 AM. If she got up at 6:30, she wasn't awake, despite having her eyes open and moving around. No one needed to get up that early there, anyway. Nothing they did all day meant anything.
6:45	Go to dining hall and eat breakfast. She didn't eat breakfast. They didn't have anything she liked anyway. All they had was oatmeal and shit. The dining room looked like detention in grade school; metal and plastic tables with benches cemented to the floor. Appetizing.
7 AM	Clean your room and make the bed. That's what maids were for.
7:15 to 9:30	Housing unit group 1. This was the first therapy attempt of the day. They got the women in her hallway to sit in a circle and talk about their feelings. Cass had been hospitalized seven times before. She knew what bullshit talking about feelings was. Who cared about *her* feelings? Who cared about truth? When she was in the hospital gaining weight before being sent to Havertin, her father lied to her. There had been a man with funny-colored eyes. He'd held her and made her feel like she had a future in this fucking, stinking world.

9:30 to 12	Clean the building. Why the fuck didn't they have janitors? Her dad was probably paying a fortune for her to be in there. Why should she have to clean toilets? Back in the hospital where she'd gained her weight back, her dad stopped answering her questions about the man. He said he was a figment of her imagination. That could be true. She'd seen enough shit that turned out to be just in her head. Maybe she *was* hallucinating, maybe she made him up, like Prince Charming. But when she believed in him, she had gotten better. After that, it was all disintegrating, drifting down, down to where she was.
12 to 12:20	Lunch and social time. Who wanted to eat that crap? Who wanted to hang with the dopes in there? And they only had twenty minutes. How cozy could they get?

	Individual counseling. They had it every day, which was evidence of Havertin's therapeutic superiority. But they hired the help from the bottom of the shrink garbage can. Individual counseling was when her counselor attempted to get her to cough up her secrets. To him? Fuck no. The guy was a sex addict. He'd be on her in a minute.
	She had to be strong. If she got through this, Daddy had told her she could come home. Maybe for Christmas. Last Christmas she had screamed all that stuff at him. She was right; it was true. But she hurt him. She didn't want to hurt him. She wanted to say she was sorry to him in person and have a nice Christmas.
12:20 to 1	But he stopped calling when she got to the Havertin Institute.
	Everything was crumbling away. The feeling she had that she could get better. That she could have a life. Everything that happened would stop waking her up every night. She wouldn't scream anymore when the memories came to her. She wouldn't do drugs. Maybe she and Daddy could find her mother. Mommy. She had to stop thinking about Mommy. If they saw her crying at Havertin, they'd up her medication.

1 to 3	Group recreation. The only place to recreate was the day room. She and the nerds sat around tables for two hours a day making "constructions" out of cardboard. They got no exercise at all. Cass wanted to run. She'd always run and worked out like her dad, but you couldn't here. There was no outlet for her fear. No punching bag. She couldn't get into shape to fight. Being able to fight was what always had saved her. She couldn't fight here. They took everything away.
3 to 5	Core group. This was the therapy devoted to treating individual fuck-ups. Cass was in five groups: 1) addicts/substance abusers, 2) eating disorders/anorexia, 3) sexual abuse, 4) trauma survivors and 5) sex addicts. That's as many groups as they had. She was in so many groups that Havertin got the great idea of rotating her from one to the other. That probably saved her. If she'd had to sit in a room with those idiots talking about that shit every day, she would have broken and spilled her guts. As it was, she never got involved enough to care about anything. Which was the way to be. Her dad had dumped her; he didn't call anymore. She didn't have anyone else. Oh, maybe Hannah. But she'd screamed at her too. She was alone.
5 to 6	Quiet time. Meditation or reading about uplifting topics. Cass did not want to be quiet. She wanted to scream. The only uplifting thing she could imagine was hearing, "Miss Duane, you're being released tomorrow."

	12 step groups. They assumed that *everything* was caused by some addiction. Yeah, she had been into heroin and coke and stuff. Meth. Anything. But they didn't get that her biggest addiction was "being raped and tortured by the devil." She kept going back and getting more; must have been an addiction. They didn't have a group for that. She wasn't going to tell them about that. Fuck. Of all people in the world, Cass knew when she was safe. Havertin was *not* safe.
6 to 9	They lied about everything. The "recent staff changes." Every fuckin' cretin who worked there had been there a week. No place she'd been in ever had that. She shut up and shut down. Safest way. During 12 step time, three hours every evening, Cass sat and listened to other women talk about how rotten their lives had been. Those dingbats couldn't have survived one day of her life.
9 to 10	Housing unit group 2. The people on her corridor got together for their eventide whining session. If the whining pigs knew what had happened to her, they wouldn't have believed it.

10	Lights out. Yeah. Her lights were out, but she had a disconcerting feeling that the sleep meds they gave her were a little stronger than necessary and that someone was in her room, touching her. What the fuck? Whatever happened to her couldn't be worse than what had already happened.
2 X per week	Individual meeting with psychiatrist. They got to get out of their other activities to meet with their shrinks. Her psychiatrist had hairs bursting from her nostrils and yellow teeth. Her clothes smelled like mothballs. Cass could not tell her how she got into drugs or happened to become a prostitute. She couldn't open up to her at all.

Cass looked out the windows in the day room at the meadow behind the building. The yard was a *big* square of grass behind the hospital. At first, it was ringed with very tall, very green trees. It had to be on the East Coast; nothing west of the Mississippi was that green. The trees weren't green now; they were leafless. The lawn was brown and looked frozen crisp. Patches of snow covered it. The patients didn't have access to the yard. She saw people out there sometimes, but they were seriously disabled, in wheelchairs or supported by nurses.

For some reason, the Havertin people seemed to think their schedule and "therapeutic modalities" made people well. Cass had been in so many institutions that she knew that they were really on the "increase her meds and maybe she'll shut up" plan. They stuffed people full of pills. If she swallowed all the crap they gave her, she'd be a zombie like everyone else. As it was, her history of bulimia held her in good stead. After drug and doze time, she puked the pills in the toilet.

Havertin had a great reputation in the shrink trade. Articles about how wonderful the place was covered the bulletin board—with anything that would allow an inmate to know where she was or the date deleted.

"Cass, it's for your own good. You need to adjust to the internal rhythms of our therapeutic environment, and to the season. You don't need a calendar; you don't need to be counting the days until you get out."

Her psychiatrist worked with her feelings of anxiety about not knowing the snow outside meant it was a very cold September or a really mild December. "Let's talk about your anxieties about time."

"Let's talk about my anxieties about where I am too. I was brought here in the middle of the night, drugged. I don't know what state I'm in. Why doesn't Havertin Institute let us know our fucking zip code?"

"No profanity, Cass. It's part of the therapeutic plan. You've not achieved such a hot record out in the world, so Havertin is your new world. When you adjust to the Havertin way, you won't question, you'll just be with us, in our nurturing family."

Like fuck. Why didn't they have mail or phone privileges? All the other places she'd been in let you take calls and have mail. You could decorate your room with posters of rock stars with hot bods if you wanted. Everything in other places was geared toward being healthy when they got out.

This was more like a prison than a hospital.

Time began to slip. She had no idea how long she'd been there or what day it was. There was snow outside sometimes. But it melted. Had it really been there? Was it winter? She wanted to run, but they didn't let them outside to run. There was a big lawn behind the place. Acres. Why couldn't she run there? Jesus Christ! She had to get out of there.

She wanted cigarettes. She found out she could get them, but she'd have to put out to one of the counselors. Cass didn't want to do that. She wanted to go straight. She wanted to get well. The pressure was all day, every day, in every way. They'd get you when you never expected it.

"Cass, you have to eat. You can't be here if you have weight problems. Havertin does not deal with eating issues." Ah. She'd thought that a bright spot. Maybe if she got anorexic again, they'd kick her back to the hospital.

The counselor leaned over her in the dining room and whispered. "If you don't eat, they'll take you to the other wing of the hospital where the real sickies are, shove a tube down your throat, and force-feed you."

Every minute was planned; every minute was with other people. The other women didn't like her. She couldn't eat. They marked down everything that everyone did. Demerits for not eating. Eating too slowly. Taking too long to shit.

Tension was building up. She would *not* explode. No. Never again. She would not blow up and tear things up, take scissors or knives to the furniture. Pull paintings off of the walls and smash them. Throw china. Destroy her father's priceless art the way she had at home. Cass was not going to do that.

"I can't stand this," she said to her counselor. "I want to call my dad. He wouldn't allow this if he knew it was happening."

"Phone privileges are earned, Cass."

"What do I have to do to talk to my dad?"

"You have to have perfect behavior for two weeks."

They wanted perfect behavior, they'd get it. She'd be perfect for two weeks just so she could yell at her fucking liar of a father. Her father had put her in this place, deliberately. She wouldn't be released. She had just figured it out.

Perfect behavior meant cheerfully complying with the schedule, which she did. Dawn to late night, she did exactly what they wanted, stupid though it was.

She did pretty well for three days.

Her counselor demanded that she sit on his lap and relax against him as "bonding therapy." He would become the good dad to her father's terrible dad. It was boner therapy. He was so hard he could come in his pants.

He did. She wiggled her butt the tiniest bit and he was bucking like a bronco. He smiled afterward, saying, "We'll have to figure out something to make you feel good."

"The only thing that would make me happy is blowing your brains out, you two-bit con. I'm telling my psychiatrist."

The counselor reported the incident as Cass coming on to him and threatening to kill him when he wouldn't perform oral sex on her. They increased her meds and gave her twice as much time in therapy with him.

A few days later, somebody got to her in the trauma survivors group. A woman told the piteous story of her horse dying. Everyone wept.

Cass snapped. She was on her feet, screaming. "You fucking idiots! You don't know what trauma is. Trauma is being locked in a dungeon and raped in the ass ten times a day. Trauma is having someone grab your nipples with red-hot tongs …"

Cass went on like that for a while, and then leapt toward the woman whose horse had died. The counselor got in front of her and grabbed her hands.

"Watch out, Cass, they'll put you in the boxes." He twisted her arm around behind her back. Cass spun, grabbed his straightened arm, and broke it at the elbow over her thigh. He screamed, groveling like a baby. She ran to the far side of the room with the entire group and the counselor clawing away from her in terror.

Cass tipped the sofa where the woman with the dead horse had been sitting on its back, and then frantically looked around the room. Spotting scissors on the desk, she grabbed them and attacked the sofa, ripping its fabric, screaming and swearing and stabbing.

When she woke up, Cass was in a part of the hospital she hadn't seen. She was "in restraints"—a straitjacket—seated on a wheel chair. She felt drowsy. They'd drugged her and put her there.

"Are you ready, little miss?" The guard was burly and had an unmistakable air of sadism around him. "You really tossed it, didn't you? We'll see that you don't do that again. Dr. Mantrell is waiting to see you. She's the new principal psychiatrist at Havertin. You're lucky to get to meet her."

Dr. Mantrell had dyed black hair, pasty skin, and a slight mustache. "Flat affect," Cass thought, drawing upon her store of psychiatric knowledge. You couldn't tell a thing about what she was thinking or feeling from her face or posture. She wore a cheap department store suit.

"Well, Miss Duane, you've created quite an impact. But then, I knew you would, eventually. I've read your *vitae*. You need to understand a few things about the Havertin Institute. You're committed for life, Miss Duane. Would you like to see your admission papers?" The goon pushing the wheelchair held them up so she could see them. "Your father admitted you as incorrigibly mentally ill, a danger to yourself and others. Read it."

Her father's signature was on the papers.

"My father put me here? Did he know what you'd do?" Cass couldn't stop the tears running down her cheeks: the straitjacket wrapped her arms across her belly and behind her. She couldn't wipe her eyes.

"Of course, he knew. He was sick of you, Miss Duane. "

Dr. Mantrell got up and marched around her desk, sticking her face in Cass's. Her breath was dry and papery. "You are here for the rest of your life, Miss Duane. You'd better adapt. While Havertin can be a wonderful place of refuge for many people, for others it can be a misery—while they live." Cass jolted backwards.

She smiled at Cass, the weirdest smile she'd seen. "You frightened your counselor and group members today, Cass. You broke a counselor's arm. This is serious. You must learn the consequences. We have many ways of countering dangerous and out of control behavior like yours. The military is experimenting with new techniques to interrogate prisoners. They can also be used to discipline wayward individuals. They call it 'waterboarding.' We call it water therapy. It's rather like drowning, but not quite. "

Cass's eyes widened and widened more. Dr. Mantrell had changed as she spoke, hissing a bit, her breath becoming shorter and eyes brighter as she described torture. She liked inflicting pain. Her tongue darted out, sharp pointed. She was reptilian. The only people Cass had seen who grew excited causing pain belonged to Enzo Donatore. He was here. This woman was his.

"Oh, yes, you will find that we have friends in common. It's impossible to really leave old friends, don't you think? Do you think I should call Enzo and tell him where you are?"

"You know Enzo? How can you know Enzo?" Cass's chest froze. She could barely breathe.

"*Everyone* knows *Enzo,* my dear. Everyone who is anyone." Her chuckle said she would call him in a minute.

"No! Don't tell him. I'll do anything, please. Don't tell Enzo."

Her captor chuckled. "All right, I won't, for as long as you're *really* good. In addition to water therapy, we also have the box. You will find out about that tonight. Quiet darkness often calms patients who can't be soothed any other way. Of course, they are often quite noisy before they settle down."

She smiled with real glee. "But we haven't forgotten anyone down there yet. Oh, maybe for a day or two. Not long. And it is cold now. It's almost Christmas. You wanted to know the date, Ms. Duane. The back garden is covered with snow today. Don't worry; we'll give you a blanket.

"And now, Miss Duane, I will leave you in the hands of my able staff. When I see you next, I hope to see you in a much more amenable mood."

"You should know that we have one other modality that we use often."

Something struck her on her upper shoulder. She rocked back, stunned by the pain. Her muscles twitched. Cass shouted, "What are you doing? Tasers are illegal."

The second and third zaps rendered her semi-conscious.

When she woke up, Cass in a pitch black place. It was cold. She figured it must be underground. A gag filled her mouth and a hood covered her head. The straitjacket wrapped her arms around her. The cold said she wasn't wearing anything below the waist.

A flashlight's beam lit the hood over her face. "Oh, there you are, you little bitch." The guy who'd wheeled her chair. "Ready for some therapy?" He wrenched her legs open. She tried to fight, but couldn't.

He hurt her. She pulled her legs up and together afterward, trembling. "Feeling more relaxed, bitch?"

She thought there were six the first night. No defense, not even a scream.

Cass knew she would die in that hole.

40

A WAKE-UP CALL

WILL RECEIVED AN email from Havertin Institute. Reaching him was hard; every aspect of his life was screened. Whoever wanted to get the message to him had done his homework to get through. It was an untraceable @numonet.com address; everyone had two or three of those. But this message had the Havertin Institute logo embedded in it and was addressed to his private code. He couldn't trace it to a specific sender, but a literate person wrote it; someone who worked there, no doubt.

Mr. Duane,

If you love your daughter, get her out. They're killing her. She's in the boxes in the back of the place.

Hurry. She'll be dead in another day.

Will went to bed and slept restlessly, starting awake every few minutes. Sweating.

The room was pitch black. Will sat up in bed. Two words came to him: Enzo Donatore.

Donatore was on his way to get her.

He called the Institute and no one answered. How could an entire mental hospital go dark? Had Donatore gotten the whole place?

Once Will got it, he jumped. He called one of his attorneys at home in New York. After all his struggling to sleep, the time was only one a.m., four a.m. in New York. "I received an email that my daughter's life is in danger at Havertin Institute. It's from inside. I can't trace it. Get a judge up and get a search warrant for that place. It's not a prank, Lewis. I'll send it to you." A moment passed while Will forwarded the note.

"OK. My computer just booted up," the attorney said. Silence as he read. "You're sure this is real?"

"'She's in the boxes at the back of the place?' What is that? Look, I think the Havertin Institute is abusing mental patients and not giving them their Constitutional rights."

"What sort of abuse? Do you have more than this?"

"They haven't allowed me to talk to my daughter. Whenever I asked to speak to her, they said she was in isolation. They didn't say why or for how long or what that was. I haven't spoken to her since she's been there. They've changed psychiatrists—or people they say were psychiatrists—on her three times. The whole place smells to me. There's no visiting. They have a song and dance about their culture. God, Lewis, they could be doing *anything*." His hands started to shake. "I admitted her involuntarily, as a danger to herself and others—you know that, you drew up the papers. But this time, I think I really made a mistake. We have to get her out of there."

"And the other patients."

"Oh, yeah." Will had forgotten about them. "There's hundreds there. It's big."

"This looks like a 'color of the law' violation. Deliberately depriving anyone of rights or privileges protected by the Constitution or laws of the United States is a *very large* federal violation. This brings in the FBI and all the feds. A judge will jump on this. I'll get moving."

Oh, God. Cass. Cass. Cass.

Will expected Leroy to tell him to fuck off. He didn't. He said, "If I save Cass, she's coming with me this time. You have nothing to say about her anymore."

"Fine, Leroy. You were right. Please save her."

41

I LOVE YOU, ARABELLA

ARABELLA SAT IN her bedroom. Leroy had left her a message that he'd recorded before the helicopter came. She played it.

"I wanted to say good-bye and thank you. This is all I got time for." His power came out of the recorder with his voice, raw power, blasting her, filling the room.

"I've loved Cass Duane since I saw a photo of her last March; a little girl jumpin' a horse over a creek. I fell for her before I knew anything about her, but I learned all about her right away. We're soul mates, my Grandfather saw it and confirmed it and blessed it. When she was a little girl, Enzo Donatore captured her. She ended up the way she is because of it.

"I saved her life. That's why Will gave me this trip and I ended up meeting you." His voice thickened. "I love Cass, even though I've only seen her broken down and close to dead. I love her and I always will.

"If you know about what she's done and look down on her, think again, Arabella. You would have been like her in a week, if you'd gone to Spain.

"Arabella, you are the leader of your family. I've given you all the power. Keep it and use it. Don't squander it trying to save your parents or the mansion or anything else. That doesn't mean you can't figure a way to keep the Manor, but a good way, that makes people happy and doesn't make you think you're better than everyone else.

"Do what you need to do, Arabella, go to school. Get expert advice from good people who care about you."

He stopped for a moment, clearing his throat. Breathing.

"Arabella, I feel like I'm bein' torn in two. I told you last night that I loved you. I do. I will *always* love you. We're soul mates, my grandfather confirmed that, too. We would have had a good life together. Maybe we will.

"I don't know how this is going to shake out. Will said that Cass is in worse trouble than before. Maybe she's dead, but I don't feel that yet.

"I can't let Cass die.

"And I won't.

"I will always love you. I will never forget you. You got my love and my blessin' as long as I live." His voice broke and the recording ended.

Arabella wiped her eyes. How was *she* supposed to live, having had him touch her and love her?

42

THE ON-GOING TASK OF
DESTROYING CASS DUANE

ENZO COULD NOT believe his good fortune. The Duane bitch, who had slipped her collar so regrettably in the New York brothel, had shown up in the place of business of one of his good friends. Should he go pick her up? Or delegate the very important task of killing her as unpleasantly as possible?

He sat in his study in front of the see-stone. It was uncharacteristically dark. "See!" he commanded it. "See, wherever you are! Show me!"

Dark and dull. The stone lit a bit. "See stone! It's in the Catskills!"

"See!" he commanded the see-stone. Greyish mist rose above it. The hospital was so far from anything that the see-stone didn't work. Or, terrible thought, maybe the crystal was getting balky. Maybe it didn't like the things he commanded it to see. Rape and pillage, that sort of thing. What they were doing to Cass Duane. He'd give pretty near anything to see that.

Screaming interrupted his happy interlude. "Shut him up! Will you shut him up!" He had so much to think about and that idiot Dashiell Pontichury—what a name—kept howling. The idiot could spend money like he was made of it, but he couldn't take a little torture. Transforming into his reptilian self in front of an internationally televised polo game! Which showed Leroy the Ape being a good guy and trying to help him. Before the robot horse and the rest of them galloped off to the Sherwood Forest, showing themselves to be as unnatural as possible. "Shut him up!"

Dashiell had shown such promise, but promise is as promise does. They all let him down, relatives and friends alike. Had his brother repented and learned? As much as stupid Pondichury would soon enough?

"Diego!" he screamed into the speaker. "Get down here! I have something for you to do."

Enzo took a moment to turn the see-stone on himself. Brilliant blue eyes, silver-laced hair that sparkled even in his gloomy study. Strong teeth, bulging muscles. Brilliance of form and intellect that no one could miss.

They still called Will Duane a stud-muffin, but that was based on his performance years ago. The term was made for *him*. He could still fuck his way to January. And he didn't care who or what his partner was. If only there was more of him to go around and he didn't have to babysit for the recruiting sessions at the castle. A big one was scheduled to start tomorrow.

"Diego. You have to take one of our planes to JFK in New York, then rent a car or find a smaller plane, and go here. The place is so small, they don't have a proper airport," he gave him the address. "It's the Havertin Institute. Cass Duane is there. Get her and bring her here." He snarled a bit at his brother, enough so that he knew what would happen if he failed again. "If you bring her back, expect good things. I want her alive."

"When should I go?"

"Now! We'll get there first and grab her before anyone knows. Will Duane will figure this out fast. Slimy bastard."

43

THE RACE

THE SULLIVAN COUNTY airport was *tiny*. It was like a toy compared to JFK. Leroy saw why he had had to change planes in New York City. He was surprised jets could fly into the County airport at all. Leroy dashed toward the only hangar. The Numenon Gullwing was tucked inside, its logo visible on the jet's nose. There was no sign of another airliner, other than his. They'd gotten there first, but anyone could be behind them. Pristine snow covered everything.

"Leroy, get in." Doug beckoned him from a black van, one of two parked near the hangar.

When they pulled the door shut, Doug said, "We got here first, but they're right behind us. The airport guy said another Gullwing was on its way in."

"Who is it?"

"Donatore, I'd say."

The snow had turned to slushy mush where tires ran over it, but it wasn't worn away. Leroy saw no evidence of a snowplow. This was a poor area, the houses along the way testified to that.

"That's the Institute," Doug drove slowly past the entrance. The gate was an elaborate wrought iron job with sharp spears at the top of each upright rod. An eight-foot high chain-link fence extended as far as they could see on both sides of the gate. The fence was topped with razor wire. A blanket of white, pure as a virgin's breast, covered everything.

"We'll get in," Hannah said. "Don't worry." She and the commandos wore bulletproof vests over their night-black garments. Hannah pulled a black hood over her head and took off with her troops.

Hannah called them a minute later. "Come to the main gate," came through a receiver Leroy wore on his ear.

Hannah and her squad stood in front of the wide open, wrought iron gate.

"It was unlocked," Hannah said. "A gate with very sharp spines, a fence with razor wire on a mental institution. An unmanned guard station. No visual surveillance that I can detect. Lights should have gone on in the building when we got here."

They walked through the gates, crunching through the snow. The party fanned out on the other side of the gate, picking their way through the darkness.

Hannah got them into the building the same way she had gone through the gate, by opening the door. "The place is wide open. It seems deserted."

They entered the building. Will had been told she was "in the back. In the boxes." That didn't make sense. They could see the snowy field behind the building. No boxes. And it was freezing out there.

Hannah easily found the wing where Cass had been housed originally. "She was in minimum security. There are no bars or elaborate security measures in this corridor," Hannah said. "I would not expect them to put their more severely ill patients up front where they might be seen." The doors of the rooms were open.

Leroy's heart raced? Would they find Cass? Would she be dead?

Hannah pushed her way into the first room. A chubby young woman lay face down on the floor, unmoving. Hannah felt for a pulse.

"Alive, but sedated. Check the rest. Feel here …" She showed them how to find a pulse on their own throats.

The rest were knocked out, some breathing laboriously. Hannah didn't know how many: dozens, maybe hundreds. She didn't have time for a count.

"We'd better call the paramedics," Hannah said. "Leroy, you and Doug find her. The note said she was in the boxes in back. That should be easy. Look for boxes."

He and Doug ranged across the vast snow-covered expanse behind the hospital. No boxes, nothing resembling a box. Just flat new snow.

"Where is she?" Doug asked. "They've got to have some sort of facility out here. What could the boxes be? It's fucking freezing. How could anyone survive?"

The baying of a pack of dogs made both of them jump. Leroy saw them coming: attack dogs, just what every mental hospital needed.

"Run, Leroy!" Doug cried, taking off at gallop.

Leroy stood where he was, feeling the dogs' energy. They were neglected and angry. He dropped to one knee and held out his hand to them.

"Good dogs," he said in his language. "You are lonely and think you want to bite. That is not true. You want to help."

They clustered around him, wagging their tails and demanding attention. "You are going to help right now." He wiped his arm against their muzzles. "You must find creatures that smell like me. They are hurt. They need your help. Go!" He waved, taking in the entire back end of the pasture.

The dogs went straight to the left side of the lawn where it met the forest. They stood in different places, six of them. The animals barked frantically, scratching at the ground.

Leroy ran over and kicked the snow away from the ground where the first dog had dug. He found a cement square flush with the ground. More kicking revealed a metal door set in the top. Opening the first one took all his strength; a weakened woman could never get out. The stench had him throw up his hands to protect himself. Hannah had completed her search of the hospital and was out on the lawn. She and her men trotted toward them.

"It's not Cass," Leroy said. "I know her smell. There's six like this."

"We'll see who's down there," Hannah said. "You get Cass. Leroy, when you find her, get her out of here. Take the van and get to the airport."

"Do you have anything of Cass's?"

"Yeah," Leroy said, pulling a wrinkled scarf from his pocket. "I took this from Cass the first time we saved her. I wanted something of hers. Been carryin' it."

He turned to the dogs and let them sniff the hat. "Good dogs. This woman needs your help. Find her."

She was in the second from the last hole. Leroy and Doug threw the door open. The stench was worst than the first one. He started to go down steep stairs.

"No. Let me." Hannah shoved past him. "You cannot see her as she is." After few minutes, she said, "You can come down now." Cass was wrapped in a blanket. The straitjacket she had been wearing was tossed on the floor.

Cass was unconscious and in worse condition than the first time he rescued her. Her face was bruised and beaten. Leroy lifted her out and up the stairs.

"They had a sack over her head and a gag in her mouth," Hannah reported. "She was wearing a straitjacket. That's all. She couldn't defend herself in any way."

Leroy took off for the van at a run, holding Cass to his heart.

The dogs clustered around the other blocks, barking and scratching at the snow. They had women in them, in slightly better condition than Cass. They were too weak to be hysterical.

"Stay here and show the sheriff this," Hannah told one of her people. "We have to go. We'll get you home later."

Leroy didn't worry about any of that. Cass was dying.

44

WHY THE HELL?

"WHY THE *HELL* did you send her there, Will?" the voice of an ancient, and angry, woman grated over the phone.

"You know, Vanessa, it's good of you to call me. I feel like the biggest shit in the world, and it's nice to have my oldest friend confirm it."

"I didn't call you a shit, Will. I said, 'Why did you send her there?' There's a difference. I don't want to beat you up. You'll do that to yourself. I want to help her. Send her to me when they bring her in."

"No, she should go to Stanford Hospital."

"If she goes to Stanford Hospital, she'll die. If not from her injuries, from Enzo Donatore's goons. What do you think happened at that Institute? They all went nuts? No. Enzo got to them. And guess who can infiltrate Stanford hospital in the blink of an eye?"

"Donatore."

"Yes. His brother Diego is after them now, and closing. Donatore knows she's alive, Will. Must have picked it up on that stone of his. He'll know if she's at Stanford. That's where you'd send her."

"Oh, God, will it ever end?" Will was weeping.

"Send her to me, Will. Tell your pilot to follow my orders."

Will put a hand over his face and let the tears fall. He'd try. He'd change. He'd take good care of Cass, if she lived.

45

DEAD IN THE AIR

THEY PILED INTO the van and raced across the silent white countryside to the little Sullivan County airport. No doubt that Donatore's men were close. The stench of evil was overpowering.

"Go! Go! Go!" Hannah admonished. "They're right behind us. Their jet is warming up over there." It was a Gullwing, but not as fast as theirs. "On second thought, we will take a moment's break."

Hannah pulled out one of her weapons, fitted it with a silencer and took two shots at the other plane. No one would ever notice the bullet holes, though they probably would notice the extreme drop in altitude in a few hours.

Their jet launched into the air, heading to San Francisco International Airport. The ultra-fast plane screamed across the country. Its custom interior was set up with bench seating in some places and a few sleeping bays, in addition to rows of seats. They laid Cass on an open area of the floor.

"Oh, Jesus," Leroy said, looking at her feet. Her toes were black. Frostbite. "She's freezing." She shivered, so deeply unconscious that she might as well be dead.

"Lie next to her, Leroy. Take your shirt off and warm her up." Doug began taking his shirt off. He opened her clothes. A vile odor filled the cabin, but he wrapped his naked torso around her anyway. "You do the other side, Leroy."

Leroy started to lie down next to her, but he couldn't. He was crying too hard.

Doug said, "It's OK, buddy. This is worth crying about." Leroy glanced at Doug and saw that his cheeks also were streaked. Doug had been in love with Cass at one time. This was hard for him too.

"I've got warmed blankets," Hannah hustled up with some folded blankets. "Lift up her legs, Leroy. We'll wrap these around her."

Leroy thrust his arms under Cass's thighs so that Hannah could tuck in the blankets.

The sewer smell became much worse. Leroy pulled his arms out from under her. They were covered with brown-streaked red liquid.

"Is that blood?" The liquid was gushing from beneath Cass. It became a flood. A tsunami. It flowed across the floor, puddling in the valleys and seams of the carpeting. Leroy couldn't move.

"She's hemorrhaging. Doug, give me your T-shirt." Hannah grabbed the shirt and cut it into wide strips with a knife on her belt. She rolled the strips into fat sausages, hands moving so fast they were a blur. "Hold her legs open." While Doug and Leroy held her, Hannah packed the strips into Cass. The bleeding didn't stop. The floor was drenched in a wide circle around Cass. The liquid stank. It was brownish red, not the red of fresh blood.

"More padding! Get me more!" Hannah's voice was shrill. Leroy kept his eyes on Cass. She had bloody crescent-shaped wounds on the lower part of her body, like chunks had been removed. The gashes were covered with pus. What were they? Why did it take so many rolls to stop the blood? Why did it smell like that?

"I've stopped the bleeding for now. It will come again and I won't be able to stop it." Hannah rose from the floor and walked stiffly to her seat in the front part of the plane. Everyone was quiet, watching her.

Hannah sat down and fell against the plane's sidewall. Her shoulders began to shake. Leroy heard her breathing, and then her sobbing. She bent, and wept as silently as she could. No one could move. No one knew Hannah Hehrman could cry.

Doug moved over to her, "Is she dying?"

"Oh, my God. She's *dead*. She cannot live. Her uterus is perforated. Fecal material has spread everywhere. That's the smell and the color of her blood. She's burning with fever. Can't you feel her heat? She's cold, but underneath, she's burning. She's so infected. No one can survive that." Her eyes raked Doug's. "They took *bites* out of her, Doug, and left them untreated so that they'd become infected. How long was she in that hole? Oh, God. They killed my baby."

Hannah began rocking from side to side, arms wrapped around herself. "They killed my baby."

The cabin was silent.

Leroy looked at Cass, barely alive. Fighting to live. He knew she would fight as long as the tiniest bit of life remained. She always fought.

"Are any of you listening? I've been trying to get through for fifteen minutes." The querulous voice of an old lady erupted from Hannah's equipment. "What's going on there?"

"Dr. Schierman. We have Cass. She is dead." Hannah put away her tears to speak.

"Dead? Pssh! I'll tell you when she's dead. She's got enough life in her for me to feel it from the West Coast. Hannah! Pull yourself together, woman, and save that girl." The raspy voice began to issue orders.

"Get her temperature down. Wrap her in wet rags. Change them every minute. Pour water on her—whatever works. Set an IV, Hannah, and blast her with antibiotics. Not penicillin. She's allergic to that.

Erythromycin. Blast her with it. And don't give up until you get her to my house alive. If you lose her, and you will have *me* to deal with. All of you."

"Who are you?" the old voice cackled. "You in the back holding Cass. With the feathers. Who are you?"

"I'm Leroy Watches Jr., ma'am."

"You're Joseph's grandson."

"Yes, ma'am. Joseph Bishop's."

"*You*, Leroy Watches, will keep her alive until you get here. That will be a bit less than two hours."

"Three, Vanessa," Doug said. "You have to count the drive from the airport."

"You're not going to the airport. I'm not going to let my girl die in traffic. You'll land here."

"You don't have a landing strip for a jet on your property," Doug said.

"Of course I don't. You'll land on Skyline Boulevard."

"Skyline? That's just a track through the trees."

"Not so. George Yeomen and his fellows have just measured a perfect landing strip right outside my door. Length and width are fine."

The pilot chimed in. "Dr. Schierman. We can't possibly do that."

"Of course you can. When you're almost here, I'll send George and the boys out to stop the traffic. They'll set up lights. You'll land. All will be well."

"We can't do that. It's illegal." The pilot was immovable.

"It's not illegal in a critical emergency. You're having a severe mechanical breakdown. I've been broadcasting your many aeronautical woes to the San Francisco control tower for an hour. They're surprised you're airborne. Keep Cass alive or there will be hell to pay. And get here!"

46

ROUGH LANDING

LEROY LOOKED OUT the window. There was nothing to see. No lights. No trees. Nothing, until the wings started clipping branches. The plane didn't slow down, but snapping sounds filled the air.

"Holy Jesus!" the pilot gasped. "That's a hiking trail. I can't land there."

"Yes, you can," the old lady's voice came over the speaker. "We can see you. Land the damn jet. Hurry. She's almost gone."

Leroy would never forget the crashing and cracking of branches. They were thrown from side to side in the cabin. The plane hit a tree or something and started to spin horizontally. But the captain got them straight and kept up his efforts when the wheels hit the ground. They bounced, throwing everyone around. They slowed. And then they stopped.

"Open the door! Deploy the stairs!" That croaking old voice.

Leroy carried Cass down the stairway. A bunch of short little men in green dresses just above their knees took Cass, put her in a van, and shot into the darkness.

"No. Don't take her …" Leroy wailed.

"Don't worry, Mr. Watches," said one of the dozen or so remaining by the plane. "You come with us." He was spirited into an SUV and flew down the black hole into which Cass had disappeared. The forest was so close that it seemed that the branches would break the way they had with the plane. But they didn't. The trees and branches seemed to move to avoid the vehicle.

"Where are we going?"

"To Dr. Schierman's house. Don't worry, lad. The lady has her. She'll be all right."

Leroy could see no reason for Cass to ever be all right. The stinking floods of blood, her wounds. The fever. She couldn't live. Hannah Hehrman was right. She was dead.

They drove straight into massed trees, crashing through the underbrush. For what? Ten minutes? He couldn't tell with all the jouncing.

Then they hit an open space; the drive went through a lawn. A gigantic black hulk rose beyond it. It was as enormous as some of the country houses he'd seen in Europe. It had two wings, one very tall and at right angles to the other, lower, longer structure. It was dark brick with stone columns. The house had nooks and crannies filled with carved gargoyles and disturbing things. Statues of dragons and things with claws. He saw one move as they drove by.

"What ..." Leroy gasped.

"Don' worry, lad. Pay the house no mind. It will pay you no mind." They pulled up in front of the house. The front stuck out with a high arch covered in carvings of bats, demons, and people with anguished expressions. Even the benign carvings of flowers and plants looked tortured.

Baying filled his ears. A pack of black dogs surged toward him. Several had heads like barrels, as big as a normal dog's body. Their faces were wrinkled up, pushed in, and equipped with large teeth.

He squatted and held his hands out. "What are nice dogs like you doing acting like that? Don't you know I'm your friend? Come here now and let me pet you."

The dogs whined and tilted their heads in one way and then the other.

The mansion's door opened. A tall, late–middle–aged woman with very erect posture stood in the doorway. "Welcome, Mr. Watches. I'm Mrs. Naughton, Dr. Schierman's housekeeper. Come with me."

"Where is Cass?"

"Cass is being cared for by Dr. Schierman."

"Is she a doctor?"

"Not a medical doctor. She's a physicist. A brilliant one. They're more useful. Come with me."

"Where's Cass?"

"You'll see her tomorrow. This way." She led him through an entrance hall that was the wooden equivalent of the carved stone exterior. This time carved plants and sort–of–cute animals cavorted on the dark walls, along with ribbon festoons and bows. All of them moved as he passed. Leroy hustled close to Mrs. Naughton.

They went down a corridor at the end of the entrance hall. More spooky carvings, but they seemed to simmer down the farther down the hall they walked.

"This is your room, Mr. Watches." She opened a door and walked through it ahead of him. It was a nice room with comfortable chairs and two big beds. "Ah, good. Cook has brought you one of Dr. Schierman's warm milk drinks." A glass of milk sat on a nightstand between the room's two beds.

"Here you go. Drink up." She stood there until Leroy finished it all. "Go take a shower. Put your clothes outside the bathroom door. We'll wash them and leave a robe for you."

Leroy did as he was told, finding an extra-tall terrycloth robe on the bed after he showered. He put it on, climbed into bed, and that was it. He was out.

47

GETTING TO KNOW YOU

WHEN LEROY AWAKENED, the clock said almost 3:30 in the afternoon. What did she put in that drink? He found new clothes, just his size, laid on the other bed. He was starving.

"Come into the kitchen. Your breakfast is waiting for you." The raspy old-lady's voice from the plane came from a speaker on the wall.

He wanted to ask her about Cass, but she scared him.

"Mrs. Naughton is outside your door. She will escort you to the kitchen."

He walked into a huge room so different from the rest of the house that *it* almost scared him. Light and bright, a wall of windows and glass French doors led to a brilliant garden massed with flowers. The room was paneled in a very pale wood with no creepy carvings. Sofas and chairs were arranged at the far end of the room. Closer was a dining table for a very large family. All of it was as of a quality as fine as the homes he'd seen in Europe. A contemporary and cultured person lived here. A wealthy one.

"Well, Mr. Watches, I'm glad y' saw fit to wake up. My scones would not have lasted much longer." A voice startled him.

Turning to the left and beyond a short wall, he found a magnificent kitchen. It was one of those kitchens that had so many appliances and gadgets that he gave up rather than trying to master even their names.

"That's right. Take a good look at the AGA range. Worth its weight in gold. I'm Mrs. Cook, Dr. Schierman's cook." She tittered. "Seems strange, but that's how my name worked out. Same as for Driver, the chauffeur. And Butler, the butler.

"You take this." She handed him a huge plate. "I just made this for y'. You're a big eater, and I made you a big breakfast."

An omelet the way he liked it, bacon and ham, both. Biscuits, pastries. A bowl of fruit salad and fresh orange juice.

For a moment, thoughts about Cass drifted to the rear of his awareness and the needs of a big man who hadn't eaten in a long time came forth.

"That's what I like to see," Mrs. Cook said smiling. "A man with a healthy appetite."

"Where's Cass?"

Mrs. Cook sucked in a breath. "Well, I'll let Dr. Schierman tell you. She's out in the sun room in the garden." She pointed at an ornate glass and iron structure that could have come from Lord Ballentyne's country home in England. "She's there, waiting for you."

He knocked on the glass door. A gaunt woman a few years short of ancient looked up. "Come in, Leroy. I'm Vanessa Schierman." He stepped over the threshold into yet another world. The light and airy gazebo was furnished with big cushy sofas and chairs. And more plants than a jungle.

The old lady was like a crow, dressed in black. Her head jutted forward and to the side alarmingly.

"I'd like you to meet someone." She waved at the settee.

He could see a slim woman with dark hair sitting on a sofa with her back to him. It wasn't Cass. As desperately hurt as Cass was, she couldn't sit with that ease even if a miracle occurred. He walked toward her, wondering what was going on.

When he rounded the end of the couch, the lady stood up and offered her hand, smiling. "How do you do, Mr. Watches? Grammie has told me a great deal about you." Blue eyes, straight dark hair, and fine, pale skin. She wasn't a beauty, but she was a very pretty young girl. The strength of her features pointed at the beauty she would be when grown. As she was, she seemed more approachable than a beauty would be.

It was Cass. She was about thirteen years old.

He fell against a big chair and plopped down, unable to move. Or anything.

"My name is Ashley Duane. I should have told you that." She leaned forward. "Are you all right?"

He tried to say something and choked.

"Here, Mr. Watches, have some water." The old lady's eyes rolled in their sockets as she turned and poured water from a pitcher. Her neck was bent so far over, it looked as though her head must have been broken off and then reattached. She was a witch for sure. What had she done to Cass?

"I'm Vanessa Schierman. Dr. Schierman. I will be your hostess for a while," she said to Leroy. He kept blinking.

"Oh, you're staying here too?" Ashley said. "Grammie says you ride horses and do all sorts of things. I was getting worried about being bored here. There aren't any young people. Grammie and I decided that I would stay here this summer while Mommy is in Spain. I really didn't want to go." She made a face. "So Grammie said that I could stay. Daddy said it was OK too." Ashley smiled, a charming, upper–class adolescent, poised and well spoken. "My parents have known Grammie forever, by the way. They'd *never* leave me with someone they didn't know well."

The old lady cracked a very unnerving smile. "Yes, Will and I are dearest friends. Have been forever. And Ashley is one of 'my girls.' She'd live here if I had my way."

Ashley smiled angelically.

His soul mate was barely a teenager.

"May I talk to you?" he asked the witch.

"Certainly, my dear. We will talk at length. But not now. Why don't you get acquainted with Ashley?" She got up and left the gazebo.

"Huh. How are you?" he stammered.

"I'm very well, thank you. And you?"

"I'm very well. How long have you been here?"

"I got here last night. I fell asleep. I don't remember the drive up here. I'm so glad I don't have to go to Spain. Mommy left today." Her mouth grew tight when she mentioned her mother.

Leroy got it as a flash. This was Cass before she went to Spain and was destroyed by Enzo Donatore. The old lady had somehow taken her back to the way she was before any of the terrible things happened to her. But how did she do it?

"Do you know your way around here? I got here late last night, too. I haven't seen anything."

"I'll show you the estate. What do you want to see?" Ashley said.

"Everything."

"The front is creepy. Grammie keeps it that way to scare off strangers." Ashley whispered. "It's because of her children. She doesn't want people to gawk at them or make fun of them."

"Oh." He raised his eyebrows.

She leaned closer and whispered, "They're all mentally ill. It's so sad. It was from a genetic problem with her and her husband. He died a long time ago. You see Grammie's children out here sometimes." They were walking along a cement path with brilliant green grass on both sides. "They're with their caretakers or in wheelchairs. Don't be afraid of them. They're not dangerous. Except Louis. He might be, but they keep him medicated."

"The hospital is right there," she indicated a warm and welcoming stucco building with lots of windows on the path ahead of them. "She has a whole hospital, with psychiatrists and doctors and medicines. If you ever get sick, you're all set. Grammie takes *very* good care of everyone."

"Is she your grandmother?"

"Oh, no. My real grandparents have passed away, all of them. She has several girls like me. She calls us 'my girls.' Alexandra vander Zandt, me, and Rosalind Roberoy. She loves us and takes care of us. Some people *say* they care for you, but then they hurt you terribly. But not Grammie." She furrowed her brow and sucked in her breath, looking troubled. Ashley turned to another topic.

"Would you like to see the barn? It's over a hundred years old. Grammie's ancestors were the first white people here. They took the land from the Indians." She gasped. "Oh. You're an Indian. I'm sorry."

"That's all right. I've heard worse."

They walked along another path for a while. Leroy had to ask. "Ashley," the name sounded strange in his mouth, "When I came in last night, it seemed like the carvings on the walls and in the house were moving. Have you seen them do that?"

She laughed. "Oh, yes. It's another way Grammie keeps strangers away. The scary house and moving statues. Creepy stuff. She's got really nasty dogs, but they're nice when they know you. Even the way she dresses is to scare people. She wants people to think she's a witch. She's not. She's a wonderful person."

"How does she do it? I felt those carvings this morning: they're regular wood and stone."

Ashley moved closer and whispered, "I think it's very well done special effects. Like from Hollywood."

"Like in movies?"

"Yes. I know having them made would cost a lot of money, but Grammie has a lot of money. Almost as much as we do." She blushed, having mentioned money. Leroy knew from his time in England and

Europe that money was one thing rich people never mentioned. "But if you go to the back of the estate, things are normal. Like the barn."

Leroy looked up, his breath whisked away by the structure. It was an ancient wood barn with carved teak beams. It soared above his head. The huge structure sat a little way from the forest that flanked the lawns. It was old, and full of power. Life force. Any animal living there would be healthy. The place was beautiful, and bewitched.

"The paddocks and pastures are out in the back." They walked through the barn. A stunning vista of manicured fences, corrals with lush grass, and large pastures out the back greeted them. There weren't too many horses. They were Thoroughbreds and sport horses. Jumping horses.

"Grammie used to have lots of horses. She bred them. But when she had her accident—that's why her head looks like that. She broke her neck fox hunting a long time ago. They couldn't fix it back then; they didn't know how. So she looks like that."

Ashley walked up to a dark horse in the nearest paddock. "Come on, Bailey, come to me." Bailey did. She petted the horse's face. "This is my horse. I keep him here because Daddy didn't like him at home." He could see sadness wash over her.

"Why not? He looks like a nice horse." Leroy stroked the horse's dark bay neck. He wondered what had happened to the mare Kathryn Duane had given Ashley. And old Lightning. Probably stuck in quarantine, if they had even left England.

"Because he's not a show horse. He's just a nice horse. Daddy has to win in everything he does and be the best. He wants me to ride jumping horses in shows. I've done it, but it scares me. Daddy says, 'If I gave in to fear, Ashley, I'd never have gotten anywhere. You have to face fear or you'll be nothing.' The show horses live at our house. My jumpers and Mommy's Andalusians. She shows those, or the trainers do. It's like always ... Mommy ..." She stopped speaking. Ashley's face contorted. She turned away from him, and took off, running.

She ran along a path toward a stand of tall evergreen trees. He caught up with her easily. "What's the matter, Ashley?" Her cheeks were streaked with tears.

"I'm such a baby. I didn't want you to see me cry." She wiped her face with the back of her hand. "I'm almost fourteen years old and I'm crying in front of you. I don't even know you."

She looked like she wanted to bolt again, so he said, "Stay, Ashley." He put some power in his voice and she did what he wanted. "Let's walk over here and sit on that bench. You can tell me all about it. Pretend I'm your cousin. Cousin Leroy."

She smiled, a quick little smile. "You seem like a cousin already. I don't have any real cousins. Daddy had two sisters, but they died. Mommy was like me, alone."

"I'm alone too. My parents just had me. Then my mom died."

"Oh, that's sad. How old were you?"

"Six. Things got worse after my mom died. My father started drinking. And then he beat me."

"He *beat* you! That's terrible!"

"He only beat me the once. My grandpa came with some men from the reservation and took me. I didn't see my dad for fourteen years. Now tell me why you were crying." Another little jolt of power and she spoke freely.

Ashley sat upright, working her hands in her lap. "It's everything. Daddy has to have his way all the time. He doesn't listen when I say I don't want to be in horse shows. Or lots of things. I don't want to go to boarding school. They're sending me to one next year for high school. Why do I have to go to a boarding school that's twenty minutes from our house?" Tears tracked down her cheeks. She wiped at them furiously. "I know why they want to send me away. They don't like me." Her chest heaved.

Leroy resisted holding her. But he felt for her. She was a sad, lonely little girl, even before all of Donatore's abuse.

"My daddy has affairs. Do you know what that means?" Leroy nodded. "Daddy does that all the time. He comes home every three days. He has condos everywhere where he can go with *women*. He pretends that Mommy and I don't know, but we do.

"I'm never going to have sex." Those lightning bolt eyes hitting him again. "Have you had sex?"

"No, I haven't."

"That's good. If you don't have sex, you can't have an *affair* and hurt your family." Her voice rose. "Do you know that people in my class have *sex?* Girls my age. With boys that they don't even love. They told me all about it. It's disgusting."

He wanted to touch her, but his better sense told him, no.

"And my mommy. I'm so worried about her. I didn't want her to go to Spain." Ashley peered into his face as though searching for permission. "Can I talk to you about something really bad? Worse than what I've said?"

"Yes, you can. Anything. I won't tell anyone."

The tears burst out this time. "Mommy's going to Spain to have an affair. She's never had one. There's a man there who has a castle. He has parties all the time and is very good looking. Mommy showed me his picture. He talked to me on the phone. He wanted me to come too. Very much. He's a bad man. I can tell. I don't know what would have happened to me, but Grammie got me and brought me here, where I'm safe. But *Mommy's* not." The last sentence was a wail.

"I'm so worried about my mommy that I could die. Something really *bad* is going to happen." She held her arms out and leaned toward him.

They grabbed each other at the same time. When they touched, the tall trees around them shook. He felt the world spin. Electricity shot through him. She clung to him, eyes wide. A blue vapor whirled around them, shot with white and blue sparkles. The pleasure couldn't be described.

"What was that?" Ashley looked surprised, but not terrified.

"I'm a shaman. Sometimes that happens when I touch people." It had happened when he touched Cass, first in the closet and then in the plane.

"What's a shaman?"

48

PAY THE PIPER

"IS SHE ALIVE?"

"Yes, she's alive, Will." Vanessa said.

"When can I see her?"

"You can't see her. She's not ready. You're not her legal guardian any more, Will. I am. I got my attorneys working on it when you wouldn't heed my advice about where to hospitalize her. Your stupidity in involuntarily committing her to Havertin sealed the deal. A judge signed off on it today. Perfect timing."

"What?! I'm her father. You have no right."

"I have every right. Did you do more than look at a brochure before sending Cass to that place?"

"Look here, Vanessa, I feel rotten enough without you rubbing it in."

"I will rub it in, Will, until the dipshit in you breaks."

"Dipshit? I'll sue you, Vanessa, and get Cass back."

"Oh, Will. *Sue* me! *Please* sue me! It will be the legal battle of the century. My lawyers are as good as yours. I will fight until *you* are *dead*."

"Have you looked at the news, dear? I won't even mention the uproar that's going on in New York. There's a judge who's raising holy hell about the hospital. The FBI found the patients were denied their Constitutional rights, tortured, and killed. If the FBI found *you* negligent for putting her there, despite my stern warnings and my Chief Psychiatrist's strong reservations, you'd be up shit's creek. So, please sue me, Will." Her laugh was a cackle. The woman seemed more witch than physicist.

He wanted to hang up, but feared he would never see Cass again. "What can I do?"

"What you are going to do for the next few years is say, 'Yes, dear,' and sign checks. You're going to be signing some big ones very soon. You are no longer in control. You've lost the right to say what happens to your daughter."

"Will I ever get to see her again?"

"What's today, Will?"

He looked on his watch. "It's Tuesday, December 23rd."

"Christmas is in two days. You are aware of that, aren't you? Time flies when you're having fun, and all that … If all goes well, you're still invited for Christmas dinner. And don't start mooning around my gates thinking I'll let you in early. Enzo Donatore knows where Cass is. He's watching the gate."

"How!? I thought that second plane went down with no survivors."

"No human survivors. Enzo's brother Diego was on that plane. George Yeoman saw tracks along Skyline in front of my property. Demons have three toes, you know. Hard to miss."

"No!"

"Yes. Cass will live on my estate when she's well. My estate is similar to the Mogollon Bowl where you went to the retreat. It's a sacred place, a protected place. Demons can't get in …"

"But they got into the Mogollon Bowl."

"Yes, but this land has more power. We are *protected*, Will. If Cass were at your place, she'd have no protection at all. If you're a good boy, you'll get to come to Christmas dinner. Goodnight, Will."

He sat the receiver down and fell back in his chair. He'd never had an argument like that. He lost hands down. She was right about everything. And he was no longer in control.

It felt really good. He hoped he could keep things like that.

49

LEROY TELLS ALL

"A SHAMAN IS a special kind of healer. The shaman goes," to the other side, he wanted to say, but how to say it to her? "to a different place inside than where most people live. A better world. It's beautiful."

"What does that mean?" Ashley's expression was so serious and intense that he could easily have forgotten she was a little girl.

"Have you ever had a dream that seemed real? Where you seemed like you were in two worlds? Not really here, but touching something wonderful? Have you felt like you knew what was going to happen before it seemed possible? Have you ever known exactly what to say to a person to make her feel better?"

"Yes. Sometimes my dreams seem like they're real. And I feel like I know what's going to happen."

"That's some of what I feel, Ashley. I feel like I go into a different world, 'the other side,' I call it. There, I can meet people and things that help me and show me what's going to happen and what to do. They come to me and take over my body. I can heal people and animals. Plants. Anything. I can ask them to help me, and they do."

Ashley furrowed her brow. "What were all those sparkles when we touched? Was that part of 'the other side'?"

"They're energy, like electricity. It comes from the other place, through me."

She looked extremely interested, but perplexed. "How did you get like that?"

"I was born the way I am. I started healing when I was four. My mother was a great healer and her father was the greatest shaman ever. We come from a lineage of shamans that go back to the beginning."

"The beginning?"

"Yes, of life. My lineage goes all the way back to when time began. My grandfather is the greatest of all of us. Was. He died at the Meeting that your father just went to."

"My father?"

Leroy realized he'd made a mistake. "Yes, your father and a bunch of his people from Numenon went to the retreat and met my grandfather and all the spirit warriors."

"My father went to a *retreat*?"

"Yes. I met him there. I liked him." Will Duane was so different than the man Ashley described that it was hard to fathom. Different at the Meeting. But Leroy had seen his darker sides.

"You *liked* him?"

"Yes. He's a warrior and he's learning how to be who he really is."

"Who's that?"

"He's a good man, Ashley. He's changed."

She crossed her arms in front of her. "Right."

Better change the subject. "Do you want to know what a spirit warrior is? I'm a spirit warrior. Many ways of thinking and schools of thought have spirit warriors. They call them different things, but it means the same. I'm dedicated to the Great One. That's what my grandfather calls God. I belong to God. And God belongs to me. The One comes to me and I have visions and ecstasies.

"Because of those and things I do—practices, like exercises for your soul—the One comes to me and helps me. It tells me what to say and acts through me, so I heal others and make people feel better. I can do more things. To earn those gifts, I have to live a certain way. I don't drink alcohol, I don't do drugs, or gamble, or do anything that will take me away from the other side and God. I don't lie or cheat. I pray and chant, the way my grandfather taught me. I help people. It's who I am. I can't do otherwise.

"Um, there's more to it ..." He blushed as he opened the next topic. "My grandfather has hundreds of spirit warriors who help him with his work. We follow the same rules. We don't have sex if we're not married. If we're married, we only have sex with the person we're married to. None of my grandfather's warriors, or any of the people that he's married, has ever gotten a divorce."

Ashley's forehead furrowed so much it looked like a washboard. "No divorces?"

"No. Not in hundreds of couples."

"And people don't have affairs?" Her forehead furrowed more, until the muscles trembled. "Can my parents join?"

"Your father already has joined. He did at the retreat. Accepting the spirit warrior's life doesn't mean we're perfect. It takes time and you have to want to follow the rules. People make mistakes, even if they're warriors."

"Oh, yeah. My dad's *really* changed. He's got condos and hotels *everywhere* so he can meet women. He'll *never* change."

"I think he has." Leroy sort of thought Will had. But he'd made an end run. But at least she wasn't talking about ...

"You said spirit warriors don't have sex before they're married?" Disbelief coexisted with wonder on her face.

"That's right."

"That's why you haven't had sex. You're really old. Most people would have had sex by the time they got your age. How old are you?"

"I'm twenty-five. My birthday was last month."

"I can't believe that. That's so *old*." Her brows bounced up and down. "You won't have affairs when you get married?"

"No."

"Really?"

"No."

"How do I get to be a spirit warrior?"

"You already are one, Ashley. That's why the energy came to us so strongly."

"When do I find my soul mate? "

He rubbed his mouth. "It can happen any time. You'll know when it happens. Things like what happened to us will happen. That's how you can tell, when you touch someone and feel like you're in heaven. Like when we touched."

Her mouth fell open. "*We're* soul mates? You're really old. I'm only thirteen. But I'll be fourteen in two weeks."

"I know. I thought my soul mate would be the same age as me, but Grandfather saw it at the Meeting. He said we were soul mates."

"How did he know who I was?"

"Your father brought a photo album of pictures of you."

Her brows knit again. "My father went on a retreat last week? He didn't say anything about it." She seemed to search her memory. "He wasn't home, though. That's not unusual. Why would he go on a retreat and not tell me?"

"I don't know, Ashley." How would he explain what happened to her?

"*I'm* your soul mate? Don't you think you're too old for me? You're a grown-up. I'm just a kid."

Sadness filled him. "Yes, I think you're too young for me."

Ashley's scowl deepened. "We can be friends."

"Sure. We can do that." Every inch of his body that had touched her screamed for more contact. "Yeah."

"I don't want you to leave." Her jaw was tight and her fists clenched. "I want you to stay with me. You can live here."

"I don't know, Ashley. I don't know if I can."

"Why? Grammie won't mind."

"Don't you feel it?"

"What?"

"Where we touched. Don't you feel it?"

She seemed to be examining herself. "I feel like I want to touch you more." She glared at him. I want to touch you everywhere, he heard her think. "What is it? What's happening?"

He sighed. "Well, one reason the spirit warriors don't divorce and are faithful is that what they have together is better than they could have with anyone else."

"What do you mean?" Her face said she already knew what he meant. She was so quick. "You mean *sex? That's disgusting!*" Ashley jumped up and ran toward the house.

Leroy chucked pebbles, bouncing them along the cement path. He'd thought the hard part was over.

What he didn't tell her was the countdown had begun. They'd touched each other. When soul mates touched each other, it was like a timer being set. The places where they'd touched would burn until they married and consummated their love.

What would he do if he had to wait four years?

50

IT'S BEGINNING TO LOOK
A LOT LIKE CHRISTMAS

THE HOUSE WAS bustling when Ashley let herself in the back door. Mrs. Cook and a crew of village people filled the kitchen, along with wonderful smells. "What's going on, Grammie?"

Dr. Schierman jumped. She wasn't used to Ashley's young voice. Cass had called her by her first name, Vanessa. "You startled me. Tomorrow's Christmas, dear. We're having a feast and everyone we know is invited. We're having a smaller gathering tonight, for the people in the house. Prime rib roast and all the trimmings tonight; turkeys, ham and everything else tomorrow. George Yeoman and his men are barbecuing the roast and setting up decorations outside. They brought in a Christmas tree while you and Leroy were talking. Where is Leroy?"

"He wanted to look at the horses some more." She hoped her lie didn't show on her face. She also hoped she never saw Leroy again. Her hands tingled where she had touched him.

Her room was upstairs next to Grammie's. She looked in the closet. Dresses so beautiful they should belong to a princess hung there. She took them out, marveling. "Oh, Grammie." She loved her so much.

Ashley's drawers were full of sweaters and nighties. An embarrassing drawer was filled with beautiful underwear. A lacey bra was on top … She didn't wear a bra. But it was beautiful.

Her tummy and arms where she'd touched Leroy ached in a good/bad way. She felt like she'd die if she didn't hold him soon. They were soul mates, that longing said. But what could they do? She was a kid.

Ashley moved to the desk in her room. A top of the line Numenon Ranger laptop was set up there. It must be a new model, because she hadn't seen one so sleek. Ashley was used to things like this. Her dad often brought home experimental computers and other things that Numenon was working on. He must have given this one to Grammie.

She powered it up and began her research. The Internet hadn't been around very long, but it was huge. In school, they told them that there were thousands websites. She didn't need that many for what she was thinking about.

What she searched for was, "How old do people have to be to get married, by state?" She kept thinking about Leroy and how he holding her had felt, with the trees whirling and sparkles and all. She wanted him to be very, very close to her.

And she didn't. Those girls in her class were *awful,* having sex and not being married. If they were married, all that would happen is they would start having affairs, like her parents. But if they were spirit warriors? They wouldn't act like her parents.

She wished she hadn't made her stupid search, anyway. She wasn't going to marry Leroy and she certainly wasn't going to have sex with him. Though she wanted to be *so* close to him. Embarrassed, Ashley moved from site to site.

He wouldn't have sex if he wasn't married. That was truly awesome. He was *really* old. Twenty five. That was … almost as old as Doug and the people who worked for her father. Too old for a little girl like her. But she wasn't a little girl, not at all.

She pushed forward and did more searches and tabulated the results. Then she wrote an essay.

Why I am a woman and not a little girl:

- I am 5' 7" tall. Many women aren't that tall. I'm bigger than most grown-up women.
- I got my period when I was eleven. That means I'm not a little girl, I'm an adult. In some countries, no one would think anything of me getting married.
- Many states allow people who are my age to get married. The people getting married have to have their parents' permission, but some states legally allow the marriages. See the attached report by state.
- I'm smart and know more about the world and feelings than many grownups.
- Leroy and I are soul mates. If we get married this young, it doesn't matter, because soul mates don't have affairs or get divorced. We'll be happier than you and Mommy are.

That isn't what she started out to research. She wanted to know if girls her age could get married and where. How did her essay change to the reasons she was a woman and could marry Leroy? She had addressed her arguments to her father. Ashley knew he would be the hard one to convince. Of what?

Her brow creased. She needed to think about some other things. Ashley had noticed facts that didn't add up.

If Mommy was supposed to come back from Spain at the end of August, why isn't she home for Christmas? If Mommy was going to be late, she would tell me. She would phone. She knows I worry about her. Ashley's brow furrowed as she thought.

Why would Daddy go on a retreat and not tell me? Why would he go on a retreat at all? He doesn't care about God.

The Numenon Ranger laptop she was working was XII. Her Ranger at home was IV. That was eight models from her laptop. *It took Daddy's people years put out a new model. It would take him almost until the year 2,000 to get to XII. That was years and years from now.*

Also, she visited Grammie's house all the time. She'd been there a week earlier. The family room, the big room with the kitchen, wasn't as large as it was now. It didn't have the whole wall of windows and glass doors, either. The walls had been lacquered a deep red with white trim. The upholstered furniture was the same red, and all the wood trim was lacquered shiny black.

Today, the room was light and bright with pale yellow floral prints. The furniture was pale wood. The room was bigger, and there was more stuff in it. The kitchen was new.

Even Grammie couldn't redecorate that fast.

Something else. She went to her computer and clicked where the date appeared on the top. It didn't. Nothing on the computer said the date.

This was so strange.

She couldn't think about anything more. Her head ached and she felt dizzy. Mrs. Naughton came with a milk drink and she gulped it down. She knew what those did.

Even sound asleep in her bed, Ashley thought of Leroy. She ached for him. She'd marry him, as long as they didn't have to have sex.

51

CHRISTMAS EVE

"HI, POP!" LEROY and his dad had played phone tag so much Leroy forgot that the man existed outside of a voice on a machine. "I'm in California. I forgot to call and tell you I didn't need that plane ticket. I hope you can get your money back."

His father was completely silent. Finally, he said, "Glad you're back, Leroy. I reckon I can cash it in."

His dad didn't get any ticket for him. He was lying. He'd forgotten about him entirely. He'd been playing polo against monsters and robots, in a game televised all over the world, and his dad didn't know or care.

"Hey, Pop," he started conversation again, "would you like to come up to Northern California for Christmas tomorrow? Dr. Schierman, whose place I'm staying at, asked me to invite you. She'll send a jet for you. I'd love to see you."

His pop's hesitation let him know he was right. Something was up. "Well, son. I'd love to come, but … things have changed. Remember the Meyers place next door where they both died and some rich folks from Silicon Valley bought it? And then they remodeled it and gave me all their old stuff for your cabin?"

"Yeah, I remember."

"They got a divorce. They put the place on the market and it got snapped up right away. I went over there to meet the new owners. Turned out it was one owner, a widow lady from back East—Connecticut. She used to fox hunt back there. Real good rider. She wanted to 'live her dream' while she could, and that was on a nice, big ranch in California. She thought that place next to us was heaven. Thing is, she didn't know a thing about ranchin' or cattle. I helped her some. Quite a bit. She appreciated it a lot. She liked me too." Leroy could feel his pop shifting from foot to foot over the phone, or shifting from something to something.

"I fell in love, son. Susan's the prettiest, nicest, smartest lady. I never knew one could be so fine—or love me back.

"When I went over to visit the first time, she said she'd heard of me. She said she was thrilled to be living near the great bullfighter! She'd been my fan for years. Leroy, Susie and I got married a couple of months ago. Flew to Las Vegas and tied the knot. It was kind of love at first sight."

Leroy froze. He blinked. "What?"

"We live most of the time at her place. That's why I missed your calls. Damned if chipmunks didn't eat the wires at our place. You know how they do that. We come over here when we want some quiet." Now, his dad was smiling so hard; Leroy could feel *it* over the phone. "She's got her ranch manager and her horse trainers at her place. And the ranch hands. She wants to start a hunt club soon. They're workin' on that. It's kind of a zoo over there. It's private at our place. She thinks it's *romantic*. Historical and all."

"Why didn't you tell me, Dad? Do you have any idea how worried I've been?" *Do you know what I've been doing? That I could have gotten killed about a million times? Do you care about me?*

"Sorry, son. Love is blind, they say. Sometimes it's stupid too."

Leroy wanted this conversation over. "OK. Can you come tomorrow, Dad? Dr. Schierman wanted everyone to arrive about three. She'll send a jet. Or a plane if the town runway isn't long enough."

"That's OK. Susie can use her plane. And her runway. Just finished. See you at three." His father went on, sounding contrite. "I'm sorry, Leroy. One thing has led to another. I'm surprised as hell myself. I didn't tell you because I was embarrassed to fall in love again, as old as I am." He cleared his throat. "And I was afraid you'd be mad at me."

"Why?"

"I thought you might think that I don't love your mom anymore. That's not true." His dad's voice went husky. "I will *always* love your mother. Emily is my one true love. Don't think I've forgotten her."

"I know how much you loved Mama, Pop."

"Well, good. We'll talk tomorrow. I love you, boy."

"What's her name?"

"Susie Watches, now. Before that, she was Susan Anderson."

He staggered into the living room as they were serving drinks.Dr. Schierman was not pleased when she heard that his father had added a guest. "He got married, Dr. Schierman. Didn't even tell me."

"Who is she, Leroy?"

"Her name was Susan Anderson. She used to live in Connecticut."

Having completed that delightful bit of information sharing and bonding with his father, Leroy went in for the Christmas Eve dinner. Ashley sat across from him. She wore the most beautiful long dress, a red and green and white plaid in some material that rustled. Her hair was swept up on top of her head with ringlets falling down. She had a little makeup on. He could barely breathe; she didn't look like a little girl at all. He couldn't talk to her much. The dining table was so wide, it made conversation difficult. He looked at her instead.

The table rivaled any of the English Lords'; vast and covered with candelabras, arrangements of holly and berries and bows, palatial silver, crystal and linens. He used everything he learned in his travels in eating dinner. He was delighted to concentrate on silverware rather than the sensations in his body and thoughts and feelings tumbling through his head.

Ashley caught him in the hallway when he was heading to his room.

"Leroy," she said. "I've been considering our situation as soul mates. I've done a study of legal marital age by state. In many states, girls who are almost fourteen can get married. They'll even allow it in California, if your parents agree. I think you have to go to a counselor, though.

"And I'm ... physically mature. In India and China, no one would care at all. I'm five foot seven. That's as tall as many grown up women. Actually, the average size of a woman in the United States is 63.7 inches, only five foot three, almost four. I'm way taller than average. I'm still growing too. I think we should get married."

She pressed herself against him and grabbed the back of his head with her hands. He had to bend over to kiss her, but not as much as he did with Arabella. She *was* tall. Sweat broke out all over him and his hands went all over her. As hers did too.

"Ashley, stop. I can't do this." She pulled away from him. He swayed, sweating, blowing like a stud horse ready to mount a mare. "Oh, God, Ashley. I have to marry you. I'm so in love with you. We have to get married. I'm going to die ..."

"We will, Leroy. We can go to Las Vegas. Grammie is my guardian. She will sign for me. We'll do it tomorrow after dinner, OK?"

He'd wanted to be married in a green, leafy wedding bower with vines reaching up and flowers trumpeting. He wanted Grandfather to marry them and all the elders to be present. He wanted smoke and feathers and all his friends chanting.

Breathing hard, he said, "Las Vegas will be fine."

He remembered Will saying long ago that they had to be in love by Christmas. He didn't mean married too, Leroy knew. But damn, you couldn't be more in love than Ashley and he.

52

MERRY CHRISTMAS

LEROY AWAKENED, RELAXING in bed lazily, until he remembered that he and Ashley were getting married in Las Vegas later that day. His father was coming with his new wife. It was Christmas.

He swung his legs to the floor and sat up. Ashley was sleeping in the other bed in his room. His eyes widened. He grabbed his clothes and ran to the bathroom to put them on.

When he was dressed, he stood over her as she slept. He was swept away by her beauty and innocence. But she shouldn't be where she was.

"Ash. Ash. Wake up." He jiggled her shoulder a bit. "Wake up! You have to leave."

She raised her head sleepily and looked at him. "What are you doing in my bedroom?"

"It's my bedroom, can't you see?"

"Oh … I sleep walked. I do that."

A knock on the door. "Ashley and Leroy, you must come out. Dr. Schierman needs you."

Leroy slipped out, blushing.

"Don't worry about me," Mrs. Naughton said. "I've seen everything in this house."

"We didn't do anything. I swear." Leroy raised his hands, protesting innocence.

"I know. Now, you're going to do something."

Mrs. Naughton suggested that he dress for dinner later that day. The village women had made him a surprise. Leroy found out there was a village behind the house, way out in the forest. Short, powerful men in muted green tunics inhabited it. They worked all over the estate, George Yeoman being their leader. They were Vanessa's ancestral people. He hadn't seen any women, but assumed they were there.

He knew the women existed when he saw the shirt. It was black cotton. Hundreds of ribbons in all colors streamed from its yokes and shoulders. It was the wedding shirt worn by his People! The women in the village had made a ribbon shirt for him.

He blinked hard, holding back his feelings. Maybe they'd be able to get married without incident. Will Duane wouldn't show up with a machete and gang of thugs. They'd eat dinner, and then fly to Las Vegas.

He walked into the entrance hall to find Dr. Schierman with her eyes closed and arms raised over her head. She was saying something in a language he didn't know, but he could understand it. That was one of his powers.

"O walls of the entrance hall, you will be quiet and still today. We are having a party. You will not scare people. Walls of the living and dining rooms, you will be still. Quiet." She turned to the door. "Oh, walls and carvings outside, today you will be like dead stone. You will not move or upset anyone. All of you walls will make your carvings into pretty things, sweet things that will not frighten people." A pause. "It's just for today. You can go back tomorrow."

The crone opened her eyes and turned to him. "Hello, Leroy. Things will start moving now. I need to go out and handle the dogs so they don't kill anyone. And there's a delivery outside for you."

"Me?"

People began to arrive, but only people close to the Schierman family and him. Will had brought a whole bunch of his People home from the Meeting the week before. Carl Redman and Roxy Crow Moon. They'd married, that was a surprise. Carl was as big and tattooed as ever, beaming. Bud Creeman and Bert walked into the entrance hall. Bert was holding a baby, but he could see she was bulging again. More people, more wonderful couples. Finally, Doug and Janice.

Leroy was practically bowled over when the big front door opened and the next guest, or guests, arrived.

"Hi, son! Good to see you." His father hugged him as hard as one of the Yosemite grizzlies would have. "I'd like you to meet Susie."

She was about five foot five, with grey hair cut chin length. Looked like a rider; athletic and strong. Like she'd be more at home in riding britches and boots than the dress she was wearing. "How do you do, Leroy? I've heard so much about you. We'll have to ride together one day."

"Um. That would be nice." Maybe.

"Susie! How wonderful to see you," Dr. Schierman appeared and saved him. "It's been so long. The meeting of the Hunt Board in Maryland." To Leroy, she said, "We've known each other for years. Since before I got this," she indicated her terribly damaged neck. "Susie is Mrs. Fox Hunting America, informally, of course."

Suzie smiled, lighting the area around her. She put her arm through his dad's, glowing with happiness. Maybe she was OK.

"I'd still be riding with you, except it might make me a quadriplegic," Vanessa said. Turning to Leroy she said, "Go to my study, dear. Someone wants to see you. Mrs. Naughton will show you the way."

"Grandfather!" Leroy's jaw fell open. He couldn't close it. His feet wobbled beneath him. "I thought you were dead."

"So did I, my son, but I wasn't allowed to stay where I was. I had to come back *here*." He sounded like being alive was a curse. "I have more work to do, helping people. Starting with you. What troubles you, my son?"

His grandpa held him as he told the horrible stories of rescuing Cass only to have her be swallowed by something worse. Of how it was to hold Cass when she was hemorrhaging. He hadn't thought of that since he'd seen Ashley, but a glimpse of his Grandpa, and it was all back. Leroy thought he was going to be sick.

He was sick. Grandfather healed him as they sat. The trauma didn't just affect Cass; it affected everyone who knew about it, but it affected those who were closest to her most. Her soul mate, most of all.

Leroy shivered, feeling everything he hadn't acknowledged since that terrible night. "How could they do that to her? How could anyone do that?"

"My son, women are raped to death every day. We just don't see it. Rape is torture and terrorism and a weapon of war. It always has been. You know what happened to our women when the Europeans came. We did the same thing to their wives and daughters whenever we could.

"You said, 'How could they do it?' They can because their goodness is covered by evil. In our lineage, we call the devil on Earth Enzo Donatore. In other places, the evil one has a different face. That's what happened to Cass. None of it was her fault. Once she entered Donatore's castle, she was doomed. She died on that plane, didn't she?"

Leroy nodded. His ribcage convulsed as he sobbed. "She died in my arms. Her blood was all over me. They killed her."

"And Dr. Schierman brought her back."

"How did she do it?"

"I don't know, my son. She has powerful magic. European magic that I don't know. Vanessa told me that she's back, as Ashley, the pure

and innocent child." Leroy sobbed harder. "Which is your other problem, isn't it? She's thirteen years old, almost fourteen, and she's your soul
mate. You've touched each other and you're both burning.

"Can you wait four years until she grows up?"

Leroy shook his head. "I'll die. I'll have to go off somewhere and not
see her. But even then, I'll die. Help me, Grandfather." He gave the shaman a rundown of what Ashley had said about not being a little girl.

"That's true: she isn't a little girl. She's the reincarnation of Cass. Cass
before she was ruined. Cass gets another chance through Ashley."

"Can she feel Cass?"

"No, but Cass can feel you. She's in love with you too."

"How do you know?"

"She's your soul mate. I know your soul." Grandfather heaved a sigh.
"An unusual case, but workable. The hardest part will be convincing Will
Duane what we're going to do is all right."

"What are we going to do?"

"You're going to marry Ashley in a few minutes. Her father is going
to give her away and be happy. Then we'll have a big party. But right
this moment, I'm going to tell you how to love Ashley so that you don't
hurt her and she remains intact until she is eighteen. And you both are
fulfilled."

"I'm here, Vanessa." Will stood in the front doorway, feeling twice as
bedraggled as he looked. He peered into the living room. "You've got a
big party."

"Yes, tonight is a night to celebrate. Come in my office, dear. We
need to have a fast powwow."

Will walked toward her office, dreading passing the creepy carved
paneling in the hall. He snuck a peak as he walked by. A carved tab-
leau of bunnies and Easter eggs covered one panel. Rudolf, Santa and
the sleigh flew across the next. A Christmas scene with a Holy Family
and shepherds grinning like maniacs filled the third. The baby Jesus

bounced up and down in his manger in ecstasy. The new carvings were worse than the flapping bats.

Will opened the door, prepared for another lambasting. A tiny figure sat across the room.

"Grandfather! I thought you were dead!" Will cried.

"Everyone keeps saying that. I was dead, and now I'm not. I'm *here*." Grandfather sat in an overstuffed chair on the other side of the room. "I'll never be able to get out of this chair. You'll have to pull me out." He frowned.

"What's the matter, Joseph?" Vanessa said, entering after Will.

"I've been teaching my grandson how to do what can't be done."

"Did you do it?"

"Of course."

"Wait a second! How do you know Grandfather, Vanessa?" Vanessa and Grandfather were obviously relaxed around each other. Familiar, even. Will's jaw had no muscles capable of keeping it closed.

"We've known each other since the 1930s. We were graduate students together in Berkeley. Physics and divinity. Perfect combination," she said, archly.

"Except we fought so much." His brow furrowed.

"We discussed issues passionately, Joseph. We did not *fight*. He really is opinionated, Will. Worse than you, but more correct in his thoughts. Let's get down to business. Will, you haven't seen Ashley since she arrived here?"

"No. You wouldn't let me on the estate." He shot a glance at her, but didn't try to make eye contact. Who knows what she might say? He jerked around. "You said *Ashley*?"

"Yes, Will. She's Ashley. Thirteen years old and untouched. Except by her parents. She had a severe alcoholic for a mother and a debauched, achievement–obsessed womanizer for a father. That's quite a load for any kid. She didn't need to be captured by the devil to have problems."

"How did you do it?"

"What I did is my business. I will never tell. Never ask me again." A hiss sizzled around the room. Some of the little forest animals carved on the wall looked fierce for a moment.

"When do I get to see her?"

"We have a few things to discuss. You know that Leroy is her soul mate?" Will nodded. "That didn't go away just because Cass died and was reborn as Ashley. Ashley loves him as much as Cass did. They've touched; they're pining for each other. I don't think either of them will last the night. We'll find Ashley in Leroy's bed and the deed will be done."

"He can't do that. That's statutory rape. It's illegal."

"Will, in many states, people Ashley's age can marry with a court order and parental approval. In Nevada, for instance. Ashley said that she and Leroy wanted to go to Las Vegas after dinner. I told her she didn't have to.

"In California, she would have to see a counselor, appear before a judge, and have one parent present when she applied for a marriage license. But she *can* marry, here and now. I have a certified copy of Ashley's birth certificate. It says she's thirty-two. And her finger prints. I obtained a marriage license from the County Clerk this morning ..."

"How could you do that if she's thirteen? The Clerk would see it immediately." Will's collar felt like a noose.

"The clerk hasn't seen Ashley, Will. Just me and Hannah Herhman."

"Hannah Herhman?"

"Yes, she helped me get the birth certificate and Ashley's fingerprints from your records. If you fire her for doing that, Will, I'll hire her in a heartbeat."

"How could you get a Clerk out here? It's Christmas Day?"

Vanessa chuckled, "Will, dear, what's the use of having influence if you don't use it?"

Will tugged at the noose circling his throat. Sweat appeared on his forehead. He was so confused. "She's a little girl, Vanessa. I remember her before she went to Spain. A darling child."

"You'll find her more mature, Will. Dying and being reborn will do that. However, she's as tall as a grown woman ..." Vanessa ran through all the points Ashley had written on her computer about why she wasn't a little girl. "So, you'll see it's not so cut and dry."

"There's more than that, Will and Vanessa," Grandfather said. "Enzo Donatore knows she's here. George Yeoman saw tracks that could only come from a demon in human form, and so did I. They have only three toes on their feet. Enzo will know about her rebirth. Say she leaves this property and he gets her again. That's not an unreasonable proposition. We know what will happen. But what if her husband, a powerful spirit warrior, was with her? He could keep Donatore and his monsters away."

"Can he?"

"He can now. He's in love with her. Love is the most powerful force in the universe. She'll be safe with Leroy wherever she goes."

"OK. We're done with all this. Let's have a wedding." Vanessa led them into the living room.

53

MERRY, MERRY CHRISTMAS

LIGHTS TWINKLED, LOGS crackled, and candles flickered. The tree was so enormous that it touched the ceiling, two and a half stories above. Every branch, every twig, bore an ornament. Pungent evergreen garlands perfumed the hall.. A mistletoe plant the size of a small car hung from the ceiling in the front of the room. Scents of turkey and gravy, mulled cider, and pumpkin pie filled the air. People were laughing and chatting; some were old friends; others had met for the first time.

An altar was set up in front of the Christmas tree: buffalo skull, eagle feathers, and more stuff. Leroy stood on its left in his wildly festive ribbon shirt. Carl Redman got up and joined him. "Couldn't let you do this alone, buddy."

All the Native Americans filled rows of chairs on the left side, including Leroy Sr. and his new wife. That was the husband's side.

The Duane side was more sparsely populated. The executives who had gone to the Meeting were there with their wives. Some moved over from the Indian side when they saw how meager Will's troops were. Hannah Hehrman came, without her mercenaries.

Will walked across the hall from Vanessa's study. A lovely young woman stood at the entrance to the living room. Tall and elegant, her dark hair was swept up on her head, with little ringlets hanging down. Her perfect carriage, the way she stood and moved a hand to adjust her skirt, said she was a lady of distinction. What he could see of her, a bit of her shoulder and neck and her upper arm, was so pale, so fair. His breath caught. She wore a wedding dress.

The skirt of her dress touched the floor and a long train flowed behind it. Layers of white silk organza created a breathtaking confection. The dress wasn't just white. Embroidered holly sprigs in red and green bordered the frock's edges and were scattered over the gown. She held a bouquet of gardenias, lilies, and holly in her right hand. Tendrils of white flowers reached the floor. A few wisps of white formed her veil. She wore it tossed back, away from her face.

He saw all that in an instant. The young lady turned toward him, letting the light fall on her pale skin and shining, dark blue eyes. She was elegant and patrician, everything he'd wanted his daughter to be. He jumped when he recognized her.

It was *Ashley*, all grown up.

"Ashley!" he cried, dashing across the foyer toward her.

She turned, saw who he was, and stepped backward. Her skin grew paler. She put one hand to her mouth, eyes widening impossibly. "*Daddy*! What *happened* to you?" She retreated further. "You're so *old*. How did you get so *old*?"

"No, no. It's all right, Ashley. I'm fine." He walked toward her, holding out his hands.

"You're *not* fine. Where's Mommy? I'm getting married. Mommy would be here for my wedding." Her eyes blazed, but tears streaked her cheeks. "Mommy would come; *nothing* could keep her away." She held her hands out to repel him. "I don't want *you. I want my mommy! Where is she? What did you do to her?*"

People stood up and started to leave the room. This was a family moment not meant for sharing.

"Something has happened. She was going to Spain from June to August. It's *December*. She wouldn't stay without telling me. Something *terrible* happened. No one is telling me. Where is *Mommy*?" Tears burst from her. Ashley did nothing about them; she was mindless of the fact she was made up for her wedding.

"Ashley, your mother divorced me. I don't know where she is."

"*You're divorced?!* Oh, no! You can't be *divorced.*" The word stretched out, becoming a wail, the wail of a child mortally wounded. "*Mommy. I want Mommy.*"

Will didn't have the faintest idea what to do. And then Leroy was there. Leroy wrapped himself around her, pulling her into his warm body, holding her to his heart. He kept her there and whispered, just loud enough for Will to hear.

"Darlin', something did happen. I'll tell you all about it bye and bye. We were gettin' married, Ashley. Do you want to do that? Do you want to marry me?"

She pulled back and looked at him with streaked cheeks. "Yes. I love you. I want to marry you."

"Come on, darlin'. Let's do it." He took her hand and walked her down the aisle. She didn't give her father a parting glance.

That was how Will Duane gave away his little girl.

54

MARRIED FOR EVER

WILL STOOD IN the back of the room, watching. Grandfather with his feathers and sage, his pipe and his glory filled the room and everyone in it. The three of them stood in front of the Christmas tree, the shaman chanting and reading Scriptures. Such a strange juxtaposition, but so brilliant and true.

He had his daughter back. His little girl, ruined so young, was whole again. She was marrying a wonderful man. Will could feel Leroy's soul when he held Ashley. He was healing her. He would heal her whenever she needed it. He would protect her from anything. She'd be safe from Donatore with Leroy.

At the end of the ceremony, after "I pronounce you man and wife," Leroy pulled away from Ashley and faced her.

"I will always love you,
"My moon and my stars.
"You're the breath that sustains me,
"The truth in my arms.
"I will never leave you.

Will didn't realize he was singing for a moment. Leroy had a huge, deep voice that rumbled in his chest. His words sounded like talking, but they weren't. Leroy was singing to his wife.

"I'm yours for this lifetime,
"I'm yours long past that.
"I'll keep you in love,
"I will keep you from strife.
"I will always love you,
"My beautiful wife.

"I love you, Ashley. I've loved you since I was born." He bent over and kissed her. Golden sparkles spiraled around them. There was a *crack*! like an electric discharge.

Will couldn't stand it. Leroy's voice fractured his soul. Everything he'd held back was loosened. His throat worked like he was choking to death. His ribs heaved in and out. He could not stay there. People could not see him like that. He glanced toward the Christmas tree. Leroy and Ashley glowed like beacons before it. She was back, and she didn't love him.

He bolted, running from the living room through the kitchen. The air was full of steam and smells of delicious food. Serving dishes piled with delicacies covered the counters. A bunch of those little village people stood around.

Vanessa had a gazebo out in back. Will made for it and locked the door. Barely aware of what he was doing, he turned to the rear of the gazebo and threw himself face down on the floor. His head was pointed toward a wilting geranium. He stretched his hands toward it.

"I'm so sorry. I'm so sorry." The sound of Ashley's cry pierced everything. If she had made that noise earlier, would it have made a difference?

Would he have stopped doing what he did to save his daughter's pain? And his wife's?

Would they have been a good family, Kathryn and he still married, and Ashley never needing to go through what she did? Would hearing her cry earlier have saved them?

He wouldn't have heard it. He was lost in himself. Lost in his endless stream of women. Lost in being the 'best of the best."

"I'm sorry. I'm so sorry. I was stupid. No, I was a shit. I was a bad man. I was a fornicator." He spoke to something that was there, around him and in him. "I wrecked my family. Kathryn could have gotten better, if I'd been home. I know that. Please forgive me."

He was panting, gasping for breath. "Ashley's back. I don't deserve her to be back. I don't deserve *anything*. I did nothing to fix things. I sent her to that horrible place where she *died*. Ashley *died*. Cass *died*.

"And it's my fault." Will lay there for quite a while, arms stretched toward the flowerpot. He grew still.

Something was talking to him. I forgive you, my child.

That was it. He was forgiven. Something touched him, a delicate touch like being stroked by a feather. It caressed the top of his head. His eyes closed, but he wasn't asleep. He dropped into something. Something he'd found at the Meeting, something he'd always known. The home of forgiveness, the home of peace, the home of joy and plenty and love. Softly suspended, it came to him, what he loved above all. He was forgiven and his dear one was there.

55

SOUL MATES

"DR. SCHIERMAN WANTS y' to live here for as long as y' want," George Yeoman, leader of the village, drove them across the lawn in a cart. They stopped at a log cabin at the outskirts of the woods. "She built the cabins for the families of the patients in the hospital. Sure 'n' her own kiddies are there, but she brings in other patients too. They need to see their families, an' sure enough work things out together.

"But they're empty now, 'cept for this one, which is the biggest." George opened the door and they entered a wooden masterpiece. Rows of stacked logs made the walls. Huge beams projected inward from their tops, creating a soaring triangle of wood, the very high ceiling. "It's not empty now, as ye'll be livin' here."

"It's like being inside a nut," Ashley marveled, raising her chin to examine the latticework of logs and their warm, light brown color.

"Yeah, it's that. We put some clothes in th' closets an' food in the kitchen. You'll be staying here a while. Fer yer honeymoon, of course." George blushed. "An' y' need to get settled as to what y' want to do next. This is yer home. Ah'll be biddin' ye g'night."

"Oh, look." Ashley and Leroy explored their abode. "Come here." She stood in the bedroom. It had the log walls of the cabin, but an amazing canopy bed filled much of the space. It was metal, wrought vines rising and intertwining from each corner, growing upward with leaves and blossoms so well made that they seemed to be real. A tiny sculptured hummingbird was attached to a blossom by its beak. The corners grew high and formed an arch over the center. A wedding bower. White silken draperies hung from the framework.

"It's so romantic. And look at the flowers everywhere. They smell wonderful." Ashley marveled at the vases of flowers. Grammie had done this, Grammie and her people. All the flowers were white. Roses, lilies, giant stars that exploded from purple centers, little bells that drooped. "It's so beautiful."

Leroy's eyes stung. He'd wanted this for so long.

"I guess we should go to bed now," Ashley said, looking determined. "We don't have to do anything. Even though I want to, and I'm not a little girl, I think we should wait until I get older."

"So do I."

"I saw a night gown in the bedroom closet. Maybe they have something for you to wear in the bathroom." She closed the closet door. She loved Leroy so much, but when the possibility of sex came close, Ashley wasn't sure she wanted it.

The nightgown was a pale blue silk with a flowing skirt. It was pretty, but not low cut. It had a fine robe of the same material, a kimono. She put both of them on and sat on the side of the bed. "You can come in now."

Leroy walked out of the bathroom and she whooped with laughter. "Oh my! What are those?"

He laughed too. He was wearing an enormous pair of flannel pajamas, bright red, printed with zany reindeer in white. Leroy said, "They glow in the dark too."

"Turn the light off and let me see. They do! They glow! Grammie must have gotten them. She does things like that. They're so funny. Oh, Leroy." They laughed together. Everything got easier after that.

Natural as anything, they were in bed, lying side by side, holding hands.

Touching him made thrills of pleasure sparkle through her. Maybe …

"Darlin', do you trust me?"

"Yes." Leroy was breathtakingly beautiful lying so close.

"Grandfather told me what to do so we can be happy while you grow up."

"What?"

"I'd like to take you somewhere. I started going there when I was four years old. It's safe, just different."

"Will it hurt?"

"No, sweetheart. Anything but that." He took her hand and kissed it. "Do you want to go now?"

She nodded.

They were in a strange space, dim and gray-green. Nothing was there. Leroy stood next to her, wearing his crazy PJs, while she wore the gown and robe. She clutched his hand. The wind moaned, but she couldn't feel it against her skin.

They moved toward something. Ashley realized it was a wall, a curtain wall the same murky color as the rest of the place. As they moved closer, the wall began to hum. Closer, and it ripped from top to bottom. Brilliant yellow light burst from it, from the other side. The light was like water, flowing into the dingy chamber.

Leroy pulled her through the opening. Light so bright and gold that it seemed a physical substance surrounded them. Went through them. It was inside her and outside her. It was like the electricity that had shocked her and Leroy when they touched. Shocking, not shocking. Exciting, calming.

She turned to him. He was illuminated, brilliant. Light shone from inside his mouth and eyes. She pulled away, but he let her know that it was safe. He pulled her farther inside. They fell down something, a tube, a slide. It twisted and turned like a waterslide in a park. It was funny. Leroy threw some gold stuff at her. She threw it back.

Fight! She laughed. They threw a brilliant substance at each other. He grabbed her and they rolled in it, gold spangles sticking to them. When they touched, bliss exploded. They were the center of the explosion, everything moving around them. Threads of bliss. Threads of meaning. Threads of love. Bound them, pulled them together.

Together—they shot together like mighty magnets grabbed them. Ashley couldn't think. Time seemed to stop. She saw Leroy, next to her, his tummy pressed against her tummy. A moaning sound, the air in a cavern, surrounded them. The light pressed them together.

Ashley felt herself enlarge, open up. Her body expanded until it was huge, then larger than that. She filled the enormous grotto. She touched its sides, and then moved past them; nothing could contain her. Chimes sounded, and bells.

Leroy pulled her to him. Then he disappeared. Where he had been was an outline in nothing, and then nothingness itself. She looked at her arm. Transparent, just moving light. She separated more, expanding, until she saw herself floating in the bliss. Vast distances in space, and a tiny nugget here and there. A hard kernel suspended in infinity floated by.

Everything was like that, nothingness, emptiness, tiny elements of … What? And then she understood. Those were molecules, her molecules, and the space was how she really was. Her science teacher had told them that their bodies were mostly water, in compounds, but if you went deeper than that, all they were was nothingness and molecules.

Atoms. Bits of existence. They were mostly nothing and could walk through walls or anything, if they got separated out enough.

Leroy was entering her. She could feel his bright dark soul, his nothingness. The joyous void. Kernels drifted by, so like her own. He was entering her, but not her body. Leroy joined with her spirit.

How long can an ocean of bliss last? How far is the universe from side to side? They lingered in paradise, mostly space with a few bits of matter. No one could be joined like a shaman and his mate.

Leroy was her, and she was him. Molecules of one were interspersed in the nothingness of each other. Up didn't exist, nor down, nor space or time.

He filled her with himself and she gave back her soul.

He was lying next to her, one leg over hers, still in his pajamas. She had never seen such a beautiful man. She hadn't seen *any* men, but even movie stars weren't like him. They were married. They were really married. People could be wed for twenty years and have every kind of sex, and they wouldn't be as joined as she and Leroy.

She watched him sleep for a while. Sunlight poured through the window. How long had they been in that place? Forever. They would live in bliss forever. That's what Leroy brought.

Ashley knew she wasn't a little girl.

56

A PRINCESS

THE SMELL OF bacon and coffee awakened her. Leroy was gone, the PJs lying on the floor. He was cooking breakfast. Ashley looked at her gown and kimono, feeling a bit embarrassed. She couldn't wear them in front of him in the daylight; they belonged to that golden world.

The closet contained all sorts of clothes for her. She'd never seen them before and they were all new, but she liked them.

She selected blue jeans and a white cotton shirt printed with red squares. A little blue flower sat on the Xs where the red squares met. She tucked in the shirt and pulled on brand new boots, then tried to fix her face. She washed her face and arranged her hair.

Leroy seemed a little scary now. They were married. That was so weird.

"Hi, sweetheart!" His smile erased any fear. He was Leroy. Her husband. He was in the kitchen standing by the stove, a frying pan in one hand and another with a lid on it on a back burner.

"You know how to cook?" It seemed an amazing feat. Her father never entered the kitchen.

"Oh, yeah. I'm the barbecue king of the universe. I do pretty much everything else, too."

Her legs seemed to melt and the room spun. Her head fell to one side as she dropped.

When she came to, he sat on the sofa, cradling her in his arms. Her face was nestled into his shoulder. She pulled back and looked at him. His were wide, terrified.

"Oh, sweetie. You fainted. I didn't know what was happenin'. You've been through so much."

Someone knocked at the door. "Rudi Heimlach here with George Zimmerman."

"Come in," Leroy called. "She's here."

Ashley jumped up, sitting erect. "Who are they?"

"I'm a psychiatrist and George is in internal medicine. We're from Dr. Schierman's hospital," said the short one with the fat stomach.

"Oh, no! *Doctors!*" Ashley leapt to her feet. Her head began to swim again. Leroy grabbed her and held her tight in his lap. She grabbed his arm, beseeching. "Never let a *doctor* touch me, please, Leroy. Please. Never!" Panic overtook her ability to think. Her eyes rolled back.

He grabbed her upper arms and held her in front of his face. "Ashley, no one is ever going to hurt you again. No one, and nothing, and no doctors. You're safe."

She started whimpering and then crying, feeling like a stupid baby, but too scared to care.

"Leroy, we can do an exam with your help. You have the sensitivity. Feel her pulse, right here in her neck." The internist touched his own neck to demonstrate. "Tell me how it counts out. Start." He hit a button on his watch. "And then put your hand around her upper arm, tightly, and then release it slowly. Tell me the pressure you feel, and when a weaker beat comes in … Listen to her heart … Feel her tummy. Any lumps?" They gave him more instructions.

"That's as much as I could do," the one called the internist said. He spoke to Leroy, like she wasn't there. Which was fine. "You'll have to stay on the estate for a while until we can evaluate what's going on, physically and mentally. You can see that some of the other is bleeding through."

"What should I do?" Leroy looked almost as scared as she felt.

"Do what you're doing. Be tender with her. Don't have inter ..."

"He did not have sex with me." Ashley sat up. "He's a very nice person and I'm too young. We're going to wait until I'm eighteen."

"That's very good, Ashley," said the fat one. "If you need to talk to me, I'm here."

"I will never talk to you. I will talk to my husband." She raised her head proudly.

They walked across the lawn toward the barn. She almost danced with excitement.

"Oh, shit, the dogs!" She cried when their baying reached her.

"Don't worry."

They gathered around Leroy, wagging their massive hind ends. Their tails had been cut off. He kneeled and petted them. "We're gonna have to do something about this attitude of yours if I'm around here, boys. Whoever bred you with your faces flat like that ought to have a good thrashing. Come here, sugar, let me fix your nose."

Ashley stared and Leroy pulled the animal's smashed in snout out to a nice, pointy dog nose.

"You'll get used to being that way. Give it an hour. See, you can smell better, and breathe better. OK, boys. My wife and I, do you know Ashley Watches? Isn't she pretty? We're going to go over here to the barn, but you be good. Don't scare good people, just bad ones. You know the difference."

Grammie's barn seemed magical. It also seemed strange. Ashley had come there all her life. Everything looked bigger and wider and higher.

So clean. Grammie's thoroughbred horses were in their stalls and paddocks. She kept the horses, even though she couldn't ride anymore. There weren't very many these days.

"Over here, Ashley. This is what I wanted to show you."

She walked to the end of the row of stalls he indicated.

"Look in there. What do you think?"

Ashley peered through the slats on the top half of the stall. Her eyes widened. "Oh, my! She's beautiful. She's the most beautiful horse I've ever seen!" A mare looked back at her, obviously a mare; every hair on her body was feminine. Her coat was almost white, just a few dapples of dark coat indicating that she had been born black. Her eyes were bright as angels' and her expression, sweeter.

"Look at her. Her eyes are so big." The animal saw Ashley and walked toward her, sniffing delicately though the bars. "She's like a princess."

"That's what she is: a purebred, Section D Welsh Cob. She's the kind of horse the English queens used to ride. I saw her in England and had to have her for you. She arrived yesterday.

"Do you want to go in and see her?" Ashley nodded, feeling afraid, the way she always did around horses, even though she didn't let it show. "This one won't hurt you." He picked up a halter and slipped into the stall, quickly haltering the mare. "You can come in now."

"Oh, she's so soft." Ashley petted the mare's cheek and then her neck.

"I've got a couple of carrots in my pocket if you'd like to give them to her. She's not grabby."

Sure enough, the grey mare gently took the carrots and ate delicately.

"I'm not afraid of her, Leroy. She's nice."

"That's why I got her for you. I knew. There's a story about her, Ashley, but I'll tell you in a little while."

Ashley spun around and grabbed him. "I love you. You're the best person in the world. No one is better than you. You make me so happy! Thank you!"

Leroy laughed. "I don't know that I'm that good, but I could pick out this horse."

A horse on the other side of the barn raised a racket, banging the stall door with its front hooves.

"Come over here, Ashley. Here's another horse I found in England." A much taller, bulkier horse stood in the stall, nodding its head up and down impatiently. His back hung a little and his lips drooped.

"OK, Lightning, we'll pay attention to you. I rode him in a polo game. He's a great horse. Still has years and years of riding in him. Which I intend to give him." Leroy laughed.

"Can we ride them?"

"That's what they're for."

"Today?"

"If you feel up to it."

"Yes. They're both grey. We have matched horses! We can ride around on matched horses!"

A shadow darkened the entrance to the barn. Ashley looked up and saw her father outlined in the arch.

57

REPARATIONS

"DID YOU BRING your checkbook, Will?" Vanessa Schierman sat at her kitchen table with Will. He'd spent the night at the estate, being too shaken to go home, even with a chauffeur driving.

"Yes, Vanessa."

"Good. Be a darling and write me a check for twenty million dollars." She smiled, looking more like the gargoyles on her walls than she would have liked to admit.

"Twenty million dollars! Are you out of your mind?"

"I told you that you would be smiling and saying, 'Yes, dear'—or Vanessa—for the next few years. And writing checks. So write me one for twenty million, now."

"What could possibly cost that much?"

"Write the check, and then sign here and here, where the tags are." She indicated a thick document. "Wait until Mrs. Naughton arrives to sign. She's a notary.

"Do it, Will, or Ashley will turn into pumpkin and you'll never see her again."

"You wouldn't do that!?"

"I certainly would, you deserve it. But *she* will be the one to reject you, not I. She has bleeding memories of what happened. She may remember the whole thing eventually. We will not talk about the Havertin Institute and your murderous predilection for putting your daughter places where they'll kill her. We *will* remember it, and the jet landing on Skyline Boulevard, and what happened afterward. And why she's alive, the reason for which you will never know. *Write the check, Will.*"

He wrote the check.

Vanessa fanned a fat contract in front of him as Mrs. Naughton entered the room with her notary kit.

"Sign on the pages with the sticky tags," Vanessa flipped through the document.

"What am I buying?"

"Read the contract."

Will scanned the first few pages. "You're selling Ashley and Leroy some of your property. I'm paying for it."

"Brilliant, don't you think? If Leroy doesn't protect her from Donatore, the land will. Leroy would never be happy in that smog-infested, over-populated Valley where you live. Silicon Valley is jammed with arrogant, excessively smart, hubris-laden clods. It's nothing like the old days down there, when people had taste and manners.

"He'll love it up here. She'll be happy and safe. Air rights to the entire estate are grandfathered in. He can commute by helicopter if he works for you. And you'll never get an inch of my land in your name ever, Will, for any amount. I'm selling it to them.

"The fact that construction is already underway for the house keeps that despicable, communist Open Space Agency away. It's a win-win."

"Construction?"

"Yes, the twenty million covers the land, plans for the estate, and early development. You'll have to cough up for the rest later. Now write me one for five million."

"This is extortion, Vanessa."

She shrugged. "Maybe. It's also the price of grandchildren. I did do a bit of extraordinary magic yesterday. You owe me."

Will cowered and wrote another check to Leroy and Ashley.

"The five million is a wedding present. Very generous of you, Will. Now, shall we go see them?"

"Yes! Where are they?"

"They're at the barn. Leroy brought Ashley the most beautiful horse in the world home from England. I pulled every string I knew to get her—them, he brought a horse for himself too—through quarantine so they could be here for Christmas. You must see them. She's ecstatic."

He got up, but she put out a hand to caution him. "She fainted today, Will. I would be as nice to her as you can. No confrontation of any sort, and for God's sake, don't tell her what happened. Leroy can do that later."

Ashley stood in the barn, hugging Leroy and looking at her beautiful new horse. "I'm sure she has a registered name, but I'd like to give her own name, one that I choose." Ashley thought. "I'd like to name her Princess, or Star, or Twinkle." She frowned. "But I can't."

"Why not?"

She whispered, "They're not sophisticated names. I should name her Anastasia or Sarasvati."

"Name her whatever you want. She's your horse."

If the heavens had opened and the Voice of God had boomed, *"It's your horse, Ashley. Name her whatever you damn well please,"* Ashley's reaction could not have been more profound.

"I don't have to be sophisticated." Her shoulders dropped and her mouth opened in a joyous Whoop! "I can do what I want. I'm free! Her name is *Princess*!"

A shadow darkened the entrance of the barn. Her father.

She shot toward him, fists clenched. "I don't have to ride jumping horses and go to shows anymore. I hated them. I was scared. I did it for you, but I was scared to death. Every single time!"

She attacked so fast and hard that she didn't notice that her father was twenty years older than she remembered and already looked like he'd been hit by a baseball pitched by a major leaguer at one hundred miles an hour.

"I hated you because you made me show horses. You didn't really *make* me. It was, 'Oh, sweetie pie. I'm so *proud* of you.' You were only proud of me when I was doing something that *terrified* me. Or made me look better than everyone else.

"I will never show a horse again. Leroy knew about me right away. He brought me a horse that I really love. She's beautiful, and sweet and not too big."

Leroy raised his hand, "Um, Ashley, I just brought Princess, but I found her in a ..." He sputtered. This was not the time to tell her about her mother.

No one paid any attention to him. Will backed out of the barn. Ashley shot after him.

"I'm not going to boarding school next year. I will *never* go to boarding school. The only reason you wanted me to go away was so you could have affairs and cover up Mommy's drinking. *Do you think I didn't know?*"

Will backed up as fast as he could, taking giant steps rearward.

"Did you know when you were out with other women, Mommy cried? And then she drank. She fell down and hurt herself. It wasn't just times you found out about, it was *lots* of times. I was scared stiff. A lot, Daddy, not just sometimes.

"*I* heard it, not you. You're a grown up. You're supposed to love and take care of me, your kid, and you're supposed to love your wife and not make her cry. *You didn't do any of that!*"

Will turned and bolted, running into an antique concrete garden bench that happened to be right behind him. He hit its back mid-thigh and flipped ass over forehead, his neck making an impossible backward curve. They heard a crunch. And then silence.

Leroy ran to him. "He's out cold." He began healing his father-in-law without any reluctance.

"I didn't kill Daddy, did I?" Ashley was beside herself.

"Well, sweetheart," Leroy said, "I've heard that the truth can't kill. In this case, I think it maimed. He'll be fine. I think."

EPILOGUE

'TWAS THE NIGHT
AFTER CHRISTMAS

DIEGO DIDN'T KNOW who he was or where he was. He didn't know why he kept walking up and down the same stretch of road. Wisps of memories came and went. He was supposed to find someone. Someone else would be very angry at him if he knew what Diego was doing. He didn't know who it was, but thinking of that person terrified him.

"I am good. I am kind. I only do good and kind things. I think good thoughts and I help people," he said to himself. That was who he really was. Someone had done terrible things to him and hurt him very badly trying to make him think he was bad.

Whoever was after him wanted him to hurt people. He'd been on this mountain for days. He knew that he had to find someone here, or that other one would hurt him very much, if he caught him.

The hill was foggy. Fog came in and went out, came in, and … Things got lost in the fog. Thoughts and ideas. Everything was a fog, except for a kind voice telling him he was good.

"You will no longer act like a monster. You will not scare people. You will keep your claws and fangs and scales hidden, because you are so nice. You will help people and take care of them, and care for your wives and children. For the wives and children of all the world. You are good."

That's what Diego remembered. That and his name, Diego. He kept walking.

A black and white car pulled up next to him. "Hey, buddy. Would you come with us?"

"All right." They wanted to put handcuffs on him, but Diego showed them his hands and wrists. They were torn up, almost to the bone. His nails were torn off. "If you put those one me, it would hurt me very much."

"What happened to you?" Officer O'Riley asked.

"When I was getting out of the plane."

"Which plane?"

"The one that crashed."

"Crashed up here?"

"No. The one in the ocean."

"The Bay, you mean?"

"I don't know. It was wet. Everyone died." That made Diego so sad, he cried.

"Maybe he was in the crash and has amnesia?" Lopez, O'Riley's rookie partner, said.

"Or PTSD or something. What's your name?

"Diego."

"Diego what?"

"Just Diego."

"Where are you from?"

"I don't know."

He had a Spanish accent. "Where are you from?" Officer Lopez asked in Mexican-accented Spanish.

"I don't know," Diego replied in pure Castilian tones.

"He's Spanish, from Spain."

"Why are you naked?"

"My clothes came off getting out of the plane." Diego remembered a little bit. Clawing through the fuselage had taken all of his strength. His clothes split and tore from his body when his scales came out. Diego's claws and teeth grew too, as sharp as they could be. He needed them; he had to get out of the plane.

"You got out of the plane that went into the Bay?"

"It was very wet." He swam from the downed plane at the bottom of the Bay to a park on the water's edge. It was the Palo Alto Baylands Park. It was dark. People were there, parked in cars, mating.

When his scales went back inside him and he looked like a human, he knew he needed clothes. He thought that he could kill one of the humans in the cars and take his clothes, but something occurred to him. He was good. He only did good things. Killing someone, especially while mating, was not nice.

So Diego left the park, silently and almost invisibly. He went to an all-night grocery store. They had no clothes to steal, but a box on the wall showed many moving pictures. It showed a plane fall into the water. He had been on that one. Another plane crashed at the same time, on Skyline.

Diego didn't know why, but he knew whomever it was that he wanted was up there, in that plane or near it. He had to go from where he was to the top of that mountain.

The store was empty; it was very late. Diego asked the man behind the counter, "Can you tell me how to get to Skyline from here?" He remembered to speak English.

"You fucking asshole! Get out of here! Stop bothering me! Get some clothes, for Christ's sake."

The man was very angry. Diego realized that there must be more like himself, wandering around without clothes.

"I'm very sorry," he said. "I lost my clothes in the plane crash. I need a map to get to Skyline Boulevard."

"You were in the crash! Holy shit! Let me call an ambulance for you."

"I'm OK. I need to get to Skyline."

"Why?"

"I'm supposed to find the other plane."

"Why?"

"I don't know. May I have a map?"

He gave it to him, but he called the police after Diego left. Diego hid and they didn't get him. He was proud of himself, because he could feel his scales wanting to come out. He didn't let them. He was good and kind and did not hurt people.

Now he was sitting in a police car on Skyline Boulevard.

"You're saying that you escaped from the plane crash and came up here. Like that? No clothes?"

"Yes. I had a map."

"You went all the way through Palo Alto, Stanford, Woodside, and then up the mountain, naked as a jay bird. And no one noticed?"

"They noticed. I was in a place called Stanford. Someone gave me something called a beer and asked if I had gone to the frat party. I said, 'Yes, I have just come from there.' He said, 'Did you get any?' I didn't know what he meant, but I said yes. He said, 'Way to go, bro', and slapped my hand. What is a bro?"

Lopez and O'Riley rolled their eyes.

"What planet are you from?"

"I believe I am from the planet Earth, though that may not be accurate."

"So you get up here and do what?"

"I walked along the road."

"Naked."

"Yes." Truthfully, Diego had been tempted. He was very hungry and cold. People were walking in these mountains and he saw many signs saying "hiking trail." He thought that killing one of these hiking people, taking his clothes and eating him might be a way to get warm and fill his belly.

But he remembered that killing and eating people and stealing their clothes was not good. So he shivered.

"Why are you walking along here? Do you know whose place this is, where you've been walking?" O'Riley thought if their weird friend knew whose house he was stalking, he'd pick up his blocks and leave the party.

"No. It is a very dark place."

"Do you know anyone in there?"

"I think the person I am supposed to find is in there, but I don't know how to get in."

"Who is this person?"

"He is my father."

"What's his name?"

"His name is Leroy."

"Would he take you if we turned you over to him?"

"I think so. He said he loved me."

A posse of Sheriff's patrol cars had gathered behind them. O'Riley turned to his partner. "Lopez, you're new to Woodside. I'm going to teach you the way I teach all of my partners. They give us courses on how to act down in the flats, in the barrio. They don't give classes on how to act here, with the rich people, *especially here*, in the place we're going. You gotta adapt to the culture and understand the customs of the people or you'll fuck up real bad. That means they'll come after you with *lawyers*. You don't ever want to see a rich man's attorney. No matter what happens when we get inside, don't tell anyone. Not your mother, or your wife, or your father confessor."

O'Riley drove south on Skyline about a mile and a half, all the black and whites following him. He pulled over, dialed a number, and was told he could enter.

"Turn in the gate, Officer," said a crackly old voice from the phone. "Your car may enter, no one else's. Tell the rest of them to go home. We're having a Day-After-Christmas party."

They turned through some gates that just appeared in the fog. Looked like they came from Frankenstein. O'Riley thought he saw trees move to get out of the car's way as they drove down a lane that showed up out of nowhere.

"You'll never see nothing like this," O'Riley said to Lopez. The forest ended abruptly and they crossed a huge lawn. Baying filled their ears. "Oh, God, the dogs are out." Hideous, gigantic dogs with misshapen heads circled the black and white as they approached the mansion. A few had pointed muzzles.

"Are those things on the walls moving?" Lopez grabbed his arm.

"Yes." O'Riley turned to Diego. "How're y' doin'?"

Diego's eyes glowed with wonder as he gazed at the mansion. "It's beautiful."

A huge African American dude met them at the door. He didn't invite them in. The guy had what seemed to be brands blazing on every inch of skin that showed. "What are you doing here, Diego?" The dogs were friendlier than this guy.

"I am good. I am kind. I only do nice things. Because of you, that is how I am. I came to you because someone very bad wants to make me bad again. See what he did to me."

Diego opened his arms and O'Riley fully saw what he'd glimpsed before. Diego's torso looked like someone had run him over with a rototiller.

"He did this to me, and much worse. But I didn't turn bad. He just thought I did."

Leroy scowled, "Were you on the plane following us?"

"Yes. I thought I could run away when we landed."

"Did you hurt her?"

"No! I would not hurt anything. I am good. She was gone with you when we arrived."

"If you'd had the chance to hurt her, would you?"

"No. I could have hurt many people getting here, if I wanted. But I didn't. I wanted to get to you."

"Why?" Leroy's eyes were angry slits.

"So you could protect me. I am very afraid. He is after me."

"Enzo, your brother?"

Diego screamed and fell on the stone porch with his hands over his ears. He groveled and wept.

"Why did you want me?" the big guy with the brands said.

"You made me. In the park. You said the good words and changed us all. I went to sleep. When I woke up, that bad person was there and caught me. All the others got away. They didn't sleep as long as me."

"How many were there with you?"

"Twenty. They got away, but I slept longer and the bad man got me."

A tiny old Indian joined the big guy in the doorway. "Twenty of your kind, good like you, are running loose?"

"Yes. They do not hurt people or eat …" Diego shut up fast. "Leroy changed us. We are good.

"I came here so he didn't get me again and make me do bad things. I am *good. Leroy* made me good. Please."

The old man approached him. "Bend down, Diego. I want to look in your mouth." Diego did and the old man looked, then stood up, nodding. "Hmm."

Then he was stern. "Did you attack my people at the Meeting?"

Diego cringed. "Yes. I did. If you want to kill me for that, you can."

"Ah. You know I can kill you. Do you know who I am?"

"Yes. I am sorry. Please forgive me. You can hurt me as much as you want." Diego fell to Grandfather's feet. "Hurt me. I don't care. I am good now; I would never do that now."

O'Riley looked at Lopez. *Holy fucking shit* hovered between them.

A woman almost as tall as the black guy, and older than anyone O'Riley had seen, inserted herself between the two men. Her head looked like it might fall off. That was Dr. Schierman, the estate's owner. He'd met her during the ticket sale for the Sheriff's Ball for the last fifteen years.

"How do you do, Dr. Schierman," O'Riley said.

"I'm fine, Ben. Are you selling tickets to the Sheriff's Ball? I'll take all of them."

"No, ma'am. We're trying to find out who this guy is." He nodded at Diego.

A black ruff of silk and glittering spikes shot from the old lady's neck. A wand—a real witch's wand—appeared in her hand. Sparks shot off the end.

"What are you doing here, Diego?" Her eyes were no longer kind.

"I need help. I am good now, but no one wants to help me. I could have eaten many hikers coming here, but I didn't."

"That's a *wonderful* recommendation, Diego. Officer O'Riley, take him to jail. I won't have him here."

"Wait, Vanessa," the old Indian said. "You're missing something. What is strange about this situation?"

O'Riley couldn't see a thing odd. A naked man, obviously a torture victim, stood in an entranceway with carved-stone snakes crawling up the walls. They faced a branded, enraged giant, a witch, and an old Indian midget. Normal as pie.

"I have no idea, Joseph."

"He's *here*. The land let him in. He can't be evil if he's here. The land would kill him."

"They got in at the Meeting just fine," the giant spit out.

"They got in because of the wrong-doing of my People. People flaunted the Rules, drank and fornicated, and made an opening for demons. Diego is here by himself."

"I am good."

"I think you are, Diego." The little guy turned to the giant, "My grandson! You have created a miracle. You have saved the most evil of all."

"No," Diego whispered, "*that's* my brother."

"Leroy, you turned a creature of the darkness into a creature of light. Let me hug you." The big guy bent about in half hugging the old man. "We will go inside and get Diego some food. We will finish our party, and I will tell you about the great event that has happened. Come!"

"He's not coming in my house without clothes," the old lady barked.

Soon, Diego was wearing a short, green wool dress and leggings.

"That's fine, boys," the witch waved at him and Lopez. "You've returned Diego to his home. We'll call you if he gets out of control." Glaring at Diego, "*Or we'll deal with it ourselves.*"

"Great, Dr. Schierman. Glad to help. Merry Day after Christmas."

"Thank you, Officer. It's called Boxing Day. You come back when you have those tickets. I'm having an Easter egg hunt on the lawn in a few months. You're welcome to that."

"Thank you, ma'am. I'll keep it in mind."

"Holy fucking shit," Lopez said as they shot for the exit. "What kind of a nut house was that?"

"The real kind, Lopez. They're all real. Did you look through the front window when we drove up?" Lopez shook his head "Will Duane was in there. Richest man in the world. The old lady owns everything on the planet that Duane doesn't. And there was a whole *tribe* of Indians behind them."

"My son, you will stay with me tonight," Grandfather led Diego to his room and sat him on the spare bed. "And tomorrow, we will travel together. We will go everywhere. Would you like that?"

"You aren't afraid of me?"

"No. You aren't afraid of *me?*" Diego shook his head. "Now my son, tell me all about what happened. What Leroy did, and what your brother did to try to make you bad again."

Diego told the shaman everything, including Enzo's reconstituting him after he ate him and shit him out.

"Oh, that's terrible."

"Yes. It hurt my feelings very badly."

"But you didn't turn bad again."

"No."

"Good. I'm going to have someone bring you some food. Then you will sleep in this bed until I call you in the morning."

"I get to stay?"

"You get to stay with me."

"Oh, Grandpa, that's so dangerous. You can't travel with Diego. Enzo will be searching for you."

"He's already searching for me, Leroy."

"What if Diego eats you?"

"Hah! If he eats me, he will eat an old bag of bones and skin. The Great One will protect my soul and I will be fine. I *am* fine. *You are not fine.*" He indicated the group assembled in Vanessa's living room, looking petrified.

"*You* are afraid of the monster, but I am not. Why?" the shaman began to speak, as only he could. Magic filled the corners of the room, draping the garlands and lights.

"I am not afraid, because Leroy created a miracle! You are great, my grandson! You will be the greatest of our entire lineage! It is true!"

Grandfather whooped a bit, which set the warriors whooping. "Let me tell you what has happened." They sat back in Vanessa Schierman's weird living room and listened aptly.

"This miracle comes at a great time. This is the day after Christmas, the day the Christ came into the world of flesh and sticks and darkness. God loved us so, that he sent—Himself. His entire Self—to this place, in the form of His son. Think of the gift that was. Light. Knowledge. Love. Forgiveness. The healing balm. God gave us *everything*, in the form of a little baby."

Grandfather's eyes swept the group. He nodded as he entered the trance state. "People forget that I am a Christian. They see how I look and think, 'Oh. An old barbarian.' I am an old barbarian too. I follow my People's ways. They are my ways.

"But I am a Christian. Jesus came to me the night I was taken from my family. He stayed with me every moment. Bad things happened to children in the Indian schools. The extent of it is just being acknowledged, but Jesus saved me from it. He is not a comic book figure for me; He is my Savior and my Lord.

"Diego came to us the day after Jesus's birth." He waved at the huge Christmas tree, bristling with ornaments and colored bulbs. "We don't really know which day Jesus was born, so we agree that it was December 25th.

"Really, the merchants and store owners picked a day so they could turn it into a sales event and make money. They make us feel—*we* make ourselves feel—'I have to get Auntie Trudy a new TV or she won't think I love her.' And I must buy everyone else something good enough, expensive enough. Then I can have a good Christmas.

"What most people celebrate is not Christ's birthday. What do you call it, Vanessa?"

"The Teutonic-pagan winter festival." The old witch smiled.

"Yes, that is what people celebrate, with their Santa Claus and reindeer and naughty and nice. And that's what it is—a pagan festival.

"What we have seen this year is *real* Christmas. We saw the decent of the dove, of our beloved Ashley, into a new life. That was a miracle.

We saw our friend Will forgiven and remade." He waved at Will in his wheelchair, a brace around his neck and his foot in a cast. "Sometimes, being remade hurts." Grandfather threw his head back and laughed. All the bells on the tree chimed with his laughter.

"We have come together for a wedding of two great dynasties. When the time comes, you will have the greatest children, Ashley and Leroy. The greatest! They will combine the best of both of you. Oh, what you will do for the world. You will be *so* happy." His eyes rolled toward the ceiling and he chanted a few syllables, lost in joy.

"You found that this old man, who everyone thought was dead, wasn't. Here I am. I get to feel the joy of this earth a little longer. Did you know that human joy humbles the angels? They can't feel what we do in our bodies of flesh and blood. *Angels* want to feel our human love.

"And now, tonight, the greatest miracle. They say that the devil, Satan, is an angel who fought with God and got kicked out of heaven." He flicked his forefinger with his thumb. "Pfft. Sayonara, devil baby." Grandfather raised his hands and shoulders and looked around in mock dismay.

"No one ever talks about a demon going the other way," the shaman pointed his finger upward and spun it in little circles. "Back to God, O fallen one. Back to your real home, O monster.

"That's what Leroy did. Who would stand on a street faced by demons that wanted to kill him and save their souls? That's what Leroy did. He set twenty-one demons free. He made them free to know their true natures, free to know goodness. Free to know God.

"We all belong to God. You know that, yes?" His eyes scanned the crowd. "We pray for sinners, that they will see their errors and repent. We pray for ourselves, that our petty errors may be erased. We pray for criminals and drug addicts, those who are truly lost.

"But does anyone pray for demons? Does anyone see a demon ready to kill him and say, 'You are good?'

"No one has done that, but Leroy. Diego tore his way out of a sunken airplane and came to Leroy for protection. He called Leroy his father. And he is.

"We rejoice when the Prince of Peace, the Son of Man, the Lord of Heaven is born, but do we recognize the miracle of a son of evil returning to the light? Do we truly believe in the miracle of redemption? This is a story of Christmas, the real Christmas, the one that beats with your heart and moves with your blood.

"That's what I leave with you. The glory of Christmas, the miracle of redemption, and the possibility of a life of exaltation beyond your dreams. That is what the Great One offers, through himself, his Son, and the love that binds us. We need only open our hearts to receive it.

"As Diego did."

ABOUT THE BOOK AND BLOODSONG SERIES FROM AUTHOR SANDY NATHAN

In Love by Christmas is Book Three of the Bloodsong Series. The way I had the Bloodsong Series laid out in my mind originally, it started with a trilogy about the richest man in the world meeting a great Native American shaman. Their lives intersect at a huge spiritual retreat the shaman holds every year in the New Mexico desert.

I wrote and published the first two books of the trilogy, and had one more book set at the New Mexico retreat to go.

But after publishing *Mogollon*, I read the book again and thought, *People will want to read more after they finish this. What can I write quickly so folks don't have to wait another year for a "big book"?*

I wrote *Leroy Watches Jr. & the Badass Bull,* a novella, which is the first time I introduced Leroy Watches Jr. The great shaman Grandfather leads the spiritual retreat in the earlier books. Leroy is his grandson. Where did he come from? In my book drafts, I found a three paragraph reference how Leroy became the FBI's Most Wanted because of that bull.

Bingo! The Bloodsong Novellas were born. I'm going to write more novellas, featuring the "faces on Bloodsong's cutting room floor"—Doug Saunders, Janice Coto, Gil Canao, Delroy West, and Marina Selene. I may write about Grandfather and his wife Rebecca. Theirs was the only marriage between soul mates that failed—but that marriage produced Leroy's mother, and hence, Leroy.

When I started writing about Leroy Watches Jr., he grabbed my soul. I wanted to find out more about this fascinating man—who is also a hunk. I've always wanted to write a Christmas book too. One of those warm, glowing things that made you feel good and had a sweet cover.

This is that Christmas book—*In Love by Christmas*, starring Leroy Watches Jr. as he searches for the love of his life. Unfortunately, I am constitutionally unable to write anything soft and fuzzy. *In Love by Christmas* is the most badass Christmas story ever written.

In Love by Christmas also rammed all other books on my hard drive out of the way, demanding to be published first. By sheer power and beauty, *In Love by Christmas* became Bloodsong 3.

This book is a romance, a biracial romance, and a Christian book. Most of my books contain powerful love stories, but in this book, the love story is a central theme.

This book is essentially, fundamentally, Christian, as I am, but it treats other religions sympathetically and as equals. One of my friends, a Christian writer who writes to a particular denomination, said it was "spiritual" because of my broad acceptance. OK. *In Love by Christmas* embodies the feelings and thoughts I have as I contemplate Christmas.

But what happened at the retreat? *Mogollon: A Tale of Mysticism & Mayhem* ends on Wednesday night. The retreat is over Saturday, *anything* could happen—and it does.

Are all those people are still camping in the New Mexico desert, dodging demons? Will they ever get home? You'll find out in *Eagle's Flight: A Tale of Mysticism & Miracles*, Bloodsong 4, which will be published in 2015.

When I sat down to write in 1995, I wrote drafts for the original trilogy and maybe seven or eight related novels. Since then, my brain has kept generating stories. I keep popping out books with new characters and locales. Because of that, the original trilogy will probably end up being dozens of books.

The coming Bloodsong books move. They don't stay in the Mogollon Bowl, however fascinating it may be. They are set in different places: Silicon Valley, southeastern Oregon, Montana, and Vanessa Schierman's magical kingdom on top of the Coastal Range in Woodside, California. The tales spin out in Spain, Italy, and Iceland, in addition to the good old USA.

The cast of characters changes and expands. In addition to our familiar billionaires and Native Americans, future works include socialites with secrets, a poet with a past, assassins, warlocks, lots of witches and demons, and musicians who rock the world.

And—while you're waiting for the fourth installment of the Bloodsong Series, I have more for you to read.

While wrestling with writer's block over the Bloodsong books a couple of years back, I pumped out another series of books.

The Earth's End Trilogy is sci-fi adventure set in a future world, right before we nuke it. The first book, *The Angel & the Brown-Eyed Boy* is about a young man trying to make sense of a senseless world, and a beautiful alien trying to save her planet.

The second book of Earth's End, *Lady Grace & the War for a New World*, features the survivors of the Armageddon in the first book. They crawl out from their hiding places and find themselves in prehistoric conditions. Also, the neighbors have mutated and are downright hostile.

Finally, *The Headman & the Assassin* is a love story throughout. It's the lifelong romance of Sam Baahuud and his soul mate. It takes place in a huge bomb shelter and features a new cast of characters, plus a few from the first book, *The Angel & the Brown-Eyed Boy*.

COMING NEXT IN THE BLOODSONG SERIES

They went to hell and back in *Mogollon: A Tale of Mysticism & Mayhem*, Bloodsong 2. Looks like most of them made it. But the week isn't over. What could possibly happen next?

Grandfather's spiritual retreat, the Meeting, runs from Sunday to Saturday, seven days. It's Wednesday night when *Mogollon: A Tale of Mysticism & Mayhem*, the second Bloodsong book, ends. Grandfather has three more days to realize his dream of creating a world where love is king.

Will Earth become a place where people cooperate and work together with mutual respect? Or will violence and corruption rule the day? Will the flawed humans who messed up creation do their own thing? Or will the Great One take the reins?

It's all in the next book of the series, *Eagle's Flight: A Tale of Mysticism & Miracles*. The suspense, terror, romance, and miracles you've come to expect from Sandy Nathan reach a crescendo as the Meeting comes to a close.

This is fantasy with a bite, bringing the gifts of insight and awe.

COMING IN 2015.

ABOUT THE AUTHOR

About the author portions of books usually are written as though the writer is sequestered on the far side of the moon, leaving an all-knowing narrator to hand out propaganda. I'm going to tell you the real story, heart to heart.

I was born to be a princess. I was a princess, for a while. My parents overcame the poverty of their youth by becoming extremely successful. My hometown was one of the most affluent places in the country. Giant oaks, old mansions, and flashy cars surrounded me. I spent my time showing horses and water-skiing behind my dad's obscenely overpowered boat.

Princess Sandy died when a drunk driver hit my father head-on in 1964, killing him. Those words aren't enough. My father died of suffocation, as bloods clots from his massive internal injuries broke loose and lodged in his lungs.

My old life vanished. Through structures and systems I will not describe, I lived at a below poverty level income for a while. What happened in the coming years opened my eyes. I've seen and lived the over-privileged existence I describe in the Bloodsong Series. I've seen how ephemeral its rewards are and how it warps those who are trapped by it. I've seen how it masks mental illness.

Want to know why a San Francisco-born, Silicon Valley-raised woman is so obsessed with Native Americans? After I'd drafted a few thousand pages of the Bloodsong books, I had this giant Ahah! At least half of the characters were Native Americans. Why? I don't think I'd ever seen an Indian.

I realized that they had lived the lite version of what happened to Native Americans. They had the kingdom—the entire continent—and lost it. I knew how that felt. They were treated abominably for centuries, and had the worst abuse hurled at them. They were asked, "What's the matter with you? Why aren't you doing better, you lazy bums?" I know all about that too.

My writing has a bite. My life has had a bite. Recovering from what happened to me has taken many years. And I have recovered. What was legitimately mine came back to me, along with the fruit of my own labor. If your life echoes mine, you might like to see how I healed; it's in my books.

My writing isn't for everyone. I write about people getting better and the world working out, but it's not always gentle and nice. A reviewer described my Mogollon as "equal parts horror, spiritual, romance, and action." If that's for you, you're my reader.

I write visionary fiction, which is about making the world a better place. Why that with the bio above? I have had huge spiritual experiences all my life, as well as gentler ongoing guidance. Whatever is behind them and this earthly life wants me to tell you about them.

Now for my "regular bio": I've been in school a very long time and have two advanced degrees. I've had prestigious careers. My writing has won twenty-six national awards. I'm very happily married; my husband and I have been together forty years. I have three grown children and two grandchildren. We live on our California horse ranch and love it.

Sandy Nathan's website: www.sandynathan.com
Join Sandy's Newsletter: http://www.sandynathan.com/contact.html

REVIEW *IN LOVE BY CHRISTMAS*

*Reviews are very important in establishing
a book's ranking. If you enjoyed*

*In Love by Christmas, please consider leaving
a review on the book's online sale page.*

www.ingramcontent.com/pod-product-compliance
Lightning Source LLC
Chambersburg PA
CBHW020504260626
47156CB00006B/1861